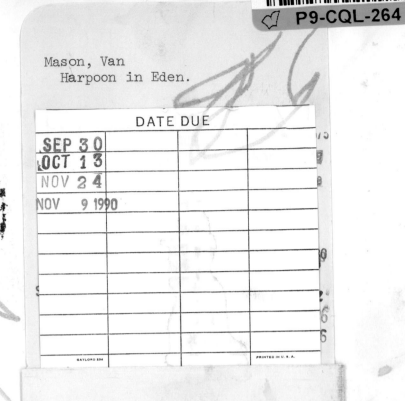

Harpoon in Eden

BY F. VAN WYCK MASON

Harpoon in Eden

Rascals' Heaven

Wild Horizon

The Young Titan

Manila Galleon

The Sea 'Venture

Our Valiant Few

Silver Leopard

Blue Hurricane

Captain Nemesis

Golden Admiral

Cutlass Empire

Proud New Flags

Three Harbours

Stars on the Sea

Rivers of Glory

Eagle in the Sky

*The Adventures of Hugh North
as Captain, Major, and Colonel*

Harpoon in Eden

F. VAN WYCK MASON

1969

Doubleday & Company, Inc., Garden City, New York

With deep affection born of long friendship
this book is
for
LeBaron and Adeline Barker

Foreword

To write on so technical, though colorful, a subject as whaling in the early 18th century called for a deal of selective research from accredited authorities in the United States and New Zealand.

Once the research material was amassed came the merciless elimination of a great deal of fascinating information which unfortunately was not pertinent to this book, or was too detailed for practical purposes.

The same problems arose in selecting appropriate facts concerning that intelligent, hardy and wonderfully artistic race—the Maoris. From the mass of notes taken from a great number of books forwarded from New Zealand by scholarly friends, I have attempted to select representative facts and incidents while playing down the practice of cannibalism and the fiendish cruelty and callous treachery practiced on occasion by this magnificently brave and virile people. The tribes mentioned actually existed in the regions where they are described as being.

The names of whaling ships and their captains are authentic—they were cruising during the years covered in this narrative but not necessarily where they are described as being. All details concerning equipment, rig and the procedure of taking whales are as authentic as a long and painstaking research can render them.

Except for their family name the Paddocks are entirely imaginary, as are Sylvanus and Abner Doane and Aimée Dumont. The entire crew of the *Gladiator* also is fictional.

I have endeavored to keep the use of Maori words and phrases to a minimum and, to begin with, have given the rough English equivalent immediately afterwards—until such words become familiar through repetition.

For invaluable assistance on the subject of whaling I have especially to thank:

Charles F. Bachelder of Newton, Mass.
Howard P. Nash, Jr. of New Bedford, Curator of the Old
 Dartmouth Society Whaling Museum
Katharine Lyford of the Boston Athenaeum
Edouard A. Stackpole, Director of the Nantucket Chamber
 of Commerce
Captain George M. Cunha, U.S.N. (Ret'd) of Topsfield, Mass.
George Bowditch of New Bedford
Reginald B. Hegerty of the New Bedford Free Public Library

Acknowledgments for help on the New Zealand sequences go to:

Alan and Doris Leonard of Auckland
Thomas and Ruth Gilmour of Waimahaka, Wyndham
Ian A. Gilmour of "The South London Times", Invercargill
Bruce E. Murray of Hawera
C. Kingsley-Smith of Whakatane
A. A. Urquhart of "Erehwon" Station, Canterbury

and to Geoffrey R. Lowton of Wentworthville, New South Wales, Australia, for his invaluable information concerning Norfolk Island

Profound thanks go to the ability, loyalty and good humor of the secretaries who have toiled so long and hard to prepare this manuscript:

Jeanne Hand Mason
Patricia Eatherley
Enid Constance Ball

Hampton Head,
Southampton,
Bermuda.

F. van Wyck Mason

Preface

A blue-bronze dusk began to close in on the village of Duc Lap lying astride one of the Ho Chi Minh Trail's main infiltration routes. Strident and varied night jungle noises arose whenever the report of mortars firing sporadically near the not-distant Cambodian border was suspended. Although the sun had disappeared, this particular evening remained insufferably hot realized Major M. T. Paddock, R.A.-M.C. (N.Z.) while concluding his evening rounds of sick and wounded Bru allies lying, sweat-bathed and insect-tormented, in various palm-thatched hovels.

After using a crooked forefinger to scrape sweat from a broad and glistening forehead the New Zealand medical officer was bending over a final patient when a Maori orderly trotted in, saluted casually. "Please to come quickly, Major. Two Green Berets have just come in with a wounded native. One of the Yankees looks in bad shape, sir."

Major Paddock, his examinations completed, set off at a dog-trot through hot, sour-smelling half-light towards his headquarters tent. Cursing, he had to wait for the passage of a line of mud-smeared water buffaloes plodding along under heavy packs containing mortar tubes and ammunition boxes. While waiting he glanced about, felt reassured that machine gun squads and sentries posted along Duc Lap's perimeter appeared alert and watchful.

Lifting a canvas panel screening the entrance of his headquarters tent the big New Zealander paused, blinking in the harsh white light of a Coleman lantern hissing steadily atop a stack of medicine chests until he noticed the Americans.

One, undoubtedly a commissioned officer, must have stood well over six feet in filthy and ragged jungle fatigues and a ponderous tangle of equipment.

Judging by their gaunt and bedraggled appearance, Major Paddock gathered these men must have been on extended patrol duty. However, the officer's leather-rimmed green beret rode at a jaunty angle upon a tangle of straw-colored hair. In his arms the big man was lugging a limp figure in jungle fatigues from whose mangled feet occasional blood drops escaped despite pressure from tourniquets contrived from strips of khaki webbing.

The third apparition was a native, flat-faced and slight of build and probably a "Yard"—Montagnard—by the look of him. He had slumped onto a box of medical supplies.

At a glance the doctor realized what had happened to him; pungi sticks, sharp as bayonets and smeared with human excrement, planted along a trail had punched deep and very septic holes in those skinny brown legs.

The American officer turned fatigue-dulled and bloodshot blue eyes. "Sorry to bother you, Major, but the Chicoms jumped us 'bout an hour ago on the way in. Bastards really clobbered us—greased both my medics."

The New Zealander jerked a nod. "Sorry on that. Let's take a look." He bent over the unconscious figure lax in the big American's arms. "Um. Land mine!" Major Paddock observed rather than queried. "Seems to have lost a deal of blood."

"Plenty," wearily admitted the American. "Reckon Hank could use about a barrel of plasma."

Two dark-faced stretcher bearers silently appeared and helped ease the senseless Special Serviceman's crumpled form onto brown-stained canvas. "Take this man to the operating tent; tell Leftenant Hawkins to get busy, *wawe-wawe*—quickly, quickly."

"Now, can you give Pay Dang a quick look-see? Sooner this Yard gets two jabs of penicillin the better. As you know, pungi sticks get infection going but fast." He nodded at a radio transmitter. "That Angry 9 working?"

"Of course. What can I do?"

"Ask SFOB to send a MED EVAC chopper to your strip—*pronto*."

Once the Montagnard had been helped out, the New Zealander extended his hand. "Sorry, Captain, I don't seem to have caught your name."

"Funnily enough, it's the same as yours."

"How d'you know?"

"Got second sight." Grinning, Captain Paddock pointed to a foot locker on which 'Major M. T. Paddock, R.A.M.C. (N.Z.)' was painted in white block letters. Below, a second inscription read: 'Maikaka Tutenekai Paddock, Takuta.'

"Gives my name and profession in Maori," explained the Major, swatting a mosquito from his neck. "Most of the enlisted men are native New Zealanders. They all can read English but it pleases them."

Then, almost simultaneously, the two began to survey one another in open interest.

From across the tent the Maori orderly's bright black eyes rounded. *Heu!* These two *pakehas*—white men—were astoundingly similar in stature, build and bearing; their features were very much of the same cast—squarish and wide-jawed; both had small, bright-blue eyes set well apart under straight and somewhat bushy brows. The only difference lay in the fact that the Major was dark-haired and golden-brown of complexion while the other was blond and fair-skinned.

The American offered a broad, blood-streaked hand. "My friends call me 'Micky'."

Over the whine of countless insects attempting suicide against the Coleman lamp, the medical officer said, "I'm called 'Mike' on account of I was christened 'Micajah'—which is a damn' sight too quaint for modern times."

The American paused while unbuckling a lightweight combat pack. "'Micajah'. Well, may I be dipped in shit!"

"Why?"

"That's *my* given name!" When he swayed a little the New Zealander for the first time noticed a small, red-rimmed tear about mid-thigh in the other's torn and stained jungle fatigues.

"What in hell made that hole?"

"That? When the Chicoms jumped my patrol some sniper must ha' got to me. It's nothing much. Just a nice, clean flesh wound."

"'Nice clean flesh wound', my arse!" grunted the Royal Army Medical Corps officer. "In these latitudes there's no such a thing. Toki!" He beckoned the dark-faced, bushy-haired orderly. "Break out a syrette of Anti-T and dressings." Curtly, he motioned the giant in the green beret to seat himself on a chest.

"No sweat," growled Captain Micajah Paddock, U.S.A.S.F.V.

He started easing off his pack. "I've had more tetanus shots than Carter's got liver pills."

"A booster shot never hurts anyone. Hold still."

Deftly the big, dark-haired New Zealander scissored away sodden fabric, swabbed clean bloodied pink skin then narrowly examined the exit hole. He smiled faintly. "You're right at that, Captain; it *is* only a simple flesh wound. All the same, I don't imagine it feels comfortable."

"Well, it does burn enough to notice."

Once both bullet holes had been cleaned, disinfected with sulpha and compresses had been bandaged into position, the New Zealander, preceded by his shadow projected huge and black on the tent's roof, sought a battered foot locker. Dropping onto one knee he unlocked it, produced a bottle of Scotch and tilted generous tots into a pair of measuring beakers.

"Seems indicated we might hoist one to Clan Paddock."

Micky Paddock sighed. "Christ, that's welcome." With the back of his hand he wiped a wide mouth framed in heavy golden stubble and winced when alcohol penetrated several deep scratches. "Well, friend, first and last I've heard about 'way-out encounters but this sure takes the rag off the bush."

The American's little bright-blue eyes, sunken and red-veined through fatigue, narrowed. "You weren't kidding just now? Your name really *is* 'Micajah'?"

A grin flitted over the New Zealander's broad, bronze-tinted features. "Guess so. At least that's what they wrote in the family Bible. Amazing you should have been inflicted with the same name. Any idea why?"

"All I know is that, for time-out-of-mind, the oldest son of an oldest son in my branch of the family has been stuck with that cockeyed label."

The insane wailing howls of night monkeys bickering with nocturnal birds swelled briefly then faded. Mike offered a cigarette, lit it, eyes still fixed on the American's features lumpy from insect-bites and scratches. "From what part of the States are you?"

"From New Bedford—that's a city in Massachusetts."

The New Zealander smiled. "Aware of that. Attended Harvard College. Didn't finish, though. Father was thoughtless, died unexpectedly towards the end of my sophomore year. Was forced to return home and take over the family business."

At some point along Duc Lap's perimeter a staccato burst of automatic weapon fire preceded the *crump* of exploding mortar shells.

"What kind of business? Where?" Micky Paddock demanded from the depths of a smoke cloud.

"Chandler's goods, plus lumber and a shipyard. We also carry on an export-import trade in general merchandise. Home office is at Waikato on the West Coast of the North Island; it's been there since the middle 1830's. Family tradition has it our business was founded by an American whaler."

The American fanned aside a halo of moths and, blinking fatigue, tossed off the remains of his whisky. "Come to think of it, while I was in college I recall hearing somebody called 'Paddock' who came from Down Under and had been in college a few years ahead of me. I was class of '61, and you —?"

"Had I finished, I would have been '57, but, as I've said I had to leave early."

He in the bedraggled jungle fatigues looked up. "How come a New Zealander went to Harvard?"

Major Paddock arose and poured more whisky. "Seems that a long time ago some remote ancestor—a rich whaling captain from Nantucket—established a scholarship there for the benefit of the eldest son of each generation descended from his twin sons. One was Jedediah Paddock who established our line in New Zealand. And you?"

The big Special Services officer briefly exposed strong white teeth while raising his beaker. "It's the same story, only I'm descended from a whaler named Obediah Paddock who must have been Jedediah's twin, I expect. So, Major, reckon we must be cousins, God knows how many times removed."

As they looked over their beakers Mike Paddock remarked softly, "It would be interesting to know how all this came about."

I
The Whalers

1

Micajah Paddock, Master Mariner

On the second storey of the handsome brick dwelling he recently had had built on New Dollar Lane, Captain Micajah Paddock lay on that same narrow, gimbal-mounted sea bed he'd occupied a generation earlier aboard his first command, the whaling brig *Bountiful*. His craggy, deeply wrinkled and parchment-hued features framed in short, stiff and iron-gray whiskers at the moment were bright with tiny beads of sweat.

As he lay propped into a near-sitting position the old man's chest was rising painfully beneath a long-tailed and sweat-drenched flannel nightshirt. Captain Paddock sighed, grimacing over vicious barbs of pain that had begun to lance through his hideously swollen and increasingly discolored abdomen. He closed watery gray eyes and, in an effort to forget his agony, forced memory to recede over the years like a tide ebbing from the yellow-gray sands of Coatue Beach.

Must have been back in 1790 or thereabouts when I captained my first vessel. What was her name? *Bountiful?* Yep. Certain-sure, she *had* been the *Bountiful* and didn't I deem her the very finest whaling vessel ever to put to sea? Well, however old-fashioned and tired she might have been we proved a lucky combination. Justified her name, she did; generally we reached home with a full hold. Because of this 'twern't over-long afore I was able to lay down and build the *Morning Star* according to my own notions; must have been sound else I'd not have fared anywhere near so well with her.

The old Master Mariner's hot, red-rimmed eyelids parted a crack permitting him to stare, blankly at first, out of the twelve-paned window opposite the foot of his bed. Then, as he began to take in the familiar view, the ghost of a smile came to curve thin, lavender-hued lips.

Well, by God, he'd showed purse-proud old Joe Starbuck his

wasn't to be the only fine brick dwelling on Nantucket! Wasn't it a crying shame that, having succeeded so well, he must die on this clear autumn day of October the thirteenth, 1830, without having had a chance really to enjoy the not inconsiderable fortune he'd amassed.

Beyond a scattering of silver-gray shingled cottages the moors were ablaze with clumps of frost-touched scarlet sumach; rises were carpeted by purplish-brown blueberry shrubs. Between such patches of color moor grass rippled like a tawny spread over a succession of wave-like, gentle low mounds and ridges which like motionless rollers stretched away in the direction of Wauwinet.

He regretted in silence. Plague take it! Why couldn't the Lord have granted me just a few more years to enjoy the rewards of toil, thrift and sound foresight?

Once, twice the dying man's bald and freckle-spotted head inclined tremulously as he mused on: Yessiree, 'twas a man-sized task to rebuild our fleet after those tarnation losses we suffered during that senseless war in 1812. But, by God, I did just that, and with no man's help, either.

Over the years our scarlet house flag has shown its black sperm spouting, bold-like, on nigh every whaling ground there is: off Greenland, the Cape Verdes, Brazil, the Sandwich Islands, the coast of Guinea and along the Middle Line. Shouldn't be surprised if by now it's not been spied flying over them new grounds discovered off Japan and 'round New Zealand. Wish to God I could have cruised them places just once, but I calculate now it's much too late in the day.

Wonder what will become of the Paddock fleet once I lie six feet under?

Still, reckon I've no real grounds to fret. Obediah's smart and has settled down fine. Ain't he over and over again proved himself fit to command? Why, during his last three cruises he ain't ever brought home less'n eighteen hundred barrels of fine sparm and spermaceti. Pity Jedediah ain't yet mastered that wild and costly headstrong streak in him and learned to look farther ahead in matters of business and womenfolk. Why don't he settle down and be like his twin?

The meaningless, strident laughter of gulls floated in through the window; that, and the acrid-sweet scent of autumn leaves being burnt somewhere.

Micajah Paddock's reflections ran on. Beyond a doubt when Jedediah learned the terms of the Will, so soon to be written, he'd feel almighty put-upon. Well, let him. So far, that brash young Captain had steered his way regardless, did just as he'd listed without thought for anyone. Let him take the consequences.

Briefly, Micajah stared contemptuously at splotched and shrivelled hands as they lay, trembling gently, on the counterpane. God above! Could these feeble fists ever have driven a lance up to its hitches into the vitals of the mightiest creature God ever had put on earth?

He sighed and his fading vision only vaguely recorded a dense flight of black ducks rising off some invisible slough or reedy pond to eddy over the moors like a shifting, dark cloud. To his surprise, the dying man clearly recalled how, long ago, Pa one day had tanned his backside plenty fervent for fetching home only *four* ducks to show for a single charge of expensive powder and shot.

In those days 'twas taken for granted a smart lad should cautiously drag a ponderous flintlock smoothbore up to a pond then scrooch down, motionless among the reeds, till the feeding waterfowl got well bunched before cutting loose. If he did this he could expect anywhere from eight to a dozen ducks—more, if he'd a dog along smart enough to track down cripples in the reeds.

The old Master Mariner's withered left hand groped towards a well-polished brass bell shaped like a dolphin fish which he'd come across half a lifetime ago in the Cape Verdes. However, he let his hand fall back onto the counterpane because he felt like some more thinking back before summoning Ben Storer whose peg leg could be heard thump-thumping about on the ground floor so restlessly that the old boat steerer must have sensed his Captain's final recall signal was about to be hoisted.

Micajah Paddock closed his eyes and smiled on beholding the likeness of Ah Kim, young, trim and flower-like walk towards him with extended hands. How delighted the girl had been when he'd bought her outright and without haggling much from a greasy Macao *comprador*.

Aye, 'twere a lucky day I sailed the *Morning Star* into Macao to refit after that God-awful typhoon which came so nigh to doing us in for keeps. How tenderly submissive that little heathen had been, so very ready to please me in *every* way. Some men, likely, wouldn't have deemed Ah Kim a great beauty, but she was pretty, excitingly built with lovely almond-shaped eyes and so very graceful in her least movements that one quickly overlooked round and rather flattish features.

Let's see now. How long did Ah Kim cruise with me? Must ha' been nigh on two years and in all that time never once did I find an excuse to beat her. Lord! Lord! How badly I felt when I ordered up the homeward-bound pennant and had to set her and our little daughter, Ah Mi, ashore on Otabiti.

Wonder how the pair of them have fared? Likely well enough, Ah Kim always was clever and by the time we touched at Otabiti she'd picked up sufficient English to take her far as a translator; and besides, I gave her plenty of cash to live on till she could find a husband who'd suit her.

From among the shifting mists of time appeared the likeness of other females he'd known very well. There was Manuela, that gentle, great-eyed Portuguese with her unexpectedly genuine red hair; and the Otahitian whose dancing was the most provocative he'd ever beheld; and Otatipi with delicate tattooing covering a beautifully rounded chin. However, once Abigail Macy had allowed she'd wed me there weren't any other lights-o'-love—well, none worth recalling.

Whatever else is set down against me come Judgment Day, there's one thing should stand in my favor; I never cheated or lied to any of my concubines; always left 'em a sight better-off than when I took up with 'em.

The shivering deep-toned *clanging* of the town crier's bell commenced to reverberate in the distance. Gradually its tintinnabulation came so close that, when the crier paused at the head of New Dollar Lane, Micajah Paddock could hear quite distinctly that President Andrew Jackson finally had proclaimed trade with the West Indies open and lawful once more.

A brief pause ensued before the crier's orotund voice resumed: "Seth Winslow's dun cow dropped a bull calf this morning. Hopin' for a heifer, Seth was sorely disappointed." The bell jangled again. "Whaler *Eliza Adams* has been sighted off Tom Never's Head; her flag's half-masted. Looks so deep in the water she's likely had a greasy voyage. Should make port come noon or thereabouts."

Briefly, Micajah wondered what sharp-eyed youngster first had identified the incoming whaler and so had won the bright new silver dollar paid for an accurate first sighting and set a square, blue flag to flying above the Port Captain's office.

If only it could have been the *Hector* or the *Cherokee* the boy'd reported. He guessed in that case he might have found strength enough to fend off the Dark-Angel till he heard how many barrels his vessel had taken. But it was the *Eliza Adams* out there, not the *Cherokee* which, as he well knew, really wasn't due home in under six months' time and the *Hector* couldn't be expected to make port before a year was up.

Gradually, he became aware of a bone-penetrating chill rising like an icy tide from already numb feet.

The lifting sun thrust a probing yellow-gold ray across the sea bed, illumined bright segments on a patchwork quilt Abbie had worked during their last voyage together.

Dear, plain, soft-spoken Abbie; she'd been every bit as capable as a ship's officer as she'd been satisfactory as a wife. She rarely made an error in navigation, could order canvas, handle sails, keep the log and set signals better than a lot of mates. No. Never had to worry when Abbie took over the vessel when me and the other officers lowered to chase whales.

It don't seem possible, does it, that nigh thirty years have sped since Abbie birthed our first get on Hiva Oa in the Marquesas with only savage black females to 'tend her? Pity little Judith had to turn out so sickly she'd perished in a few days' time. Hadn't it been just like Abbie to dismiss our loss by saying, "Well now, Cap'n, under the circumstances don't you think we'd best lay us a new keel soon's I'm fit?"

Well, we did lay that new keel and a damn sight better'n we'd bargained for because, on Tutuila in the Samoas she birthed Jedediah and Obediah 'round a year later; each one being heftier than most babies.

When I 'llowed as maybe we'd better get for home she'd said briskly, "Why's the hurry, Cap'n? You know full well we've been out two years and so far have stowed down less'n 1400 barrels. No. I'm all right and the babes are doing fine so it ain't fair to disappoint our shareholders with a lean cargo." Then she'd added with a twinkle in her steady gray eyes, "Besides, it's going to take a mort of money to keep filled mouths as ready as Jed's and Obed's.

So, Micajah Paddock, don't you dast shorten this voyage by a single day till we've made a real take."

The old man sighed, barely bit off a groan because searing pangs began shooting through his belly.

'Twas wise that I harkened to Abbie because that very same year no less'n four Nantucket whalers were reported lost whilst as many others made port with holds so near empty our oil fetched a record price.

Somewhere down the Lane a couple of dogs got to disagreeing and made so much noise that, momentarily, they interrupted the Master Mariner's recollections.

Now where was I? Oh, yes. Lydia came along five years later, but at least she made port 'midst decent surroundings—in our salt box cottage near Polpis. Queer, now that I think on it, right from the start, Lyddie didn't in any way resemble the twins or any of the rest of us Paddocks.

The boys were blond, gray-eyed and husky as bear cubs, while when born she'd black hair, was dark-complected and built along light speedy lines—like, well, say a good pilot boat; not at all like Abbie or the rest of her folk—all their women are bluff-bowed and full-bottomed, always have been.

Lydia! Wrinkles deepened across the old man's forehead. What in the world was to become of Lydia, striking, if not downright handsome, in her dark, distinctive fashion but still she was so unfeminine, set in her ways and independent as a hog on ice. Till the day of Abbie's death she'd never even pretended to understand her headstrong and always unpredictable daughter.

Another succession of savage pains racked Micajah Paddock's gaunt frame, reminded him that before long it would be time for him to slip his cable and go aloft where he hoped eternally to sail Heavenly seas with Abbie as his Mate.

The familiar clamor raised by harbor gulls being forced by a rising tide off some distant sandbar beat through the window. Gritting the blackened stumps of his few remaining teeth the Master Mariner tried to concentrate on the circling of a paper wasp in search of a place to hide for the winter. The insect ended by disappearing behind a crude watercolor, painted by a long dead female cousin, of the first *Morning Star*—luckiest ship he'd ever owned.

Why in Tunket haven't Lyddie and Jed turned out as sensible,

1

steady and reliable as Obediah? *Why haven't they?* While the children were growing up didn't me and Abbie treat them all equal—showing nary a bit of favoritism to the one or the other? According to our lights, we tried to be just, firm and impartial. Where did we go wrong?

His palsied hand sought the brass hand bell and this time rang it.

When squat-built, gray-whiskered Ben Storer came stumping in with leather-hued features deep-furrowed with anxiety Micajah spoke slowly, with frightening difficulty. "Ben, want you to trot over to Lawyer Holloway's place right now. Say I want he should fetch over his legal gear. He's not to tarry because I—well, Ben, guess I ain't feelin' over-masterly right now."

Once Sam Holloway had seated himself with battered portable desk balanced across his knees the plump little lawyer peered shortsightedly over the tops of steel-rimmed spectacles and urged, "Well, Micajah, s'pose we'd best get on with it. Can't say as I admire the way you keep catching your breath."

The sun drew tiny silver sparkles among Micajah Paddock's short chin whiskers and silvery bristles covering the rest of his still strong but collapsed-appearing features. Fixing sunken eyes on a clump of white birches gleaming golden across the Lane, the dying man began:

"I, Micajah Paddock, Master Mariner, now livin' in Nantucket Town, reckon on this Thirteenth day of October, 1830, that the Lord's recall signal is flying so I now speak out my last Will and Testament to Sam Holloway, my friend and neighbor, who I want to be its executor, along with my son Obediah."

The lawyer started to suggest a more legally worded preamble, but Micajah raised a trembling, blue-veined hand. "You can re-phrase what I say later on. Right now just you dart true and get fast to my intentions.

"Item: I direct that my ships in which I own outright, or controlling interest, namely: the *Cherokee*, the *Morning Star*, the *Hector* and the *Topaz*, shall go to my sons, Obediah and Jedediah dividing them as I now direct: All my vessels, saving the *Topaz*, together with all their gear, are to go to Obediah on account of he's better than a middling good Master Mariner who always maneuvers to

windward and steers clear of shoal waters in plenty of time." Micajah caught a gasping breath then continued, "Besides, so far as I
know, he's been just with officers and men and always pays them
their lays in full and right on time."

Lordy! Thought Sam Holloway, Jedediah's sure getting the
short end of the stick.

"I figure Obed's a deal shrewder than most captains his age;
usually he gets the jump on rivals in the vendor's market and generally picks the right whaling grounds to hunt on. He's also to inherit my wharf and counting house at the foot of Water Street."

Ben Storer crossed to look out the window so a sudden start of
tears wouldn't be noticed.

"Item: I want my son Jedediah to have the *Topaz*—which is
my newest craft—and all her gear. Is that clear? You're witness,
Ben." The old boatsteerer nodded, looking as miserable as if his harpoon just had pulled out of a fifty barrel whale.

The dying man sighed. "You can explain to Jed, private-like,
Sam, I'd have willed him an even lay with his brother, weren't he
so infernal quick-tempered, quarrelsome and over-partial to the bottle and given to rantum-scooting about with loose women.

"Item: Howsumever, I want him also to have whatever barrels
of sperm at present are lying on my wharf or are stored in my
warehouse."

Micajah Paddock's lanky frame seemed to shrink, to sink further into the mound of pillows supporting him. "Because of that scandal with Lucy Dismont, I hope Jed won't ever settle on this Island—
at least till he mends his ways. I trust he will, because Jedediah could
win fame and fortune and become a credit to this family if he ever
steadies down. Make no mistake, Jed's smart, fearless and mighty able
about taking whales."

The old man closed his eyes, then, without opening them, continued to dictate in weakening tones, "Item: Neither of my sons is
to inherit a single penny unless—they take a solemn oath on the
Holy Bible that they will name their *first-born* son 'Micajah' after
me, who single-handed, restored the family fortunes after the Second
British War during which I lost my father and both my brothers.
Also, that any and all *oldest* sons descending from Jed and Obed,
so named, shall receive free an education provided for by a fund—
you know about that, Sam—which I have set up at Harvard College

up in Cambridge—that's near Boston. Should our nation continue to prosper and the fund be wisely administered, seems likely there ought to be sufficient to educate Micajah Paddocks for time-out-of-mind."

Again, Lawyer Holloway attempted to point out that this Will would have to be re-drawn in proper legal phraseology, but Micajah muttered impatiently, "Oh, hush, Sam, when I've done I'll sign a blank paper and trust you to express my wishes according to the law. Ben, here can witness my signature." The span of his life, he knew, was growing very short.

"Item: I want that my only daughter, Lyddie, who is too confounded hard-headed and independent for her own good, shall inherit this new brick house and the land it stands on, being five acres, more or less, and everything inside it." He paused to draw a short and painful breath, "*Provided* that, within a year of the date of my death, said Lydia shall have married a sober, upstanding citizen worth not less than ten thousand dollars cash money. If she don't, then said property shall go entire to my nephew, George Macy, who is a lubber at sea, but is honest and well-intended and has a smart woman for a wife."

The voice degenerated into a whisper so faint that Sam Holloway had to bend way forward to catch what was being said.

"Item: I want my two lighters, my pilot boat and the storehouse on Shimmo Point to go to Ben Storer, who was the finest boatsteerer I've ever shipped till a bull sperm whale chawed off his leg and left him unseaworthy. When he follows me aloft I want said properties to be sold for the benefit of The Sailor's Snug Harbor of this town.

"Item: I want Lawyer Sam Holloway and my heirs to break bulk and divide the cargo between 'em as I've directed.

"Now, Sam Holloway, just you pass me a clean sheet of foolscap and I'll sign at the bottom."

The lawyer arose and put down his desk after Micajah Paddock had scrawled a signature. "Shall I send for the doctor—and maybe the minister?"

A faint smile appeared on Micajah Paddock's pallid lips, the last ever to shape them. "Why not? They're given to hunting together. One ships a man off while t'other gets him pointed on the right course."

2

Scapegrace

A late October sun shone bright and unseasonably warm. Its rays effectively gilded the trim white railing of a lookout's walk built atop the gray slate roof of the late Captain Micajah Paddock's handsome brick dwelling.

Captain Obediah Paddock stood with massive arms folded across a broad expanse of blue serge while small and deep-set steel-gray eyes surveyed the Inner Harbor. On it half-a-dozen stumpy-masted and smoke-streaked whalers, along with a clutter of untidy fishing schooners, scallopers and coasting sloops, lay moored or at anchor. Next, his gaze followed the reach of that narrow and sandy peninsula formed by Coatue and Coskata Beaches, continued past Wauwinet until it came to rest on a white-and-red painted lighthouse rising above a series of low yellow dunes marking the far end of Great Point.

A gentle breeze off Nantucket Sound stirred the young Captain's squarish golden beard and ruffled a few locks of bright hair which had escaped from beneath a broad-brimmed and low-crowned beaver hat.

Obediah returned his attention to his present command, the sturdy old *Morning Star*, which alone had survived the Second War with England. She wasn't exactly pretty but she'd sure been a fine money-maker throughout her already long life. Refitting at Pa's wharf at the foot of Water Street lay the *Topaz* which his twin had commanded during two over-long but richly rewarding voyages. Poor Jed. He'd still be in command but for that awful misadventure with Lucy Dismont and that wretched creature's subsequent self-destruction.

Um. By now a handful of wind-rounded elms which succeeded in showing above the town's pointed, pearl-gray roofs—originally Nantucket had been named "Sherburne"—for the most part had shed their leaves but here and there a few well-sheltered sugar maples continued to flaunt patches of scarlet, gold and crimson.

Turning, Obediah squinted into the sunset for sight of that chunky little schooner from New Bedford which, once a week, distributed mail, ship supplies and other freight among the merchants of Wareham on the mainland, Nantucket and Martha's Vineyard.

Would Jedediah be on board of her? Likely he would, provided he'd learned Pa now was resting in the South Church's burying ground which, like the rest of the Island's cemeteries, didn't lie adjacent to a church but was located out on the fringes of town.

A light step sounded on ladder stairs leading up to the lookout, then Lydia Paddock's sleek, blue-black head became framed in the trap door's opening. "Sight the packet yet?"

"Ain't certain-sure, but I fancy I just now spied a flash of canvas out yonder."

The huge young Captain took another turn along the length of the lookout platform which not yet, but soon, would become known as a "widow's walk".

Up on one of these lookout walks a whaling officer's wife and family could enjoy fine days and at the same time command a fine view of the moors, the beaches, the Town, its harbors and docks and a vast expanse of Sound and ocean.

When a returning whaler became long overdue, the families of such a vessel's after-guard and other interested parties would, whenever opportunity offered, mount to roof and through telescopes mounted on permanent supports endlessly scan the horizon for the first glimmer of a weatherbeaten topsail.

Everyone dreaded that moment when the vessel in question came close enough to disclose whether or not a black flag was flying at her forepeak to say that one or more of her crew wouldn't be coming ashore; if the Stars and Stripes had been lowered to half-mast it meant that her Captain or some officer had perished.

Obediah, square, red-bronzed features aglow in the late afternoon sunlight, lent a hand to assist Lydia, younger by five years, onto the platform.

Straight-away the young woman used a hand to shade faintly oblique black eyes the better to scan distant reaches of the Sound all a-glitter beyond the Outer Harbor. Lydia held her trim, muscular figure arrow-straight beneath a severely simple gown of Quaker

gray and a shawl of the same drab color she always wore—for all
Captain Micajah Paddock and all his kin many years ago had been
"put aside" by the Society of Friends for some minor infraction of
their harsh and colorless interpretation of God's will. Nevertheless,
in addition to their dress, Lydia obstinately had clung to the Quaker
way of speech, for all she secretly despised that sect's lugubrious,
self-righteous views.

As usual, Lydia Paddock was wearing straight, blue-black hair
windlassed flat against her narrow skull by means of a tight bun secured over the nape of a long yet well-proportioned neck.

Obediah's hand crept up to finger a brief, spade-cut yellow
beard while noting that subtle coppery undertones were showing in
Lydie's smooth olive-hued skin. Um. What with her thin, slightly
hooked nose and those high cheek bones she did indeed suggest that
there might be something in a carefully-guarded family secret; Great-
grandma on Ma's side had been a full-blooded Wauwinet Indian.
Strange, he reflected, why do Jed and me favor Pa and Ma, while
Lyddie, who's also their get, differs from us so much?

The young woman turned, easily, like a doe startled by a sudden
sound. "I spy the packet off Madaket. Does thee think Jed will be
aboard?"

Obed unfolded massive arms in order to grope for a short-
stemmed clay pipe which, with precise motions, he loaded from a
deer's bladder pouch. "He'll be aboard lest he's gone to sea or is
rantum-scootin' somewhere about the Mainland." Although the Nantucketer shoved his pipe into a wide, ruler-straight mouth, he didn't
light it—only sucked, causing soft bubbling noises.

Lydia turned, at the same time elevated a sable eyebrow. "Does
thee think there will be trouble when and if Jedediah comes
ashore?"

"Lord, no. Lucy Dismont ain't the only girl on this Island who's
got herself ruined. In near two years' time folks most likely will
have forgot all about that business."

"I fear thee is mistaken. People might have forgotten, as thee
says, except that poor Lucy went and drowned her shame in Hum-
mock Pond."

Obed's rugged, brown features contracted. "Expect you've a
considerable point there, Lyddie. Howsumever, let's hope that re-

spect for Pa's memory will keep the Dismonts and their friends quiet. For all he never made much mention of it, Pa did a mort of good works 'round here."

Staring out over the harbor Lydia said softly, "What happened wasn't entirely Jed's fault, Lucy Dismont always had a come-hither gleam in those wide blue eyes of hers; then again the swaying way she moved her—her bottom when she walked, was pretty much of a provocation."

Solemnly, Obed inclined his head. "—And that's not a half-truth. Couldn't help but notice it myself more'n once—so did plenty of others."

"Poor Papa. That sorry business shivered him clean down to his keelson." Her narrow lips compressed themselves, "Shouldn't wonder but it hastened his death."

"Doubt that," Obed grunted. "When Pa died he was well past our allotted three score and ten."

While resettling the deep-fringed woolen shawl over narrow but level shoulders Lydia remarked, "Be that as it may, after those near-record cargoes Jed's fetched home, *I* think Papa was a mite hasty in taking command of the *Topaz* away from Jedediah."

"I'm with you there, Lyddie. I'm certain-sure Pa must have regretted going off at half-cock like that but, of course, you know 'twern't in him to back tops'ls once he'd set his course. Wonder what Jed's been up to since he went away? Pity he ain't ever been the least part of a letter writer."

Lydia drew a deep breath which barely raised a white kerchief demurely crossed, Quaker-fashion, over meager breasts. "I'm astonished thee hasn't heard that, for nigh on half-a-year, Jedediah has been in New Bedford clerking for a firm of shipping agents."

"Which one?"

"David Coffin & Sons."

Obed snorted, "My God, what's he doing wasting time clerking for those damn' skinflints? Any numskull knows there's precious little money to be made in a counting house, lest you're an owner."

"Thy gravest fault is making hasty judgments, Obed," Lydia reproved. "Full well thee knows thy twin is no coof—as a rule he knows very well what he's about." Color invaded her smooth dark cheeks and her eyes glinted. "It might be an advantage even to thee,

Brother, if thee understood a mite more about the shore side of whaling. Land-bound owners, agents and merchants can make a great fortune without risking life, limb and ship year in and year out, to only maybe earn a profit."

Thought Obed: while Lydia's no beauty she sure looks handsomer'n a brand-new figurehead when she gets her dander up. Aloud he said, "There's something in what you say—maybe us sea captains would benefit from a better understanding of bookkeeping, banking and marketing methods."

She nodded, turned primly aside and pointed. "Look, packet's already making for Brant Point."

A row of gray-and-white harbor gulls had made bold to settle on the *Topaz*'s upper rail as she lay at Paddock & Sons' dock, careened to an angle of forty-five degrees. The whaler looked especially forlorn because she hadn't yet been repainted and her yards and topmasts were down to facilitate scraping, re-sheathing and ultimately re-coppering her bottom. Strips of new copper already in place shone rich red in the sunset.

Some perverse imp prompted Obed to inquire casually, "Figured out yet how you're going to satisfy that marriage clause in Pa's Will?"

The girl whirled hissing like a frightened cat. "Damn thee, Obed! Why does thee have to bring *that* up?"

A faint grin curved the young sea captain's slash of a mouth, and a mischievous gleam shone in small, gray-blue eyes. "Now, Lyddie, don't get all foamed up. I was thinking who just might be willin' to risk getting spliced to a—a little spitfire like you. How about Jonathan Hussey, Tobias Greenleaf or maybe—"

Never before had he seen Lydia fly into such rage. Fists doubled and eyes ablaze she started for him. Laughing, he raised a fending arm, pretended to recoil against the lookout's rail. "Hold hard, Mate! Ease your sheets. Now just you listen to me. Marriage ain't such a terrible thing as I found out. Now why—"

"Stop thy mouth!" She blazed and drummed fists against his chest until he imprisoned her hands. "Don't thee dast to mention that cursed clause ever again!"

Obed shrugged. "Of course, if you really don't *want* to inherit this fine new mansion and the other things Pa's willed you, why that's your affair, I allow. Only thought to remind you that if you defy Pa's Will you'll wind up nigh to penniless."

Lydia flung her brother a furious glance, then stepped back, thin bosom heaving. "Mind over thy own business, Obediah, and leave me to fret over mine!" Pulling full gray skirts tight about her legs, she backed out of sight down the ladder steps.

Once she'd disappeared a thoughtful expression supplanted the grin on Obed's weatherbeaten features and, yielding to a mannerism he began tugging at his beard. Lydia, being as she was, what *would* become of her? Why should she so fervently despise her sex? And could it be that fear, rather than an active dislike, rendered her so gun-shy of men? Where lay the explanation? Right from the start he'd never even begun to understand this willful, immensely self-contained sister. Maybe, as she matured, the Indian strain in her was coming to the surface?

Captain Jedediah Paddock, standing in the mail packet's blunt bow, watched a small beacon erected on the tip of Brant Point show up in sharper detail. Not counting a pair of stripped and worn-out whalers waiting to be towed beyond Shimmo, beached and left to rot, there were about a dozen ships in port; among them a quartet of recently arrived whalers. They were riding to anchor in the Outer Harbor which, if truth were told, was no harbor at all only a semi-open roadstead which afforded vessels little protection from equinoctial gales, line storms or those winter tempests which came howling out of the north or northwest. In foul weather, vessels lying in the Outer Harbor would be forced to up-anchor and run for shelter at Vineyard Haven, Edgartown or even New Bedford—expensive in both time and money, a fact which most sensible Nantucketers would admit in private.

To make the future even darker, unless the channel could be dredged across the Bar, the port's prosperity surely was doomed. But dredging would be a hopelessly expensive proposition, quite impossible without help from the Federal Government which, considering its present impoverished condition, was most unlikely.

He recognized several vessels discharging cargo or tied up to fitting-out docks along the Inner Harbor. Yonder lay the *Eleanor* and beyond her the *Glide*, both real old-timers; then there was the stub-masted *Dauphin* which, nearly ten years ago, had rescued Captain Pollard and two other scarecrows—survivors of the whaler *Essex* to end an incredible three-thousand-mile voyage in a whale boat. They had been found only long weeks after their ship had been stove in and sunk in mid-Pacific by a huge and wildly infuriated bull sperm whale; they'd managed to survive only through devouring the bodies of dead shipmates or men executed by lot.

Briefly, Jedediah wondered how Pollard and his companions were faring these days. Perhaps not badly; public opinion hadn't turned on either Pollard or the *Essex*'s First Mate, Owen Chase, in whose boat survivors also had been forced to resort to cannibalism. After all, Nantucketers lived too close to the sea and its multiple dangers not to appreciate that men in desperate straits had a right, if not a duty, to do whatever must be done in order to remain alive and continue to support dependents.

With a following breeze stirring collar-length tow-colored hair, Captain Jedediah Paddock considered the sprawling gray-and-white town. Because Pa's new house had been built of brick he found no trouble in identifying it; barring Joe Starbuck's handsome mansion, almost every other structure in Nantucket Town was wooden.

Home again. Home? After what had happened two years back would Nantucket have forgiven and forgotten? Likely he'd soon enough find out.

Massive body yielding easily to the packet's choppy motion, Jedediah recalled other occasions on which, home-bound, he'd crossed the Bar.

There was that time back in 1815 when he'd come home a passenger on the leaky and ancient *Rousseau* to face Father's wrath for having jumped the *Morning Star* on the Island of Mocha off the Chilean coast in order to enlist and serve in the U.S.S. Frigate *Essex*, 46 guns.

True, Pa had mitigated his anger because Jedediah could justify desertion on patriotic grounds. Of course, this hadn't been his true motivation; which had been a consuming thirst for action and high adventure.

For over a year he'd served in that famous man-of-war which, single-handed, had captured or burnt and otherwise harried British whalers and merchantmen of all sorts so thoroughly that they'd

shunned the eastern Pacific; like winter wolves Lloyd's of London
had howled for the raider's capture.

Briefly Jedediah Paddock conjectured on what might have become of him if he hadn't been taken prisoner-of-war on March 28,
1814 when, following a completely brazen violation of Chile's neu-
trality, the *Essex* had been cornered in Valparaiso Harbor and destroyed after a desperate action with *H.M.S. Phoebe* and *H.M.S.
Cherub*. Most likely at this moment he'd be serving as a lieutenant in
the Regular Navy.

But although matters had turned out differently, service in the
Essex had helped him acquire invaluable knowledge of navigation,
seamanship and gunnery. Also, at this early age, he'd begun to
formulate a practical philosophy: play fair so long as a venture
seems likely to pay off and the other fellow didn't try to cheat—but
if he did—forget the fair fight!

The ghost of that towering head-hunter cut down on Nukahiva
never for a minute had bothered him. Nor had those of two seamen
he'd killed perhaps with less justification.

Despite his mood Jedediah felt his heart lift once the packet
rounded Brant Point and entered a narrow channel leading to the
Inner Harbor. His pulses stirred on recognizing the sturdy outlines of
the *Topaz* undergoing repairs and those of the old *Morning Star* taking on supplies at the foot of Water Street.

As usual, the family's wharf was stacked high with oil barrels
protected from the sun by layers of seaweed spread under worn-out
tarpaulins; cordage, new spars, firewood, barrels containing salt horse,
new sails and fresh water.

He cursed resoundingly when a gull, wheeling overhead, spat-
tered his jacket with splotches of evil-smelling "whitewash" but forgot about that because he'd just noticed, to his considerable surprise
and relief, that a weathered sign on the roof of Pa's counting house
still read: "Paddock & Sons", not "Paddock & Son."

In no great hurry the packet's crew began to shorten canvas
while in leisurely fashion she headed for her berth at Straight Wharf.

Through suddenly brimming eyes Jedediah realized that although Micajah Paddock must have been under ground for all of a
fortnight, the black sperm whale spouting on a scarlet field still was
fluttering at half-mast above Pa's counting house. People surely must
be holding the Old Man's memory in deep respect.

What would be Lyddie's attitude? No foreseeing what line that inscrutable young female might take.

Um. What sort of inheritance would Pa have left her? Again, no telling; since Ma's death, Lyddie and her father hadn't got on extra well.

3

Heirs

The night proved chilly enough to warrant the kindling of a birch chunk fire in the small, cast-iron grate heating the owner's office in Paddock & Sons' accounting house. A pair of tall-chimneyed table lamps burned with the steady, clear flame given off only by sperm or spermaceti oil; it didn't sputter, give off smoke or burn unevenly like the less expensive oil from baleen or "bone" whales generally used by the less well-to-do or for street lighting.

Brow furrowed in concentration, Captain Jedediah Paddock held a copy of the Will under the nearest lamp's green-lined white china shade and without expression noted its provisions.

Lydia considered her brothers, again was impressed that the twins, although reputedly not identical bore so very close a resemblance.

Only by careful comparison would a body note that Jed's frame was a shade less massive then Obed's; his ears, lying flat against his head, were a trifle more pointed and his heavy, yellow-white hair was a shade lighter in hue and texture.

Of course the easiest way to tell them apart nowadays was in the fact that Jed was clean-shaven and, in addition to a compass card tattooed on one hand, had a small, red and triangular-shaped scar left on the point of his jaw by a Fiji warrior's spear. Otherwise her brothers, clothed, to most people, appeared indistinguishable. However, she knew better: once she'd peeked through Jed's bedroom door left open a crack and had spied a tattooed, blue-green serpent which, encircling his waist, appeared to be writhing towards his crotch with what must be lascivious intent.

Both were built in gigantic but symmetric proportions, both had large if not huge hands and feet while their deep-set eyes were quite small, round and of an identical shade of blue-gray.

In abrupt yet not ungraceful movement the dark-haired girl

arose and, on long, muscular legs, went over to use tongs on a glowing splinter of sea-coal fallen out of the grate; many black burns
checkering the flooring attested that not everyone had been so alert.

While Jed read on, Obed settled back in a captain's chair with
arms shiny through use and looked about Pa's office as if he'd never
been in it before; he noted nearly a dozen varnished half-models for
ship hulls—several of which now lay rotting at the bottom of the sea.
Others remained afloat; having been captured during the War of
1812. Even now they must be chasing whales under the Union Jack
and still manned largely by Americans. During that war captured
crews had been offered a choice of serving British owners or of being
chained and transported to endure, if they could, the bleak horrors of
Dartmoor Prison; few had elected the latter alternative.

Above the Old Man's desk hung the most recent addition to the
collection—a beautifully executed "hawk's nest" model of the *Abigail
M. Paddock*, a vessel which, under the present circumstances, probably wasn't going to be built. On a series of shelves were ranged
battered and brass-bound wooden cases designed to protect chronom-
eters, sextants, barometers, compasses and a wide range of other navigational instruments. Above these dangled a few faded and frayed
house flags plus private signals belonging to various agents.

The heirs could hear a rhythmic *lap-lapping* of waves against pil-
ings below the office's well-worn carpeting. Also could be heard the
scurrying and squeals of a multitude of wharf rats.

At length Jedediah sighed, put down the Will, then for a long
minute steadily regarded first his brother, then his sister all the while
running fingers through his hair.

He began to grin. "Well, 'pears like Pa's remembered me far better than I had any right to expect. First and last, reckon I've caused
our Old Man a packet of grief."

The others stared in amazement. They'd been expecting a furious outburst instead of this calm admission of guilt.

"In fact," Jedediah drawled with a wicked gleam in his eye, "I
think Lyddie's come off a sight worse than me in this deal."

Lydia, snapping shut her jaw, fixed bitter black eyes on the
speaker, "Thee is a spiteful devil, Jedediah, and always were. But thee
is quite right—Pa had no cause to—to punish *me* so!"

"Sure, sure, Dark Sister, only Obediah wears a halo 'round

here." Noting his twin's unhappy expression he added hurriedly. "Pay
no heed to that last, Obed, I was only funnin' you."

Slowly, Obediah shook his big head, said seriously, "No matter
what scrapes you've got into, Jed, I don't feel its right for me to inherit three ships to your one." He peered across the table. "So I want
the *Cherokee*, if and when she makes port, to be yours. I'll have transfer papers readied for signing."

Jed flashed a peculiarly winning smile then suddenly reached out
to pat his twin's broad, bronzed hand. "Mighty decent of you, Bro
Obed, and I'll never forget it." A soft note, rare with him, entered
his voice. "Howsumever, I feel that if Pa wanted his property divided
the way he said, well then—I—I figure it's an obligation for us to
carry out his intentions to the letter, but I thank you, Bro, from the
bottom of my heart. Somehow, we'll keep on together."

Gray skirts rippling, Lydia strode back from the fireplace then
almost petulantly squatted on a foot-stool upholstered in black horse-
hair. For a moment she peered intently into Jed's face as if searching
for something below the surface of his expression. "Why does thee
talk so dratted noble, Jedediah? 'Tis not in thy nature. If thee don't
accept Obediah's offer thee must be up to something."

Quite calmly Jed shook his head. "You understand me better
than most, Dark Sister, but this time I haven't the least hidden mo-
tives; only intend to respect Pa's wishes."

Obed picked up a blunted lancehead used to weigh down a sheaf
of invoices, manifests and bills of lading.

Plainly baffled, he tugged his beard while considering his co-heirs.
"Seeing as how the *Cherokee* and *Hector* are still at sea, and will be
for some time, I see small profit in locking horns over the Will right
now. So, say I, let the Will be proved as it stands—as soon as may be.

Obed smiled and, more than ever, save for his beard, resembled
his twin. "There's no law I've ever heard of forbidding a body to sell
a ship for well, maybe a dollar—plus other valuable considerations."

Jed chuckled but Lydia frowned. If Obediah was smart enough
eventually to evade the Will for his twin's benefit, why couldn't he
help her out of the disgusting dilemma in which Papa had placed her?
Men, damn them all, stuck together, always had, and probably always would; only females got left out in the cold.

"Suit yourself, Bro," Jed was saying. "We'll cross that bridge all
in good time."

Jed's hand walked on its fingers over to select a steel pen from a clump sprouting out of a birdshot-filled glass. Lost in thought, he commenced slowly to revolve it so that the compass rose tattooed in pink and blue on the back of his hand became intermittently visible. At length he considered Obed, spoke briskly, "Maybe 'tis just as well I've been forced to come home."

"Why?"

"Because I need to consult with you about another matter; it's a scheme you mayn't fall in with."

Obed smiled, "Ain't that for me to decide?"

The girl's gracefully arched black brows mounted. "What is thy meaning, Jedediah?"

"Wondered when you were going to chime in." Her brother's gaze remained fixed on a very old red-and-black house flag on which the moths had been feasting for many a season. "You've heard, I take it, I've been employed the past year by a firm of Shipping Agents— David Coffin & Sons?"

Over the shrill tumult of a rat fight taking place under their feet Obed grunted, "So we've heard. But tell me, Bro, why in tarnation are you wastin' time as a quill-pusher whilst you could ha' been to sea—Master of a well-found spouter?"

Lydia looked shocked. "Surely thee don't intend to give up whaling?" For a Paddock to desert the family's traditional profession would be worse, far worse, than turning Muslim or even dipping into capital!

Obviously puzzled, Obed blinked in the steady white lamplight. "What're you drivin' at, Bro Jed?"

Lydia spoke up, copper-red hues emphasized on the bold planes of her high cheek bones. "Let the *Cherokee* and the *Hector* come home with full holds and we—why, we stand to net sixty thousand at the least."

"—Always provided sperm prices hold up," Jed interjected.

"How can thee expect to do better than that, Jedediah Paddock?"

A rank, sour smell given off by mud exposed by a tide receding under the counting house overcame the pungent odors of cordage, tar and creosote as well as the inevitable reek of raw whale oil.

Lydia queried sharply. "Well, and what is this wonderful notion of thine? Don't just set there like a badly stuffed owl."

"For quite a spell now I've been figuring on how to beat the slow turn-over earned on money invested in whaling. Why should a really smart fellow tie up 20,000 or 30,000 good dollars in a vessel which may be away up to four years and earnin' no interest on his cash? Besides, as we know all-too-well, there's no guarantee said vessel will return with a profitable cargo—or come back at all."

"That's common knowledge. What are you steerin' at, Bro?" Obediah rumbled while Lydia cocked her sleek and narrow head to one side and with faintly slanted eyes glistening paid undivided attention.

Brushing aside the Will, Jed arose to his full six-feet-two and so cast his features into shadow above the lamp's circular green shade. At the same time he warned, "Don't either of you go off at half-cock; hear me out."

Lydia got up at the same time mechanically smoothing the gray woolen skirt which hung uglily straight down to splintered floorings. Lord's mercy! How she despised the heavy, encumbering garments females were condemned to wear. Ever since childhood she'd envied trousers which permitted a body's legs to move freely.

Said she, black eyes narrowed, "Speak thy scheme, Jedediah; perhaps afterwards you heroes will consider one of my own."

Thin, haunting music raised by wild geese passing high above the Island became lost amid a sudden crackling in the grate.

"All right, here 'tis. Once I come to own the *Topaz*, I'll sell her, but keep some shares as an anchor to windward, you might say."

Obed's bull's neck went red, swelled out over the collar of a blue-and-white checkered flannel shirt as he bellowed, "Sell the *Topaz!* Have you taken leave of your wits?"

Jed held up restraining hands. "Didn't I warn you not to go off at half-cock?"

"But *why* does thee want to sell the *Topaz?*" Lydia appeared nonplused. "Why? She's less'n five years old and sound as a new dollar in her every part."

"Oh, I'll grant she's well built. Pa saw to that. But under way she's slower than molasses in February and a regular snail to windward."

"Where's the use of speed in a whaler?" growled Obediah, brow furrowing.

"It's of no use in a standard whaler—but I mean to command a whaler of a different sort—uncommon fast and handy; bark-rigged likely."

Lydia braced hands on the paper-littered table and bent forward, Indian-like features intent. "Why does thee need such a craft?"

Jed casting Lydia a quick glance of appreciation realized that he was a lot fonder of her than he'd ever willingly admit. "I'll answer you, Dark Sister, because, for all you're only a poor, weak, female critter, you know your lines and sails; you can navigate, keep a log and account books."

"My thanks!" snapped Lydia. "But what's all this got to do with thy wanting a bark rig?"

"You ain't ever been to sea, Sissy," Obed put in, "so you don't know how tarnation difficult it is for three or four 'shipkeepers', even smart ones, to work a square rigger in a stiff breeze when all her boats are lowered and hunting to windward. Jed's right. A bark-rigged vessel's a damn' sight handier upwind."

Encouraged, Captain Jedediah Paddock hurried on. "For another thing a bark's handier to work through a narrow channel or amidst a mess of reefs; she can even be navigated up smallish rivers on which a square rigger would get nowhere." Face lighting, Jed's voice swelled, filled the whole dingy office. "I tell you, the bark rig's the coming thing in strange or dangerous waters and, if really fast she could out-foot savage canoes or other enemies even in a light breeze."

4

Bold New Notion

Near the end of Water Street, a burst of raucous singing swelled then degenerated into a chorus of discordant whoops and shouts.

Jed pulled out a pipe and lit it from a paper spill held over the lamp's chimney. "As we all know, most vessels designed and built for whaling have plenty of hold room which makes 'em confounded sluggish sailers but me *I* aim to go whaling in a ship with plenty of foot."

Obed grunted annoyance. "Which means she'd not have sufficient room below to accommodate near enough barrels to earn her owners real profits."

"That may be so—but let me point this out. If a speedy vessel was to hunt the whaling grounds and make a reasonable number of catches on her own account, what's to prevent her Master from stopping a slow ship and offering to sell, at a fair price, as much oil as the other skipper would need to round out his cargo and square away for home?"

Lydia said slowly, "Well, that *is* a point in favor of thy bold new notion."

Jed grinned, "Many thanks, Dark Sister, for those kind words. Now suppose an unlucky Captain's been away from home a fairish while and growing short of supplies but ain't quite ready to turn home, would he be likely to pass up such a chance to take on hard-to-find supplies on the spot so's he'd be able to continue his voyage?"

"—And improve his owners' chances of profit," Obed agreed cocking an amused eye at his twin. "You *have* learned a bit from Coffin & Sons."

Keeping an eye on a white-footed fawn-colored mouse which had appeared on a chest of charts to sit unconcernedly combing its whiskers, Lydia commented. "Thee is right. In such circumstances a skipper'd be a plain fool not to do business."

From the depths of a whirling cloud of gray, rank-smelling pipe smoke came Jed's deep voice. "Even if I sold odd lots of oil, I figure I *still* could fill my holds in a hurry."

"Now why'd you think that?" grunted Obed.

"Because with a handy vessel, well-armed in a small way, I'll be able to fish wherever I listed—places where many skippers daren't venture. Granted ordinary luck I could turn homeward in a hurry and save interest on my investment. Then there's something else." As if anticipating objections Jed hurried on. "On my outbound voyage I aim to make straight for Canton in China."

Obed burst out so loudly that the mouse fled. "Canton! Why Canton? For God's sake, are your wits completely addled?"

"No. I mean to do some trading there *in addition* to whaling. Lots of money's being made in the China trade these days."

Lydia bent forward, face lighting. "Pray continue, Jedediah."

"On my homeward voyage I'd take whales and buy up other Captains' oil till I'd a full hold. Figure to make the round trip in a year plus a few months, and so halve the usual time at sea. Yes, at Coffin & Sons I decided there's a fortune waitin' the first man who puts to sea in a vessel which could whale and trade on the same voyage."

"Humph!" Obed said not quite so acidly. "More likely you'd end up losing money in both directions. A while back you mentioned something about such a ship bein' *armed?*"

Jed nodded in deadly seriousness. "Yes. I mean to have my ship mount sufficient carriage guns to drive off savages, pirates, buccaneers, picaroons or any other form of rascal feeling tempted to attack me. As I said, armed, I'll be able to visit atolls, islands and ports denied to whalers showing only dummy gunports."

Aboard a ship lying to an adjacent wharf an accordion struck up a lively Portuguese tune.

Massive head encircled by drifting pipe smoke, Jedediah raised bushy brows while considering his co-heirs. "I presume the both of you deem me mad as a March hare?"

"Not I!" Lydia circled the table and, to the utter amazement of both her brothers, dealt Jedediah a timid peck on the cheek. Narrow jet eyes shining, she burst out, "I've always deemed thee to have a shrewd head on thy shoulders, Brother Jed—even when thee was making a great fool of thyself."

Back in town a deep-toned church bell commenced deliberately sounded nine times, by which hour all respectable Nantucketers should be home and safely abed. While such tolling didn't constitute any part of an official curfew over several generations this ring had served as a gentle reminder.

Standing behind Jed's chair, Lydia peered through lamp-gilded smoke. "Well, Obediah, and what does thee think of Jedediah's notion?"

Frowning and scratching deliberately behind an ear, Obediah drew a slow breath. "Could be there's somewhat of value in what Bro Jed proposes; perhaps there ain't. Anyhow, as Pa used to say, 'over-hasty judgments oft lead to expensive regrets', so I'll not voice an opinion 'till I've slept on the matter.

"Meantime—" he lumbered over to warm his back at the dying fire. "I want to know, Bro, what your immediate intent is regarding the *Topaz* because if you really intend to sell her *I'll* buy a controlling interest. Can't abide to see one of Pa's vessels fly any house flag but our own."

"Mighty handsome of you, Bro. All right, we'll plan to keep the *Topaz* no matter how badly I need money—and I reckon I'll want plenty before long."

His manner changed abruptly. "Wonder if, by chance, there's a swallow or two of Old Medford left in Pa's 'hospitality chest'?"

"Shouldn't wonder," Obed grinned. From a sea-going tea caddy —a handsome receptacle made of skillfully sculptured, painted and gilded lead—he brought out a small brass key.

Meanwhile, Jed located tumblers—so called because, their bottoms being rounded, they couldn't be put down till emptied.

From a mahogany ship's medicine chest in which Micajah Paddock habitually had kept a bottle of bland but authoritative Medford rum designed to coax agents, merchants and fellow sea captains into a pliant frame of mind, Jed removed a squat brown bottle. When he began to pour drinks for his twin and himself Lydia spoke in an edged voice. "So long as I'm deemed worthy to be present on this weighty occasion, why am I left out?"

Her brothers looked startled. On Nantucket no decent woman ever permitted herself to sample anything stronger than well-watered wine, and then only on very special occasions.

"Well, Lyddie, there's reason in what you say." Chuckling, Jed poured out a drink as strong as their own. "Mind you don't choke on this, ain't raspberry shrub."

"I'll thank thee to advise me only when asked." Lydia raised her tumbler in a quick, over-nonchalant gesture. "Well, here's greasy luck to the *Cherokee* and the *Hector* and a swift return."

Goggle-eyed, the twins watched their lithe, straight-backed sister knock off her rum and water with no pronounced effect beyond a slight watering of the eyes and an abrupt reddening of her high cheek bones.

Jed pounded his thigh, burst into roars of laughter. "'Fore God, Lyddie, where'd you learn to tipple like that?"

"Ask me no questions, Brother Jedediah," Lydia said serenely, "and I'll tell thee no lies. I've a lot of accomplishments thee'd never suspect. Come on, drink up. Then it'll be my turn to speak out and it'll prove to thy advantage to harken."

Once they'd drained their glasses Jed wiped his mouth on the back of his tattooed hand. "Fire away, Dark Sister."

"Obed, will thee be able to buy the *Topaz* right off?"

Obed, after tugging at his yellow, spade-cut beard, took a sip from his tumbler. "Wish I'd sufficient money on hand but fact is, I haven't—need ready cash to fit out the *Morning Star* against her next voyage. No. It'll take a bit of time to scrape up the purchase price and find enough shareholders to round out a fair sum."

She turned to Jed, "I take it thee's in thy usual hurry so, if Obediah can't buy right away won't thee have to sell the *Topaz* out of the family? How else are thee to purchase this wonderful bark thee is yearning for?"

Surprisingly, Jed only grinned. "I've thought on that and maybe I'll come up with an answer." Quizzically, he considered his sister. "Why'd you ask?"

"Because I fancy thy notion, Jedediah. Such a ship *might* earn her shareholders a considerable fortune." She frowned at the same time revolving her glass between supple fingers. "Willingly I would help thee in thy ambition, but I can't, thanks to that wicked clause in Father's Will. I'll be hanged before I'll marry—least of all to inherit money."

Obed straightened on his chair, spoke sharply, "Don't talk so, Lyddie. Pa might have been a mite hard on us sometimes but, according to his lights, always he was fair and generous. Pa was only thinking of the best course for you, so suppose you admit you're twenty years old and well on your way to becoming a dried-up spinster? All the girls you grew up with—even those plain as a sod house have been married long ago. So—"

Lydia's breathing quickened and her hands clenched and unclenched by her sides as she flared. "—And what are such brood mares doing now? They're witless and worn-out with raising a pack of smelly, squally brats. Such a life—if you can call it that, is not for me. I *won't*," she actually stamped her foot, "lead such a stupid humdrum, gossip-plagued life!" Her voice soared. "Do such dull creatures care about what lies over the horizon? What strange lands are to be visited? What adventures may lie yonder?"

"Why should they bother about such flighty nonsense?" commented Obed comfortably. "Take my Nancy, why she's a good wife and is content as a flea in a fox's ear in being occupied with the well-being of her husband and children.

"Lyddie, why don't you wake up and quit dreaming of high adventure, wonderful sights and exciting, strange-dressed folk? Let Jed and me who've been about a bit tell you there's no such a world! Aross the seas you'll meet with a deal more ugliness, treachery, misery and fear than all those wonderful things you've been imagining."

Stubbornly, Lydia Paddock shook her dark and gleaming head. "All the same, come what may, I intend to see the world for myself. I will! I *will!* Just see if I don't!"

Jed chuckled. "Hear! Hear!" Seldom had he beheld his sister so somberly appealing. "'Pears we've just listened to another Declaration of Independence."

Obed got off his chair, stood for a moment with hands clasped behind him staring at yellow-red riding lights glowing, scattered about the Harbor. He turned, said equably, "Jed's barely got home and we've covered a heap of important ground—too much probably to arrive at sound judgments." He lifted a cap with a cracked leather visor from its peg. "Come to my house tomorrow morning the both of you, after breakfast mayhap we'll figure out a means of keeping the *Topaz* under our flag and still get Jed that vessel he's bent on having 'thout too much delay."

Employing abrupt, agitated gestures, Lydia settled the shawl over her head. "Very well, Obediah. I'll be there but I allow that thee and Jedediah will have to stay up all night to find answers to thy problems and, more important, *mine!*"

5
Dark Sister

Jedediah and Lydia Paddock sat across from each other at the latter's abundantly supplied breakfast table. They spoke only in generalities because of the presence of fluttery, ever-loquacious Widow Hawkins, an "accommodator" Lydia had hired to do the cooking shortly before Father's death—ex-harpooner Ben Storer being no part of an artist in that direction.

Like a frigate coming to anchor the Widow sailed in to plunk down a heaping platter of golden-brown fried whitebait—Jed's favorite breakfast dish—and treated her late employer's errant son to an oblique and vaguely disapproving look. Lord, after what he'd done to poor Lucy Dismont why didn't this huge hulk of fellow have the grace to act uneasy—a little less sure of himself? Obviously, Obediah's twin hadn't yet come to suspect that public opinion for the most part hadn't either forgiven or forgotten his shameful affair with Lucy, much less the wronged girl's suicide. *Tsk! Tsk!*

From their places above a gleaming, solid mahogany sideboard fetched over from England by the *Dartmouth* on her final voyage before the War for Independence had broken out, stared a stiff portrait of Pa's stern-looking and long-jawed father, Elijah. It had been done by an itinerant and not ungifted foreign artist. Alongside hung a likeness of Lucretia Chase, his wife, wearing a crisp little white bonnet. Unlike her husband, there were fugitive lines of humor hinted at among the lines of that prim, pink mouth.

Thanks to another uncommon fine mid-autumn day, strong sunlight drew rich, red-brown hues from the late Micajah Paddock's glossy dining table of Honduran mahogany, also from chairs fashioned by one Thomas Sheraton, an English cabinet maker whose genius only recently was becoming recognized.

Lydia's ever vivacious manner was so subdued Jed reckoned she must have spent a near-sleepless night. On the other hand he'd seldom enjoyed more restful slumber than in the depths of that great double bed his parents had shared till Ma had departed this life. It was then that Pa had caused his narrow sea bed to be rigged in the "spare room" and had occupied it 'till his death.

Obed, too, probably had rested well in the large and comfortable but unostentatious gray shingle home he'd built on Orange Street.

Possibly because she'd rested poorly Lydia today hadn't skinned back quite so tight the raven hair she habitually wore parted neatly down the middle; a relaxation which effectively softened the outlines of her boldly planed features.

Leaving the scapegrace to smear gobs of honey over yet another of Mrs. Hawkin's fluffy baking powder biscuits, Lydia went over to put her head out of the window in time to watch a farmer's two-wheeled cart, nearly invisible under a mound of fragrant smelling marsh grass, go creaking by.

Presently she returned to roll her napkin with brief decisive movements and thrust it into a heavy ring carved from a whale's tooth and elaborately engraved with scrimshaw work. Keeping her voice low, Mrs. Hawkins was reputed to possess hearing as keen as that of a buck during the hunting season, Lydia opened the discussion. "Now that thee has slept has thee found solutions for thy problem— and mine? I pray thee has been successful for, as thee knows full well, *I will not marry!* Neither will I tarry in this dull, self-righteous little town one day longer than I must." Lights began to glitter in somber eyes underlined in brown by sleeplessness. "I—I feel, well, nigh smothered to death here."

Jed patted lips with his napkin then peered down the hallway to make sure Mrs. Hawkins really was at work in the kitchen. She wasn't. The Widow was in the backyard tossing scraps to fat gray-and-white hens imprisoned in a large A coop.

His manner became so markedly casual Lydia grew wary. "Dark Sister, 'tain't likely you'll believe it when I say I've found sound answers to both our problems."

The young woman's slimly muscular body straightened; she regarded him in open suspicion. "That easy? Now, Jed, this is no time for teasing."

"I'm not teasing, Dark Sister. Come along." He led her out into the front yard where tendrils of sweet-smelling pale blue smoke from burning leaves eddied about them. "Let's start by reviewing our problems. You are hell-bent to get shut of Nantucket and start traveling about the world?"

She jerked a nod. "Thee has never voiced truer words."

"As for me," he continued, "I need a deal of money; more than the price the *Topaz* will fetch even were I to sell her on the open market—which I won't do on account of my promise to Obed. So where am I to lay hands on the balance of the cash I need?"

Her dark brows arched themselves. "Why ask me? I thought thee just now said thee had found a way?"

"I have," he announced cheerfully. "It is you who are going to lend me the extra sum needed to purchase a bark which has caught my fancy!"

Lydia gaped momentarily then color darkened her clear, olive complexion as she snapped. "Has thee taken leave of thy wits? Full well thee knows that if I don't truckle to Pa's wishes I'll inherit a pittance scarce sufficient to keep me from becoming a public charge." Unexpectedly, her chin commenced to quiver. "Why does thee make such a mock of me? I—I think thee are *hateful!*"

"Belay there, Dark Sister. Now just you listen to me. Since you don't hanker to stay on Nantucket, why not sell this handsome house? Its price will bring more than enough to help buy and arm the vessel I've spoken of."

Her eyes brimmed and ran over. "*Sell* this house? Thee is a great coof! Can't thee remember that to inherit I'll have to marry within a year's time; which I won't do, not even for thy sake!"

The young Captain's little steel-gray eyes narrowed. "You'll marry, Lyddie, sure as sunrise."

Lydia's nostrils flared then grew pinched-looking; she looked bewildered, even sorrowful. "Oh Jed! Jed! Why won't thee understand? Thee whom I've always believed knew me better than anyone else in the world."

"But, Lyddie. Please listen—"

Tiny knives seemed to flash in her eyes. "Bosh! Why can't thee comprehend that the very idea of being bussed, pawed over and bedded by a man always has sickened me! I just won't waste my life raising a brood of horrible, puking babies! I want, and I *will* live my own life—just as you have! Maybe, like thee, I'll make mistakes—but I'm ready to risk that."

"For God's sake will you shut up and listen to me!" he rasped.

More kindly, he went on. "Please, Dark Sister, trust me, and if you do what I say, I promise you'll get what you want." Solemnly, he added, "I give you my word on that."

She used the back of a hand to dash moisture from long black lashes. "What is thy meaning?"

"Will you trust me?"

"I—I think so, Jedediah," she murmured in a masked voice. "Chiefly because I—I am greatly fond of thee—for all I mayn't have let on to anyone about that."

His expression softened. "I've sensed this on occasion, and I feel much the same way—up to a point. Now to business." His manner altered abruptly. "Listen carefully. I've in mind a certain young fellow who was born right here on the Island and was brought up among us. He's not lived on Nantucket for quite a spell because, like me—" Jed grimaced, "he got caught messing around with a young female."

"Thee can't mean Eben Roach?"

"None other."

"Eben Roach! Not that pale, loose-lipped tosspot of a wencher. Why I—I'd rather bed with a billy-goat."

Gray eyes intent, Jed held up a hand. "Who made mention of 'bedding'? Now, Lyddie, belay long enough to hear me out. When last I was up in Boston I saw Eben."

"Shouldn't wonder but thee did!" Lydia's straight, slightly arched nose wrinkled itself in an oddly attractive mannerism. "I've heard it said that thee and Eben are birds of a feather. Not that I've ever credited such nonsense."

A snorting laugh escaped Jed. "Aye. Pious folk are as ready here, as elsewhere, to think the worst of everyone even if they don't half-know what they're talking about. Now, as you know, I seldom drink hard except on special occasions, but Eben likes his liquor and gets drunk all the time. Still, he's never mean and he's generous when in funds."

"How does he fare these days?"

"Last time I saw the poor wretch he was wearing rags, hadn't even the price of a beer."

"But what has Eben to do with us?"

"I'm coming to that; after I've explained my views you'll understand better. I'll freely admit I enjoy full indulgence in life's pleasures." His voice deepened. "Why do I indulge myself? Life's short. Too many men fancy they're going to live to a ripe old age—but *I* know how quick and unexpectedly they can get cut down. D'you think I learned nothing aboard the *Essex* during that fight with the British? That day I saw near sixty killed and twice as many more men wounded so, ever since, my private motto's been: 'Never spoil today for a tomorrow you may never see'." His manner relaxed. "Which, now I think on it, comes pretty close to your way of thinking—for all you mayn't have realized it."

He stepped close, peered steadily into her upturned face. "Our kindly neighbors believe I've been doing naught but waste time and substance in riotous living on the mainland. Well, let them go on thinking so and be damned to 'em!" He grimaced, shrugged a little. "I've been no plaster saint but since entering Coffin & Sons' employ I've not been idle nor gone carousing except rarely.

"Aye, Lyddie, I've learned much concerning the business of whaling and trading which ain't even suspected on this Island. Night after night I've near to wore out my eyes learning how to keep books, figure dividend return rates, write profit-and-loss balance sheets and how to best figure a basis for paying lays. Moreover, I've studied the logs of more whalers and merchant ships than you could shake a stick at in a month of Sundays.

"To be sure everybody hears about two-thousand-barrel voyages—even made a couple myself, as you well know—but who thinks on ships wrecked or lost with all hands? Who remembers how many vessels come home from a skin-and-bones cruise with the hold not even half-filled?"

Jed broke off, pulled an apple from his pocket and commenced absently to crunch it. "In so doing, I've discovered and noted the profits it's possible to make in the China trade."

A faint frown marred the smoothness of Lydia's high, olive-tinted forehead as, mechanically, she re-set the angle of an un-Quaker-like gold and cameo pin securing her neckerchief.

"I'll grant all this is very likely so but, Brother Jedediah, what in thunderation does all this have to do with Eben Roach?"

Gently, Jed patted his sister's smooth cheek and when she didn't draw back he came closer and, smiling, peered into her eyes. "Dark Sister, we're both aware that to come into your inheritance—money from which I stand in sore need of—you'll have to marry. Now here's

the idea—you'll simply go through a quiet but legal marriage ceremony with Ben Roach—and no more. I undertake that you'll not be
left alone with the groom once you're spliced. Lest, of course, you
want to change your mind—" he chuckled "—which, I'm told, you
females have a right to do."

Lydia drew away, declaring icily. "I'd liefer be skinned alive and
rubbed with salt!"

"That's up to you. Main thing is—are you willing to go through
the motions and get us what we want—my ship and your freedom?"

"Suppose I agree? What will happen after the wedding?"

"No fear." He assured in a grating voice, "I promise you'll never
lay eyes on Ben Roach later."

Lydia peered up into her brother's bronzed features, was astonished to read unfamiliar and cruel-looking lines. "But what does thee
intend?"

"That's my concern. Don't question me."

He framed her long, strong face between his hands, spoke softly.
"You'll do what I ask?"

At length she nodded. "Yes. What thee proposes sounds risky
but, whatever thy faults, Brother Jedediah, I think thee is a man of his
word."

He stepped back to offer a derisive half-bow. "For such confidence I, well, I thank—thee."

Long gray skirt a-sway, Lydia for a long moment paced the
front yard. She turned, deadly serious. "However, I'll only comply
on three conditions."

"Which are—?"

"First, after the wedding Eben Roach shall never see me again,
nor shall he lay so much as a finger on my person before it."

"I've already promised that, what next?"

"That I be allowed to purchase as many shares in this vessel of
thine as I can afford."

"Granted. And what's the third condition?"

Lydia stiffened as if to steel against refusal. "Third, and to me
most important, thee must promise to let me sign articles aboard thy
vessel and sail with thee."

"What!" Jed started as if he'd unexpectedly been pricked on the
rump by some savage's spear.

"Yes," she hurried on. "I could sign on as purser, supercargo, fourth mate—whatever thee decides is fitting and useful."

"Jumping Jehoshephat! You must be daft!"

Lydia remained unshaken. "If thee wants that money as badly as thee protests, thee will sign me on for, as thee knows it. I'm an able navigator. Wasn't it thee and Pa taught me? I reckon I can order sails set a-right, and I can row and stand watch," she babbled on. "Aside from that, I'm a first-rate bookkeeper and, if called on, can do hard work with my hands."

Jed snorted, "You drive a Quaker-hard bargain. Crews are dead-set against having a female aboard. You should know that. On a long cruise a woman's bound to cause trouble sooner or later."

Lydia drew herself up, jawline hardening. "I'll cause thee never a mite of trouble, Jedediah. I'm no simpering nice-Nancy. I'll wear naught but male garb nor ask favors or consideration because of—of my sex. And don't thee imagine I can't learn to use a pistol or throw a belaying pin if necessity arises. Well?" The dark-complexioned young woman looked desperately anxious.

Jed let his sister fret a moment then, with patent ill-grace, offered a tattooed hand. "Done! I need the money and you just *might* earn your salt at sea."

Solemnly, they shook hands then went indoors to find Mrs. Hawkins clearing away the breakfast dishes just a bit too busily. How much she'd managed to overhear during their conversation in the front yard there could be no telling.

6

Uriah Dismont

Captain Jedediah Paddock quit Paddock & Sons' counting house leaving a few minor shareholders in the *Topaz*'s impending voyage arguing certain provisions included in a newly drafted charter agreement. Signatures wouldn't be applied or the document notarized until tomorrow. As matters stood, the charter agreement left him only a token shareholder in the vessel he was preparing to sell to Obediah and associates.

Briskly, Jed set off along Washington Street, which running roughly parallel to the crowded and teeming waterfront, would take him to the Anker, his favorite tavern.

Satisfaction over the way negotiations had gone were becoming tempered by apprehension. Experience had demonstrated that when affairs appeared to be going unusually well, it was time to tread warily. Indeed, it seemed almost incredible so much had been accomplished in a little over twenty-four hours.

Another pleasant surprise had come in that Obediah had come around, was prepared to admit that worthwhile profits might be earned by a swift whaling vessel like the *Gladiator*—as long ago, Jed had decided to name his "notion" ship. Never in the World would hard-headed Obediah Paddock have considered purchasing controlling interest in *Topaz* lest he'd felt confident of making money. No Nantucketer in his right mind would allow sentiment or family ties to influence a decision which touched his weasel skin—in serious fashion.

Um. With a seaman's rolling gait he swung on down the street past shops and the warehouses of coopers, iron mongers, ship chandlers, food and spirit sellers, sailmakers and cordage dealers. The familiar and far from unpleasant adumbrations of drying fish, whale oil, raw timber and boiling tar brought back a hundred memories.

Most wharfs and docks appeared to be unusually busy; on them derricks, blocks and tackles creaked and whined; longshoremen chanted discordantly as from the holds of newly arrived whalers they hoisted out, barrel after barrel. These either were lowered onto the docks to be piled under tarpaulins or swayed onto the decks of light-ers and coasting vessels waiting alongside.

Pedestrians dodged resentfully to avoid carts and wagons rum-bling and bumping between the waterfront and candle factories, warehouses or storage lofts.

Down the brown-cobbled street sauntered prosperous looking smug-faced Quaker merchants in long-skirted coats of sober brown or gray, square-toed shoes and flat-crowned, broad-brimmed hats.

Progress towards the Anker further was hampered by the num-bers of hard-looking, usually bearded characters wearing canvas pants, ragged striped jerseys or sweat-stained checkered shirts of rough osnaburg. An unusual number of foreigners seemed to be in port.

Jed encountered swarthy Portuguese in vivid shirts and gay sashes, most of them wearing small golden earrings; towering and generally fair-haired Germans and Scandinavians in rough jackets and flat, visored caps; stunted, gnarled-looking Scots and Englishmen whose complexions suggested rare roast beef. Not so numerous but certainly most distinctive were groups of bandy-legged yet otherwise well-proportioned dark-skinned Kanakas as South Sea Islanders, re-gardless of origin, now were termed.

These last went barefoot for the most part, only protected by enormously thick calluses on powerful brown feet. Some affected loose-knee petticoat breeches or kilts of fine-woven bark cloth bearing weird and usually beautiful designs. From their shoulders dan-gled capes once brilliantly colored but now faded and fraying along their edges.

On long, slightly wavy brown-black hair they wore anything from a seaman's stocking cap to a battered stovepipe or a ratty-look-ing beaver hat with broken brims.

From the nature of bluish designs tattooed on their faces and necks Jed identified some as hailing from the Marquesas, others from the Samoas, and an occasional fellow from the Caroline and Sandwich Islands but the origin of many he couldn't even begin to recognize. The South Sea Islanders seemed ready to smile while gazing in childish wonderment upon probably the first American port most of them had ever visited.

Well, it was beginning to look as if he'd now better than a half-way chance of acquiring the *Canton*, that fast-looking bark on which he'd kept a yearning eye for weeks. While her asking price was stiff it wasn't altogether unreasonable.

Her sole owner, it appeared, had died and his estate was now about ready for settlement. Cautious inquiry revealed she had been built some three years earlier by a well-known shipyard somewhere down south.

For a whaler the *Canton* showed an uncommon sharp stem with a considerable overhang forming what later would be called a clipper bow. Her masts were taller and less stubby and her yards slenderer than those usual in a typical whaler.

What had intrigued Jed most was the fact that, presumably in the interest of speed, her masts had been stepped with a pronounced rake towards her stern.

Jedediah was entering a busy little square when without warning he encountered the likeness of Uriah—eldest of Lucy Dismont's three husky brothers. In the past he'd known Uriah Dismont as a pleasant, easy-going fellow of his own age with whom he'd gone hunting or fishing many a time. Instinctively Jed put out his hand but Uriah, looking not in the least pleasant or easy-going, struck it sharply aside. "Murderer! How dast you return?"

"Steady, Uriah." He forced an uncertain smile while bracing himself. "Nothing's to be gained by getting foamed up!" The pros-pect of a fight didn't really bother him; he'd always been able to lick any two of Lucy's brothers at the same time. Uriah, tall and wiry of build, made no move to step aside; stood glowering. At the top of his lungs he shouted, "Murderer! Lecher! Get off this Island!"

"Belay there, Uriah! I was sorely grieved to learn of your sister's untimely death. Please believe that."

"Believe you? I liefer credit Satan's word."

Passersby halted and a small crowd gathered, hopeful that this confrontation would develop into a knock-down, drag-out fist-fight which rarely occurred by daylight on peaceful Nantucket.

Jed felt his neck begin to swell. "Keep your voice down, Uriah, else I'll surely take you apart. Best remember that nothing you or I can say or do will bring Lucy back to life."

Pale blue eyes glaring Uriah snarled. "Be that as it may, get off this Island in a hurry, Jedediah Paddock, and stay off so long as you live—which won't be long, I pray."

The triangular scar on Jedediah's chin turned bright red but he still spoke evenly. "Stow your gab! I'll leave town only when I'm damn' good and ready, so, Mister Dismont, stand out of my way."

"You'll regret this—and soon!" Uriah snarled, then to the on-lookers' disappointment, wheeled and made off along a narrow and uneven brick sidewalk.

With something akin to regret Jed watched him disappear; in the old days he'd been mighty fond of Uriah.

Continuing towards the Anker, Jedediah forced himself to calm down. A fellow wasn't likely to think straight when really riled up.

Could Captain Owen Chase be persuaded to command the *Topaz* on her forthcoming cruise? The last time he'd seen Owen he'd appeared to have recovered, outwardly at least, from his ghastly voyage of over three thousand miles in the Pacific after a maddened sperm whale had stove in and sunk the whaler *Essex*.

Strange, all five of the *Essex*'s survivors had continued following the sea. A single exception was George Pollard who, on his very first voyage following the loss of the *Essex*, had piled up his new command, the *Two Brothers* on an uncharted reef so hard she'd become a total loss. Small wonder Cap'n Pollard had decided that he'd been born under an unlucky star so he'd "swallowed the anchor" and never again gone to sea. Nowadays he occupied a little cottage on Pearl Street and earned his daily bread as Nantucket Town's only watch-man.

Aware that several minutes remained before the South Church's bell would boom the hour of noon, Jed slowed his pace. Behind him, he overheard voices speaking a foreign but vaguely familiar language so he turned and saw a quartet of dark-skinned South Sea Islanders wandering aimlessly down the street obviously at a loss for something to do. Two of the Kanakas were wearing what Jedediah recognized as *tiputas*—brief capes made of flax, vividly decorated and belted in about the waist. The others were clad in ill-fitting and nondescript products of some whaler's slop chest.

Most likely these drifters had come ashore from the recently arriver whaler, *William Roach*. Stub-masted and bluff-bowed she now lay at anchor, drying smoke-blackened lower canvas. Roach? How curious that a vessel so-named would make port this particular day.

Soon he entered the Anker, a long-established public house favored by sea captains, ship owners and well-to-do agents and brokers.

7

Fracas

In the Anker's smoke-streaked interior brightened by well-burnished copper pots and pans Captain Paddock recognized acquaintances, even a friend or two. On his way to the taproom's rear he paused to offer a greeting to Captain Obed Starbuck who, at sixteen, had led the *Hero*'s crew in recapturing their ship from picaroons who'd murdered the Captain and the cabin boy.

The friendly smile which lit Captain Starbuck's whisker-framed face and the warmth of his handshake went far to dispel Jed's uneasiness. Even more encouraging were greetings called out, along with a few invitations to stop for a drink.

Presently he made out bittern-thin Captain Owen Chase. He was seated by himself and hunched over a pewter mug of ale. Somehow, he'd never regained weight lost during that ghastly voyage.

Jed was seating himself when the town crier's bell began to clang down the street so vigorously it argued he must have important news. Mug in hand, men gathered near the Anker's entrance or stepped right out onto Pearl Street.

"C'n ye make what that old fool's bellerin' about?" Chase demanded, wiping his mouth on the back of a hand.

"Says he's got news concerning the *Oeno*," some called.

"*Oeno? Oeno!*" The ship's name rippled around the taproom like rings spreading from a stone cast into still water. The patrons quieted so much that the snoring of a drunken fellow slumped in a far corner sounded loud out of all proportion.

"*Oeno?*" Jed drawled. "Didn't she clear from here nigh on six years ago?"

"Aye. Thereabouts. Her owners long ago gave her up for lost with all hands."

Looking grave, Owen Chase with suddenly quivering fingers

tugged at a long and untidy brown beard—he didn't like to hear about ships being lost.

The crier's ringing ceased so close by the Anker's patrons had no trouble hearing him intone in a great, far-carrying voice, "Sloop of war *Dolphin* sent by the Government in search reports the *Oeno* of this port got wrecked five years ago among the Fijis. All her crew saving one was drowned or slain and eaten by the savages!"

Out on the sidewalk a tall young woman whose face remained concealed beneath a Quaker's coalscuttle bonnet halted abruptly and called sharply, "Who survived? My brother was aboard."

"Sorry, Ma'am, report didn't say." The crier then resumed clanging his bell and moved on with long-skirted brown coat whipping under a breeze rising out of the southwest.

Subdued moments followed the announcement; most of the Anker's patrons being familiar with the grisly fate awaiting castaways on all-too-many peaceful-appearing islands and atolls dotting the South Pacific's vast and still largely unchartered expanses.

Reports of the terrible end of the crew of the whaler *Agnes*, captured by treachery in New Zealand around the turn of the century, remained vivid in the minds of older Nantucketers. Also in circulation were more recent and dreadfully detailed accounts of unbelievable tortures inflicted by Maoris on captives from an English ship, the *Boyd*, before the poor wretches finally had been slain and devoured.

The two Captains found little difficulty in reaching agreement once Chase agreed to command the *Topaz*. He was to be paid the usual Master Mariner's lay of one barrel in twelve to be sold for his personal profit. If the voyage produced two thousand or more barrels of sperm oil he'd have a bonus of five hundred dollars coming to him.

As customary, Captain Chase would be free to select his mates and crew and decide on which grounds the *Topaz* would hunt. After finishing a pot of hot buttered rum to seal the agreement, they shook hands.

Jed said as he heaved himself to his feet, "Rest of the shareholders will be pleased to hear you've consented to command the *Topaz* this trip." Which was entirely true. Everybody knew Owen Chase to be smart, sparing with the grog and a famous driver of hard bargains. Being single, he'd likely stay at sea till Hell froze over before he'd return without earning his owners a handsome profit.

Captain Chase deliberately settled a short and faded red shawl over spare shoulders before removing a tall beaver hat from its peg. "Heard tell somewheres ye ain't taking out the *Topaz* this time account of ye've got yer eye on a certain racy-lookin' craft over to Noo Bedford. That so?"

The massive young Captain's broad, brown features remained expressionless. "Cap'n Chase, as the sayin' goes, 'There ain't much to see on a little island like Nantucket, but you can hear great and wonderful things'."

A bred-in-the-bone New Englander, Captain Chase took care to depart when Jed began fumbling for his weasel's skin purse.

Jedediah had taken only a few strides along Pearl Street before he sighted breakers dead ahead in the guise of a group including Lucy Dismont's tough old father, Uriah and two hefty brothers lining up abreast to bar his passage. Still more ominous, behind the Dismonts loitered a trio of hard-faced individuals ready to participate in trouble. Without breaking stride Jed cast a quick look about but saw no one likely to side with him in a fracas.

Pulse quickening, Jedediah re-experienced an exhilaration which seized him at the prospect of fighting against odds. A taut grin spread over his features while casting loose his jacket's brass buttons, then jerked off a neckerchief of plain linen and crammed it into a side pocket; no point in offering the enemy a useful hand hold. With the view of getting some blows in first he balled fists and started for Uriah but, before he could reach him, Lucy's father, hearty at fifty despite snowy hair and line-seamed features, held up a hand while his sons closed in on either side.

Bushy brows merged into a single line, the patriarch rasped, "Jedediah Paddock, will you agree to leave town on the packet this afternoon?"

Jed halted, lifted his jaw to a truculent angle, with its three-pointed scar blazing scarlet. "Old man, I want no trouble with you or yours, but I'll not quit Nantucket till I've finished my business. Stand aside!"

One of Lucy's younger brothers leaped forward screeching, "Murderer! Whoreson! Defiler of virgins!"

Without effort Jedediah parried the young fellow's wild swing, then, as shouts of "Fight! Fight!" commenced to arise, set his weight behind his fist, drove it smacking into the fellow's face and sent him staggering backwards into a fast-growing throng who kept him from sprawling flat on manure-speckled cobbles.

The next instant Jed tilted his head, avoided a savage punch thrown by Uriah. An experienced brawler, Jedediah kept himself under control but, coldly ferocious, he drove such a pile-driving blow into Uriah's middle that his breath went out in a mighty rush and, spasmodically, he doubled over only to be straightened up by a short but savage uppercut which dropped the big man onto the cobbles writhing, semi-conscious and completely helpless.

Nevertheless Jed, a moment later, became ringed in by the Dismonts and supporters who came surging out of the crowd. Having no time to duck Jed couldn't avoid the stinging right Lucy's father landed on the side of his jaw. Then such a flurry of punches rocked him that even his massive figure swayed and was twisted back and forth.

Surrounded by a wavering wall of glaring eyes and flashing fists he kept on doggedly lashing out at any target offered. Repeatedly he felt his knuckles crackle under an impact but his wind was beginning to give out and, under this rain of blows, he couldn't see too well.

Inevitably, he would have gone down had not a pair of burly longshoremen in striped, ragged jerseys dashed out of a grog shop yelling, "Gang 'gainst one's nigger fun!" and hurled themselves, fists and feet flying, into the thick of the *mélée*, which afforded Jedediah sufficient respite to let him land a blow on Captain Dismont's bearded jaw; it was hard enough to knock that sturdy old warrior off balance and send him lurching backwards. An instant later someone's fist caught Jedediah so savage a clip under the ear that the bleeding, breathless and now berserk sea captain's head snapped violently to one side and fiery planets commenced to swim before his eyes. The world degenerated into an insane pattern of yelling, staring eyes, writhing mouths and flying fists.

Under a torrent of blows coming it seemed from all directions, Jed, in an effort to gain fighting room, retreated until his heel struck a fallen figure. He fell heavily backwards and struck his head on the cobbles so hard that, after a blinding sunburst had seared his eyeballs, blackness enveloped him and spared him knowledge that his assailants now were using heavy boots to deal him a series of shattering kicks. These tactics proved unwise for, from the hitherto thoroughly delighted onlookers arose angry howls of protest. Joyfully, onlookers joined in a fracas which spread along Pearl Street with the speed of a grass fire under a strong wind, the street now swarmed with milling, punching and cursing combatants few of whom had the least idea of what lay back of all this.

The latest addition to the fray came in the guise of a quartet of Kanakas off the *William Roach* who, recognizing the sound of battle, ran up with long dark hair streaming in the breeze. On glimpsing a prostrate and obviously helpless figure being unmercifully kicked, their tattooed faces lit in anticipation as, led by a towering shipmate, they raised an ear-shattering warcry—*"Ki te tu parekura*—Stand firm in battle!" and plunged joyfully into the brawl.

Although unfamiliar with the use of fists, the Polynesians, quite as effectively employed the edge of their hands in delivering short, chopping blows which could disable or even kill an enemy.

Witnesses standing in doorways or viewing the scene from windows watched the tallest Kanaka—a bronze-skinned, superbly muscled fellow clad in a tapa cloth kilt and a dirty canvas jacket sizes too small for him—wade into the swaying throng of rioters shouting *"Umu potaka!"* in a voice as loud and as piercing as any brazen clarion. As the tall Polynesian fought towards the fallen man he sent assailants, one after another, into howling retreat. The battle thereupon took a new trend and shouts arose: "Kill the savages! Kill the bloody cannibals!"

Men who'd been slugging one another an instant before turned on the dark-skinned intruders standing over Jedediah Paddock's bloody and mud-smeared figure and learned painful lessons.

Women shrieked while more men and youths came pelting out of side streets. Belatedly, somebody went running for Captain Pollard, the town's only peace officer, for, unlike Boston, New Bedford or other equally thriving ports, Nantucket waterfront brawls were a rarity.

While selecting a supply of blubber spades in Silas Whippy's foundry Captain Obediah Paddock heard sounds of tumult in the distance, so ran out into sunlight flooded Union Street. Some undefinable source warned that Jed might be involved, so he called over his shoulder, "Back in a minute, Si," and began to run, lightly for a man of his size, until he encountered a whiskery acquaintance who was clutching a blood-soaked handkerchief to his broken nose.

"What's up?"

"Riot in Pearl Street."

"What's it about?"

"The Dismonts and some backers jumped yer brother."

When, like a yellow-headed Titan, Obediah charged into Pearl Street the Kanakas were being hard-pressed and barely able to hold their own now that rocks were beginning to fly and sticks to flash.

As he closed in Jed's twin quickly realized that a pair of wild-eyed seamen in torn clothes and four South Sea Islanders had formed a ring, back-to-back, above Jed's prostrate form. The Kanakas, although dishevelled, bruised and liberally bloodstained had had their queer garments nearly ripped off; nevertheless they kept sticking out their tongues and laughing while breathlessly taunting their pale-faced enemies.

Whenever an offensive move was made they sprang forward using the sides of their hands with such vicious effect that their assailants slowly began to fall back.

To have Obediah Paddock come charging in from behind, roaring like a modern day Bull of Bashan and knock several men flat, was enough to convince rioters still on their feet that little was to be gained through lingering in Pearl Street.

The largest South Sea Islander when he made out Obediah's vast outline surging into the fray threw back his heavily tattooed head and uttered a screeching warcry. At the same time he leaped high in the air and, in a curious gesture, kicked up both heels high behind him before springing at his assailants with such ferocious abandon that they scattered and, spouting curses, scampered off.

Pearl Street at once became deserted save for panting victors and a number of fallen combatants. When one of these roused and attempted to crawl away on hands and knees the biggest Polynesian used a huge foot to kick the would-be fugitive in the side so viciously that he dropped flat again. Swiftly, the South Sea Islander bent, gripped the writhing fellow by his hair and would have delivered a chopping stroke on the side of his neck had not Obed bellowed, "*Tapu! Tapu!* Forbidden!"—one of the very few South Sea words he knew; he'd never been near so handy with foreign languages as Jed who could employ several Polynesian dialects with fluency.

The giant Kanaka spun about staring in incredulous astonishment. *Tu!* Was this not the very same *pakeha*—European—who'd been lying senseless at his feet? Then his fellows began to laugh, panting *"Mahanga! Mahanga!*—Twin! Twin!"

Obediah knelt beside Jedediah and found his brother so terribly marked his face was scarcely recognizable. It was so disfigured by bloody lumps, cuts and purplish bruises. What alarmed him most was Jed's stertorous breathing and profound unconsciousness.

He motioned the big Polynesian to rest Jed's battered yellow head on his knee then set about gingerly testing for broken bones and discovered that several ribs appeared to have been cracked or broken by boot toes. Meanwhile the tattooed outlander used the tail of his shirt carefully to wipe mud and blood as well as horse manure from Jed's grotesquely swollen features.

At this moment the town watchman made an appearance, swinging his rattle. In a fine quarter-deck voice Captain Pollard ordered all law-abiding citizens to clear out.

"How bad's he hurt?" asked a battered longshoreman.

To everyone's astonishment Jedediah without opening his eyes wheezed, "I—I fine. Still c'n lick any bastard in—house. C'mon!"

"Be still!" Obed ordered. "You've cracked that damned hard head of yours 'gainst harder cobbles."

Jed's eyes opened dazedly, gradually focused until he could discern a face blue with elaborate tattooed designs eclipsing a bright autumn sky. Lord God! How'd I get back to Oceania? Jerkily, he raised a knuckle-skinned hand, *"Mihi Hoa*—greetings, Friend. Help—up."

But when his rescuers attempted to raise him, Jed uttered a whistling gasp, sank back moaning and bathed in cold sweat with so many searing, breath-taking pains lancing his left side that he all but lost consciousness again.

When he'd recovered a little he muttered, *"Wakawhetai hoa*— thanks Friend, but for you—might ha' been *patu*—killed."

Nodding rapidly several times the big Polynesian exposed irregular but nearly perfect white teeth in a great smile. "We are *waimarie* —good luck to you."

"Who—you?"

Proudly the shortest Kanaka pointed to his tall companion. "Him, Te Ponapa Kai Rangatira."

Rangatira? Kai Rangatira? With difficulty Jed tried to remember and succeeded. In Polynesia a *"rangatira"* meant a powerful chief, *Kai* meant "Heir of—"

Meanwhile Obed offered his hand which Te Ponapa accepted with immense dignity, then remarked, "Should you or your friends want for anything, Mr. Rangatira, just call on me. What are your friends' names?"

"This one is called 'Heetee.' At home he is only my slave but on shipboard he is my friend and companion. The others," he shrugged and added without malice, "they are stupid fellows from Tonga Island."

Obediah asked the rangatira, "Which Island d'you yerself hail from?"

Te Ponapa's well-shaped head went back. "I am a Maori of the Otago tribe from Taranaki, lying in the north of Aotearoa which English and Yankees call 'New Zealand'."

8

As Through a Glass, Darkly

In the main bedroom across the hall from where Master Mariner Micajah Paddock had died Lydia sat beside a mahogany four-poster bed on which lay her liberally bandaged brother. Quietly she fanned away a few sluggish but persistent bluebottle flies that so far had managed to survive the first frosts. Jedediah had fallen into an uneasy slumber immediately after consuming only a small part of an appetizing repast prepared by Mrs. Hawkins.

For the first time Lydia was regretting that she'd never taken a particle of interest in cooking; to her, food was simply fuel required to sustain one's body. Accordingly she'd always partaken without complaint of any sort of provender placed before her—provided it was clean and reasonably hot; seasoning or the lack of it didn't matter in the least.

Jed lay, broad, squarish face flushed to deep mahogany beneath his permanent tan. Although only semi-conscious he kept his breathing shallow; whenever he attempted to draw a normal breath three broken and two cracked ribs drove darts of such excruciating pain through him that he'd gasp and curse under his breath; like most seafaring Nantucketers he prided himself on being Stoic.

Aside from this, his entire head pained like an ulcerated tooth and his hands ached nearly as badly. Had they suffered broken bones? Certainly they hurt enough. How come he found himself in such condition?

As through a heavy fog his mind groped until it came on something to work from; that time he'd first taken note of Lucy Dismont. The scene returned in sharp detail; memories fell into sequence.

Lucy must have been about fifteen and growing uncommon pretty in a lush, pink-and-white way. Her melting dark-brown eyes were large enough to lend her a slightly bovine appearance. Her chestnut hair was plentiful and rich with fulvous copper tints. The girl's lips were neatly delineated and red as bleeding heart blossoms. Her pale, rose-tinted skin wasn't marble smooth in texture but bore a resemblance to fine down covering a ripe peach.

How long ago had that been? Um. About four—no, five years back. Yep. He'd first noticed Captain Dismont's daughter right after he'd fetched the *Topaz* home with forty thousand dollars' worth of sperm and spermaceti in her hold. For all his voyage had proved more than satisfactory his take hadn't come close to matching Captain Joe Starbuck's *Loper*, brought home deep to her nines under a cargo worth fifty thousand.

Along with a couple of young fellow-captains fresh in from the sea and ready to celebrate he'd hired a tip cart one fine day early in June and they'd all driven out to the Island's annual sheep-shearing festival. Customarily this was held hard by Miacomet Pond, an occasion which offered a fine excuse for family reunions and other such get-togethers.

People came in droves not only from all over Nantucket but sailed over from Tuckernuck, Maskeget and Martha's Vineyard. Some came all the way from Cape Cod, Fairhaven, New Bedford and other ports to enjoy the sheep shearing which, in many ways, compared to a county fair held on the Mainland. In addition to coconut shies, catch-penny games, jugglers, fortune tellers and giant swings there were crude merry-go-rounds to be enjoyed by the young. For their elders foot races, wrestling, weight lifting contests and a variety of rough country games brought over from the Old Country nearly two centuries earlier.

Even to the smallest detail Jed found himself recalling how, flushed with grog, he and his friends had stood watching grunting young fellows wrestle, catch-as-catch-can, for small cash prizes. When an umpire called for new contestants his companions had taunted him into pulling off his jacket to match grips with a wiry, eagle-beaked, half-breed Monomoy Indian.

The contestants had proved to be so evenly matched that a growing throng of witnesses were kept in roaring excitement; bets had flown like hailstones.

Probably because people still were talking about the *Topaz*'s near-record voyage most people cheered Micajah Paddock's massive son. All the same, he'd barely been holding his own when all at once he recalled a wrestling trick painfully acquired during the *U.S.S. Essex*'s long refit at Nukahiva.

In the end he'd succeeded amid thunderous cheers in pinning the Monomoy's shoulders to the ground, then had scrambled to his feet, slippery with sweat, his barrel chest heaving and pink as salmon's flesh. 'Twas then that he'd half-heard a girl's tremulous voice say, "Glory, Captain Paddock, you look just like Hercules must have!"

Grinning, he turned and for the first time had taken a real look at Lucy Dismont, delicate and dainty as a Dresden shepherdess in a wide straw hat and frilly summer dress.

Her mother, a gaunt, acid-faced woman standing just behind her, had looked mighty disapproving of so unseemly an outburst.

On various occasions during the weeks following the sheep-shearing festival he'd not been able to avoid noticing how often Lucy's liquid, dark-fringed eyes were clinging to him, but the chit had only hovered, flushed and adoring in the background.

For this adulation he gave Lucy Dismont no more than a quick smile and a casual nod for according to Lydia at fifteen Lucy already was reputed a natural-born flirt.

During his next two-year cruise in the Pacific he'd not granted Lucy Dismont so much as a passing thought. In the South Seas there'd been plenty of generously inclined dusky wenches anxious to occupy his attention whenever time and opportunity permitted.

Then he'd brought home the *Topaz* carrying an even more profitable cargo to find that Lucy had "bloomed" into one of the prettiest girls to walk Nantucket's streets in years. Indeed, she'd developed into a balm for sore eyes—especially those of a full-blooded young Captain fresh in from a long cruise.

Now that Lucy was eighteen she had had more access to his company, nor was he unhappy about that.

When, following a taffy-pull at Jenny Birchard's home, Lucy shyly had suggested that the towering young Captain see her home he might have declined—having sized up Peggy Greenslit as a more likely prospect—had he not imbibed freely of a bland but authoritative arrack punch concocted by Jenny's brother, a randy boon companion with whom in the South Seas he'd shared a few amorous adventures. The old saw that Yankee whalers "hung their consciences on the Horn" and only recovered them on the way home was not without foundation.

While he and Lucy were progressing along a street lined with fountain elms—still quite small—a thunderstorm which had been rumbling and grumbling across the Sound all afternoon had pounced just as they were nearing the South Church.

Despite a lashing downpour he'd noticed that its vestry room's door wasn't quite closed so he'd hauled Lucy, breathless and giggling, to shelter.

They stood alone, only slightly drenched, in a small, musty-smelling and gloomy room. They began to laugh when he used a pocket handkerchief to wipe the rain from her features.

Before he knew it Lucy's arms were about his neck and she was gasping, "Oh Jed! Dearest Jed! All these years I've been—been yearning, hungry for this moment."

Through a sort of shimmering haze he'd seen her eyes close while she lifted parted lips. Her breath, fragrant and warmly tantalizing, titillated his nostrils. "Kiss me! Oh-h! Hold me tight, Jed—and kiss me hard, *hard*, HARD!"

Events might not have progressed as they did had not a stack of new pew cushions been left on a bench built across the vestry room's rear wall.

Although Jed later on tended to blame what ensued on Johnny Birchard's arrack punch it was surging desire which carried him away. First thing he knew his arms had clamped down grinding Lucy's maddening softness against him while her lips crushed and clung to his hard, brown ones with an animal ardor he'd not experienced since that long-gone day when, as a young midshipman on Nukahiva, he'd just discovered the iridescent wonders of making love with Neti—only fourteen but already a mature and passionate expert in the subtler aspects of copulation.

Next thing, Lucy and he had been panting, struggling in a blind, delicious frenzy on pew cushions hastily ranged along the bench.

Even now he could recall how, like combers breaking over a half-tide rock, Lucy's fragrant, lace-edged cambric petticoats had frothed about his face. The two of them had been so utterly engulfed in bliss neither heard the door open to admit Deacon Philbrick, a sparse, humorless creature who'd returned in search of spectacles misplaced during a morning meeting of the Vestry Board.

Dripping rain, the old fellow at first had stood, rooted, speechless and quite possibly fascinated by this frantic coupling before he'd thundered in spluttering outrage. "Cease! What you commit is a cardinal sin but that you should commit this foulness in God's own House is an abomination! Cease, you shameless sinners and get ye hence!"

Jed had scrambled to his feet tugging frantically at his trousers while Lucy had crouched, moaning, in a corner and struggling to rearrange her garments. Jed then had committed a fearful blunder— he'd offered Deacon Philbrick a sizable bribe to hold his tongue.

More completely outraged than ever the Deacon then had run out into the storm summoning all to witness how the Lord's House was being desecrated.

Predictably, public opinion seethed and had this outrage occurred in any other part of New England—save possibly the District of Maine—the guilty couple very likely might have suffered physical as well as verbal abuse. As it was, Nantucket being Nantucket, no action was taken.

The worst aspect of the whole miserable business had been the vitriolic dressing-down delivered by Captain Micajah Paddock when he said in a voice harsh and cold as the grinding of ice floes, "You're vile and an eternal disgrace to a family that's ever been upright and God-fearing! Get off this Island straightaway and never let me behold your face again!"

Jedediah was distracted from his miserable revery when Lydia, with a swift motion, neatly caught a fly which had taken to buzzing persistently about his bandaged head.

When he continued to lie with eyes closed and breathing painfully her expression softened and she studied her brother who, in her quiet and undemonstrative fashion she'd always worshipped and admired above all mankind. Lord! Even like this he remained stimulatingly, undeniably handsome in his rugged, weatherbeaten way. 'Twas no wonder that from the time he'd won his first command till that ghastly scandal erupted every ambitious mother on the Island had intrigued to arouse his interest in a marriageable daughter. But to Lydia's intense relief Jed had evaded the most cleverly devised snares and maneuvers.

When her brother sighed and stirred she placed a palm on his forehead and felt vaguely disturbed at experiencing a sense of gratification. Hum. His skin seemed to be noticeably hotter. Was he suffering a recurrence of fever? Delicious thought; in half an hour it would be necessary to test his temperature again. If it remained high she'd start running to fetch Doctor Swazey.

Flushing, she crossed an oval braided rag rug to straighten on its stand a small model of the *Hector* delicately carved out of whale tooth ivory. How strange; whilst I understand Jedediah far better than anyone, I can't even guess what his next move will be. How can a man act so kind, generous and straightforward most of the time and also remain capable of meanness, trickery and brutality? I've heard of how Jed has saved lives at the risk of his own, also that he's killed men; a savage on Nukahiva, for example. Characteristically, she quit conjecturing. After all, the reasoning back of Jed's actions was past understanding.

Skirts rustling she then went to view the familiar vista of gray-shingled roofs, white-railed lookout walks, gables and dormers interspersed by naked, wind grieved treetops and a scattering of white-painted steeples and cupolas. Why had she come to despise her birthplace so heartily? Many strangers sang its praises.

A pair of poke-bonneted Quaker girls appeared down sandy New Dollar Lane. Heavy market baskets were causing both to walk lopsided. One cast an upward glance at Micajah Paddock's mansion but on noticing Lydia at the window ducked her head, concealing features beneath a brown sunbonnet. Her companion also bent her head. They hurried on down the Lane.

Lydia, wrinkling her thin, slightly hooked nose, gripped lips between small and slightly uneven white teeth. She shouldn't have felt surprised. Almost every female on the Island classified her as an "odd number"; she'd never been interested in feminine society or pursuits.

All through school she'd remained a thin, dark-visaged creature given to solitary walks over the moors or to combing beaches in hopes of coming across some exciting item of jetsam.

Even now she could recall the ecstasy over discovering a battered figurehead lying half-buried in the sand and, on another occasion of finding a coconut which—think of it—must have grown on some lovely tropical island.

Was it really so wicked or abnormal to dream of freedom and travel in faraway lands? Why should she instinctively rebel over having to wear the cumbersome and impractical garments of a female? As in other matters, men had so much the better of it when it came to clothing. It really wasn't fair.

Turning, she glanced at the mantel clock and saw its hands nearing four which meant Obediah soon should appear with that big brown Kanaka who apparently had saved Jedediah's life.

Jed opened his eyes, saw how effectively the sun was glistening on his sister's blue-black hair, precisely parted into twin braids. "A penny for your thoughts, Lyddie."

"How long has thee been awake?"

"Long enough to realize I've a damned handsome sister."

Narrow lips forming a flat "prunes, prisms and persimmons" line of disapproval, Lydia, though not displeased, shook her head. "Thee talks nonsense. How does thy side feel?"

"—As if a fluke stove it in. Thought Obed 'llowed he'd drop by around now. Where is he?"

"I'll go look." A glance through the window told her that Obed's towering, brown-clad bulk was drawing near in company with a Polynesian nearly as big as himself. The latter, whose skin now looked to be light tan rather than brown, was stalking over fallen leaves with the powerful and effortless grace of a prowling panther. "They're below."

Jed said quickly. "Before they get here—you've spoken to Cap'n Coffin about buying this property?"

"Yes. Seemed eager enough to discuss terms."

"I ain't surprised. He's made so much ambergris money lately I'll bet that pushy wife of his is badgering him to buy her a fancy home. You'll hold out for a stiff price?"

Lydia sniffed. "I'm not a Paddock for nothing."

9

Rangatira

The picket fence's gate clicked open, then a spring bell tinkled; Ben Storer at once could be heard thumping on his peg leg along the corridor towards the front door.

Lydia announced, "Obediah has with him a big Kanaka. I think 'twas the one led the savages who rescued thee."

"Good, but remember one thing, Lyddie; South Sea Islanders resent being termed 'Kanakas'—to them the word's as offensive as for a Black to be called a 'nigger'."

"I trust thee will reward him a good sum of money."

Jedediah shook his bandaged head. "That's no proper reward for a *rangatira*."

"*Rangatira*? What's that?"

"A title. On some islands he's only an important nobleman, on others he's the boss chief."

Lydia's bold black brows arched. "How much of their lingo does thee speak?"

"A fair amount in some dialects, but my talk's mostly concerning things a nice young female ain't supposed to hear about. Polynesians generally don't mince words and are apt to call a spade a goddam bloody shovel. Howsumever, I understand more than I let on."

"Ahoy, aloft!" Obediah's deep voice hailed from the foot of the staircase. "You fitted out for visitors?"

Jed forgot and drew a deep breath to make reply so ended by biting lips to smother a yell of pain. Lydia hurried to the hall door calling, "Patience. Thee may come up in a minute."

"Help me, Lyddie!" Fighting down a series of grunts and groans Jed struggled into sitting position while his sister stacked a bolster and a couple of pillows behind him. By the time he was able to settle back great drops of sweat were spangling his face and neck.

Presently Captain Obediah Paddock's vast frame garbed in brown serge filled the doorway. He paused to cast a quick inquisitive look at the four-poster, then strode in saying, "I've brought along our Maori friend. Thought you might want to offer thanks."

In grave interest Lydia watched Te Ponapa enter. He was clad in a pair of knee breeches but wore no stockings so muscles on his enormously powerful calves stood out impressively. Otherwise, the Maori was wearing a *tiputa*, or short striped mantle of red-and-yellow over a clean canvas shirt which lent the impression of his being darker than he really was.

His shoulder-long hair was wavy and brown-black and in it he had, by means of a broad yellow band, lodged two seagull wing feathers which rose vertically before either ear. His broad, flat feet were bare. Lydia noticed that although marred by heavy calluses, they nonetheless remained symmetrically shaped.

The Maori smiled widely then offered this tall young woman in gray a slow head-bow. At the same time his large and lively black eyes made such a frank and deliberate appraisal, that she flushed.

Lydia forgot embarrassment when the savage whose headdress was brushing the ceiling turned to the bed. He began to speak in perfect, but oddly-inflected English. "Greetings, Captain. One is pleased to hear that you have suffered no truly critical injuries."

Jed's bandage-crowned head went back. "*Mihi! Ariki Watakiapo* —Greetings, Royal First Born!"

A pleased expression spread over the Polynesian's finely sculptured light-brown features; their true proportions were disguised by an intricate pattern of tattooed blue-black swirls and coils.

"*Mihi, umu potaka!*" He padded across the bedroom offering a massive, square-shaped hand.

Lydia watched the two big men grip and became suddenly aware of an odd presentiment that this moment might bear on the fates of all those present.

Jed, unusually moved, asked huskily, "*Rangatira*, will you honor me with the *ka hongi a maru?*"

"*Hé!*" Delightedly, the giant Maori bent and, to Lydia's astonishment, several times passed the tip of a short, straight nose across her brother's.

Obed chuckled. His small eyes twinkled in the broad expanse of bronze-hued features. "Don't look so took aback, Lyddie, that's the South Seas way of greeting a friend—something like Frog-Eaters kissing on both cheeks."

Sniffed Lydia, "Wager thee has taught females out yonder a better style of bussing."

In a quick undertone Jed said something to Te Ponapa. The big Maori grabbed Lydia and before she'd the least notion of what impended he began to apply a whole-hearted *ka hongi a maru*.

Crimson, the girl braced hands against the Polynesian's massive chest and wrenched aside. "Let me be! Thou—thou stinking, over-bold savage!"

At Te Ponapa's mildly astonished expression Obediah burst into roars of laughter; his twin attempted to join in but his hurt side reduced whoops to a series of whistling groans.

Glaring like a trapped wildcat, hands clenched and shaking more from injured dignity than outrage Lydia burst out, "For shame, Jedediah Paddock! How dare thee make such shameful sport of thy own kin?"

Still guffawing, Obediah gasped, "Te Ponapa, you'd better 'defy' her lest she does you an injury."

"*Hé whakawhetai!*" Ivory-hued teeth gleamed.

The twins knew what to expect, but Lydia didn't, nor did any neighbors within earshot. Te Ponapa suddenly began to drum fists against his chest and flung his head so far back that the feathers in his hair paralleled the floor as he raised a series of howls so blood-chilling that a passing huckster's horse bolted. In the vicinity cats bottled their tails and dashed for cover; dogs raised a fearful clamor. In all directions windows started to bang up.

Three times the Maori raised his appalling cry then, goggling his eyes, rushed at the transfixed girl and with face held no more than an inch from hers ran out his tongue so far its end covered tattooing on his chin.

The Maori sprang lightly backwards and began to laugh uproariously. "Te Ponapa *hongi hongi!*—Te Ponapa salutes you. *Ata-ahua prion*—most beautiful goddess."

For a long instant Lydia could only pant, high cheeks gone scarlet with outrage. She whirled on her brothers, cried in a strangled voice, "Thee are hateful, the both of thee. Don't either of thee imagine that some day I'll not even the score—and with interest!"

Obediah tried to put a placating hand on her shoulder. "Now,

now, Lyddie, don't carry on. Our friend didn't really buss you so you can go on sayin' you're sixteen, and some over, and ain't yet been kissed."

To her surprise Lydia's anger faded while hurriedly she began to smooth her hair. An attempt to look daggers at the splendidly-proportioned savage failing completely, she ended by saying stiffly, "Finding thee, Mr. Ponapa, in such company I might have expected some exhibition of crude horseplay, but don't thee, Mr. Ponapa, ever again dare attempt such a liberty."

Jed chuckled in the depths of the four-poster, "Now that we've had our little joke I must try to thank you, O Te Ponapa; 'tis more than likely I owe my life to you and your companions. Will you do me the great honor of becoming my *tuakana?*"

Lydia, smooth, olive-tinted features still suffused, risked asking, "What might a '*tuakana*' be?"

"Something like a blood-brother," Obed explained, dropping his bulk into a wing chair. "The participants join each others' family."

Jed amplified, "It means a man must share equally whatever Fate sends to him and his *tuakana*."

Straightening his cape, the Maori said with a assumption of regal dignity. "Let it be so. Let our feet tread the same path until death claims one or both of us."

"Lyddie, we'll do this *tuakana* in style. Tell Ben to fetch up a jorum of Pa's French brandy. Maybe the gods will grant us extra approval."

When the bald old man stumped in bearing a tray and a dusty bottle Lydia shook her head. "Only *three* glasses? Thought we'd settled that matter before. Besides, aren't I fit as any of thee to toast this—this bond? Ben, fetch me a tumbler."

Once the old harpooner disappeared "below decks" Lydia surprised herself as much as her brothers by saying quietly, "If thee pleases, Mister Ponapa, won't thee relate something of thy past?"

Te Ponapa, upright feathers again brushing the ceiling, crossed to the mantelpiece from which he lifted a two-handed war club Micajah Paddock had fetched back from the Marquesas. "This is well-balanced, but my people fashion better ones."

"I think Pa picked that club up in Oparo," Jed stated. "That anywhere near the place you hail from?"

Deliberately, the tattooed giant's vitreous black eyes circled the sunlit bedroom. "No, my people inhabit the North Island of Aotearoa. My father, Te Pehi—if he is still alive, is *Ariki*—supreme chief of the valiant and all-conquering Otagos. Te Pehi's *mana*—his great fame in battle—is spoken of on both the Islands of Aotearoa. I am his *Waikatapo*—first born son."

"Mr. Ponapa," Lydia asked, "How is it thee speaks such excellent English?"

The visitor's bare feet whispered softly over the circular rag rug when he returned to the bedside. Then, in his curiously monotonous and un-inflected way of speaking, he stated: "When I was only a small *tarua* an English ship became wrecked on the coast of Taranaki near Whangaroa. Most of her people drowned. Among the few to reach shore alive was a Mr. Horatio Andrews, a college-educated scientist. While the rest of the survivors were either made slaves or killed and eaten according to our custom, Te Pehi, my father, took Mr. Andrews into his household as a free man on condition he teach sons of the Royal Family to speak English and otherwise instruct us in the ways and wisdom of the *pakehas*—Europeans." The Maori nodded to himself. "Even then, Te Pehi was very wise and knew that, to survive at all, Maoris must be able to trade and treat on even terms with *pakehas*—especially the British, Americans and Australians."

"It would seem Mr. Andrews earned his salt." Obediah went over to fill the brandy glasses.

Jed said, "Dark Sister, please bring my razor from the washstand."

More curious than repelled, Lydia held her breath when Te Ponapa made a little incision to start a thin trickle of blood flowing from the heel of Jedediah's right palm. Clumsily, because of battered hands, her brother then performed a similar operation on the Maori. The two then gripped hands, pressing their cuts so tightly together that their blood mingled, pattered slowly into a soapdish snatched by Obed from the washstand.

Ceremoniously, Te Ponapa then intoned a *karakia*—an incantation, "*Tuakana toa*—valiant brother warrior, *ki te tu parekwia*—stand firm with me in battle—and in all trials the gods send to test the strengh of our brotherhood."

In equal gravity, Jed promised, "Te Ponapa, as God is my witness, I will forever stand firm with you."

Once they had rubbed noses again and washed off a few blood-stains Lydia and Obed passed the tray of drinks. Lydia, eyes shining, lifted her glass. "I presume this is a downright un-Christian and a heathen rite, nonetheless, God send this bond between the two of thee never is tested beyond its strength."

"Amen!" muttered Obediah, "This brandy sure spreads out in a hurry."

Jed quit sucking the nick on his hand, then settled back, all at once looking wan and very tired. "Brother Ponapa, care to tell us how you come to be on Nantucket?"

Te Ponapa rested a muscle-corded brown arm on the mantel-piece and the coiling blue-black designs on his forehead became disarranged by a frown. "Four—or perhaps five years ago—I can't remember exactly when it was, I took my slave and friend, Heetee, and two others, low-class slaves to fish for kahawai off the coast in a coasting *waka*—canoe. Suddenly a storm from off the Tasman Sea blew up, and we were driven out of the sight of land. When the great *tupuki* ended no wind came for many days. The sun beat upon us without mercy. We would have died had we not brought along a small store of coconuts."

The Maori's voice lowered. "The day came when nothing was left to eat or drink so I took my war club and knocked the weakest of my slaves on the head. We slaked our thirst on his blood."

"How—how dreadful!" Lydia burst out.

Te Ponapa shrugged, "Not dreadful. The slave was ready to die. From birth his destiny was to nourish his lord in every way. His flesh fed us nearly a week."

Lydia's jet pupils became ringed in white. "Thee means thee *ate* thy companion!"

The Maori looked both puzzled and annoyed. "*Kuihi!* Speak softly, *vahine!* I ate not a friend, only a *tumau*, a slave of the lowest order. Heetee is not the same—he is of lesser rank but still of my people."

"But, but weren't all thy slaves human beings?"

Te Ponapa explained stiffly. "—To *pakehas* perhaps. No. Since the dawn of Things Remembered *tumaus* are to my people only pigs wearing the form of men."

"How awful!"

"Why, awful? Do not *pakehas* carry along supplies when they set out on a journey?"

"Of course."

"In the same way Maoris bring food of the ordinary sort but also slaves to eat if other supplies fail."

"But—but that's an abomination!"

"Lyddie, hold your tongue!" Jed warned sharply. "If you're set on traveling the sooner you learn to respect foreign beliefs the better off you'll be."

Taking refuge in logic rare to her sex Lydia swallowed hard on nothing several times and remained silent with the appalling realization that Jedediah was now blood-brother to a cannibal!

Obed prompted hastily "—And what happened after that?"

"After Heetee and I finished the last of the second *tumau's* flesh we grew so weak we were prepared to join our ancestors when a sail appeared." Te Ponapa drank the last of his watered cognac, continued in a deep monotone. "It was that of an English trading ship. Her captain, being short-handed through scurvy, took us aboard and restored our strength. In return he worked us to exhaustion." Te Ponapa scowled. "When we reached Port Jackson in Australia the brute paid us off with nothing but blows and curses."

Curlicue blue-black ridges on the Maori's features darkened, became more pronounced. "The fool even made bold to strike me, Crown Prince of the Otago Tribe; never did he suspect I could have slain him with my bare hands."

"Why didn't you?" Obed asked.

The Polynesian shrugged and his teeth flashed. "Had I done so I would not be alive and standing here."

"You acted smart."

"One dark night I and Heetee slipped overboard then swam to the *Rambler*, a whaler coming from a port called Sag Harbor."

Te Ponapa reaching under his shirt scratched vigorously, "We were lucky. Captain Worth proved to be kind and just to us. During the two years I and Heetee sailed with Captain Worth we learned to hunt the whale and I to handle a harpoon better than any boat-steerer aboard," he added proudly. "We were bound for America when a typhoon drove the *Rambler* onto reefs off an Island on which no one lived. Only four of us reached land." The Maori turned and, curious as a cat, picked up and studied a pie-jagging wheel carved out of whale ivory and liberally decorated with scrimshaw.

"For months, I have no idea how many, we four caught fish and ate breadfruit and coconuts. Finally the *William Roach*," he inclined his feathered head towards the Inner Harbor, "put in for water and took us off. I signed to replace a boatsteerer who had died. So, we hunted whales until the ship came here to finish her voyage. That is all."

"Does thee expect to sign on the *Roach* again?" Lydia inquired.

From the four-poster came Jed's weak voice. "He'll not. Not if I've anything to say in the matter—and, by God, I have!"

10

Conversation by Candlelight

Toes recoiling from contact with the cold floorboards, Lydia Paddock started for her bed but paused, shivering under a severely plain flannel nightgown. Down Silver Dollar Lane someone was singing. Immediately she recognized Jedediah's deep bass and at the same time knew he wasn't drunk; his booming voice rang true.

> *"Now this is Shearing Day, alack,*
> *And here we are around Cape Horn*
> *And we shall surely miss of this*
> *As sure as we are born".*

Jed also was mighty pleased to dance jigs learned as a midshipman in the *U.S.S. Essex*—in addition he could perform many South Sea dances, wildly war-like or undulating and suggestive of intimate social intercourse.

Lydia's skin pebbled on contact with her bed's icy sheets so while waiting to warm up, began wondering why Jed should be returning so early as nine. Usually when he dined out he'd seldom show up before midnight. She understood. Jed had been invited to dine at Obediah's. While Nancy, Obed's wife, was by no means gloomy, she nevertheless displayed a sort of serene gravity which effectively curbed her brother-in-law's hearty ebullience.

Still shivering, she heard him open the front door and call out to reassure Ben Storer, who slept in a penthouse Papa had caused to be built for him onto the rear of his mansion.

Humming "Money Musk", Jed climbed the stairs, lightly for a man of his proportions, then a wavering beam of yellow light cast by a sperm oil Betty lamp showed beneath the threshold.

Softly he called, "Lyddie? You awake?"

"Wasn't," she lied, then smiled through the dimness. "But I am now—thanks to all thy crashing around and caterwauling like a love-sick tomcat."

The door creaked open and Jed thrust his head inside. "God! It's colder in here than Christian charity with a deficit. I want a word; suppose you don a cloak and come into the library? I'll go toss sticks onto the fire."

Lydia sat up, straightening her nightcap, said in succinct tones, "Bother the library! I don't propose to warm this bed for a second time. Come in and tell me what's on thy mind."

"Come in?" Jed pursed lips in a soundless whistle. Lord God, was this chit really so reckless as to invite a young male—even her brother—into her bedroom?

"All right, but pull up the covers." The Betty lamp effectively revealed the young giant's broad, red-brown features, shock of yellow hair, even the arrowhead-shaped scar on his chin. He placed the lamp on a candlestand, then, favoring his hurt side, gingerly eased his bulk onto a ladderback rocker. At the same time he peered about with no little curiosity this being the first occasion he'd set foot inside a decent women's bedroom and immediately was struck, first by the stark simplicity of its furniture, then by the complete absence of typically feminine scents or fragrance. Nor were there visible any of those fripperies, furbelows or dainty knick-knacks he'd come to associate with white women of his acquaintance.

More for warmth than in a gesture of modesty Lydia hoisted a quilted counterpane up close under her chin while her faintly oblique black eyes fixed themselves upon Jed. "Well, Jedediah, and what brings thee here like this?"

He thrust long legs out before him, grimacing because of injured ribs. "Lyddie, I want you to pack and otherwise prepare to leave on the Boston packet tomorrow."

She stared, "Tomorrow!"

"Aye. We'll depart together."

She sat bolt upright so abruptly that twin braids escaping her nightcap uncoiled down the almost unrounded bosom of her nightdress like sable serpents. "Thee means for us to take passage to the Mainland!"

"That's about the size of it."

"Why leave in such an all-fired rush? Are the Dismonts causing fresh trouble?"

His expression hardened. "No, 'tis not that. They avoid me like the plague—as do a number of other godly folk."

"What then is thy purpose?"

"To get you married as soon as may be."

The girl emitted a sharp gasp and breath billowed momentarily about her head like a golden Nimbus. "*Married*! Well I never! What drives thee to scheme along such crazy lines?"

He eased brass buttons securing a turkey-red waistcoat then tested coils of bandage thickening his torso. "We've good reason. For one thing the town's still worked up over that free-for-all last week so 'tain't fair to Obed to keep the trouble stewing any longer than necessary. Bad for business."

"Very true. Has the *Topaz*'s charter been completed and signed?"

He nodded. "All in order. I'm free to depart anytime."

The girl peered across the chilly, shadow-ruled room. "That being that," her thin, dark lips formed a half-smile, "what's to become of thy blood-brother?"

"'Tended to. Obed's going to care for him and Heetee. They'll be waiting in New Bedford the moment we come down from Boston.

"If my calculations work out, inside a month's time I—we, that is, will be principal owners of a bark now called the *Canton*."

With a forefinger Lydia dabbed aside a sable lock dangling over her forehead. "What makes thee so dratted *certain* we'll succeed? I'd despise seeing thee make a great fool of thyself—and of me."

He jumped to his feet, cast a giant shadow on the wall behind. "Lyddie!" he thundered. "Don't you ever deem me any part of a fool—not even a little one. I know what I'm about and, by the Eternal, before I'm done I'll be a power on this Island and a greater one in the South Seas. I'll even lead troops and do battle, by God."

11

Mermaid Palace

A bone-penetrating half-gale beating in from Boston Harbor felt so bitter Captain Paddock grumbled it must have been honed on the North Pole. He quickened his pace towards the Mermaid Palace, an establishment well, if not favorably, known to the town's police.

Operated by an enormously fat "Gee", or Portuguese and the liberally mustached virago who claimed to be his spouse this establishment, termed a "tavern" but, as everyone knew, this served only as a front for depraved amusements offered on its second floor.

The place had prospered for one reason: since none of Senhor Cabral's sirens retained the flush of youth the price of their weary favors lay within reach of almost anyone's purse.

Eben Roach slumped, slack-shouldered upon a wall bench in a dingy back room where patrons couldn't too closely appraise the dubious charms of Senhor Cabral's "mermaids" as he persisted in terming his soiled doves.

Seated between a pair of bawds Roach beckoned a gaunt Negress called "Fat Lizzie". Clad in a stained yellow blouse and a sagging red skirt the slattern would serve drinks until a patron weaved in drunk enough to see in her a dusky "Venus" and soon disappear with her up the well-used staircase.

Staring emptily straight ahead Eben grunted, "'Nother round."

A red-haired harridan seated to his right slipped an arm around his shoulders and tweaked his ear lobe. "Whyn't you ask Lizzie to entertain us, ducky? She's orways good for a naughty ballad song." Betty once had been a pretty Cockney barmaid but gin and rum and Destiny had handled her not kindly.

"Maybe I will," mumbled her red-eyed and long-unshaven host. "Today I got 'nuff for lots of fun."

On Roach's other side squatted a faded and overly plump female. Boldly she slipped a grimy hand inside his shirt and commenced to rub, circling progressively downward. "God's love, darlin'! Somebody must ha' died and left you a packet! Ain't never seen you throw the oof about so free-like."

The host's bleared and swollen eyes batted. "No such luck, pet, but tonight I've money enough—treat you dollies like queens." He didn't think it worth adding that once these last few dollars were gone he'd be penniless again. Now that painful buboes were beginning to erupt on that part of his body which, for too long, had been of all-consuming interest what did it matter?

His hand closed over a nearly empty bottle and raised it to a mouth which, despite everything, remained recognizably sensitive and well-shaped. He drained it noisily, greedily. Wonder if, drunk's I am, I c'n bed both these doxies at the same time? Why not? Can't give 'em anything they not already got. To hell with 'em.

The moment Fat Lizzie placed a bottle before him Roach snatched it up and tilted back a well-shaped but deplorably frowsy head.

In heavy playfulness the former barmaid snatched away the bottle. "Cripes, ducky! Don't guzzle it all, you'll not be fit to pleasure us. Leave us pore girls a few swallows."

Nearly stupefied, young Roach became aware that the other bawd was delving into his pants' pocket in which remained exactly three silver dollars. She squealed when he slapped her hand aside, snarling, "None o' that, you ugly whore! You'll get it when you've earned it!"

From upstairs appeared a pair of bruised-looking wenches showing slack breasts half-exposed beneath opened shifts. They were wearing rosettes of bright, badly soiled ribbons in greasy hair. The younger one scanned the all-but-deserted back room then hawked loudly and spat into a box of sawdust. Summoning a dreadful smile she bore down on Roach's group.

"My Gawd, Benny, ain't you caulked them girls' seams yet?"

Colorfully, Roach's companions cursed the intruder. She took no offense, only sauntered over to accost a new arrival, probably a Brava because of his frizzy hair and thin, hooked nose. She smiled in a hideous parody of seductiveness. "Come along, brown boy. All day I been hankerin' fer a jab from a harpoon like the one I reckon you carry."

Eben Roach was finding trouble in focusing his eyes what with that last gulp of black Jamaica searing his throat which during the past few days had grown terribly raw and sensitive. He was forced to brace elbows before him to keep from slumping flat over the table.

"Cor, ducky, ain't yer forgettin' yer fine manners? Gi'e us a hearty buss." The Cockney girl pulled his head around and attempted to push her tongue into his mouth but he lurched aside at the same time shoving the bottle at her. "Lemme 'lone! I'm tryin'—remember somethin'."

While Eben really didn't wish to think back he forced himself, wondered how long it had been since he'd associated with decent, well-born folk. When last had his body been clean, healthy and free of vermin? How long since he'd worn fresh linen and unmended clothing? How long since he'd enjoyed such simple pleasures as a sheep-shearing festival, sing-songs, going fishing or shooting, playing at blindman's buff or pulling taffy with clear-eyed, giggly, pink-and-white girls? Ages.

The rum recently ordered began to take hold, warmed Eben's belly. He began to feel better, so much so that he forgot to pursue his line of thought.

A quartet of bearded, dishevelled, hot-eyed sailors lurched in, knitted caps dusted by a fine snow commencing to whirl along the waterfront.

The ex-barmaid ogled the newcomers then turned to her host, "'Ow long we goin' to waste time down 'ere, ducky? Me and Molly ain't just sittin' 'ere for our 'ealth."

"You've been paid yer time, you greedy slut," snapped Roach, "and will stay with me till I've done with you."

"No call to turn narsty, lovey!" purred Molly and at the same time succeeded in abstracting the last coin from Eben Roach's pocket. "Ye're the sweetest lad as split a pore gal apart. Now, honey, heart, you'll have to 'cuse; little Molly's simply *got* to go an' drop a tear for her dear old granny; back in a jiffy."

She started to arise but Roach's hand closed down on her wrist with a strength which surprised her, "No you don't! We're headin' upstairs; you'll earn what I've paid you."

Jerking sidewise, Molly attempted to break away but the derelict was not to be shaken off. The whore commenced to spout obscenities. "The curse o' Crummel on ye! Leggo, ye fancy, crotch-blistered bastard!"

A cadaverous, one-eyed individual with a vice-seared complexion shoved a battered tarred hat onto the back of his head and sang out, "Let her be, Mate! Yer ain't in no state to tumble even one of them wenches whilst I—"

Greasy brown hair tumbling in tousled elf locks over his forehead, Eben Roach struggled, swaying to his feet. "Mind yer own affairs, damn you!"

As balling his fists, the seaman started across the floor's damp and dirty sawdust Senhor Cabral beckoned a brawny pimp. The fellow snatched up a bung-starter and was preparing to take action when a harsh voice broke in on the situation. "Call off yer dog, friend Cabral! Yonder's an old friend of mine."

His snow-powdered sugar loaf hat brushing the blackened ceiling, Jedediah Paddock plowed through the smoke-fogged taproom like a ship-of-the-line entering port.

Senhor João Cabral's florid and rotund features lit and all three of his chins quivered with pleasure. "Be much welcome, *Senhor Capitán!* Welcome to the simple pleasures of this *posada.*"

Roach blinked stupidly at the figure towering above him. "Who'n hell might you be?"

"Jedediah Paddock. Used to know each other. Remember?"

Roach knuckled granulated red-and-yellow eyelids, muttered thickly, "Dunno you. Go 'way."

Jed stayed where he was, observed pleasantly, "My lad, that ye're stinking drunk ain't even half the truth. All the same, you're Eben Roach, whose folks live in Polpis. I'm Jed Paddock—Micajah's son and Obed's twin. Remember that time in Stonington we took the 'Bosun's Mate' apart after you set fire to the Madam's petticoats?"

Sluggishly, Roach threw back his finely formed head, stared a moment, then nodded owlishly as if to reassure himself. "Tha's right. Neva forget that won'erful night. Ye're Jed Paddock all right; friend, guide and philosopher from happier times."

Roach fluttered hands at his companions, made vague, shooing motions. "Fly away, my li'l soiled doves." Clumsily he fumbled at his pockets. "May as well. Ye've already plucked me clean."

In the front taproom an asthmatic concertina commenced to wheeze and groan.

Roach passed a trembling hand over features which couldn't

have been shaved or even washed in days. He spoke in steadier tones. "Pray join me, Jed, if you ain't too proud to be seen in company so —so disgusting."

Through force of habit, Jedediah Paddock while sliding onto the bench beside Roach checked the environs for exits, and tables at which potential trouble might originate. Then he said quietly, "By God, Eben, you've been harder to find than a whore in church. Two days now I've been searchin' the town."

The derelict's bloodshot blue eyes sought Jed's, lowered. "Why? I'm no fun any more. Look at me—pretty ain't I? And I'm flat broke; that goddam Irish biddy's just snitched the last coin to keep me free of a berth in the bone yard or aboard some stinking spouter; about the same thing."

"Shape you're in, you'd not last over-long in any fo'csle." Jed turned hastily aside. Eben's breath reeked like an open sewer. Lord God!—was Eben too far gone? Perhaps not. From personal experience he knew what miracles hot baths, clean clothes, good food and plenty of sound sleep could accomplish. Besides, Roach still was young; twenty-eight at the most—a year or so his junior.

"You really broke?"

"Absolutely and completely. That's the way it 'tiz—and there's nothing 'tizzer'. Tomorrow I must sign articles or go hungry."

"No call to go that far," Jed checked himself on noticing a circlet of angry red spots marking the base of Eben's neck, creating what the French termed "*le collier de Vénus*" and the unmistakable evidence of secondary syphilis.

He drew a slow breath. By God, he'd have to be almighty careful about bringing this fellow near Lydia.

He ordered a pair of rum toddies, said heartily, "Well, Ben, let's see what can be done. 'Twould never do to leave an old pal stove-in on a reef."

Once steaming pewter pots had been set before them he invited, "Drink up, Eben. Let's forget present worries and gam a bit. It's *just* possible I can put you into the way of finding real money."

Roach looked sidewise, a flicker of interest in his expression. "How much?"

"Too early to go into that, but it might prove sufficient to give you a fresh start and then some. Come, let's drink up and clear out of this rat's nest. Where's yer coat?"

Roach shrugged, "Dunno. Reckon I pawned it yesterday, or maybe 'twas only this morning."

He got up, weaving, "Where we headed?"

Jed put an arm about the drunkard and felt his ribs standing out like those of a skeleton. "Don't ask questions, Ben. Just come along and I promise you'll soon come up smelling fresh and clean as new yellow pine sheathing."

12

"—Or for Worse"

Worse weather for anyone's wedding day couldn't have been devised, Lydia Paddock decided while unknotting a sealskin bonnet's strings. Whew! The bitter chill from the street was slow in disappearing. Following two days of wind out of the northeast the weather at last had shifted northwest so Boston was being blanketed under a thick counterpane of fine and glistening snow which lent to streets and alleys a spurious appearance of cleanliness.

What emotions did other presumably virtuous young females experience? Were they apprehensive, expectant, eager, curious or bored and disgusted? Were she experiencing any of such sensations it would have been the last two. A good thing that Jed had warned her not to expect too much in the way of Eben Roach's appearance, hinting that her husband-to-be was no longer as she might have remembered from Nantucket—a handsome, tow-headed, long-legged and merry youth who loved to tease and pursue the girls.

Crossing the rented room to warm her backside before a blazing Franklin stove, she felt grateful Jedediah had bothered to find her such neat if not comfortable lodgings. Although, since their arrival in Boston, she and Jed had dined together every evening she'd been left pretty much to herself during the day.

On the evening before the wedding was planned to take place Jedediah finished a thumping big repast and after exploring his teeth with a little ivory pick drawled, "Well, Dark Sister, seeing as how we'll have to fulfill the provisions of the Will about your groom's being worth at least ten thousand, I—well, I've borrowed such a sum and will lend it to Eben as evidence he's no penniless fortune hunter. We'll have witnesses on hand to attest his wealth."

From an inner coat pocket he fished out a sight draft in the amount of ten thousand dollars drawn on the private bank of Messrs. Doane, Welch & Peabody of Boston. In Lydia's opinion the document appeared impressive, convincingly legal, what with all those flourishes, curlicues and signatures adorning it.

The young woman's brows assumed an interrogative angle. "Thee is not really lending all this money to that ne'er-do-well! What if he absconds?"

"Lord, no!" Jed laughed uproariously. "He won't get an opportunity. Once your wedding witnesses have left I'll straightaway return this draft to Josh Peabody and gladly pay the fifty I've promised for this er—accommodation."

"Thee means that Joshua Peabody, one of thy oldest and closest friends, expects thee to *pay* for such a favor?"

Jed said, with a flick of impatience. "Plague take it, why shouldn't he? It's a wonder you females will never understand the truth of the old saying: 'Friendship ends when there's business to be done'." Relaxing, he went to peer out of a snow-dimmed window and saw that the storm had so increased that the stark forest of masts and yards marking the waterfront had become invisible amid whirling, shifting flurries.

Lydia ventured no comment but resented the growing and revolting impression that she, Micajah Paddock's daughter, was about to be bought and sold like a heifer in a farmers' market.

Mechanically, her hands went up to smooth glossy jet hair coiled in tight, neat braids about her ears, she asked in a harsh voice, "—And in what condition does my dear husband-to-be find himself today?"

Jed smiled, put away his napkin. "I've been surprised—pleasantly surprised to note the change in him during these last few days. Ought to have—rascal's cost me near fifty dollars in repairs of various kinds. While he's still no prize-winner, at least you'll be able to recognize him as the fellow we grew up with. For a fact, Eben's looking years younger and almost handsome."

"I'll be the judge of that," sniffed Lydia. "What does Eben gain through this—this sorry masquerade?"

Jed said shortly, "Five hundred, cash on the barrel head. How long he'll hang onto it is a horse of another color."

"What is thy meaning?"

"Ever hear about a fool and his money?"

Something about Jedediah's manner and set expression prompted Lydia to become aware and dismayed by an air which she didn't recognize—something subtly cruel, overbearing and unemotional even when he kissed her lightly on the cheek. "Come now, Dark Sister, wipe off that sour expression. Know something? When you smile you're close to being pretty, which you'd better remember when you greet your bridegroom."

Next morning the blizzard had not abated, rather, it was silencing Boston under a deepening white pall. Expression coolly detached, Lydia followed her brother downstairs.

Bundled up and already assembled in the chilly little parlor were the boardinghouse keeper, a brisk and indefatigably cheery female, who with her husband had consented to be among the witnesses, and Joshua Peabody—who'd issued the sight draft. He was a tall, solemn young man who, because of flowing ginger-colored whiskers, looked older than he was. Also on hand was one Captain Ichabod Bliss, a fellow Nantucketer who'd watched Eben Roach grow up, so could vouch for his identity, even if he didn't approve of him in the least. Finally, there was an attorney, a Mr. Beresford, called in to verify the validity of the ceremony and that provisions of the Will were being complied with.

Lydia, eyes staring and bitter, halted behind Jed when, curtly, he greeted the witnesses, then said, "Well, I suppose we'd better shape a course for the chapel."

The little party stepped out into the frigid blast and were forced to bend into the furious assault of myriad small, dry snowflakes.

Fortunately, the group didn't have far to wade through the snow before it reached a small Unitarian chapel increasingly favored by couples who, desiring to be properly married, were not inclined, for one reason or another, to delay their nuptials in order to comply with stipulations imposed by the Church of England, the Church of Rome and certain other denominations.

The ceremony proved solemn but so brief that Lydia could scarcely credit her ears when she heard the clergyman conclude by snuffling—he'd a severe cold—"I now pronounce you man and wife."

This must be a nightmare Lydia Roach was thinking. Why, why, I'm no longer Lydia Paddock. Outrageous!

For the first time since she'd entered the chapel she treated the tall and slender fellow standing beside her to a steady inspection.

Jedediah had been right, she readily recognized Eben Roach. He still was unmistakably handsome and well-bred looking but his complexion was blotched and his features had a bruised and coarsened look but, say what one might, Eben Roach at the moment appeared really presentable, almost impressive in new, hammer-claw coat with gilded buttons, canary-yellow silk waistcoat and well-tailored trousers of dark blue nankeen.

Her gaze shifted. Lord above! If Eben Roach appeared almost distinguished and genteel then Jed was god-like by comparison. Why, oh, why did the laws of God and man render it utterly impossible for him to be standing in Eben's place?

From a wooden box set behind the big cast-iron stove which had been kindled in a vain effort to remove a measure of chill from the air appeared a scrawny tabby cat which stretched and yawned prodigiously while a trio of bright-eyed kittens of assorted colors climbed out of the nest to wobble after their mother, tiny spiky tails held rigidly erect.

Once bride and groom had seated themselves to sign the register the minister adjusted steel-rimmed spectacles and, in a neat Spencerian script, signed and otherwise completed a Certificate of Marriage in the names of Eben and Lydia Roach.

Without prompting from his best man Eben Roach then presented the sight-draft and called upon the witnesses to examine it and note that, under the terms of Micajah Paddock's Will, he had qualified as a man of substance.

Wide mouth compressed to suppress a huge grin, Jed watched Eben pass the sight draft over to Joshua Peabody. "You'd better care for this I expect. I'm rather inept about money."

The comfortably plump young banker nodded, stroked his fluffy and abundant whiskers. "Ahem, you will want this used to open an account in our bank, Mister Roach?"

Eben nodded carelessly. "Of course, and right away, please."

"Under what name, if you please?"

"Ebenezer Macy Roach."

Back in the boardinghouse the wedding party partook of cookies, sherry and, best of all, steaming-hot china tea.

After a while Captain Bliss and the lawyer together with Mr. Peabody excused themselves, saying they must be off before the blizzard grew any worse.

Once the other witnesses had departed Lydia's brother, wearing a particularly winning smile, clapped the new husband on his shoulder. "Come along, Eben. Lyddie's fatigued and needs repose so it's up to us to celebrate this happy occasion in fitting fashion."

"Thee won't stay out too late, will thee?" Lydia treated her new husband to a swift, embarrassed peck on the cheek.

"Of course not, my dear," Eben gravely assured. "But best not wait up for me. When Jed and I get together there's no telling what will happen."

How right you are, thought Lydia's brother.

Before going outdoors Jed paused, held out a roll of bank notes secured by a length of scarlet thread, said heartily, "Well, Ben, here's the five hundred. Good luck with it, maybe you've a future on the stage. Must say you acted your part with style."

Eben nodded, quickly pocketed his fee. "Wish to God I hadn't been such a great, giddy fool all this time. Lydia's truly lovely." He blinked rapidly, then looked away. "If only Lydia and I—oh, hell, Jed, it's too late now, far too late."

"Reckon I know pretty well how you're feeling." Jed was all sympathy. "I've acted like a bloody idiot, too. Plenty of times." Resetting his muffler, he led the way out. "Where ought we start celebrating? You name the place."

"S'ppose we try oiling elbow joints at the 'Clove Hitch'? Liquor's pretty good there—or used to be." Ruefully, added Roach, "Haven't been able to afford their prices lately."

At the "Clove Hitch" they drank a-plenty, then at Jed's suggestion, they patronized two or three other increasingly disreputable taverns—but Eben didn't notice this, nor did he care. By supper time both men were hilariously vocal, staggering and slipping ever more frequently along snow-covered sidewalks.

Even quicker than his new brother-in-law had anticipated, Roach grew expansive, took to recklessly stripping bank notes from his roll, which was noted by more than one pair of swollen and blood-shot eyes.

"Where next?" Eben belched, clutching his new stovepipe hat.

"Dunno, it's up to you. This is your party. What've you in mind?"

"Some place where there's music an' naked wenches dancin'

'round. C'mon, Jed, you name it, you know this neighborhood." Owlishly his eyes bored through the snow-filled gloom.

Swaying more than he needed, Jed pretended to deliberate. "How about the 'Hawse Hole'? Heard tell the whoremaster there's just imported a bevy of young dark-skin girls from Jamaica. Might see what they're like?"

"Sounds fine. Where's this place?"

"'Tain't but a couple of blocks away, which is lucky. I'm beginnin' to yaw a bit."

Arm in arm they started off, singing at the top of their lungs slipping, sliding and half-blinded by whirling, gale-driven snow. Once, as Jed, now snow-covered, was picking himself up from still another fall he glanced backwards, wasn't too surprised to make out a pair of figures tacking along in their wake.

By personal experience he knew that, after the "Mermaid Palace", the "Hawse Hole" was probably the vilest dive along Boston's waterfront.

A good many other roisterers must also have decided that on so wild a night the "Hawse Hole" offered as good a refuge as any. Its low-ceilinged taproom was invisible through a fog of tobacco fumes and bitter-smelling smoke that kept rolling out of a huge and badly drawing fireplace.

Once out of the icy, tumultuous wind the heat indoors impacted upon both men like clenched fists. The celebrants elbowed their way to a table from which Jed, roaring curses and threats, drove the occupants.

Even before they could order drinks a pair of skinny but not unattractive mulatto girls stark naked under gowns of black-dyed fishnet, plunked themselves down to twine arms about the new arrivals.

One pressed scarlet daubed lips to Roach's ear, gurgling, "Ah'll have champagne, boss man—beer makes me fart so."

"T'hell with c-champagne!" stuttered the bridegroom. "Bring us bottle brandy—real French brandy!"

The waiter looked suspicious, sneered. "So it's French brandy ye'll be wanting my foine buck? What're yez tryin' to do? Impress these trollops. Rum's good enough fer such!"

"Bring—brandy."

"But the brandy's so costly they ain't but two bottles in the place. Doubt if ye've got the price."

Giggling, Eben brought out his roll. "I c'n pay for best, fetch out both bottles! Ain't anything too good for me and my frien's."

After a while a young pockmarked mulatto woman, naked as the day she was born, climbed up onto a table and, thumping a tambourine, commenced a series of sluggish gyrations.

After watching a while Jed pushed aside his companion who'd begun to clap and rock her body in accompaniment for the dancer. Said he thickly, "'Ben, m'boy, reckon I've mistook my soundings. Head's ready to split, gotta clear out o' here 'fore I start pumpin' me bilges or hit the sawdust." He paused, swaying, before the table. "You comin' too?"

Eben didn't even quit fondling the pendent breasts of the hussy beside him. "Hell, no! Like our hero—'I—just begun—fight'. No, I doa't mean that. Wan' t' drink, don't wan' fight—too damn' happy —fight. Jus' wan' to love an' get loved tha's all ol' Eben wants, eh, dolly?"

"Sure, sure! boss man, that's just what you need." The girl's hard black eyes glared at the blond giant. "Clear out. Ah'll look out fo' yo' mate."

"I'll bet on that! Well, s'long, Eben, have a goo' time."

His final impression of Lydia's husband was of him showering slobbery kisses on the high-yellow harpy. Once outside, Jedediah Paddock abruptly stopped mumbling and staggering. Then, after drawing deep breaths of icy air, he set steadily off down the dim, white-blanketed alley.

Captain Jedediah Paddock wasn't entirely astonished when, late the next day, he opened a newspaper and read an item stating the body of a person called Ebenezer Roach, of no known address, had been discovered in a snowdrift; apparently he'd been robbed and beaten to death.

13

The Whaling Bark, Gladiator

The winter of 1830–31 proved bitter above average but Captain Jedediah Paddock, bundled to the ears and often numb and blue-lipped, drove riggers, sailmakers, fitters and armorers to the limit. So, during the two months since he'd bought the bark *Canton* promptly to rename her *"Gladiator"*, many interior alterations had been effected but her lovely outward appearance remained largely unchanged.

Anyone in the least familiar with ship-design would recognize at a glance that here was no bluff-bowed, stubby-masted and grace-less tub of a whaler; this Baltimore-designed vessel's spars, masts and yards were noticeably longer and slimmer than those of locally built vessels. Her only new mast was the main which had to be extra stout to support the enormous strain to be thrown upon it during cutting in.

Visitors to New Bedford's ice-fringed waterfront lingered on the fitting-out dock commenting on the racy-looking vessel's new figurehead—a work of art cut out of a single baulk of oak by Peter Gifford, the port's master carver.

His creation was that of a fiercely staring, bearded and helmeted figure wearing silver-scaled armor. In one massive hand the gladiator —in fact a Roman centurion—clutched a *gladius* or short stabbing sword with a triangular point.

So brilliantly painted was this effigy that children homeward bound from school often lingered, open-mouthed in the bitter cold to admire Peter Gifford's handiwork.

A captain just in from the "Brazeel" Grounds paused among mounds of snow-muffled gear stacked on the fitting-out wharf. "Mark you that, Lemuel?"

"Mark what?"

"Why, this Paddock fellow's got four *real* gun ports let into her streak—not just painted counterfeits!"

The other's red-mittened hand rubbed an unshaven chin. "That'll mean Paddock aims to mount eight carriage pieces. Since we ain't at war right now, what in Tunket can that crazy Nantucketer be wanting real guns for?"

His companion squirted a parabola of tobacco juice onto a piece of ice drifting in the dirty water below. "Dunno. Been wonderin' for some time what's got into a downright smart whaler like Paddock to want a Fancy Dan sort of vessel like this." He snorted. "She'll have no hold space worthy of notice."

"Lookin' for speed, shouldn't wonder; he'll get it with that rake to her masts and the shear of her bows. Wager she'll move faster'n a cat with her fur a-fire."

"But what's the good in such speed? A spouter c'n sight just as many, and maybe, more whales sailin' five knots than she c'n doin' nine. Me, I'll stick to the old style."

Captain Jedediah Paddock together with his beetle-browed Third Mate ranged the holds and 'tween decks and, with infinite patience, studied stout white oak braces designed to support narrow gun platforms running along either beam.

Jedediah narrowed small, round eyes. "Think these braces sufficiently heavy, Mister Hayward?"

Edward Hayward scratched under a knitted cap, finally nodded. "Yes, sir, so long you only mount carronades and no long guns."

"Think I've allowed the gun crews sufficient headroom?"

The Third Mate hesitated, kicked chips strewing the deck. "Well, sir, while 'tain't exactly roomy up there, I reckon there'll be as much space as we had aboard the old *Essex*. Yes, the gun crews will make out all right provided there ain't too much of a sea running or they ain't called to serve the guns in a big hurry."

"With any luck they won't ever have to." Jed climbed a workman's ladder to the gun platform and, bending, squinted through a port the lid of which had yet to be hinged and fitted. "Are these ports wide enough? Tell me true."

"Well, sir, since ye've asked, I might call 'em a mite cramped. Ought to be a foot wider at the least."

"They will be."

Descending to the fitting dock, Jed clambered over piles of

cordage and raw lumber and found Te Ponapa fully enjoying this, the first really warm day of the year.

Stripped to the waist, the big Maori went barefooted and wore only a tattered pair of old-fashioned knee breeches. Intricate patterns of blue-black tattooing rippled and seemed to come alive on his massive arms as he filed vigorously at a single-flued iron harpoon head.

Heetee also was at work. He was sharpening one of several blubber spades at a grindstone set on the port side opposite the gangway. Long since, Jed had ordered that the Polynesians, along with a few other dependables, should live aboard and guard the bark during her period of outfitting, which also largely removed them from the waterfront's varied temptations.

"You comfortable, O Rangatira? Food all right?"

Te Ponapa's big, even teeth flashed. "Never lived so well afloat. Heetee is a good cook—especially fresh pork. Can we have more? Salted is fit only for use at sea."

Jed's big laugh scared a gull perched on the bowsprit into flapping heavily away. "Pork? All right, but I'll bet you'd rather draw a ration of 'long pig'. How about a wench—say of twenty?"

Grinning, the Maori shook his head. "No. Give me one of sixteen. Such a one is more tender—and full of juice."

Dismissing Hayward, Jed sought the chilly main cabin he'd occupied ever since he'd taken title. First thing he'd done was to install Pa's old swinging sea bed using the original round stones in the counter-balancing cradle.

It had come as a pleasant surprise that the Maryland designers had been considerably more generous in designing the Captain's quarters than a New England shipwright. Further, the white painted pine paneling had been gracefully proportioned and installed.

As a finishing touch Jed had caused a scale half-model of the *Gladiator*'s hull to be screwed to the bulkhead above a narrow, knee-hole desk. On the model's backboard the bark's dimensions were listed in neat gold leaf: Displacement, 238.82 tons; Length Overall, 103 feet, 1 inch; Depth of Hold, 15 feet, 4 inches; Beam, 24 feet, 8 inches. Soon he'd have an addition reading: Armament; 8 eight-pound carronades, 4 swivel guns.

His gaze wandered out of the companionway and came to rest on the still-unpainted door to the Fourth Mate's cabin which, in fact, was but a cramped six-by-four-foot compartment equipped with a single small porthole, a short and narrow bunk and nothing else saving a few clothes pegs. The fact that a female presently would be occupying this hutch had called for no extra conveniences.

Already Jed's sextant, dividers, parallel ruler, chronometer and other navigational instruments had been ranged in well-carpentered frames or racks. The drawers in a small chart table were filled with a selection of the newest available charts of the Pacific and the western Atlantic.

Merging bushy yellow brows, Jed considered with sharp distaste a varicolored litter of papers piled on his little desk. God above! How he loathed paper work of any kind. Then his frown faded with the realization that, with Lydia serving as Fourth Mate and super-cargo he'd be spared this ordeal; also it would be her duty to keep the log. There'd be no call to train her for, even as a big-eyed and skinny young girl, she'd kept hanging around Paddock & Sons' counting house to pore over old logs and account books until she knew very well how they should be kept.

Better still, she'd steeped herself in Bowditch's *Principles of Navigation* until she could plot a course and find a vessel's position better than a good many old-time mates.

The dull rumble of a two-wheel cart conveying a load of barrel shooks alongside sounded like faint thunder.

Above his head the underside of a fine new double-card dry compass was visible through the after skylight. Its upper side was to be seen directly before and below a steering wheel of the "walking" type.

Since it still wasn't time to go ashore for supper at the "Dolphin Striker", an inn situated near the end of the fitters' wharf, he settled back into his swivel armchair and thoughtfully considered a roster of hands who'd already signed Articles.

Although not too many names yet were listed he felt satisfied of having done better than expected in signing a high proportion of veteran whalemen. What pleased Jedediah most was that these men represented several nationalities; Americans were in the majority, of course, but there were also Englishmen, Irish, Scots and Portuguese in addition to the two Maoris.

In the interests of discipline and good order he'd long since found it advisable not to ship too many hands of the same nationality.

To do so would invite trouble through the possible formation of cliques strong enough to consider mutiny. In view of the peculiar nature of the cruise he was contemplating—well, it would pay to be extra cautious.

His eye continued down the list. So far, so good. The bulk of the bark's company were dependable New Englanders headed by three of his four officers: First Mate Aaron Winslow was from New London, Second Mate Charles Coffin was a fellow Nantucketer and, so of course, was Lydia. His Third, Edward Hayward, however, hailed from Sag Harbor on Long Island or so he claimed.

Um. Coffin should be returning from Martha's Vineyard and Cape Cod by tomorrow's mail packet and should bring along a few Cape Indians. One man he wanted in particular; weazened old Tommy Blue Fox, an expert boatsteerer and harpooner belonging to the Monomoy Tribe. Also he was hoping his Second had located a gaunt but powerful Nauset Indian called John Fast Canoe. Briefly, he conjectured on how well these Indians, if they appeared, and the Polynesians might get along.

A knock sounded at the door, then Ed Hayward, the *Gladiator*'s homely and enigmatic Third, entered and Navy fashion, touched his cap's wrinkled leather visor, a courtesy uncommon aboard whale-ships.

"Come in, Mister Hayward. How'd you make out recruiting?"

"Had luck, sir. Bill Starr, that old gunner's mate I spoke of says he's willing to sign on. Better still, he's to bring along a fellow, an armorer's mate, who's served a hitch aboard the *Constitution*."

"Good. Check their papers and if they're sufficient sober, fetch 'em aboard tomorrow morning. I'll look 'em over."

"Aye, aye, sir." The ex-Navy man whose wide and powerful shoulders contrasted oddly with short, bandy-legs started to turn away but paused, batting restless pale gray eyes. "Sir, where d'you want the round shot come aboard today to be stowed? Just ain't room in that miserable little shot locker these ratted civilian carpenters have built."

Jed rubbed at his big jaw. "Stow 'em in the cable tier for the time being. When are the carronades due to be delivered?"

"Day-after-tomorrow, sir; their carriages ain't quite finished."

"Keep after 'em; no time to be lost if we're to get to sea on time."

Once the Third had tramped off Jed glanced out of the stern windows, watched a dory deep-laden with fish nets pull out from behind a battered brig hove down at the next berth to have her bottom scraped. In the distance he heard a deep-toned church bell strike six times so locked his desk and was pulling on a well-worn pea jacket when there came a trampling of feet along the deck and the sound of unfamiliar voices.

Immediately identifying Second Mate Coffin's nasal accents he summoned him below. The mournful-appearing Nantucketer appeared wearing a thin smile on gaunt features framed in dull red chin whiskers.

"You're back early," said the *Gladiator's* Master. "Any luck?"

"Fair enough. I found them Redskins you wanted so special; recruited a couple more, besides."

"Trot 'em in."

Four Indians silently trooped into the Captain's cabin. All were lean and sinewy but were short in stature—not even of average height with the exception of Tom Blue Fox, the Monomoy, whose flat, big-nosed features were deeply pitted by smallpox; nor did a drooping eyelid improve his appearance. The other Indians, all Nausets, gave their names as John Fast Canoe, Dick Sun-in-the-Eyes and Billy Big Buck; the last was a strapping, bow-legged individual who by his thick lips and bronze-black complexion must have a strong strain of Negro blood in him. The Indians stood crowded together, suggesting freshly trapped animals so restless were their opaque appearing jet eyes.

Only Tom Blue Fox spoke English with facility but his companions understood sufficient to answer routine questions such as where had they been whaling before; what were their special abilities; what were they expecting by way of a lay?

The interview at an end, Jed nodded. "They'll do. Tell 'em to make their marks."

The Second hesitated. "I'll 'tend to that but what's to be done about 'em till sailing day? Don't dast turn 'em loose; they'll sure as hell get drunk, get into trouble and maybe carried off aboard some nother vessel."

"Keep 'em on board. I'll feed 'em and pay 'em laborer's wages provided they behave themselves."

14

The Bankers

That Captain Paddock's handsome but admittedly eccentric and always aloof sister had purchased a sizeable interest in the *Gladiator* long since had become common knowledge among New Bedford's merchants and shipping agents, but never a soul suspected that she had signed articles and would sail as an officer aboard the bark. The secret had been closely held because had the news spread, many an otherwise sensible seaman would have refused flatly to sail aboard what was contemptuously referred to as a "hen frigate". Next to having a preacher aboard, the unluckiest thing in the world was to cruise with a female. Of course, exceptions had been made in favor of some Captain's strong-minded wife.

Thoughtfully, Jed made his way along a jonquil-fringed walk leading up to a gray-shingled cottage situated pretty well by itself on the western edge of town. Here the Widow Albert, pert and lively as a wren, "accommodated" a few select boarders.

From the fact that a nag, drawing a rig obviously hired from some livery stable, stood hitched to a granite post topped by a cast-iron horse's head implied that the men Jed was coming to do business with already had arrived.

His friend Joshua Peabody of the flowing silky whiskers greeted him warmly then, with a touch of deference, presented Captain Paddock to Mr. John Doane, senior partner of Doane, Welch & Peabody, private bankers. Mr. Doane was solidly built, smooth-shaven and almost bald. His aquiline, parchment-hued features suggested that his outlook on life was jaundiced. The senior partner's conservative frock coat of dark gray was set off by an opulent waistcoat of yellow watered silk across the comfortable expanse of which was looped a red-gold watch chain heavy enough to secure a skiff against a moderate blow.

Aside from Lydia, slim and austere in Quaker brown, Jed

found in the Widow's parlor—musty-smelling because it seldom was used save on holidays or when the minister came to call—there was a long-legged lad of thirteen or fourteen. He had well separated bright-blue eyes, wavy, light brown hair and almost colorless white eyebrows and eyelashes. A band of freckles crossed the boy's snub nose; a few purple-and-white pimples showed on his downy chin.

The lad's name came out when John Doane casually presented him to the towering captain. Abner, the banker announced was his nephew and only child of Sylvanus Doane, a younger brother who'd disappeared some years ago; presumably he'd been lost at sea. Jed nodded, at the same time wondered why this stripling was present. Mr. Doane, uninvited, had traveled all the way down from Boston for a conference the subject of which remained to be disclosed. He directed a quick, interrogative glance at his sister. She, however, replied only with an almost imperceptible shrug.

Josh Peabody removed a sheaf of paper from a neat calfskin portfolio and lost no time in coming to the point.

"As I wrote, Captain, Mr. Doane and I have come here to—well, to broach a matter of considerable importance. I, therefore, must ask you and your sister to pledge that you'll never reveal a word concerning the project we're about to discuss."

Jed said shortly, "That goes without saying."

Mr. Doane's pale pink lips formed a mechanical, meaningless smile. "Of course. I intend to be brief and to the point. Never found any use shilly-shallying about an undertaking. In a nutshell, what we have in mind is for you to—well, for you to transact abroad some delicate special business for our bank, which transaction would lose any hope of profit should even a hint of its nature leak out. Indeed, such a lapse of security might well bring you into the gravest of danger," the banker added softly.

While testing the implications of Mr. Doane's curious statement Jed slowly elevated heavy yellow brows. "Well, sir, as we say aboard ship, suppose you'd better 'fish, cut bait or get out of the boat'. What's on your mind?"

The banker got to his feet and commenced to pace deliberately back and forth all the while fiddling seals dangling from his massive golden watch chain. He turned to the youth, said quietly, "Abner, I want you to trot down to that little store I noted on our way out. Go purchase me a box of snuff. Here's some money, but mind they don't try to overcharge."

"Yessir." The boy, looking overgrown in his tight shell jacket and too-small pantaloons arose, a thwarted look on his good-natured, freckled face. Obviously, he was painfully curious about these mysterious goings-on.

Asked John Doane in a suddenly most effective voice, "Have we been correctly informed, Captain Paddock, that you intend sailing shortly on a voyage to the South Seas?"

"Yes. Soon as possible."

The speaker glanced at his companion as if for confirmation. "Is it true that on this voyage you intend to whale only a part of the time and will trade the rest?"

"That is what I intend." He saw Lydia sitting bolt upright, not missing a word of this conversation. He didn't notice however that her sleek, dark head swung quickly to a small noise which seemed to come from a door leading towards the cottage's rear. When the sound wasn't repeated she returned her attention to Mr. Doane.

Caressing silky side whiskers which appeared to float away from plump and rubicund cheeks Joshua Peabody took over the conversation. "If we can reach an understanding, Jed, you'll benefit greatly—and I mean greatly. Shall I proceed?"

"Fire away," Jed invited. "It don't cost me anything to listen. What's your proposition?"

"The bank wishes you to undertake the transportation of some specie to a certain port in Mexico."

"What sort of specie—gold or silver?"

"Silver dollars minted in the United States."

Jedediah Paddock drew a deep breath. "In what amount, Josh?"

The eyes of the two Boston men engaged for an instant before Peabody said in a hushed voice, "We'll be sending thirty-five thousand silver dollars aboard your ship—provided we reach agreement."

Lydia's dark and narrow lips parted a little while copper tones in her complexion became more noticeable. Thirty-five thousand! Lord above! Why, that was more than the cost of the *Gladiator*, gear included!

"Well, are you interested?" Mr. Doane wanted to know.

Deliberately, Jed studied first one then the other of these prosperous looking men. "Why single me out to help you in this scheme of yours—whatever it may be?"

Mr. Doane who'd reseated himself steepled bony white fingers under sparse chin whiskers and at the same time peered over the top of square-cut, gold-framed spectacles and said steadily, "Cap'n Paddock, you're not to delude yourself into thinking that we've reached a decision involving so much money in haste. Quite to the contrary. On your friend Peabody's recommendation I hired a couple of knowledgeable people in such matters to investigate you, your record and this vessel you've just acquired."

A flood of bright red stained Jed's bronzed features. "Can't say I admire you for hiring spies."

"Had to, considering the sum involved; 'tis only reasonable," Joshua Peabody explained hurriedly. "Besides, those men were only investigating, not spying, Jed. In our position wouldn't you do the same thing?"

Jed grunted agreement, at the same time wondered just who the investigators might have been. Hard to tell. Nowadays there were so many unfamiliar riggers, fitters, carpenters and chandlers' agents swarming about his bark.

Mr. Doane's dry, incisive tones terminated an uncomfortable silence. "Are we correct in assuming that you intend to mount a battery of cannon? How many?"

Jed snapped, "Eight, eight-pound carronades. While such ordnance can't shoot very far with accuracy they're deadly at short range."

"Um." Mr. Doane fell to playing with his watch chain again. "Will they be—er—sufficient?"

"Quite, for my purpose," rasped the sea captain. "Don't expect to engage any men-o'-war. Such armament is intended only to cope with picaroons, privateers and savages; a few rounds of grapeshot usually discourages such vermin."

Lydia noticed that now Jed was on familiar ground he was speaking both faster and louder—almost too loudly.

"You've had naval experience so I presume you're right about the carronades," admitted the older banker. "But what about fighting them? Believe it or not I served aboard a privateer during the Second War against England so I'm aware that it's one thing to carry carriage guns but quite another to have them handled well enough to accomplish anything. May I inquire what you expect to do in that respect?"

As an absurdly peaceful counterpoint to this war-like conversation the mournful mooing of a cow bereft of her calf drifted in through a half-opened window.

Jed said, "Why, I've already enlisted, I mean 'enrolled' a few former Navy men."

"You're sure about them?"

"Aye, seen their discharge papers and they were in order." Gathering authority Jed went on. "Further, my Third Mate has been a master gunner in the Regular Navy."

Unexpectedly, Joshua Peabody spoke up. "By any chance is this man's name Hayward? Edward or Ted Hayward?"

Something about the query was disconcerting. "Yes. Hayward's his name. What of it?"

"How long have you know this fellow Hayward?"

Jed hesitated, grew wary. "Not long. He's a rough sort and no beauty to look at but he showed his papers without hesitation; seemed to tell a straight story. I know that he indeed did serve in the *United States*."

Lydia leaned forward dark eyes fixed on the speaker's. "Mr. Peabody, just why are you putting such a question?"

"Don't mean to alarm you, Mrs. Roach," the younger banker assured, "but if this Edward Hayward is the same our investigators spoke of, then he was dishonorably discharged off the *U.S.S. Cyane*."

"On what charge?"

"Insolence and insubordination," came the prompt reply.

Jed's jaw tightened. "You certain about that?"

Without hesitation Peabody said, "Sorry, Jed, but our informant, who was well paid to be accurate, swore that this Ted Hayward and the man you've signed on are one and the same. What's more, he'd been in trouble before. Aboard the brig *Hornet* he earned himself a flogging so severe they say you can see the results any time he takes off his shirt."

"Therefore," interpolated Mr. Doane, "we would be considerably relieved if you would secure another Third Mate."

Uncertain what to think, Lydia watched her brother's broad face assume that stubborn look she so dreaded.

"I won't do that, Mr. Doane," Jed said slowly, "Not without better proof than hearsay. Mr. Hayward has signed Articles and, so far, I've had no fault to find with him; he knows his duties and works hard." He treated his listeners to a bleak smile. "Rest assured that if he proves to be the case-hardened rascal you say he is, I—well, I can handle him. I've dealt with plenty of harder cases than Ted Hayward. No, I won't set him packing." With a touch of truculence he added, "What you going to do about that?"

The two visitors drew aside to confer in undertones. Finally Peabody, looking decidedly unhappy, jerked a nod. "Very well, Jed. Have it your way but 'twill be your responsibility to prevent Hayward from inciting a—well, his attempting to endanger the ship— which he well may, if it ever gets out you have thirty-five thousand silver dollars on board."

Jed looked hard at Joshua Peabody. "Do you imagine I'm such a ninny that I haven't already foreseen the risks I'll face if the news gets about?" Abruptly, his manner relaxed; became less hostile.

"Now, gentlemen, suppose you explain what you want done with the specie when, and if, I successfully transport it to Mexico. Also, how much do I and my shareholders stand to profit in this business?"

To conceal sharply rising excitement, Lydia went to the nearest window and looked out in time to watch a scrawny fellow, undoubtedly the livery stable's man, wandering away from the rear of Mrs. Albert's cottage. He was whistling off-key, apparently bored with lingering indoors on so fine a day. In no great hurry the stable man stooped, plucked a spear of sweetgrass and fell to chewing its stem. Probably he'd been eating bread and milk in the kitchen, Mrs. Albert being uncommon open-handed for a New Englander. In passing he nodded to the boardinghouse keeper hanging out a basketfull of clothes she'd just lugged out of a little laundry built beside the woodshed. Since the gangling fellow in cowhide boots and with pants sagging from galluses didn't appear overly intelligent she dismissed the occurrence, soon forgot all about it.

At the end of an hour an agreement had been reached whereby Jedediah Paddock undertook to transport the money to Vera Cruz in Mexico, a port convenient for a vessel bound for the Far East. In Vera Cruz very cautiously, Captain Paddock was to approach certain agents with which the bank previously had done business. One never knew what to expect in that war-torn land.

If all went well the bank's Mexican connections would exchange the United States coins for Mexican dollars, formerly called 'pieces-of-eight'. Although identical in weight and of exactly the same size as North American currency they contained much less fine silver and so could be purchased two-for-one.

At last report, Mr. Doane assured, Chinese merchants had not yet perceived this discrepancy in value—not for many years to come would the "Dollar Mex" become valued at its true worth—fifty American cents.

It required no great effort on the part of Captain Paddock and the Widow Roach to calculate that the Bank of Doane, Welch & Peabody stood to make a very tidy profit which could be utilized and increased through the purchase in Canton of such oriental luxuries as tea, silk embroideries, camphor, carved ivory, not to forget fragile tableware which no lady of affluence or fashion could do without.

For these varied services the *Gladiator*'s owners were to share the tidy sum of seven thousand dollars plus, upon her safe return, a five percent bonus in the cargo's net profit.

Inwardly, brother and sister were all aglow. These, in addition to substantial profits to be gained through successful whaling *should* guarantee a fabulously profitable voyage.

Thought Lydia: Jedediah's notion is shrewder than anyone's dreamed on.

As for Jed, he figured this promised to be a mighty rewarding cruise for all concerned. One favorable aspect of the agreement was the stipulation that the *Gladiator* would not be expected to linger in the Far East in order to bring home merchandise selected by the bank's compradors in Canton; such imports would be sent in slower, larger ships. The *Gladiator* meanwhile would be at liberty to resume whaling operations.

"When do you expect to sail, Captain?" Mr. Doane inquired while with slow, methodic motions he put away his spectacles.

"Inside of ten days at the latest. Why'd you ask?"

"There seems to be no point in delivering the treasure till the last minute. Less chance of rumors getting started, eh?"

Vigorously Jed nodded his big yellow head. "Correct. In what guise do you propose to deliver it?"

Joshua Peabody interrupted the insertion of documents into his portfolio. "In oak kegs marked 'bar lead' which should account for their great weight; don't aim to arouse curiosity. These kegs will be delivered late the night before sailing day. You've only to set the hour." He paused, looked hard at his friend. "Where you propose to stow our specie and how you will protect it of course, is your responsibility."

Solemnly, hands were shaken all round, Lydia's included, she owning such an impressive number of shares in the bark. Thereafter, tension in the Widow Albert's little parlor lessened perceptibly.

"Possibly you've been wondering," remarked Mr. Doane, helping himself to a pinch of snuff from Mr. Peabody's handsome gold and tortoise-shell box, "why I fetched my young nephew along?"

Jed chuckled. "I presume, Mr. Doane, you aim to show the lad what the world's like outside of Boston?"

"That is correct, Captain. My plans call for him to see considerably more than he'll have noted on our way down to New Bedford."

Mr. Doane got to his feet, stood absently stroking fluffy whiskers. "Abner is a smart, good-natured lad, although a trifle overgrown for his age. He's stubborn as a mule about wanting to go to sea, like—" The banker frowned, tightened his lips, "—like his late father, Sylvanus. Wants to go searching for him."

"'Late father'?"

"No one knows what fate overtook the merchantman *Arabella* on which Sylvanus was Second Mate. He was reported in Port Jackson, Australia, about six years ago but he's never has been heard of since."

Again, Jed received the impression that something lay beneath the surface of the banker's terse statement.

"Most likely my brother's ship became overwhelmed by a typhoon with the loss of all hands. Or possibly she got wrecked on some uncharted reef or, worse still, on a cannibal island.

"I'd take it kindly, sir, if you'll sign Abner on. I'll make it worth your while. I warrant he'll prove worth his salt else he's not my nephew and Sylvanus Doane's son." Again a shadow flitted over John Doane's bony, parchment-hued features.

Aware that if things went wrong on this cruise such a favor might serve as anchor to windward with Messrs. Doane, Welch & Peabody, Jed said briskly, "I'd be pleased to take the lad along, provided he's to taste a rope's end whenever he deserves it." Smoothly, he added, "I'm signing him on *only* because I've still no cabin boy; not because he's your nephew, Mr. Doane."

15

Replacements

The first thing Jedediah Paddock did on returning aboard the *Gladiator* was to summon the Third Mate.

Edward Hayward took one look at his Captain then settled his compact body into something like a prize fighter's crouch when anticipating a blow. The former Navy man was built like an inverted isosceles triangle—broad of shoulder, long-armed and short-legged. His scarred, violence-blunted features grew expressionless but wariness shone in the fellow's cavernous dark brown eyes.

Nervously wetting his lips, the Third spoke right up. "I guess, sir, you must have been hearing talk against me." The remark was a statement not a question.

"Yes. More than enough, if even half of what I've heard proves true."

"—What did they say, sir?"

"Plenty, and none of it to your credit. Suppose, Mister Hayward, you repeat the story you told me when you signed on and this time be sure to be damned sure you fill in what you left out on that other occasion." Mouth set in harsh lines, he swung his swivel chair to face the Mate. "Proceed, Mister Hayward, I've heard about the black side of your record and," he added grimly, "I promise you'll not enjoy it if you lie to me."

The Mate dropped his eyes, commenced to revolve a battered flat-crowned straw hat between tattooed brown hands. "Well, sir, what I've already told you is gospel. I've served as Second Mate on a merchantman and I've made two cruises on whalers."

"Which ones?" Jed's voice snapped like the breaking of a dried branch.

"Why, why, the *Cyrus.*"

"Who was her skipper?"

"Captain Ben Hussey, sir."

"The other?"

"The *Rambler*. Cap'n William Worth. She was my last berth."

Jed's eyes bored into the other's. "So far so good. Now what *was* your service in the Navy?"

"Like I said, sir, I served two hitches in the Navy and sure enough got to be a master gunner. What I ain't admitted," he said in a low voice, "is that I got into trouble, bad trouble. I—well, fact is I—I left the Navy with a dishonorable discharge."

Nervously Hayward's blunt fingers kneaded his tarry hat's brim.

"Repeat what you said when you signed Articles, about serving in the Navy," Jed rasped. "I want dates, ship names and where they sailed. Try to lie and I'll catch you out and beat the hell out of you."

Long ago he'd learned liars almost invariably tripped themselves up in attempting to duplicate a detailed falsehood.

He had, Edward Hayward explained in a hopeless, badgered tone of voice, run away from his home on a farm in Sag Harbor, New York, in order to enlist and serve as a powder monkey aboard the brig *U.S.S. Lawrence*, flagship of Commodore Oliver Hazard Perry's hastily constructed squadron at Port Erie, and had been aboard when that little vessel had been bloodily pounded to pieces by the British squadron's concentrated fire.

After the battle of Lake Erie he had applied for service at sea where the chances of advancement and prize money were greater. He had been assigned to the *U.S.S. Hornet* and had been a gun captain when she'd battered *H.M.S. Peacock* into surrender.

Hayward admitted it was towards the end of this cruise that he'd first got into trouble. A fight had broken out in the berth deck over a gambling game in which fists and knives came into use. By the time the Master-at-Arms and the Marines intervened he'd suffered a considerable cut across a shoulder but the fellow who'd stabbed him lay moaning on the deck with blood pouring from between his ribs.

Hayward explained in his slightly hoarse voice. "I pleaded self-defense, which was the truth, and should have got off with nothing worse than a reprimand and stoppage of pay, but," he shrugged wide shoulders, "I'd enemies among my messmates—they owed me money. The bastards took oath I stabbed Seaman Mullins from behind whilst he was fighting somebody else; I swear to God this wasn't so at all, sir! When Mullins got knifed I was fighting on the far side of the deck." Hayward raised hands in a lifting gesture denoting helplessness. "As it happened the court-martial officers chose to believe my enemies so—I got sentenced to twenty lashes with the cat and to be drummed over the side when we reached Newport." He straightened shoulders under a ragged wool jacket. "Must I go on, sir?"

"Yes," grunted the *Gladiator*'s Master.

"Well, sir, I was still young and hadn't got my fill of fighting so I went up to Boston, changed my name to 'Joe Ballard' and enlisted as an ordinary seaman on the fifty-four gun frigate, *United States*; and I got promoted to gun captain after we'd hammered the *Macedonian* to a frazzle.

"That, sir, is God's own truth. After we brought her to New London we drew our prize money." He lifted his gaze, said miserably. "After my pay was spent I made the mistake of my life, sir. I—I deserted to the *Antelope*, privateer, in which I'd hopes of winning more prize money than a fellow could earn in a regular man-o'-war.

"To start with, sir, our cruise was lucky and we took several prizes. I was named prize master over the *Duchess* because, by that time, I'd learned how to navigate, to read charts and order sail."

"Then?"

"Sir, we got becalmed off the Virginia Capes and a British razee captured us." Anxiously, Hayward studied his Skipper's expression, found it blank and hard-looking. "Next two years I spent in Mill Prison. When the Peace was signed, I was flat broke and feeling mighty sickly—prison rations being worse than any you'll find aboard the meanest spouter you ever heard of."

Jed noted every subtle alteration in the fellow's tone and manner; found it significant that so far he'd not made a single contradiction in those parts of the account he'd already rendered. All the same, there was an indefinable restless gleam in Edward Hayward's eyes which prompted him to wonder; was this shiftiness due to a mannerism?

The Third looked like a good hunting dog who knows he's made a mistake. "Cap'n, I know I should have told you all the facts about me to start with—should have remembered a blot on one's record comes to light sooner or later. All the same," his fingers commenced to knead his hat's brim harder, almost in desperation it seemed. "I hope you ain't going to dismiss me, sir, account of I swear I've been in no trouble of any kind since I left Mill Prison."

"Except," Jed cut in, "that from Maine to Long Island you've the reputation of being the worst kind of a bucko mate. You nearly beat a man to death aboard the *Fame*, didn't you?"

"That ain't exactly right, sir, begging your pardon. That fellow aboard the *Fame* was plotting mutiny when I caught him red-handed." Hayward seemed to regain a measure of confidence. "Maybe I am a bit ready with a belaying pin but you know, sir, the sort of riff-raff that ships in spouters these days; wiser to nip trouble in the bud than risk a knife in the back, ain't it?"

Jed's expression relaxed somewhat. "I'll go along with that. A lot of hands who'll sign on will be hard cases in need of a heavy hand."

On his way back to the bark after signing his agreement with Messrs. Doane, Welch & Peabody Jed indulged in a deal of earnest speculation: the presence aboard of a readily disposable treasure was raising a host of unfamiliar dangers and possibilities. For the moment his chief concern was the necessity of keeping the nature of this cargo a tight secret.

The *Gladiator's* Master reached a decision. "Mister Hayward, I'm of the opinion you've been telling the truth. You can stay aboard."

It was touching how this ugly fellow's mouth began to quiver while his eyes filled. "God bless you, sir! You'll never regret this, I swear it on a stack of Bibles a mile high. Just say the word, sir, and I'll carry out your every order to the letter."

"See that you do, Mister Hayward; but don't forget that I'll tolerate no *unnecessary* brutality aboard this ship."

Soberly, Hayward turned away. Whether Captain Paddock was as skilled in the use of firearms or could fling a belaying pin with as much accuracy as himself remained to be determined.

A few days short of sailing day Chief Mate Aaron Winslow sought out his Captain, found him on the fore deck suppering on beer, bread and a slab of cold meat. "Dunno just what's afoot," he drawled in his high-pitched nasal voice.

Jed continued chewing but cocked a hard gray-blue eye at his short and flat-faced First Officer, "What's your meaning, Mister Winslow?"

"How many old man-o'-warsmen hev you signed on?"

"Five, not counting Mister Hayward. What for?"

Through the twilight Mister Winslow cast an eye at the dark tangle of spars, masts and rigging silhouetted above the docks against the afterglow. "Well, not bein' used to such, I bin keepin' an eye on them former bluejackets."

"Well?"

" 'Till today, I've always noted 'em somewhere along the waterfront. Today, 'round noon, I sighted but two of 'em; they both was roarin' drunk and throwin' money about. Come sundown I went ashore and hunted likely places but found no trace of them ex-Navy fellers of ours."

Jed gulped down a sizable bite of mutton. "You said they were throwing money about?"

"You didn't advance them any, did you?"

"You should know better than ask such a fool question."

"Then where d'you figure they got it?"

"What's your guess?"

Winslow tugged at a ragged fringe of salt-and-pepper hued chin whiskers. "Search me, Cap'n. There've been no robberies reported so I allow they must ha' been hired away. You know how 'tis."

"Can't be that. There's no other vessel due to sail from here within a week's time."

"What about Fairhaven? The *Comet* sailed from over there on this afternoon."

Jed swore feelingly, it being common practice for a shorthanded captain in a hurry to put to sea to hire men away or ply them with liquor and kidnap them. He'd done so himself, plenty of times, and hadn't been in the least conscience-stricken.

"What's queer is that not one of 'em was seen about this afternoon."

"Go fetch Mister Hayward; send him on the double."

When the Third appeared Jedediah demanded, point-blank, what had become of the ex-Navy men.

Hayward appeared genuinely taken aback. "Now by God, sir, it's hard to credit they've disappeared like this. Why, I hand-picked those fellers for being extra steady and reliable. What the hell has happened to 'em?"

"For one reason or another they were paid to clear out," rasped

Jed, the scar on his chin reddening. "Main question is—why have *only* ex-Navy members of the crew been bribed? If the *Comet* were armed that might offer an explanation but she's not."

Frowning, Hayward scratched his freckled, balding scalp a moment. "Suppose I go ashore and make sure they've gone—they're maybe only dead-drunk in some dive."

"Do that," Jed's small eyes glittering. "If those sons-of-bitches really have skedaddled, you goddam well better get busy and find replacements; I intend to sail on time." Although he didn't say so his chief concern was that the specie was due from Boston two nights later.

Once Hayward had trotted off down the gangplank Jed quizzed the other two Mates, but obtained no results; neither proved able to account for the desertions.

"That being that, I want you both to start recruiting hands who know how to handle a cannon."

Winslow shrugged sloping shoulders. "I'll look about, Cap'n, but I ain't over-hopeful; mighty few old man-o'-warsmen hang about this port. Mostly they head for Newport or New London."

Nor was Mister Coffin any more encouraging, only suggested that he'd better go recruiting in Newport, "Of course, that might delay our departure for mebbe a week."

"That won't do. I aim to sail come the appointed day," Jed announced so harshly his subordinates wondered why he should be all *that* determined. For a whaler a day or two's delay meant nothing at all.

"If worse comes to worst," Jed grunted, "I'll put into Newport and recruit there."

It came as a considerable surprise that, just as the first stars timidly were making themselves noticed, Mister Hayward returned and at once sought the Captain's cabin.

"Well?" Jed peered up from a pile of invoices.

"Sir! Sir! Did you note the coaster what made fast to Laird's dock this afternoon?"

"Yes, Mister Hayward. What of it?"

"Why, sir, she's straight down from Boston with a bevy of time-expired Navy seamen aboard on the way to Newport where a new frigate is waiting to be commissioned."

Narrowly, Jed considered his hard-faced Third. "You've talked to any of them?"

The Mate exposed stained and broken teeth in a lopsided grin. "Yessir, soon's I heard there was Navy men aboard I got myself rowed out and talked to 'em!"

"Are they already enlisted and under orders?" Jed queried sharply.

"No, sir. Like I said, they've only lately been discharged but are ready to sign up for another hitch—or so they claim."

"How many are there?"

"Eleven; only five acted interested."

"Who'd you talk to?"

"A tough looking fellow named Archer; said he's been serving as bosun's mate aboard the *Constellation*. He kind of heads up the party."

"What about the rest?"

"Two claim to be gun pointers; the others say they're top-men."

In the light of a lamp mounted on gimbals above Paddock's desk Hayward's battered features gleamed copper-brown. "Most of 'em can show right and regular discharge papers, of which I've seen a heap."

"'Most of them'? Who couldn't?"

Hayward hesitated an instant. "Why, 'twas Tom Archer; claimed he lost his when his sea chest got stole up in Charlestown. His mates swore Archer was speaking truth about that."

Jed experienced a rising sense of wariness. "How did these men impress you? Look reliable?"

Hayward bobbed his balding head. "Aye, sir. They're about what ye could expect; no beauties but sturdy and bright."

The *Gladiator*'s Master rubbed his chin, caused a small rasping noise. Um. Beggars couldn't be choosers; should it turn out he'd made a mistake, well, he'd cope.

"You'd advise signing 'em on?"

"Aye, sir, but not 'till you've talked with 'em yourself."

"Very well. Fetch 'em aboard soon as may be. I'll pay for grog needed to keep 'em happy and listening to you." Jed arose, head brushing the lamp. "If I don't like the cut of their jibs I'll recruit in Newport."

16
Target Practice

Those cold days which had dragged on while the *Gladiator* was being armed and outfitted were unprecedented in Lydia Roach's experience.

Lord above! Here within the space of a few months she'd been married and widowed; she'd sold her house and severed all ties with her previous existence. A most challenging prospect would be how best to adjust to living aboard a whaler.

She was being allowed aboard only rarely, and then in the role of an inquisitive shareholder, it being clearly understood no one must suspect she would sail as one of the ship's company. Unobtrusively, the young woman familiarized herself with the rigging and alterations being made on the vessel destined to transport her into the unknown.

At first she'd been aghast at the minuscule proportions of that dark little hutch designated for her use. God's love! She'd seen plenty of larger dog houses; a single porthole, the diameter of a small pie, would be her only access to light and air. There'd be space for only a very small sea chest beneath a corded bunk softened only by a thin straw mattress aptly nicknamed "the donkey's breakfast".

Prey to a sinking feeling the wiry young woman wondered how in the world she'd be able to keep herself anything like clean or obtain privacy essential on certain occasions. Only one thing stood in her favor; Jed had granted her the use of his tiny private head thus sparing her the necessity of taking her turn in the crude and drafty board "head" or latrine rigged above the bow's overhang.

She set her teeth and fought down a rising sense of panic. No. Hadn't she for all these years schemed to escape a humdrum, if comfortable existence? She'd manage.

The Widow Albert likely must deem her a trifle touched in the head because, when it wasn't rainy, she would make for a clump of pines standing a few fields distant. Usually she went alone but sometimes she'd be accompanied by her fellow boarder, Abner Doane, the banker's pale-complexioned nephew.

This cheerful youth seemed at a loss since he, too, scarcely ever was allowed aboard the *Gladiator*, so was forced to spend much time wandering about the docks or studying books on navigation borrowed from Mrs. Roach who, in the interests of propriety and legal caution, had decided to use her new name at least until the bark departed New Bedford.

When on certain occasions Abner accompanied Lydia to the pine woods he would be carrying a fine, brass-bound flat box of olive wood containing not only a pair of slim, beautifully engraved French duelling pistols but also a mould to cast suitable bullets, a worm-screw to draw balls in case of misfire, loading tools and even a *prouvette*, a cleverly tooled brass device designed to gauge the fineness and strength of ungraded gunpowder.

When neighbors complained about having heard pistol shots fired in the pine woods the Widow Albert admitted to herself she'd never begin to understand Captain Paddock's dark featured and self-contained sister. Well, so long as Mrs. Roach paid her rent and didn't hurt anything why wasn't she welcome to do as she pleased?

But the Widow would have been scandalized had she seen her boarder calmly firing at the profile of a man sketched in charcoal on a weather-whitened plank. After she'd finished shooting she'd practice throwing a dirk at the same target. On occasion she would invite a thoroughly delighted Abner to try his hand. Soon he grew fairly accurate.

Lydia reckoned she'd never quite forget the expression on Doane's freckle-peppered face the first time she'd without warning calmly stepped out of her skirt to stand, long-legged and flushed in a pair of men's pantaloons which she'd taken to wearing under her petticoats so as to become accustomed to the feel of them.

"Can't move sufficient quick in all these yard goods," she explained. "Thee will never tattle on me, will thee, Abner?"

"Oh no, ma'am, I'd never even dream of doing that." From the start of these expeditions into the pines John Doane's nephew had been her shy and adoring if somewhat mystified slave. "Wha'— what shall I do?"

"Once I've crossed that line scratched in the dirt thee is to count up to five then call out 'Fire!'."

"Yes, ma'am."

By this time Lydia had become able to plant two out of three bullets in the silhouette exactly where she wanted—at points which would either kill or disable a man. What would it be like to slay a fellow human? To start with she'd quivered at the very possibility but then she had grown quite dispassionate; of late she now began to experience a queer sense of stimulation whenever her bullet smacked straight into the center of a heart painted in barn-red on the board. At these moments she realized her breathing had quickened and her cheeks grew flushed and, most extraordinary of all, she became conscious of a not unpleasant warmth in her loins. Altogether she revelled in this glorious awareness of being young, healthy and strong.

During long spring evenings Mrs. Roach occupied herself by studying books on travel and hopelessly dull treatises on navigation; also she absorbed a good deal about the rough-and-ready medicine of the time.

On those rare occasions when Jedediah invited her to visit the bark she said nothing about how she passed the time. Always she was eager to board the *Gladiator*. Why not? Didn't she own a quarter-interest? Before mounting the workmen's gang plank she'd walk the length of the outfitting wharf familiarizing herself with every detail of the bark's outward aspect and found her lines increasingly lovely now that her hull had been painted a shining black and the gunports which punctuated a broad, bright-yellow streak running the length of her beam.

Lydia took special pride in the bark's new stern board, topped as it was, by a handsomely carved and gilded American eagle clutching a shield depicting the National coat-of-arms. She took pleasure, too, on reading the inscription painted in gilt letters: *Gladiator of Nantucket*.

The Fourth Mate-to-Be, however, wasn't as overly pleased by the figurehead. At first glance she'd realized that the effigy didn't depict a gladiator at all, but a helmeted Roman officer who, with bared teeth, clutched a silvery short sword and stared savagely straight ahead. However, she reckoned it looked fierce enough to impress savages and the like. Wisely, she made no mention of this inaccuracy to her brother; he obviously deemed this figurehead a masterpiece.

Whenever she went aboard Lydia made it a point to seek out Te Ponapa and exchange a few casual words. Quite frankly this tatooed, smiling giant piqued her curiosity—possibly he might prove helpful in introducing her to the strange, exciting world she was about to invade. Usually she found the Maori working near the blacksmith's forge putting a razor edge on all manner of lances, cutlasses, harpoons and blubber spades.

Always Te Ponapa seemed delighted to see her. His huge dark eyes shone while in his rich but curiously sing-song voice he explained unfamiliar fittings and equipment. Among other facts, Jed's blood-brother pointed out that new sails invariably were delivered from the sailmakers loft in clearly marked waterproof casks—lest they grow damp and begin to rot.

Especially, she found interest in inspecting the eight, short-barreled brown-black carronades which recently had been mounted and secured on what several old hands considered dangerously narrow platforms. These, running along the beams of the vessel, separated the upper from the lower tier in the hold.

With sailing day growing near Captain Jedediah Paddock's problems diminished as various preparations for departure reached completion. At the moment the young giant was keeping an eye on a crew of masons constructing those stout brick fire boxes over which the *Gladiator's* two try-pots of cast iron would be kept a-boiling—or so it was hoped. A generous supply of firewood already had been stowed below but as much more remained stacked on the wharf.

The Master's greatest problem apparently had been solved when, the day before, he'd interviewed former Boatswain's Mate Thomas Archer and the four ex-Navy men who accompanied him.

Archer turned out to be an alert, clean-cut appearing individual with straightforward speech and manner. What with his broad shoulders and curling black hair most girls would probably deem him good-looking above average for all he was missing a front tooth.

Questioning, based on practical experience, convinced the *Gladiator's* Master that this fellow and two of his mates indeed were familiar with the handling and use of carriage guns; the other two were topmen who also knew something of gunnery.

Once he'd examined their discharges—Archer's excepted—he'd decided to sign them on for all he couldn't shake off a nagging presentiment that somewhere a nigger must be lurking in the wood-pile.

Blankly viewing the harbor's garbage-dotted expanse Jedediah Paddock fell to speculating on how young Doane might be made to earn his salt. One thing was certain, however; he didn't want old John Doane's nephew around when certain casks from Boston were delivered. As a further precaution he'd granted the First and Second a last fling ashore and, under pretext of bringing back a spare whale-boat, he'd despatched Mister Hayward and the other ex-Navy hands over to Fairhaven.

Inexplicably, Jed experienced a sense of disquiet when the hour for the specie's arrival drew near; he was feeling, as he'd often put it, "nervous as a whore in church."

Once the last of the joiners, caulkers and carpenters had straggled over the side he instructed Te Ponapa and Tom Blue Fox to make certain no unauthorized person remained on board.

A seemingly endless half-hour dragged by while twilight deepened into dark. Finally a canvas-covered, four-wheeled freight wagon drawn by as many horses, turned off Water Street and commenced to rumble out over the dock. A single figure was occupying the driver's seat, sat humped over the reins.

Annoyance flooded Jed. Hell! Even to avoid drawing attention, Messrs. Doane, Welch & Peabody seemed to be cutting the matter of protection a trifle fine; but he then noted a group of roughly dressed individuals sauntering along in the wagon's wake and pretending, a trifle too elaborately, to take interest in their surroundings.

By the time Captain Paddock had signed a receipt for some two dozen kegs of "bar lead" and had seen them stowed under his cabin's deck in a small strong room secretly devised from the vessel's laz-arette perspiration was standing out all over his broad brown features. Lord! Now he'd become responsible for thirty-five thousand silver dollars! Pray God, no one aboard the *Gladiator* at this hour had become even remotely curious concerning the nature of this be-lated delivery.

17

Sailing Day

On June the second, 1831, the bark *Gladiator*, having left the fitters' wharf the previous day, swung to her anchor in the Acushnet River. Everyone who saw her agreed that she presented an inspiring sight what with new paint work, sharp bows, tall, white-painted and well-raked masts. Spotless new canvas lay neatly furled along tapering yards which also were painted white. From all three mastheads fluttered bright new flags: at the fore fluttered the private signal of Jedediah Paddock's agent, David Coffin & Sons. It displayed a white diamond on a bright red field and showed in its center a big block letter "C" done in black. Above the maintop floated the Paddock & Sons' house flag, the familiar black sperm whale spouting on a scarlet field. From the mizzen's gaff lazily curled a brand new National Ensign nearly as big as the maintop's gallant sail.

Like a long black sow nursing piglets the bark lay hemmed in by small boats and dories hired by shareholders, friends and relatives come to speed Captain Jedediah Paddock's vessel to the world's far side.

Abner Doane never would quite forget his sensations when a wherry conveying him and a few more-or-less drunken crew members bumped below the *Gladiator*'s gangway. He attempted a bit of swagger when, after climbing a rope ladder, he reached the deck a sea bag slung in transparent nonchalance over one shoulder then found himself gaping in wide-eyed bewilderment.

Jehoshephat! The scene suggested nothing so much as a seagoing madhouse. Every unencumbered bit of deck space was occupied by hooting, staggering whalers and equally inebriated friends. There wasn't a female in sight because, long ago, it had been discovered that it wasn't feasible for members of the fair sex to descend a swaying and uncertain rope ladder to board a pilot boat which would

return visitors to port once the departing ship began making sail for
the open sea.

The women, therefore, had done their leave-taking on the wharf
just before wherries and rowboats started to convey their menfolk
out to the *Gladiator*. Abner Doane, always noticing, observed how
often sober, decently dressed females treated their man to a radiant
smile before kissing him goodbye only to burst into tears the
moment he'd turned away—to be gone for two or three years or,
quite possibly, forever.

Cautiously the cabin boy forced his way through the convivial
swarm and gained a measure of shelter in the lee of wicker crates
containing wild-eyed chickens and a pen which, backed up against
the try-ovens, confined a quartet of completely indifferent pink pigs.

From a rack built on the stern house to accommodate spare
whaleboats dangled a red-and-white side of beef so recently butchered it still dripped slowly, redly onto the filthy deck.

Aft, a quieter group had congregated. It was composed of the
ship's officers, agents, important shareholders and the like, well-
dressed in tall beaver hats, long-tailed coats of decent broadcloth
and often checkered pantaloons strapped over well-polished, square-
toed boots. They exuded an air of prosperity, shrewdness and capa-
bility.

For this memorable occasion Captain Jedediah Paddock had
donned a bottle-green frock coat together with a crisp, ruffled shirt,
sky-blue trousers and a waistcoat of yellow-green nankeen secured
by plenty of glittering brass buttons.

He stood sipping sherry and conversing with his friend and
agent, silvery-haired and hatchet-faced David Coffin.

When someone shouted, "Avast! Yonder comes the pilot boat!"
Jed's manner underwent a sharp change. At once he beckoned
Mister Hayward who caught up a speaking trumpet and bellowed:
"Everybody ashore what ain't goin' down-river. Step lively! You
there! Get going!" He strode up to a raffish appearing character who,
glassy eyed, was finding trouble in maintaining balance. "I said, *get
going!*"

When the fellow only stared, slack-jawed, the Third gave him
such a kick on the rear that he was sent staggering across the deck.
Other visitors laughed uproariously as, draining nearly empty bottles,
they started shuffling towards the gangway and small boats waiting

below. No attention was paid to their departure by the affluent group aft.

Plenty of obscene suggestions as to how best to please South Sea wenches were shouted by departing visitors. One or two half-hearted fist fights broke out but were promptly subdued by Mister Hayward and Tom Archer the former Navy boatswain's mate. Soon the last of the crews' visitors were herded over the side.

Locked in her gloomy little cabin, Fourth Mate Lydia Paddock Roach crouched, bathed in sweat on her bunk and half-suffocated, but happier and more excited than she'd ever been. At the same time she was attempting to accustom her body to unfamiliar constrictions and the harsh texture of the male attire donned before being smuggled aboard at daybreak.

Not a foot above her head feet clumped and heavy objects were trundled back and forth. Also audible were harsh, liquor-thickened voices raised in the 'tween decks. Due to a persistent haunting of New Bedford's docks Lydia fancied she had heard about every blasphemous or obscene expression: but now she was discovering she hadn't heard even the half of them.

Gradually she was coming to appreciate how malodorous this hutch really was; what air managed to pass through the tiny porthole didn't accomplish much towards dispelling the nauseous reek of bilges and other stenches. Her accommodation was so cramped that once her small sea chest and duffel bag had been stowed, almost no deck space remained unencumbered; this bunk she was sitting on couldn't measure more than five-foot-three by two in width. How could a normal-sized human be expected to exist for months, even years, in so noisome a hole? Still, she knew this was an improvement on the steerage located just forward of her "cabin"; in it four boat-steerers would be crammed into a space only slightly larger.

Although growing hungry and thirsty the Fourth dared not disobey orders that she remain out of sight 'till the pilot had been dropped. Therefore she settled back on her single coarse blanket stubbornly refusing to admit that this was a disillusioning beginning to a voyage towards high adventure. Still, she knew she shouldn't have expected better; all along, she'd appreciated that life aboard a spouter never could be a bed of roses; however when something scurried across her trousered legs she jerked up convulsively and banged her head against a beam so hard she saw stars but not a rat which vanished behind her duffel bag. Horrified, she felt her eyes overflow but, stubbornly, she refused to sob.

At long last she heard Mister Hayward order visitors over the side. Followed a flurry of orders, then a creaking protest from the barrel winch and the rhythmic *clack-clack!* of pawls dropping into place; at last the *Gladiator*'s anchor was being heaved.

While mopping tears from sweaty features Lydia Roach recognized her brother's deep voice ordering the setting of jibs and topsails. Water began to gurgle along the side as, almost imperceptibly at first, the *Gladiator*'s fabric commenced to come alive. Hot as she was, a succession of icy shivers shook her.

In the steerage Te Ponapa, Rangitira, lay with knees flexed on a bunk which lacked several inches of accommodating his stature even though he'd persuaded a carpenter to extend its original length after having built a small locker beneath his berth. Firmly but good-naturedly he'd refused to confide what it contained.

Sailing day now was an old story the Maori mused as, hands locked under head, he dozed. How often had he listened to identical sounds on a ship about to sail? How many times since that long-gone day when the *Castor* had discovered Heetee and himself on the Tasman Sea?

He roused when the door banged open and framed a short, thick figure with enormously long arms. The intruder paused, blinking like some animal about to enter a dark and unfamiliar cave, but this fellow resembled no other Black he'd ever seen for his broad, flat features, instead of being decently tattooed, were covered on brow, cheeks and chin with designs done in tiny cicatrices—little scars which stood out in repeated chevron-like patterns. A battered plug hat rode on the back of a woolly round head and, as a further bizarre touch, a large copper ring dangled from the lobe of his right ear.

"H'lo," grunted the apparition. "Dis de steerage?"

"'Tis nothing else," the Maori said. "Who are you?"

When the Negro grinned broadly the Maori noted with interest that his teeth had been filed to sharp, dog-like points, like those of a Fiji or a Society Islander.

The Negro dropped a shapeless sea bag and thumped his chest. "Me Hercules. Best damn' steerer ever darted a harpoon!"

"You lie. You'll never match me—or Tom Blue Fox!"

The blue-black Negro relaxed, appeared not at all belligerent. "Who dat?"

"I, Blue Fox." The Monomoy suddenly sat up on his bunk, big beaked and bronze-hued features set in a scowl.

"Aw, hell, boys, we c'n settle 'at later. Le's all have a swig!" Hercules pulled a squat black bottle from his bag and waved it about in bibulous amity before thrusting it at Te Ponapa.

Once the Maori had taken a generous pull of fiery Demerera he indicated a bunk above Tom Blue Fox's. "Better you take that one, Hercules, t'other belongs to Johnny Folger—he's head boat-steerer; has the watch right now."

"Dat so? Well, me sleep now." The long-armed Negro nodded, yawned cavernously and, without removing his hat, lay down and at once commenced to snore.

Once the bark had commenced to lift and dip at a faster clip, Te Ponapa replaced hands beneath head, settled back to gaze blankly at unpainted deck beams above.

With rum warming his bowels the giant Maori found it not unpleasant to lie thus in semi-darkness to contemplate the fact that, with any luck, not many more months would pass before he'd again see the green-blue and often snow-topped mountains of Aotearoa lift above the horizon and watch long, glassy rollers go tumbling shorewards to cream and froth over barrier reefs before they rushed in lacy confusion up some dazzlingly white beach.

Maru! Then will I seek out Te Pehi, *Ariki* of the great and valorous Otagos.

The probability occurred that his father might be dead—few Maori chieftains, valiant or not, survived to a ripe age.

Could it be that five years had sped by since he, Heetee and the two slaves had been blown out to sea? Why, he'd even forgotten the taste of "long pig"—which was something like pork, only preferable. Would Te Pehi deem his heir gone soft because, in all this time, he'd not slain an enemy in formal battle?

Te Ponapa fumbled under a sweat-soaked linen shirt, gripped a *tiki* of greenstone and commenced to rub the charm's elaborately carved surface.

Would Maru, god of war, permit Te Ponapa again to sleep with many women after gorging on the flesh of warriors slain by him?

He'd been among the *pakehas* for a long time but still couldn't comprehend why they held *all* human life so confounded sacred.

If Te Pehi were dead, how much of a job would it prove to gain his inheritance? The Otagos must have believed him dead a long time ago. *Heu!* In all probability plenty of blood would flow.

Well, he'd quickly undeceive the tribe; gently if possible, brutally if necessary. The most important step, of course, would be to secure firearms and plenty of ammunition; a single serviceable musket was more to be feared than any number of greenstone axes, spears and shark-tooth-studded clubs. *Heu!* Wouldn't it be fine again to "catch the first fish"—be the first to slay an enemy at the start of battle and so become entitled later to eat the fallen warrior's heart—provided his victim proved valorous and of sufficiently high rank.

Off West Chop lighthouse amid shouts of "A short and greasy voyage!" the pilot boat, carrying the officers' guests, squared away for the long run back to New Bedford. Captain Jedediah Paddock's bearing altered as he watched her go. Briefly, he debated calling all hands on deck but he decided to delay. Right now a good many hands, veterans and greenhorns alike, were either falling-down, knee-walking drunk or much too fuddled to make sense. Accordingly, he turned the ship over to Aaron Winslow and went below to unlock the Fourth Mate's cabin.

Sweat-brightened features lighting, Lydia Roach sprang to her feet. "Oh, Jed, Jed! At last! At last! I'm so very happy—" she broke off silenced by her brother's expression.

His voice was harsh with the gritty quality of a file being passed over steel. "Avast! Now hear this and don't forget what I say. From this moment forward you'll be known only as 'Mister Paddock' and you'll address me only as either 'Sir' or 'Captain'. Is that understood?"

Eyes rounded Lydia stared through the doorway, "Why, why yes."

"*Sir!* Aboard this vessel, you'll answer not 'yes' but 'aye, aye sir!' Now, Mister Paddock, tidy yourself and report to my cabin within five minutes."

18

Under Way

Once Mishaum buoy had been left swaying astern the *Gladiator*, wearing only easy canvas, stood out into the Atlantic in slovenly disorder. At every roll empty bottles rolled and rattled from scupper to scupper; crewmen reeking of vomit lay uglily inert amid unstowed cargo.

Chief Mate Winslow remarked acidly to his relief, Mister Coffin, "In all my days at sea I ain't ever noted, come sailing day, so damn' many hog-drunk hands or a dirtier vessel."

Due to Captain Paddock's foresight Third Mate Hayward had succeeded in keeping a few hands sufficiently sober to set new courses and topsails billowing, golden-white in the sunset.

To Mister Lydia Paddock, it proved blissful to lean on the taffrail breathing air untainted by the hot stink of below decks. It also was a mighty fine sensation to feel the deck lift and fall regularly beneath new and uncomfortable square-toed brogans. Undoubtedly it would take a bit of time to accustom herself to their weight, also to the painful constriction of a specially constructed canvas vest she'd lashed cruelly tight over her breasts.

Sighing, she pulled off the wide-visored cloth cap she'd selected to conceal what remained of once-abundant blue-black hair. Peering down at the bark's hissing, lacy wake she managed a tremulous smile. Astern lay the drab existence she'd always loathed. Ahead of the *Gladiator*'s garish figurehead lay—Lord knew what?

Dawn remained a pearly-pink presentiment on the horizon when the watchman's rattle set up its sharp clatter.

"All hands on deck!" roared the Officer of the Watch. "Line up abaft the main, you slew-footed scum!"

Hung-over and ill-tempered, boatsteerers invaded the fo'c's'le then reappeared driving red-eyed sluggards with liberal use of a rope's end. Anyone too sodden or surly to move smartly earned kicks to remind him he wasn't snoring off a carouse in some brothel.

Hands clenched in the pockets of a faded blue pea jacket, Jedediah Paddock waited, grim-faced, before the mainmast; the four Mates lined up a pace behind him. Lydia, looking deceptively tall because of long canvas pants, had pulled her cap down, hoped she was looking unconcerned, strong and capable.

Ranged in a single rank to the Captain's right stood his four boatsteerers plus the gunner, Tom Archer, who, because of his unique duties had been accorded an equal rating. The remainder of the crew were drawn up in a swaying double rank which included both able and ordinary seamen. Among the latter were "greenies", landsmen with no previous experience at sea. Generally these were farm boys or runaway apprentices in search of adventure, or hard-featured characters: sots, absconding debtors and ex-jailbirds who'd found the sheriff only a short jump behind.

Running cold, experienced eyes over these individuals Jed found them no better nor worse than average. As usual, Portuguese, Indians and Britishers instinctively had collected into knots; the former Navy men, surly now that liquor had died in them, also were standing to one side.

Cupping hands, Aaron Winslow bellowed, "Off hats! Harken to the Cap'n."

On the disorderly deck descended a silence so complete that the rhythmic *shush-shushing* of waves along the bark's sides and a gentle humming of wind in her rigging could easily be heard.

Jedediah Paddock was in no great hurry to start talking. For several moments his small, steel-blue eyes shifted from one face to another, memorizing the likeness of each man.

His gaze rested longest upon the boatsteerers. Um. None were of the same race, let alone of the same nationality. Good. This would stimulate rivalry which, if controlled, would prove beneficial.

He began to speak in short, sharp sentences. "I don't aim to talk much—just long enough to tell you how my ship's to be run. First: Never forget that *I* am the Lord God Almighty aboard the *Gladiator*. You'll obey my commands and those of the Mates *to the letter*— and run to carry 'em out. Second: I will not tolerate the least waste of water and anybody caught dropping vittles overside will be put on bread and water for a month; what's more, I'll shorten the rations of his watch for the same length of time."

He paused, big body yielding easily to the bark's slow rolling. "I ain't pleased to see so many 'greenies' amongst you—means boat drills will have to start early."

Glaring, he strode along the line of new men. "Most of you look ox-dumb but, by God, you'll learn to box the compass in a week's time and know the lines by name. You fail and you'll live on deck 'till you can pass muster."

He then took a short turn which brought him before the Able Seamen. "Now you know your duties or you'll wish you did; you're to work extra hard 'till the 'greenies' catch on."

Next Jed thrust out his box of a jaw, stared hard at the boat-steerers. "I've never minded a bit of hearty competition between boat crews and I'll reward efficient work but I will *not* tolerate any dirty work. Remember this; you're not hired to work for personal profit but to forward a successful voyage."

A puff of wind stirred yellow strands of hair escaping beneath the Captain's tall and well-weathered beaver hat. After taking another turn across the encumbered deck he halted facing the entire company. "Because I've had some guns mounted I don't want you to mistake my intentions. I don't plan to privateer or go looking for trouble, but with real cannon I can do business and recruit supplies where I wouldn't dare go unarmed."

Thought Lydia Roach as she stood, thrilled to her depths, beside Mister Hayward. Aye. And said guns will help ensure delivery of certain kegs of silver coin to Mexico and China.

"Next comes the matter of discipline," barked Jedediah. "I've already said I've no intention of trying to run this vessel like a man-o'-war, but," his great voice swelled, "but, by the Lord Harry, I'll be merciless toward anybody who disobeys orders, malingers or even dreams of mutiny. He either will swing from the mains yardarm or find his back crawling under the bite of the cat."

Lydia stared, caught her breath with a small click. Could this cruel-eyed, harsh-voiced stranger actually be the brother she'd idolized?

She returned attention to that massive figure dominating the scene. Jed lowered his voice but it retained an edge. "It's time you learned that the Fourth Mate is an important part-owner. That she's my sister is something you'd better not forget." He glared deliberately along the dishevelled ranks. "Remember this: everybody aboard is required to address her as 'Mister Paddock'. You will obey her orders exactly as if she were a man and God help anyone who shows the least disrespect!"

For most of the red-eyed and still half-sodden crew it came as a shock to realize, for the first time, there was a *female* aboard.

"God above!" growled one of the ex-Navy men, "Having a split-bottom aboard is about the most unchancy thing could happen!"

The Captain's manner changed, became subtly intimidating, "Before watches are picked you'll be dismissed for ten minutes. Fetch on deck *all* firearms and any knife with a blade of six inches or longer." Jed paused, scowling. "I said *all* such arms; anybody tries to keep any back will learn what a lead-tipped cat can do to a man's back. Remember this," he added in a low-pitched but effective voice, "I'm not one to make empty promises."

Captain Jedediah Paddock grew thoughtful on surveying a more than usual number of knives and pistols which thudded onto the deck to be marked and locked away in an arms chest lying beneath the main cabin.

Abner Doane looked on when the crew lined up again, round-eyed and awed by that menace in Captain Paddock's expression. He seemed overwhelming—a yellow-headed colossus incongruously clad in a beaver hat, hammer-claw coat and checkered pants.

"Since the most of you scum haven't sailed with me before and don't yet understand that what *I* say goes, I'll grant you a second chance to fetch the rest of your contraband weapons."

He grinned like a friendly winter wolf. "This time I won't punish any man who happens to come across a piece of contraband he's missed, but if any weapons are discovered *after* this I'll make that man wish he'd never been born—by God I will!"

As, scowling, the crew disappeared below Chief Mate Winslow grunted to the Second. "Hope they believe him. 'Tis main bad luck christening a voyage in blood."

The second summons to surrender weapons brought odd results —only four pistols came to light but over two dozen dirks, knives and daggers. Jed also found it significant that on this round none of the ex-Navy men turned in a weapon of any description and looked as innocent as could be.

As a final and perhaps needless precaution he summoned the Mates then, fixing his gaze on Hayward, said crisply, "You officers will turn in any sidearms and ammunition you've brought along. They'll be returned the minute I figure they're needed."

Lydia felt her canvas waistcoat grow tighter. What about that pair of duelling pistols in the false bottom of her sea chest? What if they were discovered? She knew her brother well enough to know she'd suffer punishment—in private, she hoped; but there was no certainty of that, Jed being as he was. Paling, she looked aside, said nothing.

Early next morning Jedediah sent his cabin boy in search of the Fourth. Young Doane found her taking a solar observation aft of the roundhouse. He hesitated, unwilling to disturb her and, in deep curiosity, surveyed "Mister" Paddock. In no way did she resemble that darkly handsome young female he'd got so to admire back in New Bedford.

In a dreadnought jacket and stained canvas pants the Captain's sister appeared taller, more sinewy. Criminently! There wasn't even the least curve to her body to be seen as she stood expertly adjusting a sextant against the *Gladiator*'s easy motion.

To his astonishment the new sun's reddish rays were begining to create in the young woman's olive complexion copper tints he'd never before noticed.

Once she'd completed her observations and had listed them in a little notebook he told her she was wanted by the Captain.

She glared. "Why didn't you speak up sooner? He—he isn't used to waiting. Never make such a mistake again!"

Leaving the boy goggle-eyed she ran below, heart hammering, to discover the *Gladiator*'s Master sorting piles of documents. To one side she recognized a brand new log book bound in clean gray canvas; one of her duties she knew would be to keep said log accurately and up-to-date.

When she entered his cabin Jed looked up, frowning. Attempting to look at ease, she said quietly, "I'm sorry I took so long but Abner just now gave me your message. Why d'you look harassed, finding trouble with the papers?"

He started and reared back in his chair, brows elevated. "Did you say 'you' to me just now?"

"Yes. I did. Why?"

"Why not 'thee' as usual?"

Lydia flushed, replied defiantly. "Think what you will, Jedediah—"

"'Captain' to you, Mister Paddock," he rasped. "Go on!"

"Well, sir, I—I've decided to abandon Quaker speech for the duration of this cruise." Steadily, she continued, "Why did thee—I mean you summon me?"

In passing fingers over his chin her brother caused a small, rasping noise; he hadn't shaved. "I'm concerned, Mister Paddock—perhaps without cause—by the fact that when Gunner Tom Archer and the men who signed on with him surrendered their pistols they didn't appear surly about it—which ain't usual."

"Is Archer the good-looking, dark-haired fellow with the scar across his nose?"

"He's the one. When I quizzed them he seemed to speak like an educated man—much better than the rest." Judiciously, Jed pursed his lips. "Yes. Fellow seems to have breeding somewhere in his background. I want you to check on my impression.

"Sit down, Mister Paddock." He jerked a thumb to Pa's sea bed rocking gently on its gimbals. "There's something else frets me."

"—And what might that be?" Lydia wanted to pull off her peaked cap the band of which was painfully tight but didn't dare.

"Aboard this vessel only two people, you and I, are presumed to know about the true contents of those kegs from the bank. I've been wondering if that's still the case."

A small "V" appeared between the Fourth's level black brows. "Any reason to doubt it?"

The Master of the *Gladiator* stared fixedly at a brass-mounted barometer secured to a white-painted bulkhead across his cabin. "Damned if I can explain why, but somehow I've got to thinking that news of our 'bar lead' shipment must have leaked. So, Mister Paddock, it's most important that, right now, you think back very carefully and try to recall anything, no matter how trivial, that's been said or done which might explain how someone's caught on."

After a long pause Lydia looked her brother straight in the face. Splashes of sunlight reflected off the sea wavered about the cabin's ceiling. "I can't recall a thing—not a single thing in any way suspicious so, if there's been a leak, it must have occurred in Boston or while the kegs were on the way to New Bedford."

Her slightly oblique eyes narrowed. "Do you suppose one of the bank's guards got to wondering why ordinary 'bar lead' should be so well protected—and delivered at night? Suppose he found opportunity to satisfy his curiosity?"

Slowly, Jed shook his massive blond head. "No. I've come to believe that the secret got out—if it did—soon after we closed our deal with the bankers."

Risking a reprimand Lydia removed her cap and fell thoughtfully to massaging her scalp. "What prompts thee—I mean 'you' to suspect that?"

"Because it was only a few days after we met at your boardinghouse the first lot of ex-Navy men suddenly disappeared just as if they'd been paid to. Now tell me this: why should anyone go to such an expense and why did he bribe *only* naval characters? Damn it, Lyddie, think back. Try to remember anything even a little out of the way."

Obediently, Lydia settled onto the bed and closed her eyes to visualize Mrs. Albert's small, sunlit parlor. Step by step she recreated the bankers' arrival with Abner Doane in tow, then Jed's appearance. Thinking back methodically, she recalled how Mr. Doane had manufactured an excuse to get rid of his nephew. Mrs. Albert had been out back doing her wash so there shouldn't have been anyone else in the house. Then, suddenly, she recalled seeing lanky Jake Doolittle, the livery stable's man, wander unhurriedly away from the back door. She snapped fingers and jumped up, a trifle panic-stricken.

Jed leaned forward, small, steely eyes intent. "Remember something?"

Lydia's cheek bones became more prominent. "Perhaps. I've just recalled seeing Jake Doolittle—that hayseed fellow who drove the Boston people out from town—wander out of Mrs. Albert's back door. Come to think on it, he was in the kitchen so he *might* have overheard us in the parlor."

Jed's fist banged on the desk. "You damned stupid wench! Why ain't you spoken of this before?"

She jumped up, features aflame. "Captain or not, don't thee ever dare to curse me! I'll not abide it."

"Sit down!" he snarled. "And understand this—I'll curse you whenever you deserve it—same as anybody else. Answer me. Why haven't you mentioned this matter before?"

Stiffly she replied. "Pray tell me what is memorable about a common stable man's ambling across the yard?"

"Under ordinary conditions, nothing," Jed admitted sourly. "All the same, I'll bet a barrel *that's* how the fat's got into the goddam fire! Now get out, Mister Paddock, whilst I do some heavy thinking."

19

Whaleboat Crews

In the Captain's neat, white painted cabin, Fourth Mate Paddock cut a new point to her quill and otherwise prepared to make another entry in the log, aware that her heart was still pounding from the ghastly yet oddly exciting scene she'd just witnessed.

> 20 June, 1831. This day begins fine with small Winds out of the NNE. Course SE. by S.
> Lat. Obs. 40°31′ S.   Long. E. 65°15′
> This morn were flogged men caught with concealed weapons in defiance of the Captain's orders. These were: Able Seamen Fitch and Benton, and Ordinary Seamen Beesley and Hollis. All were former Navy ratings. These were tied up by their thumbs to the rigging and suffered 15 lashes well laid on by the Boatsteerer Hercules. I dressed their hurts which were painful but nothing serious. Weather continues Fine. Sighted the Ship *Alert* and Whaler *Fame*, of Nantucket, homeward bound; spoke to neither.

Copying a custom noticed in many of the logs she'd studied Lydia, on the page's margin, skillfully sketched outlines of a full-rigged ship and a bark. Under each she printed the vessel's name. When a ship was sighted at a distance too great to permit reading her name she would merely indicate the stranger's rig.

She blotted the entry then looked for mistakes in her neat and flowing script and, as usual, found none. Next, she riffled through a copy book marked "A Journal of Observations" in which the reckonings of various officers were listed for comparison with the Captain's findings. She took pleasure in the fact that as a rule her calculations more closely agreed with her brother's than did those of the other mates.

Once her dark eyes had flickered over the past week's entries she came to the conclusion old Charley Coffin was by far the poorest navigator among the after guard, which probably explained why he'd never commanded a ship—for all he was expert with a lance and often had killed whales with his first dart.

She squirmed in the Captain's chair suddenly aware that the boy-sized canvas pants she was wearing were too small; they bound and chafed her in the crotch. Tonight she'd borrow a sailor's palm and let them out.

Settling back, the Fourth rubbed at a nose still red and peeling from sunburn to take stock of her situation. A wry smile tightened her wide, dark-red mouth. Well, at least one fact had been established—she'd proved competent about her duties. Also, she'd learned to adjust fairly well to undreamt-of personal discomforts and privations, such as going about smelly and unwashed most of the time.

Her ears no longer heeded obscenities which ordinarily accompanied the crew's briefest observation and hardly paid any attention to volleys of searing curses when something really went wrong; recently she'd even begun to notice any piece of unusually picturesque profanity.

According to the Fourth's observation the *Gladiator* at present was nearing dangerous shoals lying off Cape Hatteras so it was reassuring that for some time she'd efficiently been standing watch along with the other Mates.

Having completed her entry Lydia skirted the after companion ladder and, reaching her airless little cabin, dropped onto her sour-smelling bunk and hurriedly unbuttoned her infernally tight canvas undervest; she sighed once wind beating erratically through the little porthole cooled her sore and rash-speckled breasts.

Relaxing, she fell to considering the all-important roles played by the boatsteerers, the only close contact between officers and crew.

Even yet, she couldn't comprehend why such men were termed "boatsteerers" because they only steered a whaleboat *after* they'd darted a harpoon into a whale thus attaching the boat to its quarry. Only then would a steerer scramble aft to exchange places with the boat's "head"—the Captain or mate who'd handled the rudder till then. The Mate then would balance in the bow with left knee hooked over the "clumsy cleat" to steady himself and await an opportunity to drive a razor-sharp lance in up to its hitches.

Abruptly her meditations ended with a shout from above, "All hands on deck! Smartly now!"

The Fourth muttered a brief curse then sat up and hurriedly tightened a length of codline to constrict her undervest until her breasts became flattened to invisibility. Next she crammed short and deplorably oily hair under her cap.

Arriving on deck she hurried to join the other Mates lining up behind the Master standing huge and tight-jawed by the base of the mainmast.

Drawn up in a slovenly rank to one side swayed the *Gladiator*'s oddly assorted and rag-clad boatsteerers, American, Negro, Maori and Indian.

Jedediah Paddock studied the sorry group assembling before the try works and drew a deep breath now that the all-important business of selecting steerers and crews for the bark's boats was about to commence. Longest of all his gaze lingered on the Third. Damned if he could make up his mind concerning the bandy-legged former petty officer. Of course it lay within his power arbitrarily to assign to each Mate a boatsteerer as well as the four hands who would row the beautifully designed but easily upset and dangerously fragile whaleboats.

Barefooted and hatless for the most part—the day being fine—men appeared yawning, spitting and blinking like so many barn owls surprised by daylight. Some, only half-awake, still were fumbling to secure sagging, ragged breeches or trousers.

Sharp black shadows wrought by shrouds, stays and other standing gear rhythmically swung back and forth across the sun-yellowed deck.

"Mister Winslow, line 'em up."

A series of barked orders ranged the crew, with exception of traditional "ship keepers"—the carpenter, cook, cooper, blacksmith and cabin boy—in a single rank along the starboard rail. Boatsteerers and able seamen were sent to larboard.

Captain Paddock, broad-brimmed tarry straw hat shoved so far onto the back of his head that tow-hued hair streamed in the wind, announced sharply, "Tomorrow whaleboat drills will be held to teach you splayfooted hay-shakers and apple-knockers what's expected. Best learn fast else you'll get hurt—even killed."

As Master, Jedediah selected first; heavy, square-toed brogans thumping softly, he moved with deliberation along the frowsy line until he came to the Nauset Indian called John Fast Canoe.

"You! Open your mouth! How many teeth you got left?"

"'Bout half, Cap'n."

"Bend your arm!" He pinched the fellow's slight but wiry biceps. "You ruptured?"

"Rupshur?" The Indian blinked. "Dunno."

To find out, Jed drove stiffened fingers deep into the fellow's lower abdomen; found it iron hard. When the Nauset didn't wince in the least Jed nodded to himself. "Good. No ruptured guts." Then he added an unusual question. "You can swim?"

"Ugh. Real fine."

Narrowly watched by the ship's company, the gigantic Nantucketer moved along the line until he'd selected three more oarsmen. One was a dish-faced Irishman with a wild red beard who gave his name as Tom Haynes, the next was another Indian called Big Buck; finally he settled on narrow-shouldered and scrawny Tony Amaral, an experienced whaleman who'd sailed with him before. Tony wasn't near as puny as he looked and was smart as a bullwhip.

To the officers' silent astonishment he concluded by selecting for his boatsteerer and harpooner not Te Ponapa—to the Maori's obvious and chagrined surprise—nor that whiskery veteran, John Folger, but Hercules, the well-muscled blue-black Negro. Selected men then went over to line up the windward bulwarks.

Next, First Mate Aaron Winslow started his selection by snapping up John Folger for boatsteerer and four other old-timers.

The Second, red-gray-bearded Charley Coffin, his face as sour as if he'd been weaned on a pickle, selected expressionless Tom Blue Fox for his harpooner and a quartet of able seamen.

Without seeming to Jed watched his officers choose as they'd been instructed and was slyly amused to note Te Ponapa's outraged scowl at being passed over.

Making a show of deliberation Mister Hayward rounded out his boat crew by first picking Abraham Fitch—ex-Navy. "You swim? Speak true, now."

Grunted Fitch, "Hell, no! No more'n the rest of us bluejackets. You ought to know that."

Hayward's next choices, nevertheless, all were ex-Navy men. They seemed downright pleased at the prospect of serving under a former petty officer.

Looking on, Lydia couldn't fathom why the choices had taken the direction they had. Why hadn't Jed chosen his blood-brother for harpooner? Why had Mister Hayward selected so many men lacking in whaling experience?

20

Shaking Down

A frigate bird cruising the skies off the coast of South Carolina could have noticed the *Gladiator* bowling along under canvas reduced to topsails, gallants and jibs over a sea gleaming sapphire-blue. Unconcernedly the bark plowed through dense patterns of bright yellow Sargasso weed, riding the long swells in easy grace.

Porpoises, always an omen of good luck, leaped and played alongside and afforded the ship's company fresh meat whenever the cook, Goober Pike, braced in the forechains, proved himself as handy with a harpoon as with a cleaver.

Old hands now were discharging familiar duties with efficiency but greenies remained as clumsy and uncertain as cows venturing out onto a frozen millpond.

While the weather warmed, everyone—the Fourth excepted—cast aside footgear and went naked from the waist up then suffered agonies through sunburn.

The fore-royal's yard having been sent down the denuded mast now swung starkly, ceaselessly nearly a hundred feet above the deck showing a pair of newly affixed wrought-iron hoops which, from below, suggested nothing so much as some giant's spectacle frames. Protected by these, lookouts during a normal two hours' trick were supposed to scan the vast and usually empty ocean for a spouting whale.

Abner learned that, the Captain and the ship keepers aside, all hands were required to serve regular tricks aloft; also that a green man's first ascent to the hoops could be terrifying. What with the ship's often violent pitching and rolling a greenie had to climb ratlines until, amid humorous obscene comments, he succeeded in squeezing, trembling and white-faced, through the "lubber's hole" to gain precarious sanctuary in the foretop.

Tanned dark as her Indian ancestors, "Mister" Paddock took a leather speaking trumpet from its rack to yelled, "Ahoy! Alow from aloft!"

Jedediah Paddock, standing near the wheel, watched his sister, on long and narrow feet, start unconcernedly for the windward foreshrouds. She was wearing slung about her neck that same short telescope Grandpa Elijah had given Pa back in 1783 when, for the first time, he'd been given command of the original *Morning Star*.

"Mister Paddock, a word with you," he called.

She drew near, quite devoid of expression, said stiffly. "Aye, aye, sir?"

"Mister Paddock, you mayn't have noticed but I've nailed a five dollar goldpiece to the mizzen to reward the first man who reports a whale." His brown broad features relaxed. "One more thing. Now that the weather's moderated I'm about to order lowering exercises. Since you are never to command a boat I want you to act as lookout whenever the boats are out for business or drill. Understand?"

"Aye, aye, sir."

Jed looked about, making sure no one could hear him above seas rushing alongside. "Now listen well, Mister Paddock, 'cause this will be a special drill. When I pull off my cap and scratch my head you're to sing out from the hoops, 'Blows! Bl-o-ows!'. When I yell 'what and where away?' you'll answer 'Sperm, ten degrees off weather bow near two miles off'. I'll allow the boats to travel only a short distance before I order the recall signal." He cast the lithe figure in dingy white canvas trousers and duroy jacket a sharp look. "What is the recall?"

"A masthead waif shown from the fore," came the instant reply.

"What's a waif?"

"A six-foot pole topped with a wire hoop covered with black canvas—sir."

"Right. Once they return I'll have 'em hoist in and lower again till they learn the knack. One more thing, while up in the hoops I want you to keep your glass mostly on the larboard stern boat and see how well those Navy men handle a whaleboat."

For an instant Lydia hesitated, then risked impertinence. "Why did you give Mister Hayward Te Ponapa for boatsteerer? Thought you'd select him yourself for sure."

A slow grin spread over Jed's wide, sun-reddened features. "Curiosity killed the cat, Mister Paddock."

Once all hands had been summoned on deck, Jed took off his cap. Immediately the Fourth's thin but carrying hail beat downwards. "Blo-o-ows! Blo-o-ows!"

Jed's tremendous voice immediately rang upwards. "What and where away?"

"Sperm. Ten degrees off weather bow."

Jed snapped over his shoulder. "Keep the helm steady as she goes, Mister Coffin!" Then he leaped into the main shrouds and swarmed up to the maintop just as if the sighting had been real.

"Lookout there! What d'you spy?"

"Ah-h, blo-o-ows! There she white-waters!"

Now astride the mainyard the Captain shouted down, "Time?"

Goober Pike, eyes round and white amid sable features, yelled, "Half-after ten, sar!"

Abner Doane, trembling with excitement, in an effort to stay out of the way climbed onto the after deck house and crouched among the spare boats in time to hear the Master's suddenly calm command: "Lower starboard and larboard bow boats! Lower larboard stern boat!" Under normal conditions by this time he would be taking charge of the starboard stern boat, but right now he'd other concerns so Blue Fox would act as both steerer and header—besides, his crew of veterans scarcely required drilling.

Wide-eyed, the cabin boy watched those sturdy cranes upon which the boats rested while suspended from davits, jerked from beneath them. The boats were lowered with only two men in each—the other four would slide down davit falls: no point in risking puncturing the bottom's white cedar planking which, only a quarter of an inch thick, wasn't sufficiently strong to support in mid-air the whole of the boat's crew in addition to the heavy equipment it carried including a pair of very heavy line tubs.

This being the first time the bark's boats had been lowered, a disgraceful amount of confusion prevailed as ordinary seamen and bewildered greenies struggled to learn just what was expected of them.

Having only one greenie aboard, Mister Winslow's boat got under way first. Despite some scrambling about, Mister Hayward and Te Ponapa with the ex-Navy men got into position and pulled away next. Jedediah Paddock's expression grew thoughtful on noting how expertly the veterans took up the stroke, pulling powerfully in unison on seventeen-foot ashwood oars which were springier and far better balanced than the short and clumsy Navy oars they'd been accustomed to.

Through her glass Lydia watched Te Ponapa's brown, blue-tattooed features take on a wide white smile and his shoulder muscles bulge as he put his back into swinging the bow oar. He'd pull this till the moment came for him to drop it and leave it trailing alongside before scrambling up to the bow where he'd snatch a harpoon from a rack and stand ready to dart the quarry.

Fascinated, Lydia watched the Third manipulate the rudder used to steer until, on nearing a whale, he would deftly unship it and, for quicker maneuvering, exchange the rudder for a steering oar which could be as long as twenty-three feet. Adjusting her body to the mast's sway she could even make out the crews' bare toes hooked over foot braces. Spray kept flying in brief bursts over the bow drenching Te Ponapa's broad and naked back.

The Third she guessed must be calling the stroke. His squat body jerked back and forth to the rhythm of the oars' power but of course she couldn't hear what he was yelling—which was probably just as well.

Beyond a doubt this boat's crew working smoothly, was well in hand.

Once the boats had been pulled or rather had struggled a mile or so to windward Jedediah Paddock ordered the recall signal made. Twice more the drill was completed from start to finish before the boats were hoisted in and secured by gripes—strong lashings—on their cranes.

Growled a scrawny, rat-faced landsman holding out raw and bleeding hands, "Look like the dog's breakfast don't they?"

"Hell!" growled gray bearded John Folger. "You think you've had it bad? Wait 'till you've towed a carcass miles through heavy seas."

21

A Whiff of Mutiny

A nor'easter struck so hard that the *Gladiator*'s canvas soon became reduced to double-reefed topsails and a storm jib, nevertheless she plunged like a wild horse saddled for the first time. At mess in the main cabin it was something of a feat to eat anything, let alone gulp or swill a cup of coffee. Mister Winslow and Lydia, gone a bit pale under her olive complexion, made excuses and on being dismissed lurched off to their quarters. Mister Hayward however lingered bracing feet against the chart chest and nursing a mug of lukewarm coffee between his hands.

Jed dropped his cup into a rack then cocked a quizzical blond eyebrow. "Well, Mister Hayward, what's on yer mind?"

"Reckon 'twill be some minutes afore Mister Coffin comes off watch," the Third observed. "Mind if I bolt the door?"

Something in Mister Hayward's tone caused Jedediah Paddock narrowly to consider that officer's battered features. He nodded then, when the Third had resumed his seat, growled, "Suppose you speak up, Mister Hayward?"

The Third batted his eyes. "It's about my boat crew."

"Spit it out, Mister, I don't admire mysteries."

"Sir, I've just come across something chancy."

"Meaning what?"

"As you ordered, sir, I picked for my boat the four ex-Navy men who came aboard along with Tom Archer. Well—" the Mate's small, bloodshot eyes flickered sidewise, then words tumbled out of his mouth like puppies from a kennel. "—Well, sir, last night Archer, after fencing about considerable, sounded me out as to whether I'd join 'em in seizing this vessel. Dunno how they found out, but they swore there's a treasure in silver on board."

"You didn't know that before?"

Steadily, it seemed, the Third returned the Master's penetrating stare. "No, sir. Until that moment I'd no idea—swear to God I didn't."

Big body yielding to the bark's frantic motion, Jed frowned. "Proceed, Mister Hayward. Give me a full and exact account. God help you if you don't."

"They aim to seize this treasure—which they think you keep hidden somewhere down there." His heel tapped the cabin's deck.

Jed remained frozen into stark rigidity, wide mouth compressed into a bleak and colorless line and hearing nothing of seas that endlessly thundered alongside, or the strident whining of steering tackles.

By the uncertain light of a lantern swinging just above their heads Jed held the other's gaze in unrelenting scrutiny.

"You're sure *you knew nothing about the silver?*" Jed's look flicked like a whip.

The fellow burst out almost in desperation it seemed. "Never a word, sir. And that's God's own truth!"

"These bastards are really determined?"

"Aye, aye, sir." Hayward insisted. "They're dead set on seizing the treasure." The tip of his tongue appeared, wetted sun-cracked lips. "Archer told me they've still got arms hidden sufficient for their purpose."

Tattooed brown hands clenching, Jed slammed back in his chair so hard it creaked. "Any idea when they'll make an attempt?"

Hayward's pale brown eyes wavered, then came to rest on the Master's. "Archer didn't say, sir. But *I* figure they'll have to make their move no later than tomorrow or the next day."

"Why so?"

The Third took his time, obviously weighing his reply. "On account of by today's deduced reckoning, sir, we're close to the coast of Georgia; 'twould prove no problem for mutineers to sail this vessel straight to the Sea Islands on which there are plenty of lonely coves and inlets. Archer's gang could plunder the ship at sea then make for the Islands in small boats."

Tautness manifested itself at the base of Jedediah Paddock's throat, a sensation peculiar with him during moments of extreme tension. "What do these fellows propose to do about the ship?"

"If Archer spoke true, sir, it's his intent to kill no one unless he has to because he don't aim to keep the vessel—all he's after is the treasure."

"Oh? Only *that?*" Jed's grin was savage. "Pray continue, Mister Hayward. You enjoy my complete attention." He crossed mental fingers before adding, "and confidence. How does friend Archer plan to go about this business?"

"When the time comes he means to surprise and overpower you and the rest of us officers. Once the ship's been taken you'll be forced to sail her wherever they want."

The whale oil lamp swayed easily back and forth on bright brass gimbals, its clear yellow-white flame creating ever-changing shadow patterns about white-painted bulkheads.

Jed shook his big head as if to rid it of thoughts buzzing about it like bothersome gnats. Mutiny, incipient and overt, he'd encountered and had dealt with before—bloodily and mercilessly if necessary. But this situation, God knew, presented unprecedented problems and implications. For instance: could the Third Mate be implicated but ready to settle for a cash reward for his information? He studied Mister Hayward's scarred features but found no answer. What bothered him most was whether to credit the Third's heated denial of previous knowledge concerning the presence of silver. Would a man, carrying a dishonorable discharge be likely to throw away a share of the loot for nothing? Still, for whatever reason Hayward *had* come forward voluntarily. Besides he made sense about the probable timing of the mutiny.

For all he'd reached a decision Jed pretended to deliberate a moment, then said over a sudden crescendo of storm noises, "Mister Hayward, for giving me warning you'll be well rewarded, and I mean *well* rewarded when dust settles on this business. Meantime, keep your mouth shut tighter'n a bull's ass in fly time. Understand?"

"Aye, aye, sir." Hayward lingered in the doorway. " 'Tis fine to feel trusted once again."

Jedediah Paddock lay on Pa's tilting sea bed fencing with a host of uncertainties until a solution came with the abrupt brilliance of a signal rocket bursting on a moonless night. From his desk he removed a pistol—just in case he'd been mistaken about Edward Hayward— and on silent bare feet made his way the short distance forward to the steerage. On easing open its door an assortment of snores greeted

him. He blinked through the ill-smelling gloom till he made out Te
Ponapa's bushy black head. To wake the Maori without arousing the
other boatsteerers posed a problem which he solved by lightly tickling
Te Ponapa's nose until he muttered and stirred.

Instantly he bent low, whispered. "Quick! Seek your brother's
cabin."

Moments later the Maori silently entered, eyes enormous and
bright as an owl's in the lamp light but his sweaty, tattooed features
were alert, questioning.

Jed motioned him to a chair. "Greetings, my Brother. There is
need to talk."

"What do you want of me?" The Maori asked softly, eagerly.
"Kill someone?"

"Perhaps, so listen well." In brief, explicit sentences he outlined
his plan.

"Ah-h." Te Ponapa made a hideous face, popped his eyes then
ran out his tongue. "There will be killing?"

Jed emitted a curiously wicked chuckle then bent forward and
said in an undertone, "Yes, O my Brother. Now here is what I want
you to do but you must accomplish the deed so cleverly no one will
suspect that what will happen wasn't an accident."

The *Gladiator* gave a particularly violent heave under the
impact of one of those occasional waves which run double the
size of the average; the sea thundered and hissed along the deck above.

By the time Jed had concluded his instructions, Te Ponapa's
eyes shone. He grinned, slowly flexing powerful brown hands again
and again, much as a contented cat kneads some soft substance.

"You understand what is to be done—and how?"

"It is clear like the pools on Otahiti. Tomorrow will be a very
happy day—for the Te Pehi's heir."

Solemnly they rubbed noses then Jed clapped the Maori on the
shoulder. "Let's hope this blow don't increase; 'twouldn't suit my
plans in the least."

After consuming a breakfast of lobscouse—hardtack and bacon
grease boiled with molasses—and coffee thick and strong enough to
float a harpoon's head, Captain Paddock appeared on deck to note
that the wind still was blowing full on the *Gladiator*'s starboard
quarter and seemed neither to have increased nor abated.

A considerable sea was running. An endless succession of short, sharp rollers were breaking into boiling whitecaps from which the wind snatched puffs of spray. All the same Jed's experienced eye told him that these seas were not really dangerous—he'd worked in worse many a time—but they still looked sufficiently ominous to scare an inexperienced hand half out of his wits.

Jed ordered the Fourth, who had the watch, to call all hands on deck then calmly informed them that a practice lowering was about to begin, adding that they'd better learn their jobs in something other than a flat calm or a Sunday sailor's breeze.

While shaggy, slovenly dressed ordinary seamen began nervously to eye one another he explained the simulated situation in short, brisk sentences: a pod of whales had been sighted but were reported to be swimming in widely separated positions. The First and Second Mates' boats were to pull smartly to leeward for the distance of a mile; while Mr. Hayward's boat would row about as far to windward. He would take his own craft in pursuit of an imaginary whale seen blowing astern.

Considerable muttering followed this announcement, especially when he told the Fourth Mate to "keep ship" with the cabin boy, cook, cooper, gunner and blacksmith in addition to a greenie who'd fallen and dislocated a shoulder. Sailing under reduced canvas like this shouldn't prove difficult to keep the bark in position.

The Second, old Charley Coffin made no comment. His gaunt features, framed in reddish whiskers, remained expressionless except for compressed lips but Aaron Winslow plucked at a stringy goatee. "Reckon you know what you're about, Cap'n, but ain't this a fairly stiff sea for men who ain't rightly broke in?"

Jedediah Paddock's voice sounded harsh as the rasping of a blade pressed too hard against a grindstone. "I ain't invited your opinion, Mister. Just follow orders and be smart about it." He turned to include the other boat headers. "Remember this: under no conditions is anyone to pull more than a mile away from this vessel." He started to turn away but checked himself. "There's one thing more. Before you turn back I want you to pretend that your boatsteerer has darted successfully and his harpoon is fast. As usual, the header will scramble forward as if to lance." Coldly, he ran small, hard gray eyes over the swaying rank of motley figures.

"The hands need to learn how to balance and manage oars in stiff weather."

Once the Fourth had brought the *Gladiator* as near to the wind as possible without the risk of being taken aback old hands began to kick off footgear—swimming shod never had been a good idea.

Jed bawled through his speaking trumpet. "Lower away! Smartly now!"

Gripped by sudden sharp and unaccountable apprehensions Lydia watched her brother, followed by his crew, lurch over to the starboard quarter boat which already had been cleared of its gripes—lashings securing the boats onto their cranes. The boat-steerers and mates then gripped davit falls, swung aboard and fended their boat free of the side while being lowered. Once the trim and graceful but comparatively fragile craft was waterborne the four oarsmen slid down the falls and tumbled about on the bottom before they got out oars.

What with the bark's violent plunging and wallowing Lydia deemed it a small miracle that all four boats were lowered without mishap.

Filled with wild exultation, Jed ignored his rudder to grab the boat's twenty-foot steering oar then clamped his left hand over a special grip rising at right angles to the oar's shaft. His shouts of "Pull-ho! Pull-ho!" started blades swinging in unison. Chortling, he set his weight to steer clear of the threat presented by the *Gladiator*'s side.

A tingling sensation began in Jedediah's hands then raced up under his shoulder blades. By God, wasn't it *fine* to feel the wind buffeting his hair again and the salty sting of cold spray against his face?

Glancing over his shoulder Jed watched the *Gladiator*, now under double-reefed topsails and a single jib, commence beating slowly to windward. It was a relief to note the other boats already plunging on divergent courses over gray, white-crested seas. With satisfaction he noted how Mister Hayward's craft, pulled by the ex-Navy oarsmen, was making good headway to windward. Intent, he watched Te Ponapa quit rowing to take the harpooner's post in the bow with faded shirt whipping wildly about his massive outline.

His own crew, all old hands, also made good progress. Because sodden shirts were sticking to them his two dark-featured Indians looked skinny, inadequate for this work. But they weren't. They were driving their blades cleanly in and out of water rising and falling capriciously, made ash shafts bend to their pulling.

The next time he looked he realized that the *Gladiator* was loafing along just about a mile distant. Mister Winslow's boat crew also had settled down and were making satisfactory progress through increasingly choppy seas.

By contrast, the Second's craft was struggling painfully along —like a crippled water bug. Its sixteen- and seventeen-foot oars often were threshing empty air or kicking up wind-twisted jets of spray.

Now the critical moment was at hand. He and Hercules must exchange places in the yawing, wildly plunging boat once the Negro had simulated making his iron fast in a non-existent whale. Mechanically, Jed checked his Indians and the other two oarsmen occupying thwarts in alternate positions next to the side: Number Two on the left, Number Three to the right and so on.

"Look alive! Once the boatsteerer yells 'fast!' you'll backwater *hard* and hold her steady whilst I go for'ard. Remember to *keep balance* when you're ordered to peak oars! Pull 'em in easy, cross 'em together then shove your handle hard into the cleat socket on the opposite side so's to form a trough to guide our line from the tubs out over the bow." He got to his feet, drenched and wild-looking. "Get ready to squeeze aside when Hercules and me pass each other. Ready Hercules? Now dart your goddam harpoon!"

The slender craft rolled heavily and water poured over her gunwales but not enough to necessitate bailing. The exchange of positions was unusually hard to effect because no whale was pulling the boat thus steadying her to a certain extent.

Hercules reached the stern and, grinning, seized the steering oar while the Captain poised a lance—six feet of finely-tempered steel affixed to a stout wooden shaft.

"Back! Back! Back!" Jedediah roared. "Quick, you ham-handed bastards!" They obeyed so readily he yelled, "Well done! Easy all."

From her position in the mainshrouds the Fourth was keeping her glass on Mister Hayward's boat, watched the Third begin to move forward just as Te Ponapa's hulking figure turned started scrambling aft. Her breath stopped with a click; the Maori suddenly lurched and began flailing the air in a frantic effort to regained balance, but the crest of a huge white-headed roller struck his boat full on its beam. It over-turned in a twinkle, spilled men and gear into the foaming water. In an instant only the white-painted bottom remained visible, along with small, dark specks made by the heads of men briefly threshing about. One of the men continued frantically to beat the water whereupon Te Ponapa's black head started in his direction.

"Into the wind!" Lydia screamed at the carpenter. "Boat over! Boat over! Stand by to tack!"

The *Gladiator*'s Master yelled at Hercules. "Third's boat's bottom up. Make for her! Put your backs to it, you lily-hand bridesmaids. Hard, else we'll be too late.

The other whaleboats also were turning, pulling for the capsized craft and a speckle of flotsam about it. Meanwhile the *Gladiator* was brought about; her canvas snapped uselessly for eternal seconds then filled and she started slowly for the scene.

Halfway to where Hayward's boat wallowed with waves breaking over her glistening white bottom Jed's chilled and streaming features relaxed. He smiled thinly; only two heads remained visible and he knew whose they would be.

Mister Winslow's boat arrived first to haul Te Ponapa and the Third, spluttering and cursing, out of the ocean. Hayward lay on the floor boards shuddering and gasping like a fresh-landed fish but Te Ponapa sat up and, to conceal a huge grin, turned his tattooed face to windward.

When Mister Coffin's boat came up it set about retrieving gear, oars, tubs and the like—even a hat or two. Meanwhile the Captain's boat took the overturned craft in tow and started towards the bark which, pitching heavily, had drawn near and was waiting under backed topsails.

Towards sundown it was still blowing hard when the *Gladiator* was brought into the wind. All hands watched the Stars and Stripes rise to the mizzen gaff's peak before being lowered halfway. Captain Paddock, looking mighty grave, appeared dressed in his best Sunday go-to-meeting clothes—clean, white-ruffled shirt and all.

Once he'd scanned the silent assembly he removed a tall beaver hat and, with the wind whipping tow-colored hair about his face, read off the names of the drowned men. After that he took a Bible from under his arm and read the Burial Service.

Mister Hayward and the gunner listened, looked mighty thoughtful.

22
The Mexican Gulf

For three days the *Gladiator* reached southward heading for the Florida-Bahamas Channel at a speed fulfilling her Master's fondest expectations; with Vera Cruz as his first port of call he'd suspended lowering exercises in favor of drilling gun crews.

Now that the only remaining ex-man-o'-warsmen were himself, the Third and the Gunner, they had patiently to work instructing the men in an unfamiliar and complicated drill, they were taught how to load, aim and otherwise serve the *Gladiator*'s eight graceless, short-barreled carronades.

Promptly it was discovered that the gun platforms constructed in New Bedford were barely wide enough to permit the use of training tackles without risk of gunners falling into the hold. Nevertheless, the promise of a modest increase in their lays kept the men eager to learn from the handsome gunner whose depth of knowledge and experience proved impressive. That well-spoken individual went so quietly and intelligently about his instruction that Jed remained more than ever mystified concerning Archer's background.

If Archer was grieving over the loss of former shipmates he kept such emotion well concealed.

By the time the *Gladiator* was plowing across the 25° latitude south into weather growing daily more torrid the amateur gunners had become reasonably proficient in the use of training tackles and in handling sponges, ladles, rammers and primers.

When at last the guns were shotted and a faulty cask had been dropped overside for a target the results bordered on the hilarious. When pieces were touched off even the dullest of the crew became aroused by the sharp, deafening reports and snuffed excitedly at billows of rank-smelling, gray-white smoke rolling back over the bulwarks.

Archer shook his head. "When you bastards first hear a whole broadside fired I warrant you'll wet yer pants!"

On the first exercise with live ammunition not a single eight-pound ball raised a water spout anywhere near its mark but that didn't seem to matter: this supplied a fine break in a whaler's dull routine. None was happier than Abner Doane, transmogrified into a powder monkey. It wasn't that the cabin boy hadn't been content—life at sea having proved all he'd anticipated he took pleasure not only in carrying out duties which he discharged smartly—but also in this wonderful new world about him.

Once the Gulf Stream was reached and the sea turned a sparkling dark-blue flecked by vast fields of gold-brown Sargasso weed all manner of unfamiliar and often handsome sea birds circled, dipped and screamed about the mastheads when they weren't diving for prey.

Even now he couldn't suppress a thrill whenever a blue-and-silver flying fish burst out of a swell to go skittering over wave crests until it vanished with the suddenness of a magician's trick. And then there were porpoises, giant sea turtles to be spied basking on the surface, and whole squadrons of Portuguese men-of-war, their bladder sails glowing electric-blue. It didn't seem right that such gorgeous creatures were reported to be dangerously poisonous to the touch.

If Mates Winslow and Coffin and other old hands wondered why the bark was sailing a course different from the one usually followed to hunting grounds off the coast of Brazil they kept their curiosity strictly to themselves.

The *Gladiator* was off the Dry Tortugas when a sail was reported—the first in almost a fortnight. From the mizzen's cross-trees Jed briefly studied the stranger, then returned to the deck. "Mister Coffin, I allow that with so much try-smoke stainin' her courses she'll be a spouter homeward bound. Hope she is. Need news from the Pacific and maybe hear what's going on in Mexico."

Bluff-bowed as a Belgian peasant, the stranger proved to be a real old-timer. Actually her keel had been laid in Pembroke, Massachusetts, during the War for Independence!

Once only a half-mile separated the two vessels they backed topsails and drifted along together in order to "gam"—exchange news.

On boarding the evil-smelling *Maria* Jedediah learned she'd enjoyed a moderately successful voyage in that her skipper had stowed down some seventeen hundred barrels of sperm. Her captain, a nearly toothless old codger, proved dour and uncommunicative. No wonder, after nearly four years at sea, he was interested only in reaching home. He did, however, admit having spoken to Obediah's *Morning Star* off Mocha Island but said the meeting had been brief because of a sudden storm.

"Where was Obed headed?"

" 'Llowed 'twas for the offshore fishery along the coasts of Chile and Peru."

"Heard anything 'bout what the Mexicans might be doin' to each other nowadays?"

The old man picked up the mug of too-well-watered rum brought on deck by his cabin boy. "Nuthin' first-hand. But I spoke a Britisher only two-three days back who'd just sailed from there."

"Where? Mexico's a big place." Jed appeared only moderately interested.

"Port was called something like 'Vera Cruz', but then, ain't much good rememberin' furrin names."

"What did he say?"

The *Maria*'s Master frowned, scratched at a dirty gray-brown scalp. "Why so all-fired concerned?"

"I'm headed there. 'Tend to some business."

"Then that's a pity, Cap'n. You'll likely run into a parcel of grief down yonder."

"Why d'you say that?"

"Well, 'tis midsummer there so it's the sickly season; likely the yellow-jack and other plagues will be raging."

"Anything else? Did this Englisher speak of fighting?"

The old man wiped his mouth on the back of a brown-mottled hand criss-crossed with swollen blue veins, stared enviously at the *Gladiator*'s sharp design.

"Now you speak of it, that Lime Juicer *did* say there was a war goin' on."

"Who's doing what and to whom?"

"Don't rightly know, but if I remember right a Gen'ral name of Santa Anna's tryin' to take the port away from the Government; the Britisher said it don't amount to much. Here, Cap'n, fill yer cup then I got to get goin'—you know how 'tis, I'm near out of drinkin' water and I've scurvy aboard."

Long after he'd been rowed back to his ship Jedediah Paddock remained in his cabin. So there was trouble in Vera Cruz? Well, maybe the fighting would be over by the time he got there; the old codger's news couldn't have been really fresh. No use worrying till he could see for himself—he'd learned that a long time ago.

Once in the Gulf of Mexico the bark's guns were exercised over many hot and exhausting hours. Finally the crew formed a committee to respectfully remind the Skipper they'd not signed articles aboard a privateer.

Since they could expect to benefit only from their lays— plus a small bonus for learning to serve cannon and the promise of a share in prize money if any—they figured the more time devoted to whale hunting the better.

Exception to this point was taken by Tom Archer, the boat-steerers, Heetee and the American Indians. Also Bert Harrington and Shamus O'Leary—the two Irishmen on board—preferred fighting men to whales.

Chiefly because Mister Hayward and the gunner felt that the crew by now had learned about as much as they were going to, Jedediah, aware that Vera Cruz lay less than four days' sail ahead and that sperm whales seldom if ever frequented the Gulf of Mexico, gave in after a perfunctory show of reluctance.

After checking solar observations against the consensus Mister Paddock concluded that inside two days time the mountain peaks of Mexico ought to lift above the horizon. Anticipation flooded her. Think of it! In a short while she was about to lay eyes on a land whose inhabitants spoke an incomprehensible language. Not many people aboard had even a smattering of Spanish. True, Mister Winslow knew a little, and Jedediah could get along after a fashion, but the only man in the least fluent was Archer whose knowledge was likely to prove invaluable.

Question: could this fellow, handsome save for his broken nose, be trusted now that the bones of his fellow ex-Navy men lay on the sea bottom somewhere off the coast of Georgia? Single-handed, would he dare to go on scheming? Lydia, after a deal of hard thinking, decided that maybe it would be wise to try to settle this point.

By cautiously cultivating Archer's friendship she succeeded in drawing him out while the *Gladiator* sped deeper into the bright-blue Gulf of Mexico. Among other things she deduced that Thomas Archer was the scapegrace eldest son of a prominent family living in Providence, Rhode Island.

One evening while Lydia and the gunner lingered to watch the wake trace dazzling green-and-white displays in phosphorus across the starlit sea Archer admitted having hurriedly left home on a horse fortunately faster than those carrying the sheriff's posse.

He stared out over the sea. "Mister Paddock, although I've given my sire every reason to be vexed he offered me a good round sum if I promised never to return to Providence." He shrugged, said wryly, "Because other gentry—creditors and the like, as well as the police, 'desired the pleasure of my company' I enlisted in the Navy. During near five years I saw a lot of the world, 'specially South America and some Spanish islands in the Caribbean."

"Do you understand Spanish people?" She tried to read his expression.

He turned and looked her full in the face. "No, and I'll hazard damned few Anglo-Saxons can. No more than I can comprehend why you chose to come aboard this ship. Would you like to satisfy my curiosity somewhat?"

Lydia started to speak but turned aside doing up her jacket buttons against the wind. "Possibly I might—some other time. I must go below now and write up the log. Please excuse me."

Grimacing, the gunner bowed. "Of course. *Buenos noches, Señorita.* Perhaps before we reach Vera Cruz you might like to acquire a small knowledge of Spanish?"

"Thank you, Archer—possibly I'll avail myself of your offer. Good night."

"Good night, Mister Paddock, or should I say '*hasta la vista*'?"

23

Fatal Mischance

Once the gunner's tall figure lost itself among the shadows Lydia made a tour of the deck and halted in a deserted area opposite the main hatch. She rested elbows on the rail and, listening to the *slap-slap* of halyards against the mainmast, considered the Gulf of Mexico's starlit expanse. *What* about Archer? Jed, of course, obviously, for some reason unknown, didn't trust the gunner yet needed his knowledge as a drill master.

A soft whistle came from the direction of the try-works. Lydia made out an indistinct figure crouched behind a great grindstone fixed to the larboard rail. She looked leisurely about, decided that the bow lookout really was peering as he should and that seamen stretched out among gear near the foremast seemed to be sound asleep.

She walked casually forward until the unknown called in a harsh whisper, "Permission to speak to Mister Paddock?"

She called softly. "Come here, you. What do you want?"

She recognized the apparition as one of Mister Coffin's boat crew, an A.B. named Harrington; a short and muscular Irishman with a flat face, button nose and enormous ears that stuck out like jug handles.

After glancing carefully about in all directions he shuffled up silently on bare feet, hair whipping about his eyes. "Please, mum—sor—I mean, kin I have a word with yez in the lee of the round house—best we not be seen together."

"You. What's this about?"

"A matter o' the first moment, sor."

"In that case, Harrington, you'd best seek out the Captain." Lydia employed the staccato level tones she'd adopted when giving orders.

"Lord love ye, sor, I wouldn't dare. Please harken." Nervously the Irishman kept craning his head about.

Surprisingly, her stomach tightened when Harrington passed so close that his curly and untrimmed beard brushed her cheek. Inside her jacket's pocket she slipped on a pair of brass knuckles, a precaution she'd never had occasion to employ thus far.

Small, round eyes set in cavernous sockets probed through the dim light anxiously. "Was I to tel yez somethin' which could save the Cap'n his ship, would—well, would yez fatten me lay?"

"By how much?"

"I'd like it doubled."

"How much is your lay?"

"One in two hundred, ma'am," said he in lilting accents. "Will yez double it? I swear on me mither's honor—it's worth it."

She drew herself up to her full five-foot-seven. "That remains to be decided. Speak up, but if I deem your information unimportant this interview will never have taken place. Understood?"

Under a sudden shift of wind yards high above creaked across their parrels.

"Ye'll double my lay if ye're satisfied?"

"You've my word on it. Now speak up and stick to facts!"

"That I will!" He narrowed little eyes. "I marked yez were talking to Tom Archer just now. Please, sor, did he say anythin' out o' the way—hintin' at somethin'?"

Lydia felt her breath quicken. "Nothing of the sort. Why do you ask?"

Again Harrington looked quickly about then drew a deep breath like a man preparing to plunge into icy water. "Last night, while we wuz standin' watch, Archer takes me aside and, very pleasant-like, asks if I'd like to make a packet of coin—not paper, but silver money.

"Sez I, 'sure, Tom, who in his right wits would be sayin' "no" to that?'" As they leaned over the rail Harrington moved so close that she could feel the heat of his breath and a knee pressed against her. "Next, I asks what he's got in mind. But before he makes answer he swears me to secrecy—and a terrible oath 'twas, too," Harrington added uncomfortably, "—likely I'll be made to pay some day for havin' foresworn meself like this.

"Sez Tom, savage-like, 'this ship's carryin' a rich treasure in silver is stowed 'neath the main cabin's decking'."

A shiver colder than an icy brook travelled down Lydia's spine, lost itself between flat, hard buttocks. In soft voice she prompted, "What is the gunner's intention?"

"He's still got arms hidden away so once t'ship stands close by the coast, he plans to take the officers unexpected-like and murder them. After the uprisin' he'll take over and head for the West Indies where he'll divide the loot and sell this vessel. Then the mutineers can scatter easy, he says, and live high on the hog the rest of their lives."

The Fourth stared unseeing out over slowly heaving seas. "What else was said?"

"Archer said he's got three hands ready to join him."

"He say who?"

Vigorously, Harrington shook his head, but then added in that almost musical voice of his, "No, 'sor', but he vowed to tell me the minute I joined up."

Lydia fell back a pace along the bulwarks to study the other's expression, then murmured. "Why speak to me? Surely, your share of the loot—if there were any—would amount to a deal more than a doubled lay?"

"Aye, that it would." The big Irishman laughed softly.

"Then why?"

"Missis Harrington's lad has led a rough life since he ran away for a sailor and he's done some things he'd sooner forget—and wishes the police would, too. But, so help me Mary! I'm drawing the line at mutiny. I've witnessed too many mutineers swing and dance the floorless hornpipe."

Heart fairly pounding, Lydia demanded a trifle breathlessly, "How many others are aware of this—this plot?"

"No tellin' for sure, sor. Whatever he is, Tom ain't nobody's fool; yez can bet he's not the lad to speak to anyone he weren't near-sure of aforehand."

For some moments they remained silent studying each other by the brilliant starlight. For all his big ears Lydia came to realize that in a rough and reckless sort of way the Irishman wasn't altogether bad looking—in fact he was attractive in an animalistic sort of way.

The ship's bell jangled to summon the new watch. Harrington said, "Please answer me quick. Do I get me lay doubled?"

"Yes, and—," her voice hardened abruptly, "a lot more besides if a fatal mischance were to befall the gunner before sun-up." She looked away, pushing a stray sable lock back under her cap. "By the way, I've just now noticed that while you're just about the same size as the gunner, you look ever so much more powerful."

A soft "Ah-h!" escaped Harrington. So that was the way the wind was blowing? Faith! What a rare, cold vixen. And her looking so calm there like she weren't doing more than sendin' me out to fetch a basket of eggs!

"Well?" Her voice sounded crisp, incisive.

"Now, sor," he grinned hugely, "'tis queer, but I've been minded of an ould saying which goes: 'Here today, gone tomorrow'."

The big Irishman chuckled, then blended with the shadows and disappeared.

24
Cannonade in the Hills

Bent to clear deck brushing his head Captain Jedediah Paddock was inspecting the *Gladiator*'s guns with unusual attention when the Third appeared.

Saluting man-o'-war style, Mister Hayward reported, "Sir, when my watch reported on deck, a man was missing." Curiously, he peered through the half-light in the hold.

"Which one, Mister?"

"Tom Archer, sir." Hayward looked for a reaction but detected none whatsoever.

"Where's he got to?" Jed forgot, straightened quickly, so cracked his head, hard. He swore feelingly.

"Dunno. We've looked everywheres but there ain't a trace of him."

To Hayward the Captain appeared genuinely surprised. "You sure?" Mingled emotions commenced to revolve in his mind like a gathering hurricane. Archer? Why Archer?

"Aye, sir, we've hunted high and low, but either Archer ain't on board or else he's hid himself so well nobody can discover his hiding place."

Puzzled that events so should have spared his taking the necessity of a cold-blooded decision he inquired casually, "You've *no* idea what could have happened to him?"

The Third shook his life-battered head. "No, sir. That I haven't. He was last seen sleeping for'ard of the try-house 'round about three bells."

"You're certain he's not to be found?" Jed spoke slowly, as if he were considering implications.

"We could look again, sir, and make certain-sure."

After a further search proved futile it became inescapable that Thomas Archer had disappeared without a trace except perhaps for a small smear of blood noticed on the larboard rail opposite the try-house. Of course, as the Fourth quickly pointed out, the smear might well have been caused by a chicken butchered the night before.

Jedediah Paddock nodded, then, without visible emotion, ordered the National Ensign lowered to half-mast. Next he ordered the gunner's sea chest and other belongings brought to the main cabin.

"Come along, Mister Winslow." Leading the way below he consulted a roster. "Seems likely when we put in to Vera Cruz you'll have to recruit replacements—'tain't advisable to continue the cruise so short-handed."

The older man tugged sparse, tobacco-stained chin whiskers. "Don't expect that'll be over-easy. This time o' year Vera Cruz is hotter'n blazes and pestilential; full o' yellow-jack and the black vomit; 'tis a real cesspool." Mournfully, the First gouged at a hairy ear. "Been there a few times so I know what I'm talking about. Hope you ain't figgerin' on tarrying long."

"I'm not." Jed's manner changed. He treated the First to a penetrating regard. "I've important business there. Any notion of what it might be?"

Winslow blinked. "I'm not supposed to, am I?"

"No, you're not."

"Then I don't know anything," came the bland reply. "And I won't go guessing, either."

On the day after Tom Archer's disappearance a feeble wind died out altogether, left sails slatting idly. The Gulf grew glassy-calm but the bark rolled heavily on an endless succession of oily swells. It grew so furnace-hot that after a while Mister Hayward, for the first time stripped to the waist, defiantly exposed a criss-cross pattern of puckered and dull-red scars drawn long years ago by a cat-o'-nine-tails.

All the same, the crew were stimulated by sighting other vessels for the first time in weeks; the topmasts of no less than four now were visible on the horizon but all lay much too far off for identification.

Towards evening when tar stopped bubbling from deck seams, an assortment of land birds, many brightly colored, appeared to perch, panting, in the rigging or to collapse exhausted on the deck.

Without fear of contradiction Abner Doane, long an aspiring naturalist, identified most as flycatchers and warblers and what appeared to be an unfamiliar species of rail.

The hairy and sun-reddened crew with inexplicable compassion, gathered up these wanderers and tried to get them to drink and offered crumbled ship's biscuits.

Lydia found a pretty little purple-and-green heron crouched half-conscious between the spare boats stowed on the round house; she set about nursing it, smoothed its gorgeous plumage.

Towards nightfall a blessed cool breeze sprang out of the east and drove the *Gladiator* so strongly along her course that, just as the sun was beginning to show above a welter of scarlet and bronze clouds, the masthead lookout bawled, "Land ho!" But an hour passed before people on deck were able to glimpse a dim and pallid triangle created by the snow-clad peak of Mount Orizaba thrusting boldly into a blazing, blue-white sky.

Other mountains lifted, one after another, out of the Gulf's heat-shimmering water. Next a long, gray-brown streak of coastline took shape, punctuated here and there by groups of bare and usually rounded hills.

Once the bark had been rendered shipshape and her canvas trimmed smartly, the Captain, a gleam in his eye, ordered gunport lids triced up and carronades run out far enough to convince everyone that this whaler wasn't relying on dummy gunports for defense.

Following an intensive study of old but presumably accurate Royal Navy charts Jedediah concluded that the approaches to Vera Cruz appeared to be pleasantly uncomplicated. This was just as well, because next morning when the whaler stood in and fired a gun, no pilot boat put out from this bleak and forbidding port. The domes and towers of some sixteen churches and similar structures could be seen rising above high, yellow-gray battlemented walls stretching over half-a-mile to connect a pair of powerful-looking forts.

Here and there tall columns of bluish smoke could be seen spiralling up in barren-looking country behind Vera Cruz.

While the *Gladiator* under reduced canvas continued cautiously to run inshore an intermittent rumbling, grumbling noise became audible. This appeared to emanate from among a cluster of low, treeless and sandy-red hills rising close beyond the port.

Mister Coffin peered up into the brazen-blue sky, grunted, "Queer. Sounds like summer thunder, but I'm jiggered if I spy so much as a single storm cloud."

Drawled Mister Hayward, keeping an eye on men furling the gallants, "Now, Charley, don't fret yourself. What we hear is cannon—a lot of 'em. Must be a right smart battle going on somewhere yonder."

Jedediah long since had identified that rumbling. Damnation! Apparently some military force must be attempting to close in on the port. How would this fighting affect his business? Probably considerably. When combat appeared imminent merchants and bankers, here as elsewhere, would secrete assets and declare themselves poverty-poor to the triumphant side.

Late in the afternoon the *Gladiator*, Stars and Stripes flying, sent her anchor hissing much farther out from shore than Jedediah Paddock had intended. As it was his bark now lay under the guns of *H.M.S. Dolphin*, brig, and *H.M.S. Hecate*, a trim, black-and-white frigate.

Acidly, Jed turned to his First. "Mister Winslow, damned if I figured I'd *ever* feel pleased about British protection, but right now I do."

"Wa-al, seeing as you've said it I'll admit the nearness of them Limeys *is* kind of comfortin'. Think we'll ever have us a Navy fit to protect our trade wherever it goes?"

"Maybe sometime," Jed said watching a long string of dirty-looking brown pelicans flap by low over the water. "'Tain't likely in our lifetime—not while so many mealy-mouthed politicians in Washington keep on lining their pockets.

"Say, what d'you make of that man-o'-war yonder?" His gaze had come to rest on a sizeable green-and-yellow-painted bark anchored considerably closer inshore than the Britishers.

The name "*Veraganza de Guerrero*" appeared floridly painted across her stern board. Her unkempt appearance and the slackness of her rigging suggested that, most likely, she must be a local man-o'-war. He became convinced of this when, through a spyglass, he made out an ensign, composed of horizontal blue, yellow and red stripes.

Since no one aboard ever before had spied such a banner it stood to reason this, probably, was that of the Dictator, Governor of *Jefe Político* presently holding Vera Cruz.

Anchored farther inshore rocked a scattering of small slovenly appearing coasters drying patched dark-brown sails. Even closer to a low-lying and gently curving waterfront lay a cluster of goletas, feluccas, xebecs and other small craft of unmistakably Mediterranean design. A few untidy little sloops and bumboats slowly were paralleling the shoreline.

Jed was tempted to order a gun fired in salute of the port but since no pilot or customs craft had appeared it would appear the port authorities either had fled or were hopelessly disorganized. Better keep quiet. No use drawing attention to the *Gladiator*'s arrival.

Although cannonading and the rattle of smallarms fire continued to wax and wane nobody aboard nearby craft appeared to pay attention.

Since H.M.S. brig *Dolphin*, the nearer Britisher, was swinging to her anchor less than two hundred yards away with a Blue Ensign curling lazily above her rigging, Jed ordered a boat lowered. Might be a sound idea to swallow his pride and appeal to the Royal Navy for information. Possibly her officers could clarify the situation on shore.

Unfortunately, the *Dolphin*'s Officer of the Deck proved to be a choleric, sheep-faced old lieutenant who stared coldly down from the gangway when Captain Paddock hailed requesting permission to board.

"Permission denied!" rasped the Englishman through a gleaming brass speaking trumpet. "Captain Danforth is ashore. Left orders no one's to be allowed on board. Come back tomorrow, my good man; possibly he'll see you—more likely he won't."

Jed felt ingrained animosity flooding back. As his whaleboat was being backed off he rasped, "See you and him in hell first! Reckon 'twill take another war to teach you Lime Juicers ordinary courtesy."

By the time the starboard quarterboat had been hoisted in, sounds of conflict had begun to fade in the distance and a faint offshore breeze began to blow bringing unfamiliar and, to Lydia and Abner Doane, exciting odors.

Even at sunset the *Gladiator*'s presence had prompted no

official reaction. Nor did signal masts on either of the grim, pale-ochre colored stone forts at each end of the waterfront betray recognition of the Yankee whaler's presence but a flotilla of produce-laden bumboats and canoes came sailing or rowing out from shore together with flights of pelicans and black cormorants with long, snake-like necks.

Before the boats drew near Jed ordered the gangway guarded with blubber spades. Pandemonium broke out when the motley squadron of log canoes, skiffs, pirogues and ordinary bumboats arrived alongside. Hungry-looking dark-faced men implored the *Americanos* to buy everything from vegetables and fruit to brightly-hued fish and wicker-trussed live armadillos, pigs and iguanas.

The Captain's orders stood: nobody was to be allowed on board until the situation ashore was estimated; if the yellow-jack or black vomit were epidemic he didn't want it brought on board. But his orders were only sullenly obeyed. All hands were hankering for a taste of fruits and vegetables: they'd dined on salt meat and ship's biscuit long enough.

Once the land wind had died out and darkness had descended on the port the squeak of fiddles and a tinkling of mandolins aboard the *Veraganza de Guerrero* floated over the harbor's placid water.

Late into the night the *Gladiator*'s Master pondered, read and re-read not only his instructions from the Boston bankers but also credentials to the firm of Gonzalez, Herrera y Cia.

Bitterly, he wished he'd done more business with Latin Americans. If only he'd more than a tavern-and-bordello knowledge of Spanish. It was hell dangerous to be lacking even the least information concerning the situation in this port.

In the face of his ignorance how in blazes should he go about opening negotiations with Gonzalez, Herrera y Cia? What sort of people would they turn out to be? Polite probably, devious certainly. Caution, caution.

Supreme question: was any senior officer of the firm still in Vera Cruz and if so, how did he stand politically?

Early next morning a gig put out from the H.M.S. frigate *Hecate*, 28 guns, rowed straight for the handsome, clean-lined whaler.

In its stern sat a gaunt, red-faced lieutenant with a thin beak of a nose jutting out from a cluster of brown side whiskers. Off the

Gladiator's port quarter he got to his feet, raised a weatherbeaten fore-and-aft cocked hat and requested permission to board.

Once on deck he saluted a non-existent quarterdeck and looked astonished when Jedediah Paddock, clad in loose duroy pantaloons and a checkered shirt because of the heat returned this unexpected condescension. The visitor looked about drawled, " 'Pon word! I've never seen so cleanly a whaler."

He was here, explained Lieutenant Channing, at the command of the Honorable Douglas Bryce, Captain commanding *H.M.S. Hecate*. He reported his Captain to be deeply distressed over discourtesy accorded by the *Dolphin*'s duty officer. Was there anything Captain Bryce could do to make amends? The visitor's voice sounded flat, dispassionate.

"Yes, sir. I need to learn what's taking place yonder." He nodded towards the town, displaced a beading of sweat which at once sketched on the deck a number of star-shaped splotches.

The Englishman mopped his brow with a crumpled handkerchief plucked from his cuff. "Sir, I will be pleased to share with you what little information we possess."

"In which case, sir, I suggest we seek refreshment below." He sent Abner running for the Fourth; an accurate and retentive memory might prove useful.

When Lydia's wiry figure first appeared the visitor failed to recognize her sex but once he did he jerked a bow, declared himself vastly honored.

He took a flat, wooden case from under his arm. "Captain Danforth's compliments, sir, a few prime Habana seegars. He begs you to accept 'em as evidence of sincere regrets over *Dolphin*'s discourtesy."

Once smoke had begun to drift about the stifling great cabin the men seated themselves. "I'd appreciate hearing 'bout what's going on here."

Lieutenant Channing pursed meaty lips to blow a smoke ring. "Why, Captain, the situation is what might be called 'normal' in this miserable, so-called Republic. Seems the fellow presently in control of this vicinity is one Antonio Lopez de Santa Anna. He's reputed to be able but cruel, and quite devoid of conscience. Saw him yesterday; darkish, rather handsome fellow. They say he's vain as a peacock about uniforms and the smartness of his bodyguard."

"You say he's able?" Jed inquired over his tumbler.

"So they say. —Knows just the right moment to turn his tunic. Personally, Santa Anna is reputed to be brave, for all he's shy a leg. Our consul here reports he has revolted against the Federal Government of President Bustamente who, by the way, is a former companion-in-arms of Santa Anna's."

"Who commands the Federals?"

"Chap name of Alvarez. It was he who assaulted the city yesterday." The Englishman undid the remaining brass buttons of his waistcoat.

"What happened?"

"Santa Anna won. At the moment Alvarez is supposed to be retreating." Apparently intrigued, the Englishman fluffed tawny side whiskers and smiled at Lydia through a stratum of cigar smoke.

"What's likely to happen next?"

"Oh, the usual, I daresay. Within a day or so peasants will bring in food, merchants will come out of hiding—along with minor officials and a salutary number of prisoners will be executed.

Lieutenant Channing flicked ashes from his cigar. "Next will come a parcel of fulsome proclamations followed by the confiscation of property of all who are supposed to have backed the Federals. The local *tavernas* and whorehouses—um, beg yer pardon, ma'am, —will be very busy."

"How recently have you been ashore?" Jed inquired of this angular figure in the faded but neatly pressed blue-and-white uniform.

"Yesterday. Captain Bryce and I went ashore tryin' to locate someone in authority. Pointless, quite pointless. We didn't tarry. This being the hot season, the place is riddled with malaria and yellow fever. Dear God! The incredible smells and stenches of that place!" The speaker pinched his ample nose.

Lydia, sitting bolt upright on Micajah Paddock's sea bed ventured to speak. "Sir, have most merchants disappeared?"

"We think not, ma'am. In this case because General Alvarez attacked almost without warning; such gentry had little opportunity to decamp. Most refugees of that sort sought safety aboard that floating pigpen of a warship showing Santa Anna's flag. Damme if I recall her name; in any case 'tis near unpronounceable."

"The *Veraganza de Guerrero?*" Lydia suggested, oblique eyes intent and shining.

"Aye, ma'am, 'tis something like that," Channing nodded. "Well, a handful of English, French and Spanish merchants came aboard us yesterday to claim sanctuary. Come nightfall they ought to be gone, provided the news of Alvarez' retreat is true."

The Englishman drew a long puff, chuckled. "They're a hardy lot, ma'am, and used to such unheavals ever since the Spanish Crown got driven out near twenty years ago. How they manage to do business these days is beyond me. Suspect they do a deal of smugglin'."

"Shouldn't wonder. Have a splash?" Jed offered a decanter.

"Why not? Dull business this, patrollin' a pestilential coast."

"Which side's likely to win out?"

"Don't know and care less. We don't meddle in political affairs. Just protect the stockholders' interests back home."

Jed said, "Mister Paddock, suppose you go find us some fans. 'Tis hotter than hell with the drafts on down here."

Once Lydia had departed Channing raised heavy sand-colored brows. "Begging your pardon, Captain, must say it comes as a bit of a shocker to encounter a female Mate."

"Why not? She's part owner—and my sister."

"Sister, eh? Well, well. Shan't forget her in a hurry."

Chuckling, the *Gladiator*'s Master heaved his enormous bulk to its feet and extracted a fresh bottle from a locked rack in the cupboard behind him. "Few people do, who know Lydia at all well."

Channing accepted a second libation, asked softly, "I say, am I wrong or *are* you a former naval officer?"

"Was. A good while back. Only a midshipman, though. Why d'you ask?"

With a hooked forefinger the visitor eased the sweaty white stock swaddling his neck, "Notice you mount real guns. Uncommon practice on a whaling ship."

For a long moment Jed hesitated then, reasoning that by offering a confidence he would risk nothing while possibly achieving a status with the Royal Navy. "I'm carrying—er, quite valuable cargo consigned to a firm of ship brokers—Messers 'Gonzalez and Herrera'. The name mean anything?"

Lieutenant Channing accepted a palm leaf fan from Lydia and commenced slowly to ventilate streaming, lobster-hued features. "Believe they're important here. Thank you kindly, ma'am."

"They reliable?"

Channing shrugged. "Can't say. Heard nothing either way."

Thoughtfully, Jed ran his tongue's tip along his upper lip. "Would you deem it safe to go ashore later today?"

The Englishman deliberated. "Venture you'd be safe enough with an armed boat party, but I doubt you'll accomplish anythin' in a business way so soon after the fighting." He finished the last of his drink and sat up. "Tell you what, Captain. Early tomorrow we're sendin' a landing party in for supplies and to try to determine which way the political cats are jumping. No reason I can see why you shouldn't join us. We know our way about the town and you don't."

Once he had treated this unexpectedly cordial naval officer to a formal salute at the gangway, the *Gladiator*'s Master decided it was much too hot to return below so sought the mizzentop as he often did to do uninterrupted hard thinking: so many uncertainties were crouched like wild animals getting ready to pounce. Sighing, Jedediah opened his shirt to let an offshore, sour-smelling breeze do what it could towards cooling him off.

Looking downwards, he took pleasure in the relative neatness of the deck and found reassurance too. Those of the crew not on anchor watch or lookout duty were engaged in homely occupations. Some were scrubbing clothes or were doing scrimshaw work; still others were splicing rigging or teaching puzzled landsmen how to tie a variety of intricate knots. One, a grizzled fellow, was leaning back against the bulwarks and, with needles flashing, placidly was knitting himself a pair of socks.

Smoke rose from the galley's stumpy stack, brought with it the odor of frying fish.

On the surface, at least, everything appeared peaceful. Ever since land had been sighted the crew had grumbled normally but had been otherwise quiet and orderly. Possibly the gunner's unexplained disappearance, in addition to the loss of Mister Hayward's boat crew, might be an explanation.

Who the Devil was responsible for Tom Archer's vanishing?

Since the event, he'd reasoned out that, at the time of Archer's loss, only one person not involved in an incipient mutiny should have known of the treasure's existence; logically, it could only be his reticent and self-assured Fourth Mate. If so, where had she found sufficient callousness to contrive a man's death? Possibly it was that Indian streak in her. Come to think about it, Lydia's Indian characteristics recently *had* become more pronounced!

Well, if Lydia didn't wish to speak, let her keep still.

Jed shifted on the narrow mizzentop, considered the sprawling waterfront. One encouraging fact remained; he'd brought the Boston bankers' money to the doorstoop of its destination.

Um. Even if the projected exchange did come off smoothly a treasure, this time in Mexican silver, would remain aboard when the bark left for China.

A disquieting possibility occurred. Suppose Lydia hadn't been responsible for the gunner's demise? Had it been someone, approached by Archer, who'd elected to murder the gunner and seize the treasure on his own?

Returning to the deck he questioned the Fourth, admired the way she looked him bang in the eye. "Yes. I got rid of him. Needed to find out if I could shape and follow a hard course on my own."

25

Gonzalez, Herrera y Cia

Shortly before sunrise on August 15, 1831, Captain Jedediah Paddock had his Fourth Mate and himself rowed by Te Ponapa, John Folger and three other dependable and well-armed seaman to Vera Cruz's water gate where *H.M.S. Hecate*'s shore party already had tied up. A mixed party of cutlass carrying, blue-and-white-clad sailors and Marines in white crossbelts and scarlet jackets were falling in beneath walls from behind which sounded the discordant braying of donkeys and the crowing of a multitude of fighting cocks.

On landing, Jed with considerable interest noted a number of broad iron bars stamped, of all things, with the British Government's broad-arrow insignia let into the quay's uneven stone surface. Most likely, these had served as ballast on some vessel's outward voyage and then had been abandoned. Where could a man travel and not be confronted by evidence of Britain's power?

Halfway down a long and nearly deserted pier which alone jutted out from shore at this point, Lieutenant Channing's gangling figure appeared in company with a short, pudding-faced compatriot wearing sweat-marked white linen suit and a low-crowned, broad-brimmed Panama hat. Over one shoulder the civilian was balancing a faded green parasol. Curtly, Mr. Channing introduced him as Paul Mercer—a merchant resident in the port. For a modest fee he was prepared to act as advisor, guide and interpreter.

Although in a rapture of excitement over unfamiliar surroundings and realization of so many ambitions Lydia hoped she was doing Jedediah credit. She'd turned herself out in a brass-buttoned blue serge coat, visored cap and spotless white duck trousers which already had become so unbearably hot that perspiration had begun to pour down her legs and between well-flattened breasts. Titillating was the pressure of a little duelling pistol beneath a broad leather waist belt.

Lord above! Wasn't this almost too much? In a few moments she was about to enter a foreign city and under perilous conditions.

A brief conference ensued with Mr. Mercer—a plump, red-faced little man whose flabby jowls hung like those of a bloodhound. As a result of the consultation the *Gladiator*'s officers ascertained that Gonzalez, Herrera y Cia was a well-established concern doing business chiefly with England. Recently, however, they had begun to traffic with French, Dutch and American merchants.

This firm's head office, Mr. Mercer averred, was situated in the Calle de la Caleta. Although it seemed unlikely business could be transacted so soon after hostilities, it might do no harm to present credentials to Don Roberto Gonzalez. A start might be made provided the bulk of the troops commanded by General Santa Anna and Colonel Barbabossa, Commandant of the city's garrison, were for some reason kept outside the walls.

Without further ado the landing party formed up and a massive, spike-studded gate of sun-bleached wood was swung open by a detail of dark-faced and scrawny little *soldados* clad in ragged remnants of red-and-yellow uniforms. The British moved off behind the *Hecate*'s lieutenant at an easy gait.

Although the sun had only just begun to illumine narrow, silent and frequently grass-grown cobbled streets, a few Indians trotted into view either bent under towering packs or leading sad-eyed burros laden with baskets of produce.

Tramping along in the wake of Lieutenant Channing's party, Mr. Mercer informed his employer that Vera Cruz was completely surrounded by high walls of massive stonework pierced by four gates which remained open only during specified hours.

Soon the Fourth realized that the great majority of private dwellings were two storeys high and built of smooth-dressed Aeolian sandstone. Most had elaborately carved wooden balconies running across the upper floor. Rows of bronze-black buzzards perched on dropping-whitened, red tile roofs, craned scabrous necks indifferently viewing the humans below.

Soon, swarms of incredibly ragged beggars materialized apparently from nowhere. They whined like hungry curs, eagerly exposed hideous running ulcers.

Good-naturedly at first Mr. Channing's Marines fended off the mendicants but soon were forced to use brass-heeled musket butts. Shrill curses and howls of pain beat through fetid-smelling air. The paupers then ceased importuning the British to devote attention to the smaller party behind them. Te Ponapa, Folger and the rest of the *Gladiator*'s party grabbed sticks from a bundle of firewood carried by a passing donkey and scattered the assailants. Mr. Mercer, using his furled parasol, layed manfully about him.

Entering the spacious Plaza Mayor, Lydia noted small groups of blue-and-yellow-jacketed cavalry squatted on their heels cooking breakfast over smoldering faggots. Others, stripped to the waist were washing at a fountain or unconcernedly were relieving themselves wherever the need seized them.

A single rank of dry and drooping palms lining this great square were the only trees to be seen and about the towers of a rather garish and badly-kept cathedral dozens of rusty-black buzzards planed lazily, ominously across a sky turning a glaring blue-bronze. The sun began to strike the earth like a succession of invisible fists.

Lieutenant Channing pushed back through his escort. "Town seems quiet, Captain Paddock, I'll bid you good morrow. Good luck to you."

"Many thanks." Making a considerable effort, Jedediah offered his hand. "Much obliged, sir—first time I've ever said that to, well—your side."

"We're not all that bad, y'know," came the dry reply. "Some day you people might even help us. Who knows?"

"Yes, Mr. Channing, you never can tell."

Paul Mercer, carrying his furled parasol like a shouldered musket, led the way under a series of low arcades, cool despite the now-shattering heat when another swarm of wild-looking beggars materialized, fawning at first but then threatening.

Lydia delayed using her stick until a one-eyed scarecrow grabbed her waist and attempted to kiss her hand. Convulsively, she lashed out and when her club thwacked home she felt unaccountably thrilled as he lurched aside and scuttled off, whimpering. So this was the sensation of applying physical power over another human?

Te Ponapa lowering his own cudgel laughed. "Mister Paddock, I am sore assailed. Please protect me!"

Like an ill-bred urchin she laughed breathlessly and stuck out her tongue. "You're big enough to look after yourself."

At street-level all windows were shuttered and blank, secured behind stout grille work of rusty wrought-iron.

Entering a street marked "Calle de la Caleta" Mr. Mercer halted before Number 6, a building little different from its neighbors. To the left of an arched carriage entrance loomed a gate secured by stout iron grille in addition to a heavy wooden door behind it. To its left was a smaller entrance bearing a highly polished brass plate inscribed in flowing script: "Gonzales, Herrera y Cia."

The interpreter mopped florid jowls, glanced at the upper storey. "Well, gentlemen, we are here. Our problem, now, is to gain admission."

Subconsciously, Jed tested his jacket's breast for the credentials: they were there all right, but sodden with sweat; pray God the ink hadn't run.

Reaching for the doorbell's brass handle Mr. Mercer hesitated. "Captain, I've a notion we might be received more readily if so many men weren't seen waiting outside. There's a *posada* down the street. Suppose you instruct your escort to wait there till summoned?"

Somewhere inside the house sounded the tinkle of a spring bell. Nothing happened even when Mercer rang for a second and third time. The Englishman shrugged apologetically. "Please be patient. People are apt to be wary so soon after er—an unpleasantness."

At last a barred spy hole's iron slide clicked aside and a single dark eye appeared. "*Quién?*" The interpreter broke into a crackling flood of Spanish but before he had finished the spy hole's cover had been replaced.

Jed tried not to show how hot and short-tempered he was becoming. "What does this mean?"

Mercer opened his green parasol against the blasting sun and shrugged. "Dashed if I can say."

"What did you tell him?"

"Only that you're a sea captain just in from Boston who has business with the firm and wishes to present credentials."

"I hail from Nantucket not Boston," snapped Jed.

Mr. Mercer laughed. "No difference. Down here everybody thinks all Americans are Yankees from Boston."

Surveyed by a quartet of wholly naked, owl-eyed and big-bellied brown urchins, Lydia, Jedediah and the interpreter lingered in the shade of the carriage entrance until a bolt *clucked* and the smaller door was eased open by a withered mestizo wearing a clean white linen jacket, pantaloons of the same material and a wide wine-colored sash.

"*Buenos dias*," he spluttered through many missing teeth. "Señor Mercer, Don Roberto is pleased to receive your Honor and *el Capitán Americano*."

The porter, disconcerted by the presence of this young woman in male attire, held up a protesting hand. "No! No! Don Roberto directed that only Señor Mercer and the Capitán will be received."

Following his shoulder the *Gladiator*'s Master pushed inside. "Mercer, tell him that this is my sister and supercargo on my vessel. As such, she is needed to deal with the business in hand."

The old servant rolled yellowish eyes then slap-slapped away on rawhide *huaracas* into the dim, cool depths of the house leaving the callers to stand in a long hallway tiled in blue-and-white and shaded by faded hangings of yellow damask. Dingy portraits of arrogant-appearing Dons in quaint, old-fashioned costumes and half-armor stared down as if in disapprobation.

For all of half an hour the Anglo-Saxons sat in steadily mounting uneasiness on richly carved but most uncomfortable benches lining this musty-smelling vestibule.

At length Jed hardened his jaw and turned on the Englishman who, having produced a folding Chinese fan, placidly was cooling himself. "Say, Mr. Mercer, just what's the idea of this delay? Who in hell do these people think they are?"

"You must learn to understand Mexican ways, sir. For Don Roberto to receive you immediately would, in his own estimation and that of his countrymen, cause him to appear unimportant."

Ever practical, Lydia resigned herself to waiting but would have given almost anything to be out of that Nessus' shirt of a canvas vest. She tried to forget her discomfort by watching graceful little emerald-green lizards skitter about the walls in pursuit of flies and other insects. At long last a portly Indian servant wearing a long green baize apron and a silver chain supporting crossed keys waddled in. He offered a profound bow, indicated a wide and ornately carved mahogany staircase carpeted in dark red. The butler paused then opened the door to a long, high-ceilinged room. Being shuttered against the heat it was gloomy except for a tall window through which the sun, shin-

ing through slatted jalousies, created a vivid pattern of brilliant yel-
low-and-black bars across a floor tiled in Moorish designs.

Seated behind an enormous carved desk was a slight but immediately memorable figure clad in black. Don Roberto Gonzalez's long,
silvery hair was neatly dressed as was his brief goatee. His nose, thin
and pink, suggested a beak jutting from a long, sad-looking face the
color of old parchment. His intense and deep-set eyes looked black
as five feet up a chimney, Jed decided, and their whites weren't
white at all—but yellow as lemon peel.

Don Roberto clapped stringy, bronze-hued hands and ordered
the wooden-faced Indian to push forward a tall-backed wicker armchair for the señorita's convenience. Next, he cast a casual nod in Mr.
Mercer's direction.

When the huge New Englander was presented the Mexican offered a blue-veined fistful of bones and assorted rings and declared
himself overjoyed. As they were gripping hands a side door opened
to admit a strikingly handsome young man of about thirty. He wore
a loose, long-skirted coat of light-gray, chocolate-hued pantaloons
and a brocade waistcoat of canary-yellow. While his movements were
graceful and leisurely they weren't lanquid—not at all. He was, it was
quickly explained, not only Don Roberto's nephew but also a junior
partner in the firm.

In a quick aside, Mr. Mercer warned, "Don't try to get down to
business in a hurry, Captain. Around here it's considered impolite."

Jed nodded absently; he was more interested in arriving at an
estimate of this tall, well-set-up auburn-haired individual whose finely
formed features barely missed being moulded in the tiresome regu-
larity of classic handsomeness.

Lydia decided quickly that here was not where the firm's routine business was transacted; rather was a place where important deci-
sions were discussed and long term policies arrived at. Recalling the
musty counting house of Paddock & Sons, she felt awed by all these
rich tapestries certainly imported from the Mother Country.

The white marble bust of some Roman patrician stared blankly
at her from a fluted pedestal standing behind Don Roberto's desk.
Abruptly she became painfully conscious of her dusty, square-toed
brogans marring deep oriental rugs of great beauty.

Only after several glasses of chilled Malaga had been sipped and
a plateful of *chirimoyas*—small, cloyingly sweet chocolate cakes—

had been consumed did the old man signal the servant to offer a canister of long, black and very slim cigars. Once these were well alight Don Roberto settled back in his high-backed, tapestried armchair and murmured to his nephew.

Don Jaime arose and, crossing the room, held out his hand and invited in almost unaccented English, "Please. The letter of credence from our banking friends of Boston."

While her brother was fishing out a pair of sweat-marked brown envelopes Lydia sensed, rather than noticed, a penetrating curiosity on Don Jaime's part concerning her presence. A moment later when she chanced to glance straight at him, a flush mounted to her high cheek bones; beyond a doubt Don Jaime mentally was undressing her!

Once Don Roberto had donned a pair of enormous spectacles rimmed in tortoise shell in preparation of studying the documents from Messrs. Doane, Welch & Peabody, Jedediah Paddock turned to the nephew and inquired, deviously for him, into the political situation—especially about its probable effect on the success of his mission.

The young Mexican, stroking dull red sideburns running low on his cheeks, treated him to a flashing smile; it appeared genuinely reassuring.

"As undoubltedly you are aware, Captain," Don Jaime began courteously but with a watchful glint in fine, dark-blue eyes, "Anastasio Bustamente at present is President of our Federal Government. He is reasonably honest and well-intended, but, I fear, not sufficiently firm or ruthless to deal with the ambitious rascals who surround and oppose him." Airily, he waved a be-ringed hand exposing a froth of lace in his cuff. "In Vera Cruz General Lopez de Santa Anna governs in President Bustamente's name."

"What sort of fellow is this Santa Anna?" Jed queried so bluntly that Mr. Mercer winced.

Don Jaime obviously rehearsed his reply. "General Santa Anna enjoys the reputation of being an excellent politician and a most capable if unpredictable soldier who is quite merciless to his enemies."

A lean, pale-gray greyhound appeared, claws clicking on the tessellated floor tiles, looked about, then went to rest his head on Don Roberto's black silk clad knee.

"Enough, my friend, of General Santa Anna; the important figure for you to deal with is Colonel Hector Barbabossa, Commander of the city's garrison." The young Mexican continued. "He is no better nor any worse than most officials. Colonel Barbabossa, if it pleases him, can, without trial or legal right, confiscate property, plunder businesses and order men imprisoned, shot or tortured."

Lydia Paddock, sitting erect and darkly unobtrusive in her big rattan chair, made mental note of the name; experienced a fresh sense of exhilaration. Imagine becoming involved in so potentially perilous affairs!

Out in the street a donkey commenced to bray as Don Roberto put down and smoothed the letters before him. Like a fluid mask a meaningless smile slipped over sere and bony features. "Your credentials appear to be in order, *Señor Capitán*, but, before we proceed further in this—er, most delicate transaction—if indeed it is at all possible—I must consider your credentials and the proposed negotiations at leisure. Perhaps in a few days—?"

"But, sir," protested the New Englander, "there is no time to waste. Every day I delay increases the risk and expense."

Don Jaime raised a placating hand. "One appreciates this. Please, Captain, I will talk with my uncle and possibly speed matters up." He seemed to be pleading for understanding beyond the huge American's immediate perception. "Is it not apparent that business of so complicated and dangerous a nature should be approached with much caution? I am sure Mr. Mercer appreciates this." Don Jaime spoke without removing his gaze from Lydia whose slim and sinewy figure appeared to fascinate him as if she had originated on another planet.

"I would be greatly honored, Captain, if you would dine at my home tonight. I seldom sit down before ten but please come at eight in order that we can discuss affairs and possibly make plans. Then," he flashed a quick, white smile, "perhaps we will turn our attention to pleasanter matters."

26

Bull Dance

Jedediah Paddock was long in forgetting his dinner with Don Jaime Muñoz; which proved a quietly elegant affair. Just the two of them sat at the table. The butler and a soft-treading blank-faced mestizo footman, spotless in white uniforms and cotton gloves of the same color, served a plethora of dishes he never before had experienced in an amazing array of silver, crystal and lace tableware. Massive candelabras of pure silver supported dozens of exquisitely sculptured spermaceti candles.

He and his muscular, red-haired host garbed in turquoise and yellow, occupied a ponderous refectory table decorated by a linen cloth of intricate lace work. Clumps of poinsettias—named after Mr. Poinsett, a recent American Minister to Mexico—flamed in a bowl of Venetian glass while an impressive rank of wine glasses stood in gleaming order before each setting.

Twirling a tiny glass of aged French brandy between supple thumb and forefinger Don Jaime finally and, with apparent reluctance, approached the real matter in hand. "One hears that your so-beautiful ship mounts real cannon. Is this true?"

Jed sighed, put down his glass. "That's so."

"But, surely, is it not most unusual for a ship pursuing the whale to be armed?"

Some of Jed's sense of well-being departed—albeit unwillingly—as he forced himself to try to read beneath the surface of the other's words. "Reckon so. Howsumever, I've reasons."

"The shipment of silver, perhaps?"

"No, I'd decided to mount guns long before the bankers approached me."

"Ah, I see." By candlelight the Mexican's sideburns gave off faint, reddish-gold tints when he selected a long, black cigar from a humidor offered by his butler.

"Doubt if you do, so I'll tell you. By carrying real guns my ship can enter a lot of dangerous places and ports where ordinary whalers daren't venture. Nor do I need to fear attacks from picaroons, pirates, savages and the like, who will veer off at the first sight of a cannon ball."

Once the meal came to an end the Mexican led into a room where Don Jaime sought a chest of drawers strapped in iron. After unlocking a pair of padlocks he lifted out a drawer lined in green baize and containing stacks of coins secured in position by beautifully tooled and fitted wooden frames.

Don Roberto's nephew then quickly described the relative fineness and market value of coins used in Mexico; these included piasters, doubloons and pieces-of-eight which recently had been termed "dollars."

Don Jaime held up a gold coin, heavy but bearing a crudely executed profile. "Here is one ordered struck by the late Emperor Iturbide." He grinned like a friendly fox.

"Never heard of the gent," Jed admitted drawing deeply on his fragrant *puro*.

"It is no wonder for his empire endured barely three years. Foolishly, we thought to have had more than enough of kings, queens and emperors."

" 'Foolishly'?"

He shrugged, lifted his hands. "We have learned that dictators and self-appointed governors can be far worse."

Deftly, Don Jaime made a selection of coins of varying sizes, placed beside them a second row of similar denominations. He beckoned. "Now, *amigo*, for your own good, note carefully. These examples in the upper row are of full weight, but these below them have been debased through sweating or clipping. Others also are of less value because they have become worn through much use. Therefore, great care must be exercised to determine the true value of each piece."

Finally, agreement was reached: a new United States dollar would be exchanged for two-and-a-half sound Mexican dollars, the discount being due to the latter's lesser content of pure silver.

The host's expressive dark-blue eyes became veiled. "Such a rate of exchange satisfactory?"

"I expect so."

Learning rapidly, Jed pretended to hesitate, for all Doane, Welch & Peabody would have been satisfied with an exchange rate of one-for-two. After counting to ten slowly, Jed nodded, picked up his cigar and drew on it leisurely. "Don't want trouble with the Customs. What's to be done about 'em?"

Jaime declared with perfunctory detachment, "That, Captain, is my responsibility so please do not disquiet yourself. Colonel Barbabossa is a friend and so also his Chief of Customs." He settled back, blew a smoke ring and stared at painted beams above him. "My uncle has made them several small goodnesses. Nevertheless, I must be discreet."

The American thrust long, white-duck-covered legs out before him. "What's to be done?"

"For many weeks the troops of General Santa Anna have not been paid. This for him is not comfortable since we merchants in Vera Cruz have lent him all that we can or will. I imagine, also our *Liberatador* finds it difficult to keep his favorite mistresses in the usual comfort. In short, for funds he is desperate."

"That's good," Jed said solemnly. "What do I do?"

"Beneath our warehouse on the harbor lies a little slip. You will recognize it by a castle and lion carved on the—on what you say—the main stone of an arch?"

"Keystone."

"*Bueno*. Tomorrow night, then, you will in the greatest secrecy bring the Boston money there. In the morning, by a fish pedlar, I will send instructions to your ship to set the hour and establish recognition signals. Meantime, I will arrange for clearance papers."

The American, small gray-blue eyes intent, sat forward, said flatly, "Please fix things so I can leave by dawn the day after tomorrow. Considering the cargo I'll have taken aboard that will be imperative."

Don Jaime looked a trifle annoyed. "Does not our firm have as great a need for you to get safely away? Everything will be done to make this possible."

"Meant no offense," Jed grinned, offered a conciliatory tattooed paw. "Let's shake."

Immediately their hands had met the red-haired Mexican's manner underwent a change. "Now to seal our friendship!" From a yellow-and-green decanter Don Jaime refilled the brandy glasses, then, grunting in relief, loosened an over-tight stock of Mechelin lace. Meanwhile his gigantic guest was casting adrift brass buttons securing a white linen waistcoat.

Jed grinned. "Here's to luck and love!"

He in the turquoise jacket laughed softly and raised his glass. "But of a certainty. As is said in my country: '*Salud y pesetas y fuerza a sus pelotas!*' You have been long at sea, no?"

"Aye, too long." Esoteric understanding passed between the two. Lazily, Jed laced fingers behind his shock of yellow hair. "I'd admire to—well, explore the town."

Jaime sipped from his glass; a lazy smile shaped his lips. "No need for that, *amigo mio*. Soon we will drop in for polite conversation with a señorita of my acquaintance; with her sister she occupies a small *pied-à-terre* of mine. —And will you do the honor of calling me 'James'?"

The American grinned like a happy dog while refilling his glass. "Now that, friend James, is the brightest notion I've heard of in quite a spell—and, for the benefit of good friends I am called 'Jed'."

By the time Don Jaime bent to unlock the door of a narrow-fronted dwelling in the next street they'd discovered more than a few common interests: hunting, gaming, sailing for pleasure, fishing and, of course, the matter in contemplation.

Warmed by liqueurs and that rare fine dinner, Jed really took to this courteous yet thoroughly manly young fellow; no common Latin stud-buck preoccupied with females, he seemed a lively gentleman of uncommon discernment and apparently possessed of considerable imagination.

The moment they entered a short, faintly illumined hallway cool scented air greeted them like the caress of affectionate fingertips. Eyes glinting, Don Jaime motioned towards a staircase, then led the way upstairs to a fairly spacious salon in which a pair of uncommonly lovely but quite dissimilar young women were smiling demurely. Neither, it would appear, had celebrated her nineteenth birthday.

The walls of this high-ceilinged room were decorated by several embossed and well-polished salvers of brass interspaced by vividly colored shawls of Chinese silk. In one corner stood a huge red clay *olla* sprouting a tall clump of pale-buff pampas grass plumes. A sulphur-crested cockatoo, perched in the background, cocked its head

sidewise, surveyed the intruders with a glassy and knowing jet eye
rimmed in vivid yellow.

Smiling Don Jaime slid arms around the waists of both girls, led
them forward. "Jed, may I present Señorita Raquel, a very dear
friend and playmate."

Possessed of cool ivory beauty, Raquel was fairly slim, with
large, light-blue eyes and masses of elaborately dressed pale blonde
hair to attest that, centuries ago, Visigoth barbarians had conquered
and, for many generations, had lingered in northern Spain. The girl
was dressed in a tight, low-cut jacket of yellow silk and wore a
bouffant ruffled skirt of brilliant emerald green supported by an
unguessable number of flounced and ruffled petticoats. A tall, jewel-
spangled tortoise-shell comb towered above the back of a small and
delicately proportioned head.

In no time the sea captain sensed that this was Don Jaime's current mistress so took care to concentrate attention on Raquel's dark-
haired and slightly taller companion.

Don Jaime swung the brunette forward gracefully, as in a dance
step. "My friend, this is Raquel's 'sister'—Estrellita. This is my
amigo, el Capitán Pad-dock." In as aside he added. "This baggage will
please you, I think, especially as she comprehends sufficient English
to permit an understanding of your pleasure."

Red in the face and with mouth loosening, Jedediah gripped the
girl's hands, but kept her at arms' length long enough to permit a
frank and thorough appraisal.

Black-haired, and more fully figured than her companion the
girl called Estrellita had lively, lazy-looking black eyes and a
squarish mouth freshly tinted a vivid cardinal-red; full breasts strained
visibly beneath a tight, black-bordered bodice covered by glittering
sequins. Flashes of scarlet suggested that, beneath her flaring skirt,
rustled numerous petticoats which, like her silver-buckled and high-
heeled slippers, matched the blazing hue of her lips.

"Now that protocol has been observed—let us forget such
nonsense! *¡Vámonos!*" He dealt the stately blonde such a smack
on her bottom that she squealed and the comb fell out of her hair.
Next he swept Raquel clear of the waxed tile floor and rained kisses
on the girl's pale hair, lips and down to the base of a generous
décolletage. He set her down, flushed, dishevelled and breathless,

then snapped fingers. "Let us celebrate, let us drink pleasure to my new friend!"

"*Sí*, Don Jaime, *bebemos*—let us drink." Still dabbing her disarranged coiffure the blonde, dignity abandoned, whirled over to a marble-topped table covered with bottles and glasses. She caught up a bottle of sauterne but her patron called in boisterous good humor, "Such slop is for old ladies and little boys. *Nombre de Dios!* If you have not sufficient champagne chilled, your bottom will smart!"

"But of course, *mi amor*, I go fetch it." She glided out of sight.

A tiny marmoset with tufted ears startled Jed by suddenly poking its head out of the Chinese jar in which it must have a nest. The diminutive creature stared timidly up at this huge, flushed figure in the unbuttoned blue coat, wrinkled duck trousers, black scarf and already sweaty white shirt.

Estrellita, shiny full lips parted, held out a small, liberally beringed hand saying gravely, "Good morneeng, *Señor Capitán*. How are you? I am ver-ri well!"

"Come here, Buttercup!" Jed swept her off the floor and crushed her against his chest. Giggling, the black-haired wench wound cool, pale-brown arms about his neck then gently rotated her bosom against him while gluing her lips to his.

Once Raquel had filled delicate glasses with champagne laced with cognac, Don Jaime drank deep then sent buttons flying by ripping off his frilled shirt to expose a hirsute and well-muscled brown torso. He raised his glass, finished the wine in a single gulp. Teeth flashing, he turned to Jed. "You find favor with the brunette? If not, I will be honored to bestow Raquel upon you." He laughed a trifle loudly. "But it is for this night only. Every *caballero* about Vera Cruz envies me my lovely *rubia*."

Um. Why was so much being done for him? He'd heard it said that Spaniards could be the most lavish of hosts. But this!

Luxuriously, Jed ran fingers through his mop of tow-colored hair. "Thanks for the offer, Jim, but to me this here Estrellita's triple-distilled catnip. Ever since I went to sea I've always been partial to big tits, dark hair and matching eyes."

"That is good. *Pues, chiquita, ¡un poco de música!*"

Raquel nodded and from a chest produced a guitar tied with yellow-and-green ribbons. She struck up a brisk *jota* that set the cockatoo to elevating its crest and rocking jerkily on its perch.

The Mexican sprawled onto a settee. "You, Estrellita! Dance us a *pasa doble*."

Jerusha! All these liquors were beginning to take a real hold. Feeling finer than velvet, Jed lolled in a wicker armchair, bloodshot gaze fixed on the scarlet and black shod dancer. Fascinated, the huge New Englander watched Estrellita bend, whirl, stamp, gesture imperiously then toss her head making her hair fly like a tattered sable gonfalon. She commenced to spin faster, more furiously, until her whirling skirt and lace-trimmed red petticoats rose to a level with her garters then her stocking tops, up, up until they spun about her waist, and disclosing the full length of slender legs, ivory hued thighs and the fact that she was wearing no undergarments whatsoever.

Although the guitar music ceased abruptly Estrellita kept on spinning—over to Jed's armchair to collapse, panting and palpitating onto his lap.

"You find amusement, friend Jed?" Don Jaime inquired over the rim of a goblet the blonde had refilled. Laughing he raised it to his lips.

"Never better. This beats even the *vahines* of the Marquesas." Jed fumbled through a tangle of generously perfumed black hair until he found the girl's lips and stopped talking.

Presently Don Jaime heaved himself to his feet. "As yet you have beheld nothing. Now we will perform *el baile del toro*—the bull dance, a *pasa* of my own inventioning."

He disappeared and returned almost immediately carrying a torero's black, cocked hat and a pair of bull horns—small but sharp—affixed to a wooden crosspiece with a handle; a device employed to train apprentice fighters in the art of managing capes and *muletas*.

He tossed the hat to Raquel who, blue eyes shining, placed it on her tumbled ash-blonde curls at a deliciously jaunty angle. Meanwhile, Don Jaime kicked off his slippers then backed into a far corner at the same time raising the dummy horns before him. Then, bodice straining, Raquel drew herself to full height like a capeador taunting a bull.

Laughing, he called out. "Play, Estrellita! *¡Por Dios!* How can one dance without music?"

Once her pick began to flicker over the strings striking a rhythmic *zarzuela*, Don Jaime, hair tumbled over forehead, began to prance and paw like a bull preparing to charge. Raquel's hands busied themselves, undid ties holding in place her skirt of flowing emerald taffeta. Swaying in time to the music she shook it, swung it in a wide and graceful arc in the manner of a capeador. Nostrils flaring, Raquel then arose on tiptoe.

Then Don Jaime quit swaying and, snorting realistically, levelled the horns at arms' length and rushed towards his partner so swiftly she barely succeeded in twisting out of the way. Still dancing, she flourished her skirt.

To furious bursts of guitar music the "bull" spun lightly and swayed in some very complicated steps. Don Jaime then lowered the horns and charged once more. Raquel turned "in profile" waving and alternately shaking her "cape" repeatedly calling "Ho! *Toro!*"

The young Mexican charged and this time a horn caught the shimmering green skirt causing a small snarling sound as it ripped the cloth from Raquel's hand.

Shrieking excitedly, the cockatoo ran back and forth across its perch. The marmoset disappeared. Estrellita, in mounting excitement, picked up the tempo to a gale of jangling chords.

During a few obviously improvised steps which kept the dancers circling about each other Raquel undid her topmost petticoat—she must be wearing five at the least—and resumed citing the "bull". Jed gulped huge swallows of champagne, belched and then yelled. "Money's on you, Jimmie! Hook her again!"

This time Raquel, although she danced lightly aside, lost her "cape" on the first pass but swiftly replaced its loss with another petticoat.

"*Olé! Olé!*" screamed Jed's girl. "*¡Viva el toro!*"

By the time Don Jaime, dancing with ever-increasing abandon, had hooked aside the last petticoat his hair-matted chest and shoulders were gleaming with perspiration; his eyes sparkled; his mouth worked revealing pointed, very white teeth.

A swooping rush removed the last of the blonde's nether garments so, dancing all the while, she spun aside at the same moment tearing off the sequined bodice. Naked and lovely as an animated marble nymph she used it in a final attempt to baffle the "bull". Of course she failed and, laughing uproariously, Don Jaime made a token thrust which briefly imprisoned the girl's breasts between dully gleaming black horns.

Breathing in deep, quick gasps Don Jaime bowed, "You never have seen such a bull fight?"

"No, and by Jesus, I don't want to watch any other sort."

Pale-pink-and-white body glistening, Raquel gracefully retrieved a petticoat and with an air of pretty solicitude tenderly wiped her partner's torso free of perspiration.

Enthusiastically, Don Jaime returned the attention—took special care with bust and back. "Perhaps you will do one of those South Sea dances you spoke of?"

"Hell no! That'd be a waste of good energy." The *Gladiator*'s Master nevertheless struggled to his feet. Holding his giggling, half-dressed partner clasped in a muscle-corded embrace he spun furiously around the room until the floor seemed to sway under him.

"You find Estrellita pleasing?"

"Hell, yes!" he gasped. "Liveliest white girl I've ever met out of bed."

Don Jaime broke into laughter so uproarious that the cockatoo uttered a series of deafening screams. "In that case, *amigo*, why do you not explore her abilities in such a place?"

27
Specie

Captain Jedediah Paddock grew increasingly anxious while he and the Fourth were being rowed as silently as possible over glassy water towards a low, black-mouthed ellipse barely visible beneath a stout stone warehouse rising some distance to the left of the municipal pier. Oars dipped and splashed softly in rhythm while the riding lights of ships receded. A quarter-moon having set, only brilliant starlight glinted now and then on a number of cutlass hilts and carbine barrels.

Um. The fact that this matter of currency exchange had progressed thus far without a hitch was at once reassuring and disquieting. Yet, rack his imagination as he would, he still hadn't discovered grounds for apprehension.

Once the flat arch bearing a lion and castle on its keystone became recognizable, Jed at the tiller, called in an undertone. "Easy all. Manage those oars!"

By starlight he glimpsed his Fourth, a blunderbuss held across her lap, crouching in the bow among kegs of "bar lead". The four boatsteerers stopped pulling then shipped oars in almost complete silence. Bending low, they then tested locks of pistols shoved into their belts.

Once buildings on the shoreline were looming in irregular silhouette not fifty yards away, the boat's crew fixed their attention on the dim outlines of the warehouse belonging to Gonzalez, Herrera y Cia. Minutes, eternally long, dragged by before, in an upper window, two half-masked red lights commenced to glow beneath a faint green one.

A long sigh of relief escaped Jed as he hand-signalled to resume rowing cautiously towards a heavy iron grating which rose, clanking and dripping, like the portcullis of some medieval stronghold. If this was a trap into which he was venturing, it would be difficult to imagine one more perfect.

Noiselessly, the whaleboat coasted into a narrow and rank-smelling berth lined with masonry into darkness barely relieved by a feeble lantern whose light only emphasized the extent of what looked like a huge, low-ceilinged and shadow-ruled cavern. The smooth and slippery stone sides of this slot or sleeve ran about level with the whaleboat's gunwales.

"What the hell?" Jed rasped when the portcullis began to descend, effectively imprisoning the boat party.

Convulsively, Lydia's hand sought the grip of a duelling pistol.

"Please, my friends, do not disquiet yourselves. There is nothing to fear. We take precautions only against interruption." Don Jaime Muñoz with dramatic abruptness, stepped out from behind a row of enormous wine casks. Once a stained canvas curtain had been dropped before the portcullis more lanterns began to gleam. Don Roberto raised one while making his way towards a counter at the slip's squared end. After him came a trio of Negroes, armed to the teeth, and a mestizo in rusty black who had "clerk" written all over him.

Don Roberto hurried to assist Lydia ashore. Bowing, he said, "Everything proceeds in good order, no?"

Still in the whaleboat, Jed motioned his crew to begin unloading onto the sleeve's stone border.

Lydia, slanted eyes huge in the half-light, already had placed a brass-bound travelling desk on one end of a rough, freight scarred counter and, outwardly calm, became engaged in unlocking it.

"*Señor Capitán*, our friends in Boston did well to select so bold a man as you to conduct their business," observed Don Roberto.

"How so, your Honor?" Jed thought the title might be pleasing.

"The cannon you mount are so few and small." He smiled thinly. "One wonders why you have dared, so lightly armed, to bring a cargo of such value into these troubled waters."

"To make real money a fellow must be willing to run a calculated risk now and then."

"One observes that you also are—er, prudent, *Señor Capitán*." Don Roberto gestured first towards the brace of boarding pistols in Jed's belt then at the boat's polyglot crew, similar only in their formidable appearance and a capacity for action. Armed with cutlasses in addition to pistols and handling short-barreled carbines, all appeared alert, ready to cope with trouble.

Presently the negotiants ranged themselves around a pair of delicate balance scales and wooden frames containing graduated cylindrical brass weights.

After a boatsteerer had broached the first keg Don Jaime and the clerk deftly arranged glistening new dollars in stacks of ten. Together, Don Roberto and Lydia checked the contents of each pile.

Rats scurried and rustled, water lapped softly along the whaleboat's sides and gigantic shadows projected by the lanterns moved back and forth across the ceiling.

Meantime, the Negro porters trundled in a number of low carts piled with sturdy wooden cases of Mexican money. While the doubloons closely resembled American-minted dollars both as to weight and size, they weren't of comparable fineness. These also were arranged in stacks of ten on the opposite side of the scales.

Lydia, alert but less tense, seated herself on a keg opposite the scales and poised her pen over a slim account book, reassured by the pressure of the little pistols in a broad waistband of black cotton.

"Now, *Señor Capitán*," said Don Jaime in a suddenly flat and incisive voice, "is it clear beyond doubt that this exchange will be based solely on the measured weight of each coin, regardless of its denomination? Two-and-one-half dollars in our currency to be paid for one minted in the United States."

Don Roberto raised silvery brows. "Is that rate not excessive?"

Lydia shook her head, said briskly, "No, sir. Not at all. The dollars we offer are uniform and fresh from the mint; all weigh exactly 416 grains and contain 371.25 percent pure silver; while your doubloons and pieces-of-eight may be as big and weigh the same, I doubt if most are as much as 338 grains fine. Besides, many are badly worn or clipped."

Don Roberto jerked a nod, "That may be the truth, but please to explain something." Don Roberto removed dark rimmed spectacles and rubbed at a red mark on the bridge of his beak of a nose. "Why do none of your coins show the least sign of having been in use?"

"The answer is simple, Mr. Gonzalez," Lydia said promptly. "Few American dollars are in circulation because, in 1807, President Jefferson ordered no more dollar pieces struck."

Don Jaime peered across the counter. "Why did your *Presidente* do that?"

"Because our coins were of such a fineness that, as fast as they were put in circulation they disappeared, were hoarded. His order forced our people to use French, English and Spanish coins of lesser fineness."

"Is it really so no American dollars have been minted since 1807?"

Lydia flashed him a little smile. "Yes, sir. That's gospel truth."

Jedediah Paddock considered his sister with surprise verging on respect.

In rapid succession gleaming stacks of American dollars crossed the counter; hours hurried by, pens scratched and coins clinked. An amazing variety of foreign coins were dropped one by one into a scoop at one end of the scales until they exactly balanced a selection of bronze counterweights.

In the background Jed's men disposed themselves on freight as comfortably as possible and, in silence, watched the proceedings, weapons unobtrusively handy.

Cocks began to shrill all over Vera Cruz and a clock had sounded five resonant notes before the last of the Mexican silver had been stowed on the *Gladiator*—excepting four small wooden cases of specie which no amount of shoving and levering could be made to fit into the lazaret. Jed ended by secreting these under a row of kegs in the powder magazine.

The eastern sky was commencing to pale when Jed appeared on deck relieved that so far matters had progressed with an un-anticipated lack of complications. He had opened his shirt and was enjoying the cool wind beginning to blow in from the sea when he became aware that that slovenly sloop-of-war, the *Veraganza de Guerrero* was shaking out topsails and getting under way. Why should she sail so early? It wasn't usual for Latins to forgo sleep, especially when the tide presented no problem.

28
Regalo

Because he needed to replenish the *Gladiator*'s water casks and take on livestock and fresh provisions Captain Paddock, after brief deliberation, caused his command to be tied up alongside the Embarcadero Municipál—that same long stone pier on which he and Lydia first had set foot two days back.

If the bark's company believed they'd been unbearably tormented by insects, heat and humidity while at anchor, they quickly became disillusioned and, grumbling incessantly, went about their duties barefooted and streaming sweat.

Sometimes rain would fall in brief, lashing cloudbursts which, when the wind died out, caused an atmosphere like that of a steam bath. Additional swarms of roaches and other uncleanly insects crawled out of produce brought aboard, flies and mosquitoes appeared in droning, stinging myriads.

Incredibly gaunt and ragged hucksters crowded out along the pier bent under bundles and baskets of fruit and vegetables and squealing little pigs trussed with vines.

A quartet of sandaled *soldados* in dirty blue tunics were on duty, ostensibly to keep order, but they seemed only interested in finding shade or shelter as the weather dictated. The only order in the *Gladiator*'s vicinity was maintained by the half-dozen armed crewmen assigned to restrain and regulate the passage of pedlars over the gangway. Others patrolled along the bulwarks away from the wharf to club off vendors who, swarming up from a flotilla of canoes and bumboats, attempted to climb the sides or to crawl through ports left open for ventilation.

It didn't take long for the Fourth and Goober Pike, assisted by Te Ponapa and Hercules, to select an ample supply of lean but healthy livestock—turkeys, fowls, goats, pigs and even a flea-bitten calf. These were secured in pens built next to the try-works.

Except when it rained, the hubbub was as deafening as it was unbroken.

In the early afternoon a pock-marked, saddle-hued captain of infantry escorted by a squad of ragged little Indian soldiers appeared at the gangway and demanded permission to board. He was wearing a shako adorned by a plume of scarlet flamingo feathers and much tarnished gold braid looped across a surprisingly clean uniform jacket.

The visitor, when Paddock came forward hot and short-tempered under mounting tension, gravely introduced himself as the Port Captain. He then stated it was the Governor's order that the *Americano* bark must remain tied up until clearance formalities had been completed.

And when would clearance papers be forthcoming? Jed was at pains to appear confident and polite at the same time. Very soon, assured the Captain; would *El Capitán Americano* remain patient a little longer? How unfortunate that affairs in Vera Cruz were in much disorder. The Mexican's dark head in its plumed shako had swung in the direction of the Castello de Santiago when several volleys of musketry rattled sharply and echoed through the town.

"They execute traitors captured in the battle," explained the Port Captain.

"Hope, sir, you'll do everything in your power to speed things up." Jed noticed the visitor's eyes sweeping the deck, the boats, the rigging. Good thing his carronades were mounted below decks and not in sight.

Furtively, the Mexican considered this yellow-haired giant. "And why is the distinguished *Capitán* so impatient to quit our lovely port?"

"Only because there's plenty of smallpox and the black vomit around and it's spreading fast. I don't want it on board."

"One comprehends your anxiety, Señor," admitted he in the shako so tall it only seemed to emphasize his meager stature. "It would appear that our English friends, too, have taken alarm."

For the first time the *Gladiator's* Master became aware that H.M.S. *Dolphin* and H.M.S. *Hecate* were heaving anchor and the dark outlines of topmen were moving out on yards to unbrail gallants, royals and topsails. Jibs commenced to climb jerkily into sight.

Both men-o'-war got smartly under way and disappeared in the heart of a violent silver-gray rain squall. With the *Veraganza de Guerrero* already departed, the Bay of Vera Cruz now lay destitute of warships.

His temper like a dark town full of armed men Jed, towards sundown, finally granted permission for hands to go ashore and do business with an importunate mob of hawkers, curio dealers and vendors of pets.

Those dealing in monkeys, jewel-brilliant parrots, parakeets and other bright-plumed birds met with the most success. Abner Doane became owner of a yellow-headed green parrot which to his delight proved able to swear in French, Spanish and English; returning aboard with the bird balancing on his shoulder he felt quite the old salt.

Te Ponapa bought a pretty little orange-and-black monkey principally because he enjoyed stroking the creature's fine and silky fur; it reminded him of a young *vahine's nether hair.*

Only when a vicious thunderstorm swept in from the mountains and pounced on the port like a hunting *tigre* did bargaining come to an end. Lightning repeatedly stabbed the steaming earth with dazzling blades.

Darkness closed in, dripping and smothering, but no word came from either Gonzalez, Herrera y Cia or the Port Captain's office.

When, by eight o'clock of the following morning, there still was no sign of clearance papers Captain Jedediah Paddock, cursing softly, struggled into a linen suit reeking of mildew and, after locating Mr. Mercer, was guided to the offices of Gonzalez, Herrera y Cia in the Calle de la Caleta where he found Don Jaime Muñoz seated at his desk and apparently hard at work.

Don Jaime leaped up, teeth flashing, and held out both hands. "Ah! My friend Jed! Such pleasure to greet you. Be a thousand times welcome!"

"How d'you do, James? All right, I hope." Jed's tone was flat and sour though he'd have given much to appear unruffled.

Nodding pleasantly at Mr. Mercer, Don Jaime Muñoz shoved aside a small snowdrift of papers. Then his radiant smile became supplanted by an anxious expression. "Why are you here, *amigo?* By this time you should have sailed."

Jed removed a wide straw hat purchased the day before, then, mopped streaming red-bronze features. Said he, narrowly watching the other. "How can I leave without clearance papers?"

Don Jaime appeared genuinely perplexed. "What! You did not receive your *despacho de aduana?*"

Jed strove to control his temper. "Ain't seen hide nor hair of any."

"But this is amazing! Did not the Port Captain pay you a visit?"

"He did. But nothing came of it. He just stalled, then ordered me to stay tied up to the Municipal Wharf."

The young Mexican elevated slender reddish brows. "Ah! I think I have it. Did you fail to send his Excellency, Colonel Barbabossa a *regalo*—a suitable gift by the Port Captain?"

"No. You've told me nothing about that sort of thing. Haven't you done anything for me?"

"*¡Seguro!* Long since our firm has paid the customary gratitudes to the Customs, the *Guarda de Costas* and to the naval authorities." He struck his forehead a sharp slap. "*¡Ay de mi!* How could I have forgotten to fee Colonel Barbabossa? Yes. This unfortunate lapse of memory is clearly my fault."

"—Which could prove a damn' costly piece of forgetfulness." Jed's steely little eyes explored the other's expression but detected nothing beyond apparently genuine concern.

Frowning, Don Jaime plumped himself down, stared into space. "Even so, I cannot understand this—this unfortunate delay; our firm already has contributed most generously to General Santa Anna's war chest. Perhaps the explanation is that Barbabossa, who is a creature of his, and who also is his brother-in-law, did not receive a satisfactory share of our contribution." He nodded to himself several times. "I should have foreseen such a possibility."

"Damn' right." Ignoring a warning gesture from Mr. Mercer, Jed used a sodden handkerchief to mop his face wishing to hell he was clear of this stinking port. "Well, Mr. Muñoz, what's to be done? You know damn' well I've got to get out of here instanter."

" 'What is to be done' you ask? The moment Colonel Barbabossa receives a handsome contribution to what he calls his 'Soldier's Compassionate Fund' your clearance papers will appear and you will be free to depart."

A flush crept along Jed's wide cheek bones. Innate New England thrift bothered him until he reasoned that Messrs. Doane, Welch & Peabody—even if they hadn't broached the subject—must know that any traffic with Latin Americans must entail the occasional greasing of palms. Grimly, he inquired, "How much d'you think it would take to square Barbabossa? Five hundred doubloons?"

Don Jaime parted well-kept hands and shrugged delicately, "Double that amount, my friend, and you will come closer to the mark. He would feel insulted by a lesser sum."

"I'll take your word on that." The big New Englander surged to his feet. "How quick can I expect action?"

Don Jaime's smile grew vast. "My dear Jed, send your contribution to me as quickly as you reach your ship. I, personally, will arrange matters and deliver the clearance papers."

"When can I count on sailing?"

Delicate furrows creased the Mexican's smooth forehead. "Ah, as to that, *¿quién sabe?*—who knows? All will go well, *provided* the Colonel has not taken offense over your failure to approach him."

"—And if he has?"

"He will delay. An aide will explain that he is busy hunting down the defeated *Federales*."

Jed's big jaw tightened. "Come what may you'd better fix things in a hurry. I don't intend lingering in this pesthole much longer."

"Do not concern yourself." Don Jaime put an arm about the American's shoulder.

Mr. Mercer assured: "Things will quickly be arranged to your satisfaction, Mr. Muñoz is well-experienced in such matters."

Jed permitted himself to look reassured, though he wasn't. "All right," said he crisply, "How do I get the bribe money to you? Certain-sure, my ship is being watched around the clock."

Don Jaime's ready smile reappeared. "I believe I have a practical solution."

"—Such as?"

"This evening I will send aboard a party of singers and dancers to entertain your people." He almost smirked. "During the entertainment it should be simplicity itself for you to pass me the *regalo* unnoticed. Of course your payment should be made in gold. It is not of such great a bulk."

"Gold!"

The young Mexican looked startled. "Surely you have some?"

"A little," Jed admitted. "But it's only for use in emergencies."

Some of Don Jaime's stiffness departed. "But is this not an emergency?"

"Reckon you're right. To make the transfer safe and easier you'd better come aboard ahead of the entertainers and sup on board."

"*Magnífico!*" Don Jaime clapped Jed's shoulder. "The troupe will not appear until after dark."

Captain Jedediah Paddock on reboarding the *Gladiator* found Mister Hayward together with a pair of armed deck hands waiting by the gangway. Navy style, the Third knuckled an old tarpaulin hat, muttered, "Please, sir, come straight-away to the steerage."

Without hesitation the Captain followed his Third below and out of sight of idlers lingering on the pier.

Shifting weight uneasily from foot to foot in the steerage's cramped confines stood a round-shouldered, pinch-faced and completely bald individual wearing the blue-and-white jersey and bell-bottomed trousers of the Royal Navy.

"Who's this? What does he want?"

"Sir, say's his name's George Purvis. He claims to have deserted the *Dolphin;* came aboard out of a bumboat just a little while ago."

For a long moment Jed considered this fellow standing at rigid attention, noted wide-set and restless brown eyes. "Well, my man, why are you here?"

"Trying to save m' life, sir."

"So you're a deserter? Why'd you risk getting flogged to shreds?"

"Why, sir, I found a handkerchief in the 'tween decks and delayed searching out its owner which, sir, were a bad mistake 'cause it belonged to the Captain. Since I were seen picking it up and made no report right off I were charged with theft." The deserter grimaced. "I were mastheaded and sentenced to eighty lashes."

Mister Hayward muttered, "You mayn't know what that many lashes means, sir, but *I* do. 'Tis terrible hard to bear."

"I presume so. Now you, Purvis, what's your rating?"

"Gunner's mate, sir. Signed on as such in Portsmouth."

"Gunner's mate, eh?" Jed tilted his head to one side and briefly fingered his chin. He shot the Third a glance.

"Since Tom Archer ain't with us any longer, sir, it might prove profitable to have a real gunner aboard."

"True enough, though I don't fancy harboring a British Navy deserter; could bring on a heap of trouble. You—step closer."

The fellow advanced, round hat clutched over his chest with rigid fingers. "Yessir?"

"Your name again?"

"George Purvis, sir."

"Your age?"

"Don't rightly know, sir, but I figures I must be 'round forty."

"You can captain a carriage piece?"

"Oh, yes, sir. Mine were top gun o' the starboard broadside. Won the Admiral's prize for marksmanship, we did. I've also served as master gunner aboard H.M. sloop *Kestrel.*"

Purvis's lips beginning to quiver, he dropped his hat, knelt and clasped heavily tattooed hands in an agony of supplication. "Please, sir, for God's sake sign me on! I swear to serve you well and true, sir."

"Get up, man. Get up! Very well, you'll be signed as gunner—on one condition."

The Englishman's joyous expression faded. "Aye, aye, sir. And what may be that condition?"

"On the voyage down here, through a regrettable accident I lost four experienced cannoneers—they drowned when their boat capsized so I'm in need of trained replacements. Bring me two or three reliable men and I'll sign the lot of you. Can you do that?"

The deserter delayed reply long enough to convey a semblance of honest doubt. "I dunno much about this 'ere pest hole of a port but since we've been stationed here I've heard about others who've jumped his Majesty's service. How much time d'you grant me, sir?"

"'Till daybreak tomorrow."

Purvis looked fearfully anxious. "That ain't over-long to ferret out good men in a furrin port, sir."

"I'm aware of that," Jed fumbled in his pocket, passed over a few doubloons. "These may help you to find 'em. Get going."

Don Jaime Muñoz, dapper, reassuringly at ease and, neatly dressed, took dinner in the main cabin together with the *Gladiator*'s Captain and officers. Abner Doane, scurrying about the table, was fascinated by this elegantly attired and well-mannered foreigner who spoke such excellent English. Criminently! He'd never seen so many beautiful rings, nor a watch of heavy gold all covered with diamonds. Why, this distinguished-appearing gentleman surely would feel comfortable amid the most exclusive circles in Boston!

He became even more delighted when a troupe of singers and dancers in bright, tawdry costumes came aboard laughing and babbling like a cagefull of parrots. They arranged themselves about the deck forward of the main hatch, began to strike tentative, shivering chords on guitars and beating tambourines and on little tom-toms.

Once the officers, with the exception of Lydia, had disappeared on deck, Jedediah produced a lumpy leather bag containing approximately one thousand dollars in rich, red-gold English sovereigns.

"Count 'em out. Mister Paddock," the *Gladiator*'s Master directed. "Let's have no errors at this end!"

Don Jaime colored, said stiffly. "Nor will there be a further mistake on my part. You have the word of Muñoz y Herrera."

"No offense intended," Jed grunted, "but it's best to keep our transaction ship-shape."

Pulses quickening, Lydia pushed forward a receipt. "A mere formality, sir, only designed to reassure the gentlemen in Boston their money has been well spent."

Don Jaime's eyes narrowed as he took the pen but he smiled and quickly scrawled his signature with a flourish. "Were the circumstances different I would resent such a request but, as matters stand, I deem it a pleasure to accommodate so gracious a lady."

As he rose to leave the Mexican's left eyelid flickered. "*Amigo*, soon you will discover how well I am about to repay your *regalo*."

29

Measure for Measure

By daybreak all preparations for precipitate departure had been taken. Jedediah Paddock and his officers kept anxious eyes on the water gate just opening for the day. Through it drifted a scattering of ragged fishermen and a party of sleepy looking soldiers who shuffled to the Embarcadero Muncipal's far end, built a fire then stolidly set about cooking breakfast.

Next to appear was a group which attracted Jedediah's immediate attention. George Purvis, followed by a pair of furtive-looking fellows, could be seen advancing in elaborate casualness towards the *Gladiator*. At well-spaced intervals three deserters from the Royal Navy slipped aboard and were at once hustled below.

Still there came no sign of a uniformed customs official nor of any well-dressed civilian who might be representing Gonzalez, Herrera y Cia.

It added to Jed's already mounting disquiet that a *Guarda de Costas* sloop mounting ten guns presently dropped anchor off the Embarcadero's seaward end. Significantly perhaps, her crew then brailed up her canvas so loosely she could quickly be got under way.

George Purvis and his evil smelling companions, concealed in the forehold, were sweating from more than the growing, penetrating heat. What if the *Dolphin* or the *Hecate* reappeared? Worse still, what if the whaler came intercepted in international waters and, as they often still did, the men-o'-war insisted on making a search?

While sweat began to darken his blue cotton shirt Jed wrestled with a mounting fear that he'd been a great fool to trust any Mexican—even one so companionable and straightforward as Don Jaime Muñoz.

The clocks of the port had begun to dispute the exact moment of one o'clock when on the Embarcadero appeared two burly individuals. Brandishing staves they made their way towards the *Gladiator*. Between them walked a tall female figure in a long gray cape the hood of which had been pulled far forward.

From beside the bark's taffrail Jedediah Paddock watched the trio make their way among heaps of produce, piles of coconuts, bundles of vegetables shaded by palm leaves and heaps of brilliantly colored fishes.

Since they appeared to be heading for the bark a sudden possibility occurred; was Don Jaime Muñoz, who no doubt had sound reasons, employing this unorthodox means of delivering his clearance?

When they drew near Jed called, "Mister Coffin! If that woman and her niggers want to come aboard, let 'em. Send 'em straight to the main cabin."

Um. One of this slight, gracefully walking female's escorts was carrying a cloth bundle. Suspicion mounting, Jed went forward in time to watch the Negro drop his bundle on deck then turn and run back down the gangway in a big hurry, and with his companion, disappear among the swarms of vendors.

He arrived at the gangway in time to hear the visitor say to Mister Coffin, "Please, *señor*, I bring important papers from Señor Jaime Muñoz for your *Capitán*."

Although the speaker did not throw back her hood, Jed started. Why should that rich, slightly husky voice sound so familiar? Instantly, he guessed and felt his pulse rate quicken. "Mister Coffin!" he spoke sharply, "show this lady to my cabin at once."

Men working about the deck grinned. Lord, yonder went a dainty bit of stuff!

Lydia, working on accounts, looked up and stared when Jed entered followed by a tall full-skirted female. "What is that—that creature doing down here?"

"Don't know yet, so clear out whilst I learn what's afoot."

Once the door banged shut Jed uttered a flat laugh. "Better shed your cloak, Estrellita; you'll find it hot below."

Expressive dark eyes round with anxiety, the girl unclasped and whirled aside the cloak in a graceful flourish reminiscent of the bull dance.

Breathing accelerated, Jed held out a hand. "Now's not the time for nonsense so excuse my lack of courtesy. Hand over the papers Don Jaime sent."

"Oh, yes-s." Disconcerted, the girl delved into the front of her frilly yellow blouse and pulled out a single and thin envelope sealed in green wax.

"Is this all he sent?" —Clearance papers would certainly have been more bulky!

"*Si, señor.* This is all." The girl's lips commenced to quiver as harsh lines abruptly aged the *Americano's* powerful features.

Swamped by chill misgivings, the New Englander broke the seal and read in script so perfect as to resemble copper-plate engraving:

'Much my friend Jedediah. It is with much deep grief I inform you, first, that despite my best efforts I have failed to reach Colonel Barbabossa. It is that he is away in the mountains inspecting troops. Alas, your clearance papers cannot be issued until the Colonel returns—and no one will say when that may be.

And there is still worse news. Our business of the other night no longer remains a secret. I have learned that a rumor you are carrying treasure became known *almost as soon* as you arrived in Vera Cruz. Who can have betrayed us? I am completely desolated.

Therefore Don Roberto and I feel you must, for your own safety, quit Vera Cruz *this very night!*

Another word of warning: Be on the lookout for *la Veraganza de Guerrero*, the Government ship-of-war. We have had secret information she lies in wait to seize you.

Since, unfortunately, I am unable to return the gold you entrusted to me therefore, I send you, my dear Jed, Estrellita in exchange. I feel confident that, since she so much delighted you on a certain occasion, you will not feel cheated.'

Jed drew a slow breath and read on:

'In case, my Friend, you feel inclined to send back Estrellita please do not do so. The moment this girl attempts to re-enter the city she will be arrested on a charge of treason against the Government.

Confident that a gentleman of your fine sensibilities could not even contemplate such a fate for a lady so charming, I have no fear for her future.

May the continuation of your voyage prove prosperous beyond your fondest hopes.

> Your humble, obedient servant, who
> kisses your hands,
>
> J.M.'

Once the sun had set behind Vera Cruz casting its domes, battlements and towers into stark silhouette Jed summoned all officers to the main cabin where they collected half-dressed, and patently uneasy. Seldom had they seen the Captain appear so taut, so tight-lipped. Lydia wondered what could have become of that cloaked female whose cloying *frangipani* perfume continued to permeate her brother's quarters.

In brief sentences Paddock admitted to having been tricked, then added, "We'll do nothing but wait 'till I feel ready to make a move. Listen closely. When the time comes I want you, Winslow, and you, Hayward, to lower the larboard boats very quietly. Once we cast off you will tow the ship, on very short lines, away from the dock." His gaze swept the semi-circle of sunburnt faces glowing under the gimballed lamp. "With that damn' guard boat lying so close I won't set even a rag of canvas till we lengthen the range."

"What about the guns in the forts?" Mister Winslow asked calmly, as if addressing a vestry meeting. "The ones in that big fortress on the island to the north are sufficient heavy to range the whole inner harbor."

"They are," Jed agreed grimly. "That's one chance we'll have to take. But in darkness maybe their gunners won't shoot too well."

He turned to the Third. "Now, Mister Hayward, just in case the Dons try beating us to the draw, I want all guns manned and charged with grape and matches will be lit, but I don't want any port triced up until the word is passed; even after that, there'll be no firing 'till I say so. Everyone understand?"

To be on the safe side Jedediah Paddock delayed ordering boats lowered until the hour of ten, by which time most of the town's lights had blinked out and silence was descending upon Vera Cruz.

Because of superior night vision Jed ordered his sister and Tom Blue Fox to the foretop. Climbing the ratlines, Lydia Paddock Roach realized that at this moment she really stood in danger of losing her life—especially if that bland villain, Don Jaime, had compounded his treachery by alerting the forts.

However, neither lookout peering hard through the half-light, could detect activity aboard the shadowy *Guarda de Costas*, now lying barely fifty yards away.

Making soft rustling noises shore lines were cast off and snaked inboard; only faint bumping sounds attended the lowering of whaleboats but creaking caused by their davit tackles sounded appallingly loud.

Aaron Winslow hissed like an angry tomcat when someone's oar blade failed to dig quite deep enough into the harbor's stygian, garbage-dotted water. "Blast you! Quit splashing."

Almost imperceptibly the gap separating ship from shore widened. Soldiers, crouched about a fire smouldering before the water gate never even turned their heads.

The shadowy whaler, rigging a sable network against a clouded sky, was pulled in almost complete silence past a scattering of fishing boats on which everyone appeared to be asleep although the embers of cooking fires still glowed dimly on sand boxes built on deck.

To Jedediah Paddock's inexpressible relief a breath of air caressed his cheek. Hope arose that, a few hundred yards further out, off Lavendera Reef, the bark's canvas might catch the off shore breeze which usually began to blow after sundown. Steadily the tow moved towards the outer clumps of fishing vessels and coasters.

All might have gone well beyond expectation when, unexpectedly, a boat from the *Guarda de Costas* pulled out from the lee of a sizable schooner; someone commenced to shout, "*¿Quién pasa? ¡Detenga Vd.!*"

"Damn!" growled Hayward, peering at his gun crews crouched, tense and ready, among the carronades. "Now that's torn it! Stand by to trice up port lids."

Out of the dark sounded a flurry of footsteps and the dull clank of loading implements.

Jed picked up a speaking trumpet. "Please speak English. We don't speak Spanish. We're shifting to a cooler anchorage."

"*No comprendo. ¡Detenga Vd. immediatamente!*"

Lights began to glow aboard the coast guard sloop. Jed roared at the crews, "Pull hard! Put your backs to it." Down the after scuttle he shouted. "Below there! Raise port lids but don't fire!"

"*Hacer alto!*" A shrill voice insisted from the *Guarda de Costas'* small boat.

"Balls to the lot of you! Helmsman! Steer full on 'till we gain headway!" Primordial, nearly forgotten impulses began to course like sailing currents.

Hands, hitherto concealed behind the bulwarks, swarmed up the shrouds and out along the yards as nimbly as so many overgrown apes threatened by a prowling leopard. Almost immediately dim blurs of canvas materialized but only rattled gently therefore, to the *Gladiator*'s harassed Master, it became painfully apparent that there was but little more air blowing aloft than was on deck.

The gloom to starboard suddenly became raked by a slender, dazzling streak of flame followed by a report. Another musket blazed, then several more. Lydia felt her stomach contract spasmodically when a bullet went "*thock!*" into the foremast just below her. The effects of these scattered shots were immediate and considerable. On nearby boats lanterns began to glimmer, strident voices rang out. In the town a deep-toned bell began clanging, then others joined in sounding the alarm.

Jed cursed at a sudden intensification of starlight. Why the hell couldn't one of these rain squalls, until now a plague, close in?

As if relenting, Fate sent a series of strong puffs offshore to start the bark slipping along so rapidly that soon the whaleboat crews were ordered to belay towing and stand by to be picked up. The wind continued to increase until the freshly spread canvas filled and rounded and waves began to slap comfortingly alongside.

The *Guarda de Costas*, a big one crammed with armed men, put out sweeps, began pulling on an intercepting course.

Jed turned the wheel over to Mister Coffin and, supremely calm, ranged the deck to muster and marshal to best advantage excited, white-eyed crewmen armed with lances, harpoons and razor-sharp blubber spades. To the few who'd been issued firearms he rasped, "Remember, no shooting without orders! I'll skin alive anyone who disobeys."

Lydia, not receiving orders to return on deck, reckoned she'd better stay where she was. Along with Blue Fox she breathlessly watched the Mexican craft thresh nearer. Meanwhile royals had been unclewed; they filled at once and perceptibly increased the *Gladiator*'s speed.

By straining her vision she made out outlines of a swivel gun mounted on the cutter's bow and beside it the dull glow of a slow match.

She cupped hands and yelled downwards at the top of her voice: "Boat five points off larboard bow! Collision course!"

"Keep her steady as she goes!" Jed snapped at the Second then devoted attention to swinging in the boats.

The wind freshened so much so that the Mexican coxswain miscalculated the bark's speed and, before he could veer aside, found the *Gladiator*'s figurehead glaring down upon him. Venting a small scream he flung himself against his boat's tiller barely in time to avoid being crushed and ground under the bark's stem; nevertheless it suffered a glancing blow which tilted the craft onto its beam's end and spilled its squalling occupants into the harbor's warm and phosphorescent waters.

At this moment a battery in the great castle of San Juan de Ulúa opened fire. Lightning-bright flashes flickered along its sable battlements and thunderous reports rolled over the harbor but only one round shot came anywhere close and that raised a miniature spout well wide of the *Gladiator*'s port quarter.

Jedediah Paddock through night glasses saw that the *Guarda de Costas*' sloop was beginning to sail but, after watching her rate of progress a few moments, he quit worrying; once the *Gladiator*'s courses began to draw there was small chance of being overhauled. He experienced vague chagrin because apparently he still wasn't going to find out whether his gun crews could hit what they shot at.

The bark now began running so crisply before an ever-stiffening offshore breeze that, soon after leaving Galleguila Reef to port and Balanquilla Island to starboard, the lights of Vera Cruz disappeared.

A bleak set to his mouth, Jedediah Paddock ordered a course bearing north, northeast. Long since, he'd figured the *Veraganza de Guerrero*'s commander aware that this whaler was destined for the Pacific probably would attempt interception off Cabo Catoche at the extreme eastern tip of the Yucatán Peninsula.

30
Little Star

Stretched on her narrow, sour-sweat-smelling bunk, wearing only a long-tailed shirt, Lydia Paddock Roach struggled to shake off a torment of cold rage mixed with pangs of jealousy. Worst of all was her sense of helplessness—as unfamiliar as it was infuriating.

What was going on? Why should her carefully planned existence thus become so profoundly shaken?

Grimly, she set about trying to foresee what effects the presence of this foreign female in her brother's cabin would have. Odd, mused Lydia, she'd no real idea of the hussy's likeness. During the past two days this so-called passenger hadn't once come on deck, even put foot outside the great cabin.

Why had this creature been hustled aboard only to be hurriedly deserted by her escorts? Of only one fact did Lydia feel confident; Jed *had* recognized the hussy at once and immediately had ordered her below for all he'd pretended to be disconcerted and taken aback.

Resolutely the Fourth tried to suppress a growing sense of outrage; the sensible course was to reason the matter out before deciding what should be done.

After a while she came to a fairly firm conclusion the presence of Estrellita Vasquez—Jed had given the "passenger's" name as such—must in some way or another have to do with the gold so wryly entered her in the ledger as "Payment for Customs Clearance."

For a while longer the Fourth Mate, streaming perspiration, twisted fretfully on her bunk, lamented that, in all likelihood, this stifling heat would continue another twenty-four hours. Miserably she attempted to conjure up visions of activities taking place in the main cabin.

Long since she'd ascertained from several sources that, at sea, her brother acted far less inhibited than on land. Poor Lucy Dismont!

Staring miserably into gloom only slightly relieved by the tiny porthole Lydia fell to wondering what sort of a depraved creature this Estrellita might be, so, 'Estrellita' meant "Little Star" in Spanish? Um. Pity she'd such a pretty, romantical name in two languages. She'd been so well cloaked and hooded that first and only time she'd beheld her so all she knew for sure about Jed's "companion" was that she stood half-a-head taller than herself and probably weighed half-a-stone more.

In deep relief she heard the helmsman's rattle sound just above her head summoning the larboard watch to duty. Sighing, the Fourth slid out of her shirt and sat a moment, jay-naked, mopping her body with a damp rag. She set her teeth in preparation to lacing up that infernal canvas vest. And to think once she'd been proud of devising such a garment! Nowadays she didn't bother with hose or shoes so, after belting on a pair of lightweight duck trousers, she thrust none-too-clean feet into native sandals of rawhide purchased on the Embarcadero.

Arriving on deck she noted that a half-moon had disappeared leaving countless great tropical stars to throb and illumine the sea. Best of all, a strong cool wind was driving the bark along at a smart clip.

Once Mister Hayward had turned over the watch he didn't go below as he usually did, lingered, pretending to check the compass course, then sauntered over to the weather rail where Lydia, with neatly-sculptured narrow head tilted back, stood studying the set of canvas. A few strands of sable hair had escaped her cap and were curling gently about her cheeks.

The Third after lighting his pipe at the galley fire remarked drily, "Well, Mister Paddock. Seems like we got us a passenger for a spell."

She jerked a nod, shot a searching glance at Mister Hayward's battered features. "What can she be doing on board?"

Diamantine sparks snatched from Hayward's pipe bowl whirled over the rail. "Your guess is as good as mine," he evaded. "Got a good look at her yet?"

The slim figure turned as if to study the *Gladiator*'s lacy wake and attempted to sound casual. "No, have you?"

"Yes, I have. In a dark sort of way she's prettier 'n a red-wing blackbird on a cattail. Speaks a little English, too."

Lydia was surprised to hear herself inquire, "Where's she berthed?"

"In the main cabin. Fancy the Skipper's making her—well, real comfortable every way he can."

Lydia's composure cracked. She spat over the rail like an angry fo'c's'le hand. "How disgusting! Shameful!"

Mister Hayward chuckled softly. "Depends on the point of view. Your brother wouldn't agree 'bout that."

"But he—he's so, so brazen about this."

"What has he to fear? Captain ain't married or even pledged so I hear."

Squirming inside, Lydia sensed, rather than saw, this hard-bitten figure grinning slyly. "Don't know why you act so taken aback, Mister Paddock. Surely, you lived on Nantucket long enough to have heard all about 'sea wives'. Such come aboard a lot of vessels ye'd never suspect would tolerate 'em—even Quaker ships. Would you believe it? 'Tis common practice for a whaler to touch at the first likely South Sea Island she sights and recruit sufficient native girls to satisfy all hands? Naturally, officers get the pick of the lot."

Lydia nibbled at her lower lip. "Where do such creatures live?"

"In the boats, on deck, in the fo'c's'le; anywhere there's room for 'em to—to lay down. Make 'emselves useful, too, sewing, cooking and such-like."

"What becomes of these poor savages?"

Mister Hayward tapped pipe ashes over the side. "Depends. Unlikely ones are got rid of quick—get put ashore at the first opportunity. Pretty, extra-agreeable females get traded or sold off just afore the ship makes for whaling grounds. Women get in the way when there's heavy, bloody work to be done—you'll see."

A pig penned aft of the try-pots for some reason squealed, set fowls crated alongside to cackling. When the noise subsided, Hayward resumed. "But I can name some ships whose skippers won't ever allow a female on board so whenever they make port they get crippled through desertions. Why? 'Cause a man can't go against Nature, Ma'am." Softly, he added, "*You* understand, I'm sure."

"No, damn you, I don't!" She stalked forward, eyes filling.

Towards midday, Goober Pike, his round, good-natured black face shining with sweat shuffled up to the *Gladiator's* Master, mumbled, "Cap'n, suh, dinner am ready."

Jedediah jerked a nod then, following a set routine, crossed to the compass to check the course. Next he studied the set of canvas before saying to his First, "Mister Winslow, dinner is on."

The First Mate said, "Thank you, sir." Then, in the same fashion, Winslow notified Coffin. Hayward, having the watch, was omitted, so he notified the Fourth. On the way below each officer made a pretense of checking the ship's position chalked on a slate beside the helmsman.

Last to descend the after-scuttle was Lydia, steeled against the ordeal of sitting for the first time at table with Jed's harlot. By the time she took her seat in the main cabin her cheek bones were standing out like hatchet blades. Jed, Mister Winslow and the "passenger" had knotted napkins about their necks and were consuming salt pork and rice heaped indiscriminately on knife-scarred tin plates.

Nobody looked up when Lydia entered until the Captain announced in a attempt at heartiness tinged with warning, "Mister Paddock, this is our passenger, Miss Vasquez. Trust you will make her feel welcome aboard. Pass the relish, Abner!"

Lydia managed to mutter in a suffocated voice, "How do?" before sliding into her seat at a skillfully hinged circular table ringing the mizzen mast's base. She discovered that she'd an unimpeded view of the "passenger."

While choking down a few mouthfuls she stole a quick look and was surprised at the fineness of the girl's light-tan hued features and modest yet lively air. Only faint traces of rouge showed on the young woman's lips and cheeks while her gleaming blue-black hair was plaited into neat twin braids secured by yellow bows, crisp and dainty as little butterflies. She was chilled, however, on noticing that, when the door to her brother's clothes locker swung open to the ship's gentle rolling, several bright and generously ruffled items of feminine apparel were hanging among masculine garments.

Towards the end of a silent repast punctuated by the Captain's brief sallies of forced conversation Lydia forced herself carefully to consider the interloper and felt somehow relieved that her first fleeting impressions hadn't been in error.

This Mexican wench was by no means as coarse-looking or bold-mannered as she'd anticipated. Señorita Vasquez's nose was straight and slender and so short it just missed being snub; actually, it was quite attractive as was an intriguingly short upper lip which, naturally red showed a streak of dark fuzz which, when she grew older, probably would develop into a definite moustache; this was some consolation. However, there could be no denying the appeal of the girl's gracefully flaring black brows or the amazing length of eyelashes which, for the time being, Estrellita was keeping discreetly lowered.

It hurt Lydia to admit to herself that the "passenger's" hands not only were small, well-shaped but equipped with slender tapering fingers with which she ate almost to the complete neglect of knife and fork.

All in all, this young female was completely unlike the brazen baggage she'd anticipated, which only fanned smoldering resentment into a blaze. When lying on her bunk, she heard singing and Ordinary Seaman João Fuentes playing his fiddle in the main cabin.

Throughout her brief but chequered career Estrellita Vasquez never before had felt anywhere near so wholly pleased with life as during these halcyon days following the *Gladiator*'s escape from Vera Cruz. Her situation amounted to the blissful fulfillment of rich and hitherto unattainable ambitions. *¡Aye de mi!* How often and how heartily could this burly giant make love! Always she roused to palpitating anticipation whenever she heard the great cabin's door bolt shot home.

Plumbing the depths of experiences which, for a girl not yet eighteen, weren't inconsiderable, Estrellita strove to anticipate, stimulate and satisfy this huge Yanqui's sometimes extraordinary desires. Also, she felt inordinately proud that this wonderful Norte Americano should have accepted her, a miserable, nameless little *puta* in even exchange for a *thousand gold dollars! ¡Madre de Dios!* Successive shivers of delight rippled down her satin-smooth back, set her loins and buttocks to tingling. The only serpent in this maritime Eden was the presence on occasion of a steely glint in the Fourth Mate's eyes.

She guessed she'd never forget how that impassive, self-contained and unbelievably flat-chested creature had reacted when, in her presence, *el Capitán* had admitted that this phenomonon *was his sister*. The Fourth Mate had said in a deadly undertone, "That was quite unnecessary, but I suppose every swine fancies himself lord of his wallow."

While Estrellita's English wasn't sufficient to encompass the Fourth's meaning, the gist of her remark penetrated. She was amazed that *Señor* Jed only burst into roars of laughter and dealt his sister a resounding smack on the bottom.

"Could be the truth, Lyddie, but never forget we're of the same strain; some day I warrant you'll thaw out and maybe learn to enjoy life while you're able."

Thereafter Estrellita never quit the main cabin during daylight hours, only ventured on deck after all saving the watch had turned in.

31

Sloop-of-War

After three days' sailing a northeasterly course the *Gladiator*'s figurehead was swung sharply about to commence the long run down the coast of South America. During this interval Jed spent the bulk of his time below, entrusting the bark's navigation to his officers.

All went well except that Mister Coffin committed an error in calculation so trifling that, while it went unnoticed, it served to divert the whaler from a course designed to carry her comfortably clear of the Yucatán Peninsula.

The only time Estrellita was left to her own devices for any length of time occurred whenever a gun drill was under way. At such times the new gunner's British accents and profanity rang through the 'tween decks; solid wooden carriage wheels rumbled like distant thunder and breathless shouts came from crews working at training tackles or handling loading instruments.

The Fourth continued to exist in a state of sullen indecision. For instance she still couldn't convince herself that, whatever Jed was doing with his mistress was none of her business. The Vasquez girl didn't give the impression of being in love with Jedediah—yet *could* she be? Why hadn't she, Lydia, long ago attempted to understand rather than despise her sex?

Curiosity plagued her. Just exactly what *was* taking place in the main cabin? During night watches she'd overheard a deal of bragging and lurid descriptions of strange and unlikely amusements indulged in on South Sea Islands.

At odd moments she'd taken to wondering just how much of such disgusting and disquieting talk had foundation in fact.

Dawn of the fifth day since leaving the Mexican coast proved unusually beautiful. The rising sun tinted the under sides of woolly,

low-lying cumulus clouds scarlet, gold, yellow and even green.
Schools of delicate shiny flying fish burst from wave crests or fled
the dolphin-striker's empty menace; a host of seabirds swooped or
planed about the royals. Squadrons of porpoises sported alongside;
some came so close that Goober Pike climbed into the knight heads
and, to the crews' delight, succeeded in harpooning a couple—even
fresh out of Vera Cruz they revelled in the red and tasty beef-like
meat.

The sun was nearing its zenith and beating down with a
vengeance when Jedediah Paddock sought the deck to await the
"Doctor's" summons to dinner. He found satisfaction in the way the
Trade Winds, with unvarying force steadily were driving the *Gladiator* towards the Channel of Yucatán separating the peninsula of
that name from Cabo San Antonio on Cuba's western extremity.
Might as well enjoy this fine warm weather for within weeks the
bark would be entering those dangerous and altogether forbidding
latitudes at the tip of South America.

Having doubled the Horn on four occasions Jed wasn't looking
forward to this inevitable ordeal which would include blizzards,
freezing storms of sleet and screaming, tearing gales which buffeted a
ship with colossal waves and vicious cross-seas. God send that on this
passage his masts and spars never became so sheathed in ice as to
render the bark top-heavy and ready to capsize.

Right now he'd be glad to sail the Channel well clear of Cabo
Catoche and enter the Yucatán Basin, where he should be safe from
interception.

Balancing easily on the brilliantly sunlit deck, he squinted aloft
in time to see the lookout turn to bellow downwards; "Sail ho-o-o!"

Jed's sense of relaxation evaporated. "Masthead there! Where
away?"

"'Bout twelve points off'n stabboard bow, sir!"

"How does she sail?"

"Too far off to make certain. Can't count her masts so she
must be makin' straight towards us."

"Helmsman! Steer ten points to larboard."

"Aye, aye, sir. Ten points to labboard it is!"

Uneasy but still not really concerned the *Gladiator*'s Master
secured his telescope and was climbing to the maintop to examine

the stranger when the lookout hailed for a second time. "Land ho! Land to stabboard!"

Jed quit climbing. "*Land!* Look again, you damn' mole! You *can't* be sighting land! We sail near a hundred miles *east* of Cape Catoche!"

"Mebbe so, sir, but all the same there's a streak of coast showin' beyond the stranger!"

"Beelzebub's balls! You positive?"

"Certain-sure, sir," shouted down the man in the hoops.

Jed wasted no time and descended the ratlines roaring, "All hands on deck! Down the wheel! Brace all yards to windward."

The forecastle disgorged the watch below. The *Gladiator's* bow was turned away from that inexplicable coastline and the distant ship bearing down under a full press of canvas.

Before long the bark's company became aware of two dismal facts: wind in her vicinity had begun to falter while the stranger, identified as a square-rigged three-master, still was enjoying strong winds blowing from another direction. Was this a frigate or a sloop-of-war? As yet there was no telling. For a space the *Gladiator's* after guard silently but fervently prayed that yonder might sail *H.M.S. Hecate* but this hope faded once the stranger's hull lifted far enough above the horizon to reveal a green hull streaked in yellow.

A half-hour later Jedediah Paddock could make out through his glass a horizontal tricolor of red yellow and blue stripes snapping at her mizzen's gaff. Another half-hour brought home the sickening fact that this man-of-war was the *Veraganza de Guerrero*. Also, it became inescapable that she was fully able to intercept the much smaller whaler. Her broadside guns could be seen peering out of their ports. Jedediah Paddock wholeheartedly, cursed the hour he'd ever done business with Gonzalez, Herrera y Cia.

Before long it became evident that even when the *Gladiator's* wind picked up this slatternly but clean-lined man-o'-war undoubtedly would have the foot of her, no matter how shrewdly the bark's sails were set and trimmed.

Hands in their usual grubby garments lined the side and anxiously watched the Mexican vessel close in, tricolor bright in the dazzling sunlight.

Tight-jawed, Jed ordered the Stars and Stripes run up then summoned Mister Hayward and Purvis, the new gunner. "Lay a glass on her, you two," he rasped. "See what you make of her battery."

The Englishman spoke first. "Looks to me like she's mounting twelve-pounders, sir. Twelve to a broadside."

Mister Hayward agreed, then growled. "Means if she wants, she can stay at long range and pound us to pieces 'thout our popguns even scratching her."

Feverishly, Jed racked his imagination for some way out of this predicament. Surely there must be some dodge he could employ?

"Shall we man the guns?" Mister Winslow demanded, a nerve beginning to tick in his unshaven, mahogany-hued cheek. "Maybe if we fire a few rounds we can bluff 'em off; Spicks being as they are."

"Hell, no. That'd only invite slaughter," snarled the *Gladiator*'s Master, eyes gleaming like knife points. "He's got the range—has us dead to rights."

Rasped the Third, "Why not let her close in if she will—then cripple her with our smashers sufficient to get us free?"

"She won't venture close enough," was Mister Coffin's opinion. "Lest her Master's coon-cub crazy."

Lydia spoke for the first time. "Neither will he try to sink us at long range—not right away, at least."

"Why not?" snapped her brother, gaze fixed on the onrushing sloop already running out bow chasers.

"Because of what's in the lazarette."

"You're right," Jed grunted. "They know about it, thanks to my dear friend Don Jaime. Helmsman! Keep her steady as she goes. Hell's fire! If *only* this damn' wind would freshen I'd point up and try swapping tacks."

But the breeze continued light; the pursuer closed in steadily, became revealed in ever-increasing detail.

By the time the coast of Yucatán again had disappeared below the horizon's glowing blue the *Veraganza de Guerrero*'s straining canvas brought her into what George Purvis estimated as extreme range for her long guns. Meanwhile a hoist of signal flags, bright as butterflies, climbed jerkily into the green-and-yellow man-of-war's rigging. Not understanding their meaning, Jed ordered his colors dipped as if in salute.

Te Ponapa and Heetee, the American Indians, the ex-naval ratings and a few others who would enjoy nothing better than a good fight began to cast hopeful looks at the Captain up in the main shrouds with yellow hair whipping as, stonily, he studied the sloop-of-war cruising under full sail less than a mile astern. She made a beautiful sight with diamantine spray flying in regular bursts from beneath her figurehead, a full-bosomed and raven-haired sea nymph.

Following a brief delay the *Veraganza*'s string of signals were lowered, then a second set climbed to her signal yard.

Purvis broke taut silence prevailing on deck. "Suppose, sir, we was to pretend surrender, heave-to and let fly when she closes in?"

Temptation racked Jed. Why not? But the inescapable fact remained; the fire of four eight-pound carronades, no matter how expertly served—which, of course, they couldn't be—would not inflict decisive damage. Should such a maneuver fail he'd lose both ship and cargo, and what would his fellow owners have to say about that?

Innate caution which for three generations had kept the Paddock house flag flying decided him.

Over a shoulder he yelled, "Wheel, there! Bring her into the wind!"

Once wind had spilled from the bark's canvas and her topsails were backed men furtively started below in search of hiding places but, on Jed's sharp command, mates and boatsteerers leveled pistols and put an immediate stop to the movement.

Lydia, standing straight and silent by the taffrail, for once was glad of her accursed canvas vest. True, she'd hungered for adventure but this fare was proving over-rich. Miserably, she recalled tales concerning the horrible fate suffered by females captured by pirates, mutineers and letters-of-marque bearing commissioon of questionable validity. What was about to happen to the *Gladiator*, to the crew and to her?

Almost mesmerized, the whaler's crew watched the sloop-of-war pass to windward. Smartly enough, she came into the wind with stained canvas flapping and gun muzzles showing black and menacing.

The *Veraganza* promptly lowered her longboat which rode, gunwales nearly abrim, under a motley assortment of dark-faced men. In her stern balanced a tall, very thin officer wearing a cocked hat plumed in yellow and green; a white tunic adorned by a crimson plastron showed above blue pantaloons striped in yellow.

Entering the whaler's gangway the officer, to the astonishment of everyone, introduced himself, courteously enough, as *el Tienente* Luis de Cordoba of the Republican ship-of-war, *Veraganza de Guerrero*—Avenger of the martyred President Guerrero.

In broken English he informed the *Gladiator*'s Master that his commanding officer was in possession of irrefutable information that this bark recently had taken and illegally exported a cargo of Mexican silver.

In effect the *Gladiator*'s officers must know that the *Veraganza* had been despatched to make certain this treasure would be returned to Vera Cruz.

The hawk-faced officer's features was scarred by a sabre slash which puckered his mouth into a permanent, sardonic grin. Surprisingly, he added, "Not fear, *Señor Capitán*. Surrender silver quiet—we not hurt you. You free to continue sailing." His teeth flashed as he spread hands. "We not want troubling with your so-glorious American Republic."

Jed, going purple-faced, roared, "Damn it, sir! All I did was to exchange American currency for Mexican—all fair and square. For such a transaction no export license is required!"

"*Señor Capitán*. I am not patient mans. I come not to argue but for silver. I advise not delay, not provoke!" The Lieutenant's eyes were of a vitreous brown-black and for all his courtly air and neat well-fitting uniform Lydia decided that here was a cruel, hard-looking individual. She didn't fancy the way he began to finger the ornate and heavily gilded hilt of his sword.

"*Pues!* Where is silver? I wait no long more."

"But the deal was entirely legal," Jed insisted.

"My Commander was told different."

Jedediah raised his big chin, attempted to stare down this gaudy intruder. "Mister, let me point out that we're far outside Mexican territorial waters and since our countries are at peace you've no right of search or seizure on the high seas."

The Mexican's scarred upper lip lifted in a sardonic smile. "You make mistake." He indicated the *Veraganza* and the row of black gun ports gapping her streak like missing teeth. "We *have* right. More heavy cannons. My Commander, most reasonable, offers you choice."

The deep breath Jed drew could be heard all over the deck. "What choice, Mister?"

"Silver is surrender here, or we take, then sink you and your ship. *Entiende, Señor Capitán?*"

To Jed it was becoming apparent that these people weren't keen on destroying the *Gladiator*. Most likely, the sloop's officers were only intent on grabbing the loot for themselves; probably it would never be seen by Santa Anna, who, if even half of what was said about him was true, would be disinclined to share such plunder.

Cock feathers in his hat whipping smartly, the Lieutenant stalked over to the rail and called down to the four boats now bobbing and swaying alongside. "*Aquí, ¡pronto!*" a pack of barefooted sailors swarmed over the rail to cover the whalers and order them, wide-eyed and apprehensive, to line the port rail amidships.

Abner Doane, standing goggle-eyed and shivering with excitement, watched his Captain's hand start towards his pistol's butt but he ended by snarling, "I protest! My Government will hear of this at the first possible moment. However, I won't have my men killed in vain and it's my duty to my owners to continue this cruise. So steal my silver and be damned to you!"

The Mexican's scarred features hardened and he glowered. "Watch words, *señor*. We confiscate—not steal!"

While the last cases of specie were being handed over the whaler's side and members of the boarding party had begun to scramble into their boats Mister Winslow's smoldering rage suddenly flared. He shook a gnarled fist under the Lieutenant's nose. "You'll be made to pay for this piracy, never doubt that, you damn' greasy rascal. The United States won't tolerate such goings-on!"

"See how I tremble in fear?" jeered the Mexican. "Your country she talk tall but she have few warships."

Lieutenant de Cordoba then resumed an air of courtesy so exaggerated as to be insulting. He lifted his cocked hat, feathers gaily flashing and curling and jerked a little bow. "*Señores,* thankings for such good reasoning. I now bid *buen viaje.*"

He was making for the gangway when Lydia Paddock who'd been standing among the crew, sex undetected, stepped into the gaudy officer's path and pulled off her cap to loose her long hair. Eyes bright she said in a clear contralto, "Maybe you don't know it, Mister, but you've overlooked something of value which belongs to Mexico."

Thinking that his sister must have suddenly gone mad to mention those four cases of silver in the magazine Jed thundered, "Hold yer tongue!"

"*¿Cómo?*" The Lieutenant looked startled. "Have you not surrender all silver?"

"Oh yes."

"Then of what valuable remains?"

In a flat, strained voice Lydia replied, "If you'll look in my cabin you'll discover a very pretty whore lady and a compatriot of yours hiding there."

The Mexican blinked. "What is one more *puta*? Already we have plenty on board."

Before Jedediah could erupt into a string of amazed curses the boyish figure said quickly, "No doubt. But Miss Vasquez is a Mexican citizen who boarded this ship illegally in Vera Cruz. Moreover, she's a very dear friend of Don Jaime Muñoz. He undoubtedly will want her returned now that she has served her purpose."

The Mexican began to chuckle, winked elaborately. "*Por supuesto*. Don Jaime has spoke of such a *hija*, but the matter escaped the memory of me. *Muchas gracias, Señorita*. Don Jaime will find much pleasure to see his *amiga*."

32

Retrenchment

During the rest of the day Captain Jedediah Paddock sulked in his cabin licking wounds to his self-esteem. How could he, a presumably smart and experienced sea captain, have been such a ninny as to have been so completely taken in back in Vera Cruz?

In fierce disgust with himself he downed one beaker after another of watered rum until he lapsed into unconsciousness. Hours later he woke with a splitting head by way of catharsis.

After gulping quantities of scalding coffee he sponged head and chest with cold seawater, then towelled unmercifully.

What had become of those brilliant prospects for this carefully planned cruise? Red-eyed and puffy of face, he roared for the cabin boy and ordered something to eat.

On entering the main cabin Abner Doane was startled by the changed appearance of one he deemed little short of an omnipotent demi-god. He couldn't help noticing a yellow petticoat and a bright red skirt swinging jauntily among the Skipper's sober-hued coats and pants.

Criminently! Hadn't those greasy foreigners bundled the Captain's pretty passenger, kicking, biting and shrilling like a shoat stuck under a fence, overside in jig time? The Skipper's profanity at the time had been really inspired, perhaps because the Fourth had giggled all the while like a mischievous schoolgirl.

Following the lad's look Jed snapped, "Pitch those damn' underpinnings overboard!" But then he held up a hand. "Hell, no! Wash 'em out, boy. Those are of lawn and nothing makes better bandages. Now fetch me Mister Paddock, quicker than quick!"

Because a half-gale was blowing, Abner made his way forward, with attention, knocked diffidently on the Fourth's cabin door.

"Cap'n wants you, Mister. Better hurry!"

"How is he?"

"Awfully grouchy, sir; meaner-acting than a bee-stung bear."

"Very well." Silently she thought, have to face the music sooner or later; now what in Tunket possessed me to betray that poor foreign baggage who'd done me no harm? She always acted quiet and well-mannered. What's come over me acting like a jealous, hot-bottomed wench over-hungry for a husband?

Fingers trembling, Lydia Paddock Roach secured her vest over an odoriferous chemise which should have been laundered days earlier; viciously she jammed her hair under a big cloth cap. Wonder what Jed will do? Try to whip me? He'd better not; I'll kill him an he tries. Of course he'll never forgive what I did. Why have I ruined our—our understanding over something which pleasured him and didn't truly affect me?

On her way to the main cabin she wondered how many men a girl, as young as Estrellita, might have known. What was it like to be made love to? Was the act altogether disgusting or supremely blissful? A pity she'd never encouraged confidences from her few female friends.

She found her brother's massive figure sprawled in his armchair, mouth ugly and the expression in his bloodshot eyes ominous. "Take a seat, Mister."

Quivering imperceptibly Lydia obeyed. She must have paled for her brother commenced to laugh. "Suppose you think I'm about to deal you the hiding of your life. If you weren't such a miserable, bloodless substitute for a female I'd enjoy whaling your bare backside bloody-red."

Abruptly he sat up. His expression altered. —"But I ain't going to because, though you didn't intend so, you did me a good turn— in another few days that piece of luscious bit o' cunt would have frazzled me silly. Besides, once we start catching whales she'd have been in the way."

A sibilant sigh escaped Lydia. —To think she'd once thought to understand this tow-haired giant!

"Point is," Jed was saying, "I've acted so 'cute as to lose around thirty-five thousand dollars Boston money—and me already up to my ass in debt."

The Fourth licked dry lips. "What do you aim doing?"

Wrinkles laddered Jed's bronzed forehead. "Suppose, Dark Sister, we strike a balance? Debit: five men dead, above two weeks' time wasted: six men down with intermittent fever and shy thirty-five thousand, cash money."

"Hold on!" Lydia roused shaking her head. "Hold on. Those pirates didn't find all the specie. What about the cases in the magazine?"

"B'God, I'm still so muzzy I clean forgot. What d'you calculate they're worth?"

She barely heard herself say, brightly, because he'd called her "Dark Sister" again, "No telling the exact amount 'till we count. Still, I'd hazard you've kept maybe five thousand."

"Hope so. We'll make a tally durin' the dog watch." Jed stroked his chin on which its triangular scar remained unusually noticeable. "Before you came in I was figurin' on whether it'd be smarter to make straight for the Pacific or to stop and fish the Brazil Grounds for a piece; season there's nearin' its peak." He slapped his knee. "Yep. The Brazil Grounds it is. With any luck we'll stow down plenty of barrels."

33

Brazil Grounds

While the northeast trade winds drove the *Gladiator* at a smart clip across and out of the doldrums and across the equator, an atmosphere of tension which had permeated the ship evaporated; with no specie known to remain on board plotting came to an end—to the after guard's silent but unfeigned relief.

On fine evenings fiddles squeaked once more. Lige Lovewell pumped a wheezy concertina and João Fuentes strummed his guitar. Other crew members more or less melodiously bawled out an assortment of ballads and chantys: some were jolly; more were sentimental or downright lugubrious; only a few were in any way obscene.

To his considerable surprise Abner Doane discovered he'd a fine tenor voice—when it didn't crack embarrassingly on occasion. He quickly memorized such prime favorites as "Bengal", "William Taylor", "A Young Virgin", "Shearing Day" and "Heathen Dear".

On other occasions Te Ponapa and Heetee sang in Maori and swayed, arms held overhead, while stamping broad feet in a distinctive and captivating tempo.

Best of all, Abner liked "The Coast of Peru".

> *"Come all you young fellows*
> *That's bound after sperm*
> *Come all you young fellows*
> *That's rounded the Horn*
> *Our Capt'n had told us,*
> *And we hope 'twill come true*
> *That they's plenty of sperms to be found*
> *On the coast of Peru.*
>
> *"We've weather'd 'e Horn*
> *And now are for Peru*

We're all of a mind
And endeavor to do.
Our boats is all rigged
And our mastheads all manned.
Our riggin's rove light
And our signals well planned.

"Now the Chief Mate he struck him
And down went the whale!
The Capt'n pulled up
And tried to bend on
But 'e whale begun to vomit
And blood for to spout
And in less'n ten minutes
We had him fin out!"

Both of George Purvis' recruits were Irish and solemnly had signed as "Big Pig Monahan" and "Beefy Pickleman". To the new gunner's outspoken disgust exercises at the guns now had been abandoned in favor of boat drills.

Sudden shouts of "All hands on deck!" "Prepare to lower!" might come at any hour between dawn and dusk.

While the hump of South America loomed on the western horizon an ever-increasing number of sails were sighted and afforded Lydia excuse to draw delicate but accurate representations of passing vessels on the log's margin.

Today she wrote:

'Bark *Gladiator* off Coast of Brazil.
August the 8th, 1831. Latitude obs. 6°.00.00S
Longitude obs. 31°.10.30E
Today sighted and logged the Scottish Brig
Bannockburn, passed 1 mi. to windward on a northerly Tack.'

Twice the bark overtook American whalers bound for the Pacific. Jedediah Paddock, however, made no effort to speak to them, but when a third ship hove into sight flying a "homeward-bound" pennant in addition to the Stars and Stripes he altered course to indulge in a gam.

She proved to be the *Reaper*, a very small full-rigged whaler which, sailing deep-laden, looked badly weatherworn. On closer inspection, she proved dirty as any pigsty. Sag Harbor turned out to

be the *Reaper*'s home port so Nantucketers aboard the *Gladiator*
classified her as an "outlandishman"—only a few cuts better than an
out-and-out foreigner.

The moment the stranger's smoke-darkened Stars and Stripes
was run up Jed ordered topsails backed and his vessel brought into
the wind.

To Abner Doane, clinging to the foreshrouds, this meeting on a
vast and lonely ocean was a sight he'd never quite forget. How
sharply contrasted were the trim and freshly painted *Gladiator* and
the *Reaper*, a slovenly, weed-draped veteran of nearly four years at
sea.

When only fifty yards separated the ships Jed, carrying his brass
speaking trumpet, climbed the mizzen shrouds. Meanwhile, the other
skipper, a stoop-shouldered individual with a great bushy brown
beard clambered onto his rail and steadied himself against the starboard quarter boat's davit. "Ahoy! Who's in command?"

"Cap'n Paddock of Nantucket."

"Which Paddock? Seas are sick of 'em!"

"Jedediah! —And up yer arse with a blunderbuss, you damn'
Long Island herring choker. Who might you be?"

There was no trace of irritation in the Captain's reply—such
pleasantries played a time-honored part of any gam. "Silas Swan."
Then derisively, "Lord! Lord! Fust took you fer a privateer all
trigged out purty-like and carryin' real guns. Surprised ye'd even
speak to a dirty old spouter."

"Maybe, like the singed cat, ye're better than you look. 'Ppears
you've enjoyed a greasy voyage."

A smug grin spread over the Long Islander's brown features.
"Nigh-on eighteen hundred bar'ls and that's a fact." Captain Swan
then offered the age-old gibe. "How'd you leave Nantucket? Sunk
yet?"

Jed laughed, "Reckon 'twill still be above water when Sag Harbor's been forgotten. Think likely we'll find much on the Brazil
Grounds?"

"Likely," Swan drawled, "But 'tis lonesome yonder. Didn't
spy 'ary a tops'l in nigh-on a month."

"Whales about?"

"Enough to fill me up so's I've had to drain some water barr'ls."

"Right or sperm?"

"Sperm."

"What's the easiest course?"

Captain Swan tugged at his ample beard. "Wa-al now, were I standin' in yer boots I'd head for about latitude eighteen degrees and twenty-four degrees longitude. But then I was huntin' the Grounds above a fortnight ago; critters may have shifted. You know how 'tis."

"I know. How fared you doubling the Horn?"

"'Twas rugged, but not over-severe in the Straits."

Under a gust of wind the Long Islander's coat skirts stirred. "Oh, by the bye. Just afore we entered the Straits I spoke a British packet for Liverpool. He'd news."

"Good or bad?"

Lydia, standing at the rail between Mister Winslow and the Third, strained to catch the reply.

"Lime Juicer allowed picaroons and the like lately ha' been plunderin' and burnin' vessels off the Gulf of Penas—that's in Chile. Murdered men, too."

Abner cupped an ear. Criminently! Sometime soon the *Gladiator* would be cruising those waters!

"Britisher 'llowed they found the burnin' wreck of a whaler and rescued survivors. Maybe you won't be sorry ye've sacrificed hold space for them pop guns of yours."

34

Blo-o-ows!

Two days after the *Reaper*'s weathered and smoke-soiled canvas had dipped out of sight the crew were crouched about the deck noisily consuming a midday meal of porpoise scraps, white beans and broken hardtack, when from the maintop gallant hoops—the royal spar having been sent down to permit a wider field of vision—came a long anticipated bellow. "Blo-o-ows!" The other lookouts instantly joined in, "Aye! There she blo-o-ows! Ah-h, blo-o-ows!"

Jedediah Paddock appeared on deck, jaws still working, a food stained napkin fluttering about his neck. Through cupped hands he shouted, "Where away?"

Eyes showing suddenly extra white in his gaunt brown face, John Fast Canoe yelled, "Her two points off lee bow, sar!"

"What is she?"

"Sperm I thinks, ain't sure."

Hurriedly Jed wiped his mouth on his forearm then swarmed up the shrouds to the maintop. "Keep her steady, Mister Coffin! You! Fast Canoe, how far off?"

"Two, mebbe three mile. Her white-waters!"

From the maintop. "Doctor! What's the time?"

"Quarter-past noon, sar!" yelled Goober Pike following quick consultation with the helmsman.

"Whale sound, sar!" called the Nauset.

"Below there! Clear to lower! Hump yerselves!"

Under a hurricane of orders the crew galvanized into action; shouting men, after kicking off shoes and pulling off jackets, raced for their stations while the Mates and boatsteerers unneccesarily checked gear long in readiness for this moment.

Surges of satisfaction swept Jedediah's being. "Brace the yards around!"

Satisfied with the progress of the orderly confusion below Jed then scanned the glinting, Prussian-blue ocean to windward 'till a dark line materialized and a great black head lifted majestically to blow a thirty-foot stream of vapor into the air. But the distance remained too great to determine whether yonder gray-white plume was shooting skywards from the single spouthole of a sperm or the twin spiracles of a bone whale.

"Boat crew men, alow from aloft!"

By now one thing was certain; yonder was swimming a huge bull sperm whale.

"Best take care," grunted the Second to Mister Hayward. "Likely yonder's a loner and meaner than a bitch wolf with pups!"

Even as the First's boat was being swung out came a fresh hail, this time from the foremast head. "Blo-o-ows! *Two* spouts to looward!"

On reaching the deck Jed shouted, "Christ a-mighty! *Where* away?"

"Side by side, mebbee him mile away!" Hectce's high voice screamed.

Jumping off the rail, Jed almost felled Lydia. She was huge-eyed and her now much longer hair was streaming smartly about her features. "Get aloft, quick now. Yonder whales ain't just loafing along. May lose sight of 'em when we lower. Sure of the signals?"

"I can recite 'em backwards!"

"Don't try." He flashed her a grin but his small steel-gray eyes stabbed like knife points. "Just keep ship and look alive. I'm leavin' you the cook, carpenter, Abner and the hands we shipped in Mexico. Think you can make out, Mister? If you ain't certain-sure for Christ's sake say so!"

The Fourth swung easily into the rigging. "You go and catch those whales, Capt'n; no call to fret over what I'll do."

Before scrambling into his boat, already swung free of her cranes and swaying from its davit falls, Jed called. "You! Carpenter! Keep her full and by! What d'you want, Bub?"

"P-please, sir," Abner Doane's freckles were showing dark in his pallor. "Mayn't I go in Mister Winslow's boat?"

"Hell, no! Wait awhile. Right now, son, you ain't strong enough to pull a sheet off a virgin."

Abel Starbuck who, thanks to a sprained back, was serving as foremast lookout reported all three whales swimming to windward, well separated, into a freshening breeze already beginning to snatch silvery spray from the crests of heaving, disorderly rollers.

"Deck there!" he hailed, "First whale's sounded again! Ah-h, there go the others!"

Quickly, all four boats were swung out but with only leaders, Mates and harpooners already aboard. Rowers stood ready to slide down davit falls the instant their craft hit the water.

From his place beside the starboard quarterboat's falls Jed glanced up and recognized Lydia's wiry figure in the main hoops. Already she was scanning the sea through a short telescope.

"All set, Mister Coffin? Mister Winslow? Mister Hayward?"

A ragged chorus of "Aye, aye, sirs."

"Ten dollars to first boat makes fast!"

"Below there! I sight a spla-s-sh!" The Fourth's hail sounded clear but distant above working canvas being braced for full effect. "Smallish whale's swimming upwind."

While his half-naked, shaggy and delighted crew came sliding down, scrambled to their seats and caught up beautifully fashioned sixteen-foot oars, Jedediah rigged his rudder. At the same time another shrill shout came from the lookout. "Sounds! Must have seen us!"

"You! Carpenter! Brace yer lower yards about and ease the jib sheets. Don't risk over-running."

Abner, his eyes round, glanced about, saw that the carpenter had the wheel with George Purvis standing by. Other ship keepers stood grouped to work sheets and braces.

Once the boats had been pulled a short distance from the *Gladiator* crews rested on their oars, listened for reports from the hoops. The Captain's huge voice called, "Look sharp, you lookouts! Sing out when a whale breaks water. Cook! Ease your helm a mite."

During this hiatus the *Gladiator*'s speed gradually diminished but she still was moving right along, broad on the wind.

Jed, balancing in his boat's stern, glared at his ship. "Carpenter! How long's that buster been down?"

"Close on half an hour, sir. Damned if he ain't the original long-winded old sinner! Shall I wear, sir? I'm fearful of forging past."

"No, keep—"

"Blo-o-ows!"

Starbuck screeched, from the foremast. "The big one! Straight ahead, near mile off!"

Jed roared, "Mister Hayward and I will chase him. Mister Coffin and you, Mister Winslow, ride close by the bark till the other two get sighted. Then hurry to 'em. Don't want we should get too spread out."

Abner Doane dashed down to the Captain's cabin and made bold to borrow a spyglass. Criminently! With the greatest moment of his life coming up he sure didn't intend to miss any details. He was just in time for the first time to witness a whale's breaking. A vast, blunt-headed black creature suddenly shot straight up, entirely cleared the sea. It didn't dive gracefully at an angle like a porpoise but hung an eternal instant, enormous flukes flailing, water cascading back onto the surface, then fell flat on its belly causing a report as loud as a big gun's report.

"No use getting all worked up, lad!" grunted Big Pig Monahan. "An that there whale's nigh as big as masthead says, he won't surface again short of an hour."

Abner stared in sudden respect at this powerfully built Irishman, amber-hued teeth revealed in a wide grin. "How'd you know that?" He almost added "sir" but caught himself in time.

The new man pulled a solemn wink. "Faith, for all I've signed on for a gunner, 'twas two years I've spent on the Greenland whale grounds." He eyed the boy sharply then his gaze flickered sidewise. "Don't tell nobody that; I'm mortal fearful of whaleboat work. Me mither's favorite son near got killed when me boat broached and a great hill of a beast chawed it to splinters. Ye've no idea how very frail such a craft is till ye've seen one stove in."

Big Pig was pleased to appear knowledgeable. "Once ye've chased whales awhile ye'll learn 'tis rule o' thumb; a sperm can tarry below 'bout one minute against each foot o' his length. Suppose he's sixty feet long? Why, then he can stay down close to an hour and he often does, account of sperms always feed deep.

"Another thing me lad, when he surfaces again—provided he ain't gallied—disturbed, that is—he'll spout just about sixty times before he sounds again."

Eager to add to a growing store of knowledge, Abner demanded breathlessly. "Suppose he's—gallied?"

"Then he'll sound and swim fast but, before long, he'll surface again to finish his spouting."

35

First Blood

Feeling as if cut in two by pressure of the main hoop against her waist Lydia Paddock watched the boats scatter and oarsmen swiftly settle down to a powerful, body-swinging beat. On this bright and cloudless day one could see every detail of the boats' progress. At this stage harpooners pulled hard on their boat's bow oar, keen to sink their irons at the first possible moment.

Spray spurted rhythmically over the boats' bows; long oars flashed and dipped; flying fish skittered away like tiny silver-blue darts hurled across the wave tops.

Far ahead, the dark bulk of the great whale lazed powerfully along.

Hercules, great muscles bulging with effort, risked a break in rhythm by stealing a quick glance over his shoulder. He grinned ferociously. Jaw locked and jutting, Jedediah Paddock felt blood being driven through him in tingling surges while he chanted, "Stroke! Stroke! Harder! Pull harder! Come on, lads! Third's gaining."

Knowing that sperm whales possessed amazingly acute hearing, the Nantucketer lowered his voice for fear of gallying the quarry so it continued to swim, quite unalarmed, about a quarter-mile ahead and spouting every few minutes.

Now Mister Hayward's boat gradually began to fall astern as the experienced power of the Captain's crew began to tell. From his position at the tiller Jed stole an occasional backward look, noted the *Gladiator* cruising along under easy canvas then saw a jib briefly lowered to signal that the smaller whales had reappeared and were swimming downwind.

Winslow's boat, thanks to his quick hoisting and skilled use of a leg-of-mutton sail, had opened up a long lead on the Second's laboring craft.

Once the bull's broad and barnacled hump showed less than two hundred yards ahead Hercules quit rowing, and left his oar, secured by a thong to be towed alongside; then, turning about, he rubbed his copper earring for luck before standing in the bow left knee braced over the clumsy cleat which was a short, post-like device, carrying a crosspiece, designed to lend purchase to, and steady the harpooner for his dart. Deliberately the big Negro selected a broad-headed, long-shanked, two-flue harpoon from the rack beside him. Deftly he bent on the bight of the whale line then tested the knot securing it to the head's hitches—rings welded into the weapon's head shaft.

Swiftly Jed's boat closed in. The wind had freshened so much that a couple of straining men lost their hats and Jed's shoulder-length tow-colored hair, escaping from beneath a broad-brimmed straw hat, began to lash his face. Normally taciturn at such a moment, he commenced to talk:

"Put yer backs into it! Third's gaining. Don't let him beat us to the dart!"

He watched Te Ponapa, a feather in his shapeless felt hat whipping strongly, leave off rowing and select a harpoon. The Maori's nostrils flared, his tattooed cheeks flattened while he raised a paean of battle. "*Ki te patu nui tohora*! I will slay a great whale! Hue-ee!" His whole aspect was changing; soon he would draw blood! Much blood! Great brooks of blood!

Bronzed body asway, the Maori hefted his weapon and braced when, quite without warning, the monster whale veered to the left thus shortening the distance so much that, barring a miracle, the Third would be first to arrive within darting range.

To make matters worse the Skipper's boat lost more ground for even as he was unshipping his rudder in favor of the steering oar—handier for quick maneuvering at close quarters—his Number Three oarsman caught a crab.

Hercules shook a fist at Te Ponapa, roaring, "Stay clear, man!" Derisively the Maori ran his tongue out all the way before returning his attention to the business at hand.

Number Two in the Captain's boat snatched a glance over his shoulder, gasped, "Christ above! His back's like a ten-acre lot! Bet they's a hundert barrels 'neath all that black skin!"

The boats now were pulling almost abreast, spray flying, to close in on the still unwary monster.

Furious, Jed kept his eyes on the dark hill of blubber boring steadily through the sea just ahead—now he could even count the rhythmic beat of massive, fifteen-foot-long flippers. B'God, he'd made a mistake in picking Tony Amaral and Big Buck for his crew; although strong and experienced they simply didn't carry sufficient beef to bend oars hard enough.

Body jerking to each stroke of the oars, Hercules with muscles beneath his satiny, blue-black skin rippled and bunched got set for a thrust.

"An you don't get fast, Hercules, yo'd better go overboard and never come up!" Flecks of spittle were bursting from the Captain's lips and the triangular scar on his chin blazed scarlet. "Short strokes now! Harder, goddamit! Can't you lubbers see Third's gainin'? Ah-h. Better! Another spout and he's ours."

Mister Hayward cursed ferociously when a panting and bug-eyed greenie in *his* boat caught a crab which cost the Third a full length. In a paroxysm of disappointment Te Ponapa howled like an enraged banshee.

While clamping his knee tighter over the clumsy cleat the big Negro's fist tightened over the wooden shaft supporting his dully gleaming six-foot harpoon. Poised, he watched a mountainous black side speckled with barnacles and trailing tendrils of seaweed loom high, higher, before him. He glimpsed the beast's massive right fluke working and, through flying spray, strained for clear sight of his target—a small space back of the eye and just forward of the flipper's hinge.

Jed quit calling the stroke, barked, "Hold hard 'till we pass his hump! All right, boys, one more stroke. Get ready to back for your lives!"

Eyes gleaming, aware that the Third's boat was closing on the whale's other flank, they all heard him yell. "Stand by your iron, you goddam Kanaka! Dart him! Dart him!"

But Hercules' massive shoulders were bunching as, momentarily he balanced, poising his harpoon a few yards short of that streaming, wall-like black side. Venting a loud "Ha!" the Negro then flung his whole weight behind the weapon and drove its broad head deep, all the way to the hitches, a split second after the whale, making a mournful, sonorous whistling sound, spouted and enveloped the heaving boat in a cloud of humid evil-smelling vapor.

The instant he felt his weapon solidly set Hercules whirled and, while the oarsmen backed frantically, plunged towards the stern to exchange places with the Captain already charging nimbly forward.

The Maori darted an instant later. His blade met momentary resistance then sank smoothly, sucked, it seemed, deep, deep into that vast body. He experienced a flash of sublime ecstasy such as when he pierced a young and unspoiled *vahine.* "*Ka tota au! Opu nui!* Bleed, Big Belly, bleed a river!" Te Ponapa screeched.

"Fast! B'God!" howled the Third before scrambling forward to change places with Te Ponapa.

Suddenly a vast, cyclopean tail shedding sheets of water lifted so high into the sky as to seem to erase the sun. Then its flukes descended making a tremendous, crashing report easily heard aboard the *Gladiator* now wallowing along at a distance of more than three miles.

While lurching forward Jed yelled, "Turn oars! Stern all! Clear your line tubs!" Then, as he reached the bow he bellowed at Mister Hayward's boat. "Keep clear, damn you! Foul my line and I'll surely spill your guts!"

Hercules meanwhile had seized the steering oar and now both boats were scrambling to back out of reach of that devastating tail; they swayed and lurched through clouds of cold spray.

"Peak oars! Peak! Quick!"

Rowers pulled in and crossed their oars above their seats to create a rough trough through which the line might speed forward without risk entangling men or gear from tubs placed aft.

Gaining the bow, Jed grabbed a long chanked lance tipped with a razor-sharp, leaf-shaped steel head. This weapon no more resembled a barbed, broad-headed harpoon—designed only to attach a boat to the prey—than a plow horse looks like a thoroughbred.

Followed a swirl and a rush as the leviathan breached clear of a crater of broken water and started for the horizon with such incredible acceleration that Mister Hayward's line, inexpertly coiled, snarled and snapped with a sharp report; its backlash knocked a couple of oarsmen sprawling onto the bottom.

The Captain's line of best manila cordage, long-laid and thirty-nine threads to the strand, began to hiss through a guide mounted on the stem; equipped with a roller and a chock designed to keep the manila in place it allowed the line to pay out at smoking speed.

Even before the whale took off, Fast Canoe, rowing in Jedediah's boat as after oar, threw two turns about the loggerhead—a short snubbing post set in the stern and designed to slow loss of line.

Like an uncoiling snake the whale line whirred out of the stern tub then began to hum as tension became applied. The whaleboat began to leap across the waves like a sportive porpoise and water came boiling over the bows as a real "Nantucket sleigh ride" commenced.

"Wet that line!" roared Jed. "Steersman! Throw on another hitch! Want me to lose all my line? Bail, the rest of you. Bail like hell!"

The rowers obeyed, began bailing frantically amid half-floating gear. Jed's mouth tightened over the way his line kept on smoking out—at this rate the contents of the midships tub would have to be bent on very soon.

If and when the second line neared its end, Mister Hayward would, if he could, pull alongside and bend his line onto the Captain's bight or Jedediah Paddock would be forced to use a hatchet always kept ready in the bows to cut free.

The line now was wailing like a siren around the loggerhead and escaped so fast that spirals of blue smoke commenced to rise above that sturdy oaken post.

Knee hooked over the clumsy cleat, Jed rasped, "Damn it! *Will* you lubbers water down that line!"

Fast Canoe bailed steadily onto the flashing line while Hercules applied still another turn which somewhat slowed the rate of escape of the half-mile-long manila a moment before its backing started to hiss out of the waist tub.

Braced against his boat's wild yawing and plunging, Jedediah jerked free thongs securing a leather sheath over a second lance's head. Casting an eye aft, he swore feelingly.

"Beelzebub's balls! He's close to taking all my line. Big Buck, get ready the drug! Bail harder!"

But then, to Jed's vast relief the bull took to swimming in a deep semi-circle back towards the Third's boat. Even so, he still was losing line at a dangerous rate.

"Mister Hayward!" he bawled across heaving seas, "Stand by to throw me your bight. Spring hard, do!"

Only a few flakes of manila remained in the waist tub when Hercules noticed that the terrific strain on the line was lessening; it no longer was escaping with such breath-taking speed. He flung up a hand bawling, "Eases! Eases! Him slowin' down."

"Never mind!" Jed yelled at Te Ponapa making ready to throw over the bight of his boat's line. Then to his crew when his boat began to settle a little, "He's coming up. Stand by to haul in."

Feet braced on the thwarts, the rowers, gasping and purple in the face began to heave in line. Deftly, Hercules cinched their gains about the loggerhead while at the same time Number Four coiled the recovered line into the tub by his feet.

"Come up!" Hayward exchanged his lance for a harpoon there being no time to allow Te Ponapa to scramble forward to dart for a second time. "Pull along Cap'n's line. Hard!"

The Third's boat shot forward and pulled abreast almost alongside the Captain's boat which rapidly was slowing its rate of progress. Jedediah Paddock, granite-jawed, barked, "'Vast hauling. Grab oars!"

Awareness that their most perilous moment was at hand gripped both panting crews.

Once a vast dark shape became visible beneath the surface both boat headers got ready. Paddock stood with wickedly slender lance poised for the killing thrust. Scarred features working, Mister Hayward got set to dart his harpoon and make fast again.

Amid a welter of foaming water a massive, blunt head appeared, then the whale started swimming slowly to windward. The breath-taking proportions of the barnacle-grayed monster seemed unbelievable, its immensity rendered the hovering whaleboats as insignificant as two string beans lying near a watermelon. Everyone could see Mister Hayward's first harpoon trailing its broken line over the creature's side.

Abruptly the whale stopped swimming, then, as if confused as to the nature of its danger, it wallowed briefly in the trough of the seas before "milling"—a move feared by any whaleman worth his lay. Standing upright with its whole head out of water, the sperm deliberately looked about in all directions then disappeared beneath the surface.

Jed snapped. "Watch out! Critter may try to jaw-back. Now pull so's I c'n grease my lance before he tries it."

Immediately, the Third ordered his boat forward but paused, waiting to dart till Paddock could use his lance. The Captain surely would have his scalp if the chance of making a thrust which might terminate the battle then and there were spoiled.

"Pull ahead 'till I get a set on him," Jed ordered. "Hercules, a mite to port. Ah-h. Lay forward hard, right on for his fin. So! Way enough. Hold water!"

When the boat's forward progress faltered Jed looked for his target, that space almost midway between the creature's right eye—hardly larger than an ox's—and the leading edge of the gigantic flipper.

"Ha!" Breath exploded from Jedediah's lungs as his lance sank in a full six feet.

Simultaneously Hayward seated a broad-headed harpoon. The Third instantly grabbed up a lance and also drove it deep. Before he was forced to let go he gave his steel a brief but savage churning to increase damage to the quarry's lungs.

"Stern all! Stern all!" yelled both boat headers.

Ponderously, the tortured leviathan lurched up, then down, as if rallying to escape his tormentors; it lifted huge, fan-like flukes sky-high before diving. His plunge created a small maelstrom of crimson, whirling, madly frothing water.

"Hold her so!" cried the Captain as again the line began snaking out of the stern tub. This time, however, the half-inch manila disappeared in a downward direction rather than streaming out nearly horizontal.

Water streaked with dark-red currents heaved and boiled about both boats which, being well fast, waited, oars poised, for the sperm's next maneuver. Balancing in the bows of their boats, both Jed and the Third held new lances half-cocked, hopefully awaiting that moment when the whale would cease sounding and, hurt and vengeful, start back to the surface.

The enormous bulk reappeared and at enormous speed shot straight up until it towered above the wind-whipped blue water higher than a two-storey house. Body almost clear of the water, the quarry stood on end a long instant before crashing back into the ocean with a tremendous report and causing a circle of high waves to shake the whaleboats.

"Haul quick! Get that stray line in!"

Shouts arose when the bull blew; this time the jet was laced by thick skeins of scarlet blood.

"Dart! Dart! Right on for his fin!" The boats dashed in until it became a case of "wood to black skin"—with the prow actually in contact with the sperm's side. Both lances flashed, were driven in right to their sockets.

"Ha! D'ers de red flag fly'n at he nose!" chortled Hercules. Oar blades were reversed in preparation of backing away in a scrambling hurry.

"Yep, his chimney's damn' well afire!" roared Number Four.

"Back! Back for your lives!" thundered Jedediah. "He's goin' to flurry, maybe jaw-back."

Gasping, scarlet with exertion, the oarsmen did their best—well aware that during a leviathan's death flurry their peril was most extreme with the dying whale "fighting at both ends." Flailing fins madly in all directions the monster could, and often did, stove in a boat and mangle its crew. If it "jawed back" the sperm would roll on its side then its enormous jaw, lower mandible studded with huge, conical ivory teeth would snap again and again, crunching anything encountered in its convulsive sweeping.

"Back! Back for Christ's sake," yelled Hayward.

Following so nearly perfect an attack, all should have been over in a few minutes, but the whale, although deeply pierced in three places and spouting clotted blood, suddenly hollowed his back then turned in a half-circle with enormous fins showering cascades of water onto the bobbing, already half-swamped boats. For eternal seconds that great black tail swayed against the bright afternoon sky then slewed above the Captain's boat. Jedediah screamed, "Jump! For your lives!"

In a twinkle a massive fluke smashed the boat into shapeless wreckage, sent screaming men spinning through the air or beat them, half-stunned, below the surface.

Jedediah Paddock was hurtled on high, only to be immediately engulfed in a smother of salty froth. Faintly, yells and howls rising nearby could be heard. He tried to draw breath but only bitter water entered his lungs. Hell! Was this an end to everything? Spasmodically, he struggled, kicked and flailed towards the surface. Finally his head cleared the surface amid a welter of wreckage and he was able to breathe.

Although coughing violently he oriented himself sufficiently to realize that the great bull was sure enough dead. Rolled onto its right side it lay, wallowing sullenly, with a fin sticking straight up like a vast black trysail.

Still dazed, he grabbed a floor board then glimpsed Mister Hayward's boat pulling in his direction; it paused now and then to haul inboard a limp, dripping figure. Next, he sighted the shattered stern section of his boat drifting by a short distance away. Damn! Smashed like that it would be beyond repair, but maybe some of its gear could be salvaged.

The Third's boat came up, lurching through tangles of wreckage, then brown, tattooed hands reached out and hauled him aboard. Alternately cursing and spewing seawater, Jedediah joined others of his crew gasping upon a mad tangle of gear on the floor boards.

"You all right, sir?" inquired Edward Hayward, his battered features betraying apparently genuine concern.

"I'll do! How about—others?" He'd already recognized Hercules and the two American Indians.

"All here savin' the Gee," grunted Tom Haynes testing a great bruise bleeding and streaking his shoulder.

"No sign of Amaral?"

"None yet, sir."

Painfully, Jed, still nauseated by all the seawater he'd swallowed hoisted himself onto a thwart. Looking about, he could see nothing of the two other boats but the *Gladiator* was lying, hove-to, nearly three miles to leeward with a big red-and-black flag rising and falling from the mizzen gaff to tell the other boats—if the Fourth was signalling correctly—that their quarry were rising between them and the ship. Judging by the signals, no attention was being paid to what was taking place to windward; the main thing was to kill as many whales as possible.

Hayward ordered his boat over to the great carcass riding half-awash, then planted a "weft"—a small black flag lashed to a lance—to mark the dead whale's position.

Said Jedediah, viewing oars, line tubs, bailers and other equipment drifting about, "First, we'll salvage gear then hunt for Amaral's body."

Mister Hayward bit off a chew. "How in God's name did you get by losing only one man? Way them flukes came down, sir, I figgered you'd mostly be crushed flatter'n halibuts."

Jed forced a bleak smile. "Devil caring for his own, I reckon."

Wincing against the bite of the main royal hoops Lydia Paddock at long last diverted her attention from the boats to leeward, tiny specks near the horizon; they were sailing back and forth, so must have lost sight of their prey. Likely they'd keep on that way. Since Lydia had shown the black-and-red flag the whales must have taken alarm, sounded and swum off God knew in which direction.

Face aflame in the hot sunlight, she from time to time called down changes in course and to shift the set of sail.

Finally the Fourth returned attention to the boats to windward where all had appeared to be going well. Instantly she experienced agonizing pangs. Lord above! Only *one* boat was working about the carcass of a big dead whale.

Throat muscles tightening, she then made out bits and pieces of wreckage floating to leeward of the prize. *Whose* boat had vanished?

36
Doubts

Tony Amaral's mangled body was discovered over a quarter of a mile away only because it had become a focus for shark fins. By the time the corpse was hauled into Mister Hayward's boat it lacked both legs and an arm; the head had been smashed so violently its blank black eyes were popping out like those of a hanged man.

It was unfortunate that the Fourth should be at the gangway when Mister Hayward's boat came alongside, almost awash under the weight of a double crew and a short and shapeless bundle of blood-stained canvas—a shroud improvised out of the boat's jib.

The body was being hoisted inboard when a lanyard securing the shroud went adrift and spilled Tony Amaral's gory remains at Lydia's feet. The Fourth stood, small hands clenched by her side, staring out to sea and struggling to keep from vomiting.

This hideous lump of flesh was all that remained of Tony of the flashing teeth and lively eyes. Tony, who had owned the sweetest voice on board. Turning aside she buried face between hands and, yielding to a hateful feminine reaction, commenced to sob in silent spasms.

She heard Jed snarl, "You can quit that snivelling, Mister Paddock! Come below. Haynes's arm is badly hurt; needs attention."

Haynes's luck was in. He'd suffered a clean, transverse fracture —no complicating bone splinters broke the fellow's leathery skin. When traction was applied Lydia succeeded in joining the broken ends on her first try. Before long the swollen limb was swathed in cotton batting. Then with Jedediah's help she bound hickory splints into place; altogether, she did a deft, ship-shape job, but reading agony in the hurt man's eyes she became soaked in clammy sweat.

"Thank'ee, ma'am, sir, I—I mean. Ye've lovely light hands," wheezed the patient.

Before returning on deck Jed took a great pull of Old Medford, then passed the bottle. "Have some, Lyddie. You've earned it. Mister Winslow! Steer straight for the carcass; want it alongside in a hurry. Glass is droppin' faster'n I like."

To Lydia's astonishment, no one, with exception of the cabin boy, appeared affected by Amaral's death. While the remains were being stitched into a worn-out staysail there was no comment. Once a ballast stone had been sewn into one end of the tragically short canvas cylinder it was balanced on a plank thrust over the larboard rail. Without saying so everyone hoped the body would sink fast enough to cheat sharks which appeared from nowhere to circle expectantly about the bark.

The sun's lower rim hovered on the horizon as Jedediah Paddock removed a crumpled felt hat and in a flat, unemotional tone read an abbreviated burial service. This done, the plank's inboard end was raised. Abner gulped, felt shivers flash through him like icy needles as, smoothly, the body slid off into the deep. A general sigh arose. Haynes was the only one to wet an eye. The Stars and Stripes to a gentle creaking was hoisted to full mast.

Gruffly, Jed remarked, "Reckon we'd all feel better if we splice the main brace."

Her easy canvas—topsails and gallants—glowing in the sunset the *Gladiator* plowed leisurely towards the black weft flapping above that vast carcass some two miles away. Hands were busy lowering and rigging the cutting stage outside the gangway. The carpenter's grindstone began to whine and screech putting fine edge to blubber spades and horsing knives.

At the mainmast's head men, under Mister Winslow's direction, set about busy rigging ponderous sheave blocks and tackle to control a huge cast-iron blubber hook which, attached to a travelling black, could accommodate a manila cable often eight inches in circumference.

Thought Abner, Lordy! were any creatures more essentially repulsive than those sharks cutting swift circles about Mister Coffin's boat, which recently lowered, laboriously was towing the dead whale up to the *Gladiator*'s starboard beam.

Once the carcass had been towed alongside, it was secured to the bark by a fluke chain belted about the small of its tail to lie, heaving leadenly beneath the cutting stage.

"For a starter," observed Mister Hayward squirting a brown stream over the rail, "this is a damn' greasy-looking sperm."

Mister Winslow nodded. "Aye. Might go nigh on ninety barrels, shouldn't wonder."

"Stand by to splice 'e main brace!" yelled Goober.

Although greenies in the crew looked exhausted and glum, old hands eagerly lined up at the galley door to draw mugs of well-watered rum.

With the glass holding steady after falling all afternoon, and with so many of his crew new to the intricate business of cutting-in, Jedediah decided to wait for dawn. An announcement to that effect was greeted with a wholehearted cheer.

Pretty soon a fiddle commenced to squeak forward of the barrel windlass whose cable now held the carcass bumping heavily alongside.

A voice, neither as true nor as rich as Tony Amaral's, raised a ballad in which Abner joined softly.

> *"Farewell to a mate, a right fine lad*
> *Who made us sing, now makes us sad*
> *Like us from home he's gone adrift*
> *And without ballast learns to shift*
> *And steer against the tides so dark and mad.*
>
> *"Farewell once more*
> *A rude tough tar*
> *Requests the parting tribute of a tear*
> *And should my bark on this voyage be lost*
> *We hope in Heaven to meet at last."*

Jed tramped down to his cabin with his right side aching so badly he wondered if perhaps he'd once again cracked a rib. He found Lydia, looking mighty solemn, seated at his desk to complete the day's entry in the log. Over her shoulder he saw she'd sketched skillfully enough, on the margin, a funeral urn decorated with a neat T.A. Right now her pen was enclosing it in a wreath of weeping willows.

Without looking up, Lydia queried, "How old would you say Tony was?"

"Maybe twenty, twenty-five—hard to tell about Gees. They age quick."

Lips compressed, she wrote below the urn: 'A.B. Tony Amaral killed by a whale, August 15, 1831. Aged twenty-two years. RIP.' She then sanded her design and fetched a deep sigh.

Jed came to rest a hand on her shoulder, said gently, "Don't take on so hard, Dark Sister. Maybe you haven't heard, but whaling's a hard and perilous way to earn one's bread. There'll be more men die before we next raise Cuttyhunk. Come, we'd better sample some Medford."

The young woman's slanted dark eyes wavered upwards. "I— I guess I don't feel like drinking."

"Maybe you don't, Lyddie, but you're going to—orders. It'll be a hard day tomorrow and uglier than you've any notion."

37
Cutting-in

For some reason the ribs injured last winter began to ache in sympathy with his latest hurt so Captain Paddock's sleep proved fitful and unrestful. Towards dawn he was tempted to draw on a slender supply of laudanum in his medicine chest but decided not to; before this cruise ended someone would need such relief a sight more than he did at present.

He sought the deck and cast a morose nod to Mister Coffin whose watch it was, then stiffly went over to survey the barnacle-studded carcass tethered, almost awash, along the *Gladiator*'s starboard beam.

It came as a measure of consolation that, in exchange for a boat smashed beyond hope of repair, the largest whale he'd seen in a very long time had been taken.

Of Mister Coffin he demanded, "How many barrels d'you figger he'll try?"

"Wa-al," came the familiar nasal twang, "I'd hazard we ought to stow near eighty barrels."

"What! Only eighty? Looks closer to a hundred."

The Second's whisker-framed features assumed a lugubrious expression. "Mebbee. Provided we're able to try-down the whole of him. Never did see so damn' many sharks about. What they'll do once we start cutting and blood flows only God knows how much they'll cheat us of."

"Mister Coffin," Jed's manner brisked. "Come sun-up I'll want all hands on deck, the blubber hook rigged and hoisting tackle set and ready."

When the eastern sky showed a few streaks of color the watch below appeared spitting, coughing and knuckling red-rimmed eyes to line up. The temperature continuing mild, all were wearing a minimum of their very raggedest clothes; the old hands knew what they were in for, greenies followed suit.

"Mister" Paddock now took over, ordered the setting of jibs, staysails and spanker to start the *Gladiator* sailing slowly, close on the wind.

Meanwhile a folding cutting stage—a long and narrow platform some fifteen feet in length and composed of three planks and a hand-rail—was lowered opposite the gangway.

"Haul on that starboard guy a bit more." Mister Winslow, who as Chief Mate, would be in charge of cutting-in. "Don't want the stage bunged up first time it's used." He ran his eye over the men. "Who's for overboard? Step forward!"

From veterans who volunteered, with the reward for such hazardous duty strongly in mind, the First selected the brawny Irishman called Bert Harrington. He grinned and joshed while a "monkey rope" or lifeline was secured about his waist.

Carrying freshly honed blubber spades, Mister Winslow and Mister Coffin, both wearing safety ropes, then stepped nimbly out onto the sharply swaying cutting stage and set to work.

Wide-eyed greenies, the cabin boy and the Fourth—clad in her oldest shirt and pants she'd allowed her lengthening hair to escape unrestrained from under a wide straw hat purchased in Mexico —looked on while the mates carved a "U" shaped pattern around the base of the whale's upright fin. Again and again razor-sharp blades sank in with surprising ease. Boatsteerers, working from the rail, assisted in the work. Soon the squarish "U" shaped incision was completed, clearly visible in the dull black skin which, as Abner had heard, quite without belief, really was so thin it could easily be scraped off with a fingernail.

Both carcass and ship barely "cutting to windward" rolled heavily from time to time and on occasion the dead leviathan actually brushed the under side of the cutting stage which, on its outward sides was equipped with collapsible handrails to protect the cutters.

Once the blubber coat began to be separated from flesh beneath, dark-red serpentine patterns of blood began to coil away from the incision and stain the restless water; swarming sharks seemed to go mad. Snapping and writhing, they often slithered high up on the carcass. Every now and then the Mates on the stage and boatsteerers, quit cutting to lean far out over the side and slash and stab at those hideous gray shapes. When they found a mark the wounded shark would turn aside, streaming blood to be quickly torn to shreds by its fellows.

After two holes had been cut near the middle of the "U" the Second, greasy, reddish-gray hair streaming in wild disorder, peered up from the stage, ordered quietly, "Hook over!"

Immediately, Jedediah ordered, "Windlass men! Lower away and don't you dare tangle those damn' falls."

While a ponderous blubber hook, controlled by leadlines, commenced to be lowered, Harrington jumped down onto the carcass about which sharks continued to make the sea boil. Steadied by his monkey rope, the Irishman stood swaying, waiting to guide the descending hook which easily could have brained him. The moment became critical because the vast bulk beneath him kept shifting and rolling.

From on deck the Third yelled, "Get ready, Harrington! Only small waves coming, now's your chance!"

At his first try Harrington missed passing the hook through a hole in the blubber because it hadn't been lowered quite far enough and at the same time the carcass twisted under a low swell.

On deck the Skipper looked about. "Where's the doctor? Tell that damn' nigger to raise a chanty the minute hook's seated."

Eight men stood grouped about the great barrel windlass intently gripping bars they'd use to operate it.

Came a sudden cry from the cutting stage, "Hook's in!"

"Sure the hook's taken well?" Hayward wanted to know.

The First told him, "Yep! Tighter'n a duck's foot in the mud!"

Immediately Jed rasped, "Heave on that windlass! Heave hard, you ham-handed bastards!"

Immediately the cutting falls stiffened into rigidity and the windlass' pawls started *clack-clacking*.

"Damn it, Goober, raise that chanty!"

The cook commenced to bawl out "Captain Bunker" accentuating the rhythm on a barrel head while the top of the first blanket of pearly-gray blubber, roughly four feet in width, commenced to be ripped from the carcass.

> *"De waist boat went down an'*
> *Of course got de start,*
> *Lay me on! Cap'n Bunker,*
> *I'm hell on de dart.*

"Now bend to de oars boys,
An' make dat boat fly,
An' mind just one t'ing now,
Keep clear of de eye."

Quickly Abner grasped how the operation of stripping off a blubber blanket was accomplished—it was absurdly like peeling an apple in a single spiral to be cut off at a desired length. Thus the whale was kept revolving slowly while its blubber continued to be stripped off.

Under the great weight of the blanket stripped free of the carcass the ship gradually heeled to starboard and its mighty mainmast began to creak and protest. The windlass, driven by panting, sweat-drenched men, inexorably clacked on and on.

Copious rivulets of blood dyed the water as more flesh became exposed offering a maddening attraction for frantic, ravening sharks.

The Mates, relieved from time to time by boatsteerers, plied often-replaced blubber spades to continue the long "scarf" or incision in a blubber blanket averaging six inches to a foot in thickness. Once the blubber hook, lifting the first strip, had risen to a point just below the main crosstrees to which the cutting tackle had been rigged, Jedediah sang out, "Way enough!" The windlass at once stopped and left the lower part of the suspended blubber blanket slatting ponderously against the gangway.

At this point Hercules and Te Ponapa hacked two holes in what presently would serve as the top of a second blanket piece. The end of a length of chain was passed between these holes and linked to a second blubber hook to which it was attached; immediately its falls tightened.

Te Ponapa, tattooed face and torso blood-smeared, used a boarding knife as large as a small cutlass to cut the original blanket piece free of the newly attached section.

"Sway away!" ordered Jed, for the moment forgetting the pain that kept gnawing at his side. Now that the upper blanket piece was swinging free, men working around the gangway scattered in a big hurry.

An incautious fellow could get knocked overboard, senseless, or crushed to death against the bulwarks or deck gear, or be crippled for life should he get in the way of that huge hunk of blubber now starting to swing like a monstrous pendulum.

From her station in the fore-gallant hoops, Lydia watched the initial blanket piece being lowered with the aid of guide lines through the main hatch into the blubber room just below; there, it would be hacked into "horse pieces" then sliced into even smaller "bibles"—chunks small enough to be easily forked into the *Gladiator*'s bubbling try-pots.

Long since the "goose pen"—a deep pan set below the oven fires to keep the deck from catching fire—had been filled and fires of pitch-pine kindled; streamers of pungent black smoke were pouring furiously through the try-works' two squat chimneys. A pair of four-barrel cast-iron try-pots were beginning to give off billows of steam.

By noon the whale's thick, oleaginous and very close-fibered covering of blubber largely had been stripped off leaving the huge, red-and-pink carcass bereft of flippers to ride alongside fully exposed to the sharks' redoubled fury. By the time that prime delicacy, the tongue, had been hacked out along with great chunks of fresh meat for the crew, the deck was running with grease, water and blood rendering it tricky for a man to keep his footing during an unexpected pitch or roll. By now the entire crew, with the exception of the Fourth, the cook, the cooper and the cabin boy were blood-spattered, their ragged garments dripping sweat and oil.

Towards midday the blubber hunters' attention became absorbed by the difficult task of severing that vast blunt head from the rest of the whale, an operation directed by the grizzled veteran, John Folger.

Selecting a newly honed spade, he dropped onto the carcass and cut through several feet of flesh, coarse-fibered muscles, rope-like tendons and hose-thick blood vessels until vertebra attaching skull to spine was reached.

Dashing sweat from his forehead and panting heavily, he called up to Te Ponapa, "Take over, I'm pooped!"

The Maori, grunting delightedly over such quantities of freely coursing gore, expertly severed the last tendons. Then, on noticing Jedediah looking down at him, he did a curious thing. He bent, wetted his hand in blood, then snapped it at the ship's side to sketch a splatter of drops in Jed's direction. At the same time he broke into deep laughter. "Hail to thee, my Brother! We'll draw richer stuff soon, eh?"

The detached head rolled slowly over until its lower jaw was uppermost. The crew treated this part of the head with special care for, since time immemorial, a sperm's ivory belonged to them. During idle hours the big, conical teeth would be engraved or carved into scrimshaw work, into sometimes artistic, but generally practical articles such as piecrust foggers, busks to support some sweetheart's bosom, paper knives, ditty boxes, buttons and a host of other semiuseful items.

Abner Doane gaped in awe on viewing that long rank of huge white teeth exposed when the wishbone-shaped jaw was hoisted clear and, dripping cascades of bloody water, swung inboard amid a chorus of whining creaks and protests from various blocks and tackles. He was further amazed to discover that sperm whales had no teeth at all in their upper jaw.

Next, the tail was amputated and those gigantic flukes which had killed Amaral were cut away at the "small'—the tail's narrowest point.

Morosely, Jedediah Paddock watched the tail's shank join the lower jaw on the *Gladiator*'s encumbered and dangerously slippery deck. There'd have to be one hell of a lot more of these brought aboard if Messrs. Doane, Welch & Peabody were to be compensated —more still, if the owners were to receive a half-decent return on their investment. Hell! How could his grand plans have gone so incredibly far astray? Still, this cruise wasn't over. Not by a damn sight.

Just before the mangled remains were cast adrift a banquet for sharks and swooping, screaming seabirds—the carcass was turned belly-up and then disemboweled.

"Holy Mither!" chortled Big Pig. "And will yez look at the cock on the brute! 'Tis easy ten-foot long."

"Don't look jealous, ye dirty Roman Catholic harp," boomed Harrington, who was one himself. "Just thank the Saints you don't have to carry one 'round the size o' that!"

A search of the entrails was begun for ambergris, that exceedingly precious ingredient in expensive perfumes. Not for many years would it become known that this rare, mysterious, greasy and unattractive substance was secreted to coat-over and heal wounds scored in a sperm's intestines through passage of innumerable fearfully sharp squid and cuttlefish bones—creatures on which this species fed almost exclusively. Lacking a quick secretion of soothing ambergris, a whale often weakened and died.

To the profane disappointment of all hands no trace of the precious stuff came to light, search as they would.

Once the last of the blubber had been lowered through the main hatch nightmarish figures, working by globe lanterns, set to work in the blubber room busily slicing blankets into "horse pieces"—strips about four feet long by two wide. Preparations also were made for the important task of bailing out the "case" or bulging brow of the cetacean. First the great head was windlassed upwards until it bumped, half-suspended and half-awash, against the gangway where it became divided into "junk"—pieces which consisted of skull and lower part of the head—and the "case", that huge, wedge-shaped mass of flesh forming the massive forehead in which was stored spermaceti—a highly concentrated oily pulp.

Abner, who'd been busy collecting scraps of flesh for dinner paused long enough to ask Big Buck, "What're they about?"

"Why, young sar, we about to bail spermaceti out of 'e case."

"Spermaceti?"

The Indian's bright little black eyes narrowed. "Whale keep dat stuff in big cave in head for when food get scarce. Spermaceti make very finest oil."

"How much can he carry in there?"

The Nauset grunted, hitched up sagging breeches. "We in luck we find mebbee thirtee barrel."

The cutting stage having been hoisted out of the way, two men, Beefy Pickleman and Sun-in-the-Eyes, oblivious to, or possibly relishing the presence of straight-backed and wide-eyed Lydia Paddock stripped, naked and grinning. Next, armed with broadheaded axes then leaped onto the head and set about hacking a hole in the forehead surging lazily in seas which, providentially, were remaining moderate.

John Folger, seated on the rail and enjoying a brief rest was joined by Abner and Billy Big Buck. Together they watched a gang haul forward a number of tubs designed to receive spermaceti as it was bailed out of the case and passed, bucket brigade style, over the rail.

Jedediah's angular and hatchet-faced Second remarked, "Naow, if yonder case was smaller, which I'm pleased it ain't, we'd swing her right on deck and work easier, but as it is, there's small use risking a sprung mainmast or straining the cutting falls. You mightn't think so, but that there case likely weighs close on twenty tons."

Meanwhile, smoke and flames fed by scraps of blubber were roaring out of the two, four-sided bronze chimneys rising above the try-works, whirling upwards it was beginning to blacken staysails and topsails. Other clouds eddied about the oily, blood-splotched deck and stung the workers' eyes.

The bailers, looking as if they were at work in the heart of a vast honeycomb, now were working, waist-deep, in the great red hole hacked into the case; they scooped full and passed upwards bucket after dripping bucket of spermaceti, a fatty, gelatinous substance which glistened pearly-white and quivered like jelly while being hoisted on deck by means of a lanyard. The slopping receptacle then passed from hand to hand until blobs of spermaceti could be dumped into a rank of waiting tubs. Scupper vents had been stoppered lest even a little of this precious matter escape overboard. The men emitted grunts of satisfaction; so generous a take of spermaceti as this certainly must show up when lays came to be calculated.

The lowering sun didn't look overly healthy during its descent into a bank of woolly, copper-yellow clouds so when the chore was completed everyone looked pleased as that many cats inadvertently locked in a creamery. Mister Coffin estimated, and Winslow agreed with him, that not less than thirty barrels of pure spermaceti oil would result once the matter had been boiled down and poured, hissing-hot, into cooling vats below ready and able to accommodate up to fifty barrels.

Ordinary blubber, diced into books, already was beginning to decompose and give off an insufferable stench but it would have to wait its turn until after all the spermaceti had being forked into the seething try-pots.

If Lydia fancied she'd already encountered the vilest possible sights and smells, she promptly became disabused. Her every sense was outraged, sight, hearing and smell: nauseating odors of stale blood and boiling blubber; bawled orders, loud, perpetually obscene talk; dirty, unlovely, foul-smelling fellow humans everywhere. Even Jed was looking, talking and acting like a savage, openly revelling in this ghastly scene.

Tried-out blubber rind was being fed so fast into the try-works bricked furnaces that cloudlets of silvery steam from the goose pen mingled with the try-smoke.

Gradually the stench became so indescribable that Lydia, head swimming, held her nose and, gagging, sought the windward rail but on the way slipped on slime and fell so hard onto her lean bottom that bright little stars revolved crazily about her eyeballs and for a moment she nearly lost consciousness.

Never, in her most imaginative mood, had she dreamed that the taking and trying-out of a whale could be so utterly revolting. Rallying to an innate stubborn streak, she thought numbly: and to think of all I plotted and *did* just in order that I might sail on the *Gladiator!* Well, I've had my way, so, God willing, nobody's ever going to suspect, let alone make me admit my mistake.

All night long watches alternated every six hours. The weather continued so unusually fine old hands muttered a tempest must be brewing. Everyone hoped this wouldn't be so. Suppose a whale raised and got killed with a heavy sea running and it came time to cut-in and try-out? Then was when men suffered broken limbs or got knocked overboard to get torn to shreds by tirelessly patrolling sharks.

When night fell great, curling flames continued to writhe out of the chimneys like flaming serpents. Their glare colored toiling men, lower sails and rigging a diabolical red-bronze. At the same time it powdered deck houses, boats, gear and canvas with a coat of fine black soot which even laborious scrubbing and repainting never could quite remove.

Driven frantic by the terrible heat and smoke generated by the try-fires huge, loathsome, brown-black cockroaches swarmed into the fo'c's'le, into the steerage and even into the main cabin. Increasing numbers of brown rats, tempted by heaps of rapidly decomposing blubber grew bold, deserted their habitual haunts.

In these latitudes, close to the equator, the heat of the try-fires finally became so intense no one could sleep below and men snored about the malodorous deck in awkward and unnatural attitudes suggestive of corpses on a stricken battlefield.

During the course of the night seething oil was ladled out and conveyed to capacious tanks below decks, there to remain until sufficiently cooled to be poured into barrels marked with a big white "S" for ordinary sperm oil, or "S.P." for refined spermaceti.

By dawn of the next day blubber waiting for the try-pots really began to rot, giving off a nauseous, sickish-sweet stench which sometimes would linger in a man's nostrils for days on end. Only the American Indian and Maori members of the crew seemed oblivious to it.

Like everything else the trying-out process came to an end and all hands felt mightily cheered to learn that seventy barrels of ordinary oil either lay gurgling in casks hastily assembled by the cooper, or still were cooling out. These, plus thirty-one barrels of pure spermaceti already stowed down brought the take to a total of ninety-one barrels from a single whale!

That night Lydia in India ink sketched a sperm whale's silhouette on the log's margin taking care to leave a blank white circle in the center of the great blunt head. On this she entered the numerals "91".

John Folger while wiping grease from straggly chin whiskers, shook his head, drawling, "I allow ninety-one bar'ls *do* make a fine start, but 'tain't likely we'll come across many more critters size of this."

38
Off Soundings

The weather grew colder and though it continued to threaten nothing worse than a half-gale developed so it proved relatively easy to cleanse the bark and fit out one of the two spare boats as replacement for the Captain's craft.

The weather continued moderate. A couple of days later lookouts found no trouble in sighting a distant pod of sperms. For some reason these cetaceans proved so uncommonly unwary that the bark's four boats in rapid succession got fast to different whales.

Mister Coffin killed a cow and her calf so before darkness fell five carcasses lay rafted alongside—the half-grown calf, two large cows and a pair of sizable bulls. Together they yielded almost three hundred barrels.

The only enjoyable reaction Lydia experienced from this exceptional haul—to her disgust she still couldn't stomach the ghastly sights and smells of cutting-in and trying blubber—lay in sketching five black silhouettes on the log's margin.

Later in the week for the first time she had occasion to draw the conventional symbol for a whale struck but lost: this was an upright set of flukes with a broken line trailing from a harpoon.

During the following weeks the Fourth saw little of her brother by remaining as far removed from the foul and sanguinary business as duty permitted.

The quality of Goober Pike's cooking deteriorated, he being forced to work endless hours feeding weary but always ravenous try-crews. Abner Doane, learning to handle a ladle with the best also served as dicer and general utility hand, stumbled about so exhausted as to appear drunk. He looked twice his age.

Lydia felt these days as harassed and uncertain as the master of a ship being driven relentlessly onto an uncharted lee shore. So many cherished dreams were evaporating.

She couldn't have foreseen how many ugly injuries would have to be dressed and disgusting illnesses treated. Everywhere, it seemed, parts of butchered carcasses lay about. Blood, blood and more blood! Brutality, filth and the try-pots' never-ending stench. No privacy whatever and little fresh water remained available for ablutions. Voracious sharks and barracudas continually alongside. Rats, roaches, fleas and lice everywhere. Try as she would, Lydia never could succeed in ridding herself of body vermin.

Naturally she manufactured excuses to seek the clean and private haven of the hoops. Up there she could let out the laces of the vest against increasingly sensitive breasts straining so painfully she'd soon have to fashion a bigger cinch. Unwelcome changes were taking place in her amidships; what once had been a minor inconvenience every twenty-eight days now was becoming an ordeal replete with agonizing cramps, swellings and hemorrhages so copious they were difficult and embarrassing to cope with.

At the same time Lydia was mystified that, subconsciously, she should have begun to compare the manly attributes of crew members who, stark naked, bailed a case or hosed down after a day's labor.

She'd come to the conclusion that, aside from her brother, the most powerful and best-proportioned men aboard were Te Ponapa and Bert Harrington; below the belt, however, they were nothing compared to Beefy Pickleman and Hercules. Aware of such observations her cheeks would grow hot and her breathing quickened; successive small shivers rippled not unpleasantly from her shoulders to her fingertips and down into her loins. Angrily, she would try to think of other matters—her duties for example.

One possibility gnawed ceaselessly at her peace of mind and hitherto well-ordered outlook on life. Were these changes altogether unperceived? Why had certain of the ship's company recently begun diffidently to offer "Mister" Paddock small pleasantries and courtesies customarily reserved to her sex?

The weather continuing warm, sunburned hands went about even after nightfall clad in loose-fitting trousers or breeches. But the officers, following some sort of tacit agreement, wore shirts in various degrees of disintegration. Even they went barefoot.

Tonight she fancied she'd detected a speculative gleam in Bert Harrington's eye when he appeared to stand his trick at the wheel.

Te Ponapa's attitude also seemed to be undergoing a change.

Quite often when she was standing a night watch the hulking Maori had taken to manufacturing trivial excuses just to loiter nearby. Could he have sensed that she no longer considered him just a handsome savage?

Other members of the crew when Jed was below furtively touched headgear as if—why—as if she were only a good-looking female. Perhaps this was because, for some time, she'd quit snipping her hair.

One day she appropriated a bundle of garments left by Estrellita. Examination disclosed a bolero jacket of glossy black velvet, a generously ruffled blouse of white silk, several bright-yellow petticoats and a sweat-marked linen undershift.

October faded into November. After a fortnight passed without a spout being sighted Jedediah Paddock ordered the *Gladiator* put onto a southwesterly course. The Brazil Grounds had yielded about all that could be expected—and then some; above five hundred barrels of sperm and spermaceti lay below, well-secured by chocks, cuntlines and lashings.

Following a series of restless nights Jed concluded his best chance of making good at least part of the pirated silver lay in selling oil to homeward bound vessels which, out beyond their time, hadn't stowed down sufficient barrels to satisfy crew or shareholders.

Since boyhood he'd heard plenty about unlucky ships—the whaler *Franklin*, for example. She'd cruised over four years only to come home carrying less than one hundred barrels!

Full payment wasn't to be expected; part would be paid in supplies like cordage or shooks to make new barrels. Some buyer's agent would sell the *Gladiator*'s oil on commission. The results then should be forwarded to Messrs. Doane, Welch & Peabody.

Doane. The name lingered. He'd taken quite a fancy to his energetic, cheerful and intelligent cabin boy. What could have happened to the lad's father who'd sailed on the *Arabella*, reportedly lost with all hands?

Had Sylvanus Doane drowned or had he, like so many others, been cast away to survive forgotten on some remote island? Though he never said so, it seemed more likely that Mr. Doane's younger brother long ago had been killed and devoured by cannibals.

Jed settled back in his armchair, joined tattooed hands under

his chin and absentmindedly cracked their joints. For sure it was piti-
ful to hear young Abner's eager questions whenever a gam took
place: hadn't anyone heard of Sylvanus Doane from Boston? The
cabin boy remained so pathetically expectant of encouraging news.

Why such dogged persistence? Sylvanus must have departed on
his last voyage long before his son could have come really to know
him. Perhaps it was the lad's mother who kept fanning fading
embers of hope?

Through force of habit the *Gladiator*'s Master cast an upward
glance to satisfy himself that the course indicated on the dry compass
was correct. Hum. Abner was shaping up considerably better than
anticipated; never had he had a lad aboard so keen to learn everything
about navigation and the business of taking whales.

Thank the Lord the youth's complexion was clearing up and
nowadays he was moving like a man instead of lurching about like a
splay-footed puppy. Moreover, his self-confidence seemed to increase
with his height.

The rudder post was *bump-bumping* more noisily against its
pintles for with sundown the wind had stiffened until a full gale was
whistling through the rigging.

Now that he'd decided on heading for the Straits of Magellan
Jed felt better pleased with his prospects—but only a little; memories
of the fiasco in Vera Cruz still rankled.

Wouldn't it be fine if he could double the Cape in a hurry, reach
the coast of Chile and start hunting the Off Shore Grounds without
undue loss of time, men and gear? Before making for the Grounds he
reckoned he'd better water and revictual at the Galapagos, lying
astride the equator. Then, if his recent luck held, he might come
across a concentration of sperm.

He continued to muse. Well, there'd been at least one good result of the *Veraganza*'s interception; with the loss of the specie in-
centive to murder and mutiny had been removed.

Bitterly, he reflected that conservatives in New Bedford possibly
might have been right; maybe he *had* been ill-advised to arm his
vessel—at least so weakly. Um. So far his costly little battery had
proved inadequate while its presence robbed him of storage space and
had wasted valuable time in futile gun drills.

Still, all-in-all, things hadn't gone too badly now that he'd around five hundred barrels already in the hold and with *Gladiator* not yet out five months. The tip of his tongue wetted sun-cracked lips; Estrellita. Lordy, Lord! Would he ever again experience the likes of her?

A few evenings later someone knocked. He nearly cracked his chair so hard did he rear back when the white-painted door swung open to disclose Lydia Paddock Roach clad in a salt-stained pea jacket down the front of which frothed a lace-trimmed white shirt. The Fourth also was wearing a yellow skirt rendered bouffant by several petticoats and on her small and narrow feet were high-heeled slippers adorned with silver buckles.

Lydia hesitated, smiling uncertainly. Her olive cheeks glowed and her faintly slanted black eyes sparkled brighter than he'd ever seen. Going red in the face he saw she'd washed and combed her dark hair which by now had grown long enough to brush her shoulders; whatever she might be wearing beneath that ruffled shirt certainly wasn't her canvas vest.

"Evening, sir. I've come to complete today's entry in the log," she announced in a tremulous voice. Quickly she closed the door and made for the chart table.

Jed surged to his feet growling, "By the blazing balls of Beelzebub! What in hell's the meaning of this—this silly masquerade?"

Lydia seated herself and, smiling faintly, selected a pen. "Dear Brother, need I remind you that officers, off-duty, are allowed to dress as they please?"

Utterly flabbergasted yet not wholly outraged at her transformation, Jed burst out, "You—you shameless baggage!" He towered over her. "Clear out of here this minute and get rid of those—those female garments! You look silly. What ails you, you crazy goose?"

Lydia remained where she sat, gripping her chair's arms so tight her knuckles shone ivory. "*Nothing* ails me, Jedediah," she announced evenly. "It's only I've discovered that despite my notions to the contrary, I'm a female and intend to remain one."

"—Not at this late date, you don't!" Nostrils flaring, he wagged a blunt finger under her nose. "You signed on as a man, able and willing to do a man's work, so by God, you'll go on acting and dressing as such. Understand?"

Under the menace in her brother's steel-gray eyes Lydia recoiled. "But, but, Jedediah, what does it matter how I dress off-duty so long as I well and truly discharge my duties; you'll have to admit you've no honest fault in that direction. Where's the harm?"

"Harm? HARM? Why, you silly ninny, minute the hands spy you switching your rump about in a female rig there'll be packets of trouble. I won't have it! You've no notion of what can happen when a man who ain't laid an eye, let alone a hand, on a female in months takes a notion to, well—to get friendly. I *do!* I've been one."

Jet eyes narrowing, the seated girl glared at the flaming, contorted face above. "Harken to me, Jedediah Paddock. You may fancy yourself God Almighty aboard this ship but there is a limit to your authority. I'll not allow you to tell me what to wear off-duty." She actually tossed her head as she'd seen schoolmates do. "When it pleases me to dress like a—a female, I will!"

Breathing hard, Jed stepped back, an evil grin spreading over his features. "Ye're wrong there! Now, you take off those fooferaws right now. I'll lend you a cloak or, if I have to, I'll strip 'em off myself. Then, you hard-headed brat, I'll deal you a spanking you earned off Yucatán!"

"*I won't!*" She shook her head so violently shining, blue-black hair waved like a wind-tossed gonfalon. "You wouldn't dare!"

"Wouldn't I? Well, let's find out." He jerked her to her feet, a massive arm clamped her little body to him, pinioning her arms at her sides. Then his free hand fumbled for and jerked undone ties securing the skirt and a pair of petticoats beneath.

Whenever the *Gladiator* rolled they swayed and staggered back and forth across the cabin as in grotesque dance steps. Lydia struggled furiously, futilely, dark features twisted into an outraged grimace all the while hissing forecastle obscenities Jed had no idea she'd picked up.

Before she knew it the last petticoat and her ultimate undergarment went sailing across the cabin whereupon Jed laughing uproariously lifted his sister clear of the deck and carried her kicking and squealing to his sea bed. He seated himself on it then, with irresistible strength swung her across his lap and imprisoned with bare bottom up, and legs caught between his knees.

Momentarily a temptation seized him but he shook off the appalling impulse and pinning Lydia by the neck and ignoring frantic flailing of legs to deliver a succession of smacking blows on those quivering pink-and-white mounds; swiftly these went red then crimson. Suffering in more ways than one, the Fourth submitted but never cried out or begged for mercy.

Finally, puffing like a grampus, Jedediah put her on her feet, snatched a cloak from his closet and wound it about his half-nude sister. "Now, Mister Paddock, pick up those clothes and don't you dare ever to try wearin' such again aboard this vessel.

The sheer venom in the dishevelled girl's swimming eyes was something to behold—and to remember with caution.

Pulling the cloak tighter about her, Lydia at last commenced to utter dry, racking sobs. "Some d-day, Jedediah Paddock, thee—thee will p-pay *dear* for this! See if thee don't!"

39

Full Moon off Staten Island I

Off Argentina's bleak and forbidding southeastern coast the *Gladiator* encountered a succession of fierce gales which, screaming out of the southwest, forced her to reduce canvas to jibs, staysails and double-reefed topsails and then tack painfully towards the Straits of Le Maire at the eastern approach to Cape Horn and the Straits of Magellan.

Thanks to Jedediah Paddock's skilled and experienced navigation at November's end the jagged, treeless and otherwise desolate black coast of the Tierra del Fuego showed far off to starboard.

Long before, the ocean had lost its clear deep-blue to turn an icy and forbidding shade of slate-gray.

The day before Staten Island, which for generations had been known to seamen as "Hell-on-earth" was sighted, the wind inexplicably lost much of its frigid velocity. The sky turned a pallid blue and the sun came out for the first time in a week as if to announce that spring had arrived in these latitudes.

The *Gladiator*'s Master, however, refused to be cozened into neglecting the precautions usual before entering the Straits of Le Maire. All boats, including the remaining spare, were made extra fast through the application of double gripes and lashings; top-gallant and royal masts were sent down, spare spars shackled in place and important stays and braces doubled. Stout new hemp replaced running gear worn thin since West Chop lighthouse had been left astern.

Under the Captain's personal supervision oil casks, each containing about six barrels, were further immobilized in the main hold. Chocks were driven tight and dunnage—bolts of wood—braced them against the bark's sides.

The carronades, grindstone and anvil were lashed into immobility along with any other gear which might conceivably fetch loose.

Pig and poultry pens, long since emptied, were knocked down and stowed below.

By the time Staten Island's sable, pointed and otherwise inhospitable outlines were reported, all was secure leaving the ship's company free to lounge on deck, do washing, mend clothes, work scrimshaw and otherwise enjoy this fine, almost balmy weather.

Many, Abner included, took to hanging over the rail to view jagged little ice islands drift by. Sometimes there were live things on them—seals and funny-looking up-standing black-and-white birds. Mister Coffin informed the boy that these were penguins. The seabirds were different, too. Bigger, darker and less graceful in flight —gulls, frigate-birds and wide-winged albatrosses and any quantity of shags and petrels.

On the evening of the day the *Gladiator* entered the Straits of Le Maire it chanced that Mister Paddock stood the second dog watch—from six until eight. Various species of seals, huge sea elephants, a few small baleen whales and clouds of seabirds had appeared to frolic about as if intending to convoy the bark through the Straits.

Satisfied with the set of sail, Lydia tramped aft to heave the log. Probably because of service in the Navy, Jedediah Paddock insisted on this practice when cruising for long distances or navigating dangerous waters; precious few spouter captains bothered with such a tedious routine.

Shortly after the sun had disappeared below the coast of Argentina a glorious full moon—as if eager to replace her resplendent consort—lifted above the horizon. A pale effulgence rapidly increased until lookouts could make out the shore of Staten Island and see surf battering it furiously, eternally. It was, as one of Commodore George Anson's officers nearly a century earlier had written in his journal, "A scene of pleasing horror."

After chalking the rate of progress on a slate slung to a nail beside the wheel, Lydia pulled off her hat, allowing the wind to caress well-lengthened hair, a pleasure enjoyed only when Jedediah was not in evidence.

She rested elbows on the taffrail and for a space enjoyed the moonrise, then went to check the course with the helmsman, Harrington. Abruptly uneasy, she wondered why, never by word or look, had this big Irishman made reference to that night Tom Archer had disappeared once and for all. Why?

Harrington with long hair tumbling about his forehead stood straight as a pikestaff, feet well braced apart. Perhaps because of the narrowness of the space in which he stood the fellow's shoulders appeared even broader than they actually were. Under a shapeless watch coat he was wearing a tight blue-and-white-striped jersey which effectively revealed a pattern of magnificent chest muscles.

The Fourth halted where she was, tried once more to estimate Harrington's true worth. By now she'd found him fascinating in several respects. For instance he could sing as sweetly as any linnet; he could, lightly and gracefully, tread intricate jigs and dances especially, she suspected, when he glimpsed her among the onlookers. By now she could tell the moment he saw her by the bold way he'd toss his head in her direction; although keeping his gaze averted.

The moonlight grew sufficiently brilliant to create faint but fascinating silvery tones in Harrington's curling reddish-yellow hair. Before she realized it, she was commenting, "A most lovely sight."

Without turning his head Harrington replied, "Aye, sor, and what about it pleases yez the most?"

"Why, the way moonlight casts yonder island in silhouette at the same time ringing it with flying silver sparks from the surf."

"Sure, sor, and 'tis indeed a rare, fine sight. Mary send we get more weather the likes of this."

With ease Harrington's bulk compensated to the bark's leisurely pitching, then she realized he'd kicked off heavy brogans and was steadying himself by means of broad toes hooked into the wheel grating.

A cheerful atmosphere pervaded the bark. The squeaking of a fiddle playing of all tunes, "A Young Virgin" and the thumping of a hand drum drifted aft as a rough voice, singing deplorably off-key, began to chant:

> *"This young virgin as we understand*
> *Took a trip to a foreign land*
> *Wheras forty young lovers a-roving came*
> *To some of their callings I long for to name."*

The words were clearly distinguishable above the rush of waves alongside so the Fourth and the helmsman missed never a word as the singer told off in verse after verse various attempts against the lass's virtue made by a merchant, a doctor, an apothecary, a tailor, a fiddler. Then in conclusion:

> *"The next was a sailor bold*
> *With his pockets lined with gold*
> *She waited not but ended the dispute*
> *Sir, here is my heart and maidenhead to boot."*

As the singer fell silent Harrington chuckled. "Well, weren't she the smart one?" He sighed. "And there would I have been without a penny to bless me with."

Maidenhead? mused the Fourth; men set such store by 'em it's a wonder I've kept mine.

Moonlight beating through the main shrouds etched a stygian, net-like pattern shifting in slow rhythm back and forth across the well-scrubbed deck. Curling wave tops, snowy in the moonlight, passed endlessly along the *Gladiator*'s beam as uncountable galaxies of unfamiliar constellations added fresh radiance to the night's beauty.

Lingering behind the helmsman she felt her heart beat quicken, then she drew a series of deep breaths and ran fingers through breeze-whipped hair, allowed it to coil almost caressingly about her neck. Despite a new and larger canvas vest she felt her breasts becoming constrained so, with trembling fingers, she groped under her shirt furtively to ease its lacings. The relief was so gratifying that for the first time in months she ceased thinking about men who'd perished on this voyage; Tony Amaral, the four would-be mutineers drowned through Te Ponapa's cunning clumsiness and Tom Archer. Her gaze shifted to Harrington's broad back. Odd, until lately she'd not experienced an instant's remorse over the gunner's murder. But now, well, she didn't like to visualize Archer's body dropped overside into eternity.

With the chill wind probing inside her coat and shirt she shivered. What now did she want from life? Whaling and trading? So far, at least, these pursuits offered little of the high adventure she'd craved. Quite the contrary. How could she have anticipated such violence, brutality, treachery and ugliness of so many sorts?

For a space Lydia fixed her attention on the moon; it appeared huger and more radiant than she'd ever seen it. Quite without conscious intention she crossed to stand close beside the helmsman as if to check the course then she heard her voice say, "Tell me. Wherever did you learn to sing so beautifully? Who taught you?"

Harrington's powerful, flat features became disclosed faintly by a light illumining the compass's card. "Why, sor, where I hail from most everybody sings true and well, though niver a soul gets a bit of teachin'. Like the Welshies, my people have *got* to sing and let others know how they're feelin'—be it happy or sad, hatin' or lovin'."

"—And from what part of Ireland do you come?" Lydia's voice was softly rich.

"—From Glengariff on Bantry Bay; 'tis in County Cork, mum —sor, I mean." His eyes flickered back to the compass card. "'Tis a rare beautiful place."

"Then why did you leave?"

Harrington's lumpy hands tightened over the wheel's handles to make a minute correction. "Why, sor, I ran away from home ere I was fourteen. Why? First, because in our cottage there wuz ten of us and niver enough to fill our bellies. Second," the helmsman's voice hardened, "because, in a bicker over the ownership of a brace of rabbits I'd snared, I licked the whey out o' our landlord's youngest son."

Lydia's trim dark lips formed a fleeting smile. "You weren't poaching by any chance?"

The big Irishman chuckled. "That I wuz and no two ways about that. Anyhow, us poor bog-trotters hated the guts of the foreign landlords whut owned every rood and perch o' decent ground about us. So, three jumps ahead o' the bailiff, I ran off to sea. What other choice was there for one of my race and religion?" Turning, he allowed the back of his hand to brush the hip of the slight figure beside him.

"—And you've been seafaring ever since?"

"Aye, that I have, ma'am."

"Then you must have seen many strange and wonderful things?"

"Aye, ma'am; a fair share. I've whaled from the Arctic to the Middle Ground which lies 'twixt Australia and the New Zealand Islands—'tis from there me friends Te Ponapa and Heetee come—or so they claim."

"I—I presume you've had your fair share of women, too?" It was out before Lydia realized it; heat flooded her chilled features.

"I expect so being of the forward sort who ain't afraid of odds when a likely wench is at stake."

The roughness of his hand closed over hers, she shivered but made no effort to break contact. "Then you—you've known a lot of girls?"

"Sure and I have; for if there's anything sweeter in this life than rolling a lusty lass God's kept it to Himself."

Stealing a sidewise glance to make sure they remained alone he realized that the Fourth's sooty eyes were fixed on him, wide-open and as bright as polished onyx seals adorning a rich man's watch fob. When he noticed through opening in her shirt that what he took for a corset had been separated far enough to reveal the beginnings of a shallow cleavage he caught his breath. Arragh! How would this lean and sunburnt female look wearing dainty slippers, a saucy chip hat, and a silken gown like Lady Kaulback's and with lace-trimmed petticoats a-froth about her ankles?

Jaws beginning to work a little, Bert Harrington and Mister Paddock for a brief interval continued to stare intently on one another. God's teeth! He couldn't credit that here stood that same hard-voiced, sharp-faced vixen who customarily barked orders brisk as any bucko mate. His grip tightened on the wheel's handles. When the Fourth dropped her gaze and fell back a step he for the first time became aware of the remarkable length of her eyelashes.

"I seem to have distracted you," Lydia remarked in a flat voice.

"Why, sor?"

"You're near two points off-course." Turning aside, the young woman hurriedly jammed hair up under cap, next she stalked back to the taffrail and, turning her back, savagely hitched tight her canvas vest.

Only then did she realize not only that the sing-song forward was continuing but that the nature of music was different. The tom-tom's throb now was louder and beating a quick, pulse-stirring rhythm. Even before Te Ponapa began to sing she sensed his awareness of her presence. To her surprise the towering Maori began to sing in English.

"She stepped up to me and took hold of my hand
Saying, 'You look like a stranger away from your land.
But if you will follow you're welcome to come
Where I live by myself in a snug little home.'

"Just as the sun set behind a blue sea
I wandered alone with my little Mowee.
Together, we rambled, together we rove
Until we came to her house in a coconut grove.

"With fondest expression she said unto me
If you will consent to live along with me
And never shall go roving upon the salt sea
The language I'll learn you is of the Isle of Mowee."

Still disquieted by her encounter with Harrington, Lydia edged along the weather rail and obtained a clear view of a strip of moon-brightened deck running athwart ships just aft of the fo'c's'le companionway.

Most of the shadowy onlookers either were squatting on the deck by the foremast's foot or sat hunched on the bulwarks. Thick-bodied Heetee was thumping a drum improvised from a hide of some sort stretched over a nail keg. The Maori was holding it between his knees using fingertips and sometimes the palms of his hands to extract from his instrument a now sensuous, now staccato rhythm which varied abruptly in tone and tempo.

She soon noticed that most of the time Te Ponapa kept his flattish dark face lifted towards the moon, eyes half-closed. Once his chanty ended the Maori threw back his powerful head and with blunt, bare feet commenced beating a furious and complicated cadence. He sprang back and forth, sinewy and lithe as a leopard, taunting invisible enemies, then raised a barbaric war chant, *"Homai taku maro! Kia huruwa! Kia rawea!"*

Tattooed features quivering, he ran his tongue so far out that its tip wet the point of his outthrust jaw then in a frenzy ripped off his shirt to dance clad only in frayed canvas knee breeches.

Chanting all the while, Te Ponapa spun, jumped simultaneously kicking heels high up behind him before sinking into a crouch and glaring about with eyes become concentric circles of black and white. As war club he brandished a stick of firewood at the Fourth; a slight, shadowy outline beyond the outer ring of spectators.

He checked a bounding, howling rush with his tattooed face gibbering not a foot from the tip of Lydia's nose.

The drumming slowed, Te Ponapa, streaming sweat, retreated all the time grinding his pelvis in an erotic orbit. He halted and, swaying gently to the *Gladiator*'s motion, looked straight at Lydia. "*Aroha marama!*" Laughing, he raised arms towards the bark's moon-silvered top canvas then, vast chest heaving, Te Ponapa dropped onto the barrel windlass and peered out to sea.

Shaken, delightfully confused, Lydia Paddock Roach retreated until she encountered Mister Coffin checking the course with a new helmsman. The Irishman had disappeared.

To regain a measure of calm, Lydia sat on the main transom and clasped her knees as she'd used to when a little girl.

Te Ponapa materialized out of the shadows, confidently, as if by prearrangement.

"You liked my war dance?"

"Yes, very much. You did it wonderfully well. Don't know how to put it, but I found it quite—quite exciting. Do you dance like that often?"

"At home, yes," the Maori admitted. "You liked my song?"

She looked out over the heaving moonlit ocean. "I—I really don't know. Your song—whatever you intended by it, was pleasing, but—I," she continued with a rush, "I think I liked your dancing best."

His teeth glinted. "That is good. But what I danced is nothing to the way we really dance when we prepare for battle. Perhaps some day, Princess, *Vahine Rangatira*, you will see for yourself."

Never had Jedediah's blood-brother appeared so handsome, so distinguished a predatory animal. This was odd because all at once she no longer felt repelled by that complex pattern of tattooed whorls and curves on his features. Te Ponapa moved closer. He still was breathing quickly and exuding a faint, musky aura reminiscent of a freshly-washed hunting dog.

"Tell me, Te Ponapa, that song you sang to the moon, you intended it for me?"

A rich, low-pitched laugh escaped him and his towering bulk advanced, seemed to eclipse the moon. "Only for you did I sing '*Aroha Marama*'!"

"What does '*Aroha Marama*' mean?" she whispered.

"'Moon of Love'," he explained in a musical undertone. "You cannot understand what one is till you see a true *Aroha Marama* shine, golden as honey, over Taranaki. It is then people of all castes lose control so often that many of our people are named 'Child of the *Aroha Marama*'."

Before long the *Gladiator* left Staten Island's forbidding silhouette astern. As, close together, they leaned over the rail Te Ponapa picturesquely described the rich and varied beauties of his homeland; to his pleased astonishment his blood-brother's sister made not the least effort to draw apart.

"You—you are impatient to see your people once more?"

"Of course! I shall not rest until I rule over Taranaki."

Aware that Mister Coffin's square-toed boots were drawing near, Te Ponapa breathed, "*Me te mea po Kopu ka reri i te pae*," then disappeared in utter silence affording no hint as to his meaning.

40

Full Moon off Staten Island II

Once the wick of the fist-sized brass lamp balanced on gimbals commenced to give off uncertain amber hues, Lydia Paddock Roach sank onto the edge of her bunk to stare blankly at grimy oilskins swaying from pegs let into the bulkhead.

Again she wondered why so many changes were occurring in Micajah Paddock's daughter? It was unnerving that she no longer could feel confident of life stretching ahead, predictable, to be followed by one sure step after another.

Nervously petulant, she slid off her jacket then rid herself of graceless brogans and scratchy woolen stockings. Next she pulled a small mirror from a ditty bag kept under her bunk and studied her face as if she'd never seen it before by the clear, faint light of the sperm oil lamp. All at once she stuck out her tongue just like the Maori and jeered her image. Look at you! Studying your reflection like a love-sick moon-calf, like some silly, romantic heroine in a second-rate novel! What's become of "Mister" Paddock?

Above the persistent creak and groan of the *Gladiator*'s fabric she heard, through a thin bulkhead, every detail of rasping snores raised by the Third whose cabin lay just aft of her squalid hutch. Nonetheless, she forgave Mister Hayward because he seemed so eager to teach her the fine points of sailsetting or whenever he could spare her some particularly disagreeable duty. By now she'd decided that the ugly Third was more intelligent and better bred and educated than he'd ever let on. Else why should he keep in his quarters a volume of "Josephus", some of Shakespeare's plays, Plato's "Republic" and "The Travels of Pliny the Elder?"

Beginning unaccountably to shake she undid her shirt, stripped off her trousers and man's underdrawers to stand for a long moment poignantly aware of the fact that she was stark naked. Next she shook out a nightgown she'd contrived out of Estrellita's petticoats. Too bad her mirror was so tiny: what did she look like full figure. Was she well—attractive? Hardly. Probably most men would deem her too thin, too muscular, flat-chested and dark-skinned to be truly appealing.

The sight of silken ruffles fanned a burning resentment she'd retained ever since her spanking. Even now could she hear her brother panting, "You signed on as a man, so by God you'll stay like one 'till this voyage is over!" The fact still continued to escape her that Jed was entirely right by insisting she continue her masquerade.

She laid out the nightgown and stood looking at its bright softness, then experimentally caressed herself with long, rough hands, cupped them under small, erect breasts. After that the Fourth almost defiantly stroked her thighs inside and out wondering why she'd never before noticed her skin's warm, satin-smooth texture.

Luxuriously, she ran fingers through her hair, smoothed and then using a dingy pink ribbon secured it above the nape of her neck. Finally she sighed and ended by donning the nightgown.

Boots clumped along the deck just above her head; someone bellowed an order indistinguishable in the steady wash of waves along the *Gladiator*'s side.

Balancing on dirty tiptoes she blew out the light and stretched out on the rough, sour-smelling bunk. For a while she lay reviewing the progress of this remarkable evening. Her reflections formed no logical pattern nor had she arrived at any conscious conclusions by the time her eyes grew heavy and she dozed off, deeper and deeper. She was on the verge of true slumber when a calloused hand settled firmly, gently over her mouth.

"Sh-h-h. Keep quiet," came an unidentifiable whisper.

Her eyes, wavering open, found the darkness so complete she couldn't have seen more if she'd been immersed in a cask of tar. When she attempted an outcry the unknown's fingers tightened, effectively silencing her; at the same time the pressure started her confused consciousness to whirling like a hard-spun top.

She ceased to struggle once the unknown's considerable weight began to pin her down. All at once she realized her sensations were more of curiosity than of fear. Like a bright sunbeam shooting out of a welter of storm clouds came a realization. Hadn't Jed insisted on her continuing to act like a man? Men took what *they* wanted, didn't they? "Well, by God and by gravy," as Papa had used to exclaim when deeply moved, she'd do what suited her—man-like. If she was fit to discharge a man's responsibilities—she was fit to enjoy his prerogatives!

Chaotic, ecstatic, painful moments followed, resolved into sublime, undreamt-of satisfaction. Her visitor uttered never a word—his only sounds were of quick-drawn breaths ending in a prolonged, quivering moan.

When at length a measure of reason returned, Lydia lay alone, trembling, blissfully satiated and, for the time being, quite unrepentant.

41

New Year's Day: 1831–1832

The whaling bark *Gladiator* finally won her westing and emerged from the Straits of Magellan on the thirty-first of December 1831. For over twenty-one days she'd been mercilessly battered, tossed and tormented by a series of howling, frigid gales which so heavily sheathed spars and rigging in glistening ice that more than once the bark had threatened to capsize; only eternal hours of frantic chopping preserved her.

The *Gladiator* emerged from the ordeal ice-scarred and otherwise weatherbeaten but intact save for the loss of her mizzen topmast. Her figurehead had suffered most having been chewed and gored by floe-ices through which the bark had been driven. Great patches of red, blue and silver paint had been scraped off and, in effect, both the *Gladiator*'s eyes had been extinguished and part of his head hacked away.

The crew commenced to thaw out, unfeignedly thankful that not once during the passage had the cry of "Man overboard!" been raised. True, certain of the ship's company had suffered from frostbite, bruises and one a broken arm. Even so, Jedediah Paddock, had he been a religious man, would have raised hosannahs of thankfulness. This, by far, was the easiest doubling of the Horn he'd ever made.

Warmed by a draught of Old Medford Jedediah lingered watching Goober in the galley preparing a holiday pot of dandy funk for supper. Now the old year was about to slip into the eternity carrying with it memories of Pa's death and of his own tumultuous return to Nantucket. In sardonic satisfaction he recalled Lydia's ephemeral marriage and felt no compunctions on that score; Eben Roach for a long time had been heading for self-encompassed perdition.

For a little Jed wondered where Obediah might be cruising at the moment. Probably he'd be hunting sperms somewhere along the Line. Damn! How he missed his twin's steadying commonsense.

Mechanically reassuring himself that the main staysail was drawing efficiently he, with less confidence, reviewed his undertaking with Messrs. Doane, Welch & Peabody. Yep. For sure he'd slipped up badly in that direction. Profit or no profit, he never should have been party to an enterprise courting troubles so varied and unpredictable. Without the specie's lure he'd never have been forced to lose—he hadn't ever thought of those deaths as murder—all those men.

Taking a short turn across the spray-splotched deck he considered a dim, gray streak on the horizon which was the coast of Chile.

On the other hand certain disasters couldn't be blamed on anyone but himself: in Vera Cruz he'd been taken in and artistically hornswoggled, he'd dallied so earnestly with Estrellita he'd failed to detect Mister Coffin's error in time to avoid the Yucatán Peninsula. Smart alert Master he'd proved. Like hell!

Against these incidents remained the fact that, against long odds, he'd succeeded in securing and equipping the *Gladiator*. And then there was his successful cruise on the Brazil Grounds.

Nonetheless, massive problems persisted: even if he returned with a record cargo of oil it still wouldn't reimburse the Boston bankers and leave sufficient to satisfy his crew, his fellow shareholders or himself. The prospects therefore weren't bright if he hoped to establish a truck house on the Bay of Islands in New Zealand.

Irritably, Jed spat over the rail. Nevertheless, come hell or high water he'd have a go at it.

He returned to find the "Doctor" peeling the last of the Mexican oranges and lemons and heating water for a traditional New Year's rum punch. Good. On this particular eve of the New Year all hands ought to celebrate not only the occasion but also having so easily rounded the Horn.

By tradition, only the helmsman and the Officer of the Watch would stay sober and gloomily watch shipmates get drunk, sing, dance and participate in horseplay which easily might degenerate into senseless and sometimes deadly brawls.

Jed watched the Fourth come on deck to hang washing in the rigging and was startled to notice the unconscious grace of her movements. Um. Why did Lyddie no longer stride about?

What in Tunket had come over her since leaving the Brazil

Grounds? Of course she'd never forgiven him the humiliation of that
licking; he felt uneasy because, before long, he'd have to warn her to
keep her hair shorter and throw some reefs in that contraption she
wore. Of late it had betrayed the proportions of twin roundnesses
so clearly that hands moistened lips and stared whenever they dared.

The carouse on New Year's Eve proved to be all Jedediah had
anticipated—and more besides. By nightfall a visitor could have believed himself aboard a vessel manned by lunatics; boatsteerers, the
gunner, cook, cooper, and seamen were staggering about singing
long songs on two notes, or capering about in grotesque dances with
arms draped about each other in maudlin affection.

Wide-eyed, Abner Doane watched men drain dripping tin cups
at a gulp only to return again and again, and dip into the barrel of
punch presiding in state upon the main hatch.

Tom Blue Fox, John Fast Canoe and the other Indians soon
began acting crazy—no other word could have described their frenzy;
they acted even wilder than Te Ponapa and Heetee who scarcely
were behaving like lads at a Sunday school picnic. Egged on, Maoris
and Indians pranced, shrieked and with shouted insults offered to
fight anybody who felt like taking them on.

Tempted to assert his approaching manhood, Abner, suddenly
daring, found a half-filled mug on the grindstone's seat, grabbed it
and carried it forward of the try-house.

"Here's blood in your eye," daringly he toasted someone
sprawled inert in the scuppers. He took a big mouthful and all-but
choked but, eyes streaming, he managed to keep it down. Encouraged, he finished his tin pot and after joining hands with Big Pig and
Goober began to prance about until, without warning, the deck
began to shift, heave and sway as if the bark had been struck by a
hurricane. Soon the cabin boy gagged, let go and started teetering
towards the lee rail but tripped over a fallen figure and fell onto all
fours. Head spinning, he added copiously to the mess polluting the
deck. Last thing Abner recalled was praying God to end his misery
in a hurry!

Just before darkness fell a heavy rain storm closed in, then,
after it had passed, a dank, dense fog enveloped the bark. Jedediah,
pleasantly jingled but far from drunk, wasn't worried. He was sure
that the *Gladiator* was so far offshore this gloom didn't matter; with

Mister Coffin in charge and sober as a barnful of owls, there should be no danger.

Soon the weather thickened so much that even if the ship's company had been stone-cold sober they couldn't have noticed a faint, rosy glow throbbing somewhere ahead.

Lydia, disgusted with the noisy saturnalia on deck, in lonely rebellion sought the main cabin and there helped herself to two generous potions of the Captain's best brandy lightly laced with water. In a gesture of purely childish defiance she plunked herself down in Jed's chair, put feet on his desk and sat sipping steadily, listening to the jangle of guitars, the wheeze of a concertina and the wild thudding of feet.

For a while she almost enjoyed the racket aloft and the unaccustomed stimulating warmth spreading so pleasantly through mind and body. Even yet, she hadn't adjusted to that visitation off Staten Island; to have no idea who her visitor might have been remained deeply disturbing, no less than worry over possible results. Ever since, she'd tried stubbornly to assure herself that she'd been outraged, that the experience had been hateful and disgusting. Still, *had* she been completely revolted? At times it was odd that her thoughts strayed in surprising directions.

On occasion she even took to sleeping in the ruffled nightdress but always bolted the door whenever she did so. Who, *who*, WHO? All she retained was a certainty that she'd been ravished by someone both heavy and very powerful. Who qualified? Harrington, Te Ponapa, Hercules for a starter, and then occurred another possibility. She sat bolt upright gasping, "No, no, no! It can't be! Utterly impossible!"

After a bit the Fourth, still shaken, helped herself to more brandy but soon became aware that this had been a mistake. Feeling dizzy, she lurched out of the cabin and barely reached her bunk before losing consciousness. Her sleep was so profound that a soft *click* made by the door latch went unnoticed and she made attempts to waken only on becoming dimly aware that she no longer was alone on her bunk.

Attempts to rouse and shake off a paralyzing lethargy failed completely; her head spun so wildly Lydia felt she was whirling, disembodied, through lightless space. She attempted to cry out but couldn't make a sound before lapsing into unconsciousness.

Light, slanting through the cabin's porthole, roused the Fourth to a painful realization; her head was throbbing like an Indian tom-tom and nausea threatened whenever she made the least effort to move it.

Gradually she became aware of a number of unpleasant facts. The trousers she'd been wearing lay crumpled on the deck and so many buttons had been torn from her shirt that her breasts lay bared; also she was feeling aches in a region well removed from her head.

Furiously angry, Lydia made hurried efforts to remove evidences of what had occurred. How dreadful to have no more idea of who had violated her on this occasion, than she'd had off Staten Island. How right Jed had been.

The Fourth still was cleansing herself with a damp rag when Mister Coffin clumped below and began to bang on the main cabin's door.

"Cap'n, sir! Cap'n! Lookout's reporting a ship on fire!"

42

Picaroons I

What the *Gladiator*'s blear-eyed lookout had sighted at dawn appeared to be a full-rigged ship lying dead in the water, down by the head for half her length and spewing great clouds of smoke. Flame and sparks were soaring high into a pleasant, early morning sky. She must, Jedediah determined, have been afire a considerable time since her foremast steppings, now under water, had burned so much that the mast was canting over the submerged bowsprit at a drunken angle.

By the time the bark arrived close enough to make out details, flames were licking up well-tarred main shrouds and running out along her yards.

Right away the *Gladiator*'s after-guard badly hung-over, lined the rail or clung to shrouds and agreed that this handsome vessel was no whaler; she'd more likely be a merchantman homeward-bound.

Presently it appeared that at least two men had remained on board; they could be seen waving frantically from the stern. Jed ordered the helm put down and topsails backed then worked the bark slowly through a wall of acrid, eye-stinging smoke until it became possible to read on her sternboard beneath a handsomely carved and gilded American eagle and Stars-and-Stripes shield, the name *Amanda Alexander of Baltimore*.

What at once seized Jed's attention was the fact that the blazing vessel's smallboats remained smouldering or burnt in two but still fast to their davits. He brought the *Gladiator* close under *Amanda Alexander*'s port counter but the crackle of flames was too loud to permit understanding of what was being shouted by the two wild-eyed men.

The merchantman being obviously past saving, Jed ordered Mister Hayward's boat lowered. Shortly before it took the water a sharp explosion sounded aboard the clipper and great pillars of fire shot vertically through her main hatch. Thereupon the *Amanda Alexander's* mainmast began to sway, reeled drunkenly a few instants then, causing a thundering crash, it toppled over the starboard bulwarks and sent sheets of water flying sky-high.

After a space the Third's boat returned, bearing not only the men who'd already been sighted but a third—a scrawny, saffron-skinned fellow the outlines of whose pointed features were disguised by a scraggly black beard. Anyone could tell at first glance that this mestizo's chest had been so caved in by a heavy blow that he could breath only shallowly with blood-speckled foam bubbling at the corners of his mouth.

Barely had the boat been swung up onto its cranes than great blasts of air began to escape the *Amanda Alexander's* hull causing weird, whistling noises. Grandly, smoothly, the ship's stern, cascaded water until, almost straight up it towered above the ocean like a grotesque steeple. Spare spars and a torrent of loose deck gear continued to tumble into the Pacific. On reaching the perpendicular the beautiful vessel paused an eternal second before commencing her trip to the bottom with the ease of a dirk slipped into its sheath.

Shimmering swirls of spume briefly veiled a deep whirlpool created by the *Amanda Alexander's* disappearance. When they dissipated nothing remained to mark the spot beyond a litter of debris and a single smallboat bobbing lonesomely about—a fact which pleased Jedediah Paddock's thrifty Nantucket soul; it looked large enough to serve as a gratis replacement for that boat stove-in on the Brazil Grounds.

One of the stunned-looking survivors identified himself as Adam Masters of Old Saybrook, Connecticut; the other, Murdo Morrison, was a rawboned, bandy-legged little Scot who, judging by the harsh lines about his mouth and eyes, must have led a hard life.

The wounded man, they mumbled, was one of those picaroons who, by using sweeps mounted on their schooner, had pulled up alongside the evening before to overwhelm the *Amanda Alexander's* crew while she lay hopelessly becalmed.

Jed snapped, "Where were you from and where bound?"

"Out of Canton and Port Jackson for Philadelphia, sir."

Jed jerked a nod in the stricken pirate's direction. "This critter speak English?"

"Nae, sir-r," said Morrison. "Only Portuguese."

The wounded picaroon sprawled limply on a wornout staysail appeared to have so little life left in him Jed rasped, "Doane! Go find Manuel Fuentes, quick, quick!"

"'Doane', did ye say?" Dully, the survivor named Adam Masters blinked after the hurrying cabin boy but everyone was too preoccupied to heed his query.

Pleased by this unexpected acquisition of two hands and a free boat Jed turned to the hollow-eyed survivors. "How come you two are still alive?"

"We found time to hide i' the car-rgo, sir," averred the Scot.

"What about him?" he indicated the bearded picaroon now drawing breath even more laboriously. "Come on, you! Pull yourself together."

"He fell down 'e main hatch during 'e fight we put up when 'em devils swarmed aboard," the Scot explained in a weary, toneless voice. "Reckon his fellow rogues deemed him done for, so when they finished murdering the rest of us and plundering the ship, they cheated him o' his share and left him behind. Lord! Lord! The awful sounds Adam and me listened to."

While shuffling towards the galley Adam Masters mumbled, "Doane? Doane?" several times, but any connection with the name escaped him.

Lydia, having made a hurried examination, arose from her knees shaking her head. "Rate this rascal's bleeding he can't last very much longer. Hurry your questioning the best you can."

Fuentes ran up, knelt beside the dying pirate.

"Tell him to name his ship and Captain."

Following a burst of Portuguese and a labored reply from the dying man, Fuentes reported. "He say, him Cap'n called El Funesto —the Sinister One—him brig called *El Sangrador*—the Letter-of-Blood."

"His own name?"

"Pablo Rego. Him say him from Bahia, Brazeel. No real Portuguese, only stupid Colonial."

"Where does this Funesto hang out?"

The stricken picaroon's eyes rolled so far back in their sockets as to hide their pupils; trickles of blood escaping his lavender-hued lips forced him to cough several times before gasping, "Isla Chiloe."

Jed broke in. "Anybody know where Chiloe Island lies?"

Surrounded by a curious crowd, Mister Winslow nodded. "Aye; lies near the entrance of the Gulf of Ladillero—at least I *think* so."

"Do other picaroons use this base? Ask him!"

The dying man's lips barely moved and his voice faded so much that when Fuentes bent low the tail of his faded stocking cap brushed the other's forehead.

"Him say only El Funesto use thees place."

"How many guns on his schooner?"

Fuentes counted twelve on his fingers.

"Heavy or light?"

The picaroon tried to say something but could only gurgle, drowning as he was in a flood of scarlet.

Frowning, Jed stirred the scrawny, leather-hued corpse with his boot's toe, growled, "Damn' inconsiderate of the bastard to die so fast. Now there's no telling whether land batteries guard the El Funesto's base." He turned to Mister Coffin. "Drop this dogsbody overside and clean up the mess he's made."

Abner Doane was receiving instruction from Mister Winslow in the art of celestial navigation when summoned to the Captain's cabin. He entered, a shapeless cloth cap clutched over his stomach, to find the Captain cross-examining the *Amanda Alexander*'s survivors and arrived in time to overhear that the clipper had been carrying a rich cargo from China; tea, silks—plain and embroidered—porcelains, tableware and carved ornaments in ivory, gold and silver.

Captain Paddock's penetrating eyes considered Adam Masters. "Presume you've no idea what this cargo was worth?"

"No, sir, and that's a fact. Still, I guess it was plenty. Pirates must have found that out 'cause they never bothered with no tea which was lucky for me and Morrison who only escaped havin' our throats cut account-of we wuz hiding 'mongst the tea chests."

The Scot rolled sunken, bloodshot eyes and growled deep in his throat like an angry airedale. "Aye, but for that, we'd have been murdered like the rest. Losh! I'll ne'er forget those waesome screams frae the deck. God send the day comes I can even scores wi' El Funesto."

"Mayhap you'll find opportunity ere long." Jed remarked. "Morrison, you're dismissed. Go find 'Mister' Paddock, say you're to sign articles. You, Masters! Stay here and tell young Doane what's on yer mind."

Adam Masters, a small man with a flat brown face framed in grayish chin whiskers, eyed the cabin boy. "Did I hear aright yer name's 'Doane'?"

Abner nodded.

"Yer Pa's Christian name wuz 'Sylvanus'?"

The *Gladiator*'s Master stopped calculating the ship's position and settled back in his chair to listen.

"Yes, my father was so christened."

"He hail from Boston?"

"Why yes, sir; my family's always lived near there."

"Did this here feller Sylvanus Doane ship six—maybe seven year' ago 'board a Boston vessel in the China trade named the *Arabella?*"

"Oh yes! Yes!" Abner burst out. "Please! Please, sir, did you know my father?"

"Aye. Him and me wuz shipmates and good enough friends to boot."

Breathlessly: "When did you last see him?"

"In Port Jackson—that's in Australia."

"Is—is he still alive?" Abner drew a deep breath and held on tight for the answer.

"Now as to that, young feller, I can't rightly tell for reasons I'll explain. Why you so keen to learn of him?"

"Because we, my mother, my uncle and I that is, haven't heard a word or any report of him in over seven years." Hesitantly, he added. "Why haven't we? What's become of Father?"

"Dunno," admitted Adam Masters wearily. "After he signed off the *Arabella* I heard somewhere he'd got to be Third on the *American Star*—another China merchant." He considered the youth's gawky and angular figure. "Exceptin' for the set o' yer face, ye don't favor him much; 'Vanus wuz big, tough, full-blooded and ever ready to join in a fight, footrace or a frolic wi' the doxies."

Impatiently, the *Gladiator*'s Master snapped. "Get on with it, man. Talk facts or stow your gab. Can't you see the lad's on tenter hooks?"

"Aye, aye, sir. 'Twas back in twenty-nine—or were it twenty-eight?—the *American Star* put into Port Jackson where the *Ara-*

bella was takin' on cargo and supplies. So far, we'd had an unlucky cruise; lost near a dozen hands in a typhoon off Macao."

Abner, faced drained of color, stared at the survivor with the intensity of an accused man awaiting the jury's verdict.

Again, the rugged little man scratched at lank and greasy hair. "Lemme see, lemme think back. Yep, like I said, we wuz layin' in Port Jackson to revictual and recruit. 'Twas then I heard yer pa'd got himself mixed up in a tavern brawl and wuz in prison awaitin' trial."

As if seeking encouragement the speaker cast a glance at Jed's big bronzed face. "Of course, I weren't a witness—the fight had took place a fortnight earlier—but I talked to some of his shipmates who took oath the Third wuz only defendin' himself. Howsumever, and I hate to say this, young feller, the heft of the witnesses declared 'twas 'Vanus provoked the brawl and stabbed a man to death."

As Abner's eager expression crumpled, Jedediah directed sharply, "Go on. What happened then?"

"Why, sir, after a lively fight 'Vanus wuz arrested and hauled off to jail."

A sensation as if the deck was buckling beneath him seized Abner. Lord! Lord! This *couldn't* be so.

"What happened to Doane after that. They hang him?"

Adam Masters shrugged. "No, sir. Just before we cleared for home our Skipper heard Doane got convicted of murder in the second degree and wuz sentenced to fifteen years' hard labor on Norfolk Island."

"Oh-h, then Pa's still living! Thank you, good Lord! Thank you! Thank you!" Abner dug fists into his eyes and commenced to blubber like a small boy.

Surprised at himself, Jed got up and went over to pat the youth's quivering shoulders. "Don't take on so, Bub. Just be glad yer pa got off with fifteen years; the Australians are a hard lot."

The survivor shook his head. "Maybe poor 'Vanus weren't so lucky as you let on. Ever heard tell about that convict colony on Norfolk? Well, I *have*. If you ask me 'Vanus would have been a heap better off if they'd stretched his neck."

"Belay such talk!" growled Jed. "Why was no report made on the matter to the ship's owners?"

Adam Masters made a sucking noise through amber-hued teeth.

"Why, sir, I allow 'twas probably because the *American Star* on her homeward voyage was lost with all hands on Vanua Leva Island, a cannibal isle in the Fijis or so a British man-o'-war reported just a while ago."

43

Picaroons II

Soon after the *Amanda Alexander* had disappeared Jedediah Paddock, brow furrowed, went below and remained there scheming, calculating risks involved in somehow profiting from what appeared to be a God-sent opportunity. 'Twasn't easy to arrive at a decision so critical; at sundown he went on deck and curtly ordered a change in course.

Mister Winslow felt fairly confident, provided the wind held fair, that the Island of Chiloe at the entrance to Ladrillero Bay would heave into sight at the end of a three days' run to the east-north-east.

How big was El Funesto's schooner? If what the survivors said proved true, Jed reckoned she must displace about two hundred tons; this tended to back up the dying picaroon's assertion that *El Sangrador* mounted twelve cannon.

Other important questions remained unanswered: for example of what weight was the picaroon's ordnance? Was their base protected by land batteries of any kind? How close inshore would he dare take the *Gladiator?* Considering the limited range of his carronades this was a vital problem.

At first Jed thought to keep his plan to himself but soon realized he could only gain wholehearted and intelligent cooperation through making his intentions known.

To his surprise the company proved almost unanimously enthusiastic—possibly because they still were outraged over the burning of the China trader and the cold-blooded murder of her crew, but more likely because they were hoping for shares in the recovery of the *Amanda Alexander*'s cargo; plus, perhaps, loot taken from other ships.

Hour after hour Mister Hayward, Purvis and his fellow deserters drilled amateur gun crews who this time labored without complaint.

Brows knit, Jedediah in red circled the Island of Chiloe on an old Admiralty chart. "Main question is, will we find El Funesto's ship in port? Next, how many picaroons may be living ashore and how well-armed are they?"

The Third canted his head, scratched a cauliflowered brown ear. "While I've never been there, sir, seems to me I've heard or read something about Chiloe. Um. Ye-es-s, a Spanish fellow in Vera Cruz let drop that a parcel of old-style Royalists revolted against the Republican Government which is running Chile nowadays."

"What happened?"

"The Republicans got chased out, sir."

"Are the Royalists still there?"

"Fellow didn't say, sir; reckon it's anybody's guess." The Third fingered his scarred chin a moment, looked up. "I'd say they're not, or the picaroons wouldn't be basing yonder."

Jed nodded. "That makes sense, still, it don't guarantee Chiloe's been altogether deserted by a Government. Even so, shouldn't be much of a population on a hole-in-the-wall island which this chart indicates."

He used a pair of dividers for a pointer. "Notice? There's only one bay which the Britishers have named 'The Cove of Oxen'. Since that's the only sheltered anchorage shown I figure we'll find El Funesto's base there." Jed glanced at Mister Hayward through whirling billows of bluish-gray smoke. "Well, and what are our chances of catching El Funesto and Company off-guard?"

"Fair to middling, sir. Lawless men ain't much for keeping a sharp lookout 'specially along a lonesome coast like this where there ain't a Government man-o'-war likely to be seen."

A burst of smoke escaped Jed's lips, rose towards the skylight. "Back in New Bedford you were right. I *should* have mounted heavier cannon but since I didn't we'll have to make do with carronades. Want you and those Limeys to keep working the hands or come pay-off day their lays will be smaller than a schoolboy's prick. Meanwhile, I and the new man Morrison, who seems knowledgeable, will teach 'em the use of smallarms."

For two cold and blustery days the *Gladiator* ran parallel to the desolate, mountainous and otherwise inhospitable coast of Chile while the crew learned how to load, aim and fire pistols and muskets at marks tossed over the side.

While a few hands became fairly proficient the majority remained dismally slow and inaccurate. The marksmen of course were Jedediah and Mates, then Harrington, Te Ponapa, Big Buck and Sun-in-the-Eyes, but it was the Fourth and the cabin boy who astonished everybody by the speed and accuracy of their fire; naturally, no one suspected their practice on the outskirts of New Bedford.

Everyone admired how dexterously Mister Paddock could handle light duelling pistols and hit three out of four times a box tossed overboard. Abner, thrilled to the core, did almost as well and gained a deal of stature among the crew who, as Purvis said disgustedly, handled muskets like a parcel of charwomen sweeping a poorhouse floor.

Gun crews excused from drill for so long remained deplorably inefficient despite the profane best efforts of their instructors.

In these chill, gray waters not even the sail of a coaster or fisherman was raised.

If the old Admiralty chart proved accurate, three, pointed peaks of nearly uniform altitude soon should appear to identify the southern entrance to Ladillero Bay.

When they showed, Jed at once sent the *Gladiator* speeding out to sea; only after dark did he intend to risk making for the coast; no use running the chance of some craft hidden under the land spying a speck of canvas on this vast and apparently empty ocean.

If his calculations were correct, the bark should nose into a narrow strait separating Chiloe Island from the Mainland just about dawn. Aside from such a hazard, God alone knew how many unmarked shoals and reefs lurked around the entrance.

Towards sunset a thick fog closed in, necessitated frequent heavings of log and leadline plus calculations to fix the bark's position after a fashion. Explicably, the crew all became tense and apprehensive, profanely protesting they wanted no more of this business; but they continued to obey orders.

Their anxiety lessened somewhat when, shortly after midnight, a warm wind arose and swiftly dissipated the dank, blinding vapors.

Not until around four of the morning did a three-quarter moon dimly reveal the coastline's jagged black outline dominated by the three peaks of Chiloe. Soon it became possible to make out a low silhouette fervently hoped to be that of Chiloe Island.

When cutlasses, firearms and knives were issued, Abner Doane ceased worrying about his father. Wait 'till the folks, Mother and his friends in Boston learned how he'd taken part in attacking a genuine pirates' nest! Suddenly he swallowed on nothing; suppose the picaroons had been warned and were ready? Where lay a guarantee against this?

Suppose their den on the cove was protected by a heavy battery? It could blow the feebly gunned *Gladiator* to kingdom-come. In the cold wind the cabin boy shivered. In that event he couldn't go on searching for Papa.

Swaying in the fore-hoops alongside Sun-in-the-Eyes he offered a silent prayer that the picaroon schooner hadn't yet returned to base.

Lydia, laying out medical supplies in the main cabin with her initial zest for adventure recaptured, was feeling equally taut.

The false dawn was fading when the *Gladiator* under jibs and lower sails poked her bowsprit into a narrow, half-seen strait. No point in showing easily visible top canvas.

Men blessed with extra-good eyesight were sent into the rigging, tried to penetrate the gloom and decide the approximate nearness of land looming ever closer off either beam. Here and there breakers created pale lines along some otherwise unseen beach, or ringed invisible rocks.

Taut, and grimly alert, Jedediah Paddock with pistols hung by hooks to his belt, posted himself in the foreshrouds, listened to the rumble of surf and the angry barking of a multitude of invisible sea lions. With assurance he conned the *Gladiator* into Ladillero Bay. One thing was all to the good; nowhere was even a pinpoint of light to be sighted on land or water.

Pearl-pink rays announcing the imminence of dawn were improving the visibility by the time the bark weathered a finger-like peninsula to enter Ladillero Bay which, it seemed, was hemmed in on all sides by treeless, stony hills and mountains. Nowhere was there any sign of human habitation. Clouds of seafowl arose from the surface, commenced shrieking and screaming overhead. Penguins, seals and a few sea elephants swam up to gaze curiously at this ghostly apparition.

Silently, men disappeared below, wondering what was going to happen before long. Would they be alive this time tomorrow? Lowering for a whale in stiff seaway was one thing but, by now, all hands understood the dangers inherent in such an operation. Here they were, about to be called upon to fire cannon they secretly were afraid to serve. Of course everything depended on whether they'd find *El Sangrador* lying in the Cove of Oxen.

Everyone started when a lookout shouted down, "Below there! I spy a light—sev'ral lights!"

Jed tilted back his head. "How many and *where?* Be precise, damn you!"

"Five lights behind a little low island, sir, 'bout ten points off larboard bow!"

"Mister Coffin. Ease tops'l sheets till they sag, then cant our upper yards, sloppy-like. Want to look like a coaster blundering about in distress."

In Abner Doane's imagination the bark shrank magically until she suggested an overgrown chip moving slowly over silver-gray waters. Heart lifting, he watched the Captain's huge figure mount to the foremast's lookout hoops. There, he trained a spyglass.

What Jedediah Paddock saw was a cluster of faint, yellow-red lights showing above a low and rocky point. All at once he felt years younger. By God! His heart hadn't thudded like this since *U.S.S. Essex*'s crew had manned guns to take her richest prize, the *Georgiana*.

Well, before long he should learn how effective Mister Hayward and George Purvis' drilling had been; it was entirely possible such half-trained amateurs, after firing an initial broadside, might become rattled on being deafened by crashing reports and swirling billows of choking, eye-stinging burnt powder fumes.

He ordered staysails set to overcome what appeared to be a stiff current rushing out to sea then returned attention to a low lying shore looming roughly a mile to port. He then made out an opening to what he hoped would prove to be the Cove of Oxen.

Once the bark sailed into a small bay he knew he'd made no mistake; along its shores loomed the outlines of five or six stranded wrecks.

Jedediah traversed his glass searching for evidence of a large vessel at anchor. His breath came in with a rush on making out the topmasts of a large three-masted schooner; it must be *El Sangrador*.

Nothing would seem to indicate the picaroons were on the alert. To his infinite relief Jed failed to detect any sign of harbor defenses but made out a few fishing smacks and small coasters anchored between *El Sangrador* and a wide sandy beach on which smallboats and canoes lay pulled up like drowsing sea elephants. To his satisfaction he recognized the outlines of whaleboats which had no business to be there.

Aware of a familiar deadly calm he studied *El Sangrador*. Sure enough, she'd been pierced for six guns to a broadside.

The only structure of any size appeared to be a box-like, two-storey stone building which in no way resembled a fort. It had, however, a square watchtower too low to have been effective as a look-out with what looked like a pair of swivel guns mounted on its roof.

He also found satisfaction in the fact that not more than three dozen shacks, cabins and shanties built of wood stood at irregular intervals above a wide gray and sandy beach divided by a short wooden wharf.

The country behind the settlement appeared supremely bleak, stony and forbidding. Only a few wind-stunted trees were to be seen.

Turning the conn over to sharp-eyed Tom Blue Fox, Jed slid down a stay to the deck. To effect the surprise he'd envisioned he ordered the topsails clewed up so that Chiloe's rock-studded shore could be hugged through the harbor's entrance.

Now possessed of a reasonable understanding of the situation, as well as of the lay of the land, the *Gladiator*'s Master implemented a swiftly improvised scheme of attack: no land batteries being in evidence, it stood to reason his first broadsides should be concentrated on *El Sangrador*. Once the schooner had been disabled or sunk it shouldn't prove over-costly—always provided his crew remained steady—to swarm ashore and carry El Funesto's base with pike, cutlass and pistol.

Mister Winslow strode up, craggy features contracting, "Don't like way the wind's dyin'. If we run into trouble in the harbor 'twon't be easy to clear out."

Jed jerked a nod. "Right, but that's a chance we'll have to take."

Steadily, the *Gladiator* glided towards the Cove of Oxen's narrow entrance. Great flocks of waterfowl roared into the air, skimmed past rigging and topmasts; seals poked heads above the surface and with soulful black eyes followed the bark's noiseless progress. Still, the presence of the whaler remained unnoticed in the gray half-light.

Only when the *Gladiator,* lower canvas turning pink, actually entered the harbor did dogs set up a furious clamor.

Jed, muscles standing out rigid along his jaws, took the wheel and steered straight for the schooner's stern; it should prove simplicity itself to rake the unsuspecting *El Sangrador.* So he passed word below for Mister Hayward to order gun pointers to aim at the picaroon's waterline and to keep firing till she started to sink: no point risking casualties by boarding a ship as completely surprised as this one seemed.

Unnoticed save for dogs running along the beach and fairly barking their heads off, the *Gladiator* glided silently across the Cove of Oxen straight for the schooner.

Much credit became due to Mister Hayward, Purvis and the other instructors that the carronades remained silent, when the bark entered into musket-shot and then into pistol-shot range.

Just before the *Gladiator* closed to point-blank range Jed ordered topsails backed in order to allow the gunners time to pound the enemy while they simply couldn't miss.

The bark, big and black in the half-light, had shoved her figurehead to within a hundred yards of *El Sangrador* before the first startled outcries arose.

To Purvis, standing straight and alert as ever he had on a British man-o'-war the Master snapped. "Prepare to fire!"

"Aye, aye, sir!" Out of habit the gunner saluted before repeating the order.

Some seventy-five yards off the big schooner's stern Jedediah Paddock, heart soaring, shouted, "Fire at will!"

At this still hour the broadside of carronades, small as they were, sounded outrageously, unduly impressive. Under the recoil of her four little guns the whaler shuddered and rolled a few degrees to starboard as gray-white clouds of smoke gushing through triced-up gunports started to drift back over the bulwarks. Seabirds screamed while below decks sounded a rumble of wheels and barked orders of Purvis and Mister Hayward. "Run in! Wet that swab! That's it, now drive home your charge! Round shot. Lay onto those tackles! Hit her 'twixt wind and water!"

Coughing amid clouds of rotten-smelling burnt powder smoke Abner and selected younger crew members, big-eyed with excitement, pounded back and forth below decks to fetch fresh charges from the bark's miniature magazine. There was no need to carry round shot, these having been secured in rope circlets designed to prevent them from rolling about; a good supply already lay beside each piece.

Sponges and rammers were swung and driven home by grunting whalemen. "Everybody yell! Yell like hell!" Jed roared. "Scare turds out o' those greasy, murderin' bastards!"

The *Gladiator*'s company complied and created enough racket to suggest that a frigate was closing in.

Because of the breeze's lightness, agonizing moments of uncertainty elapsed before gunsmoke cleared away sufficiently to estimate the damage done by carronades. A puff of wind obligingly moved the fumes sufficiently to reveal a series of jagged yellow-white holes punched through the picaroon's stern.

Inexorably, the whaler closed, spouting dazzling brief spurts of flames as her carronades smashed at their most effective range.

The sharp crackle of timbers being riven, shrieks, screams and shrill commands given in hysterical accents could be heard beyond a drifting wall of smoke which, when it again dissipated, disclosed figures running about *El Sangrador*'s deck in panic-stricken aimlessness.

Amazed and delighted that not even a musket yet had been discharged by the enemy Jed snatched up a speaking trumpet, shouted below "Mister Hayward! Canister, if you please! Sweep her decks."

At the same time he spun the wheel and, because not a gun yet had been manned aboard the picaroon, steered the *Gladiator* along the schooner's beam allowing his carronades to hammer her unmercifully at point-blank range.

The Fourth, alone in the main cabin, readied medical equipment while trying, with some success, to conquer unexpected qualms.

Causing a whirring noise suggestive of a covey of giant quail being flushed, canister raked *El Sangrador*'s deck, smashed spars, boats and severed plenty of halyards and braces. A chorus of shrill cries and wails swelled to a crescendo aboard the schooner, then a mob of hairy, wild-eyed figures appeared, scrambled onto her bulwarks to dive or leap into icy gray water.

By the time the whaler's guns had fired a fourth broadside it was seen that the schooner, half-seen through drifting smoke clouds, must be taking plenty of water through her riddled stern she was settling so rapidly. A big man in vivid green shirt scrambled up on the rail waving a white cloth and screaming, *"Merced! No más, por piedad! Merced! Entreganos!* Mercy! No more, for pity's sake! Mercy! We surrender!"

Murdo Morrison, perched in the maintop, shot the fellow, dropped him, arms flailing, into the harbor. "There's the sort o' mercy you desairve," he snarled. "Ye bluidy-handed rogue!"

Satisfied that the schooner not only was disabled but sinking, Jed sheered off, then, after ordering round shot, set his battery to firing at the settlement. At the same time he commenced to work the *Gladiator* closer inshore.

Because the wind was failing fast Jedediah further reduced canvas and wore, placing the *Gladiator*, almost motionless, with her larboard broadside fronting the settlement. Its first salvo effectively shattered the nearest row of hovels and shanties, sent broken boards and bits of furniture flying high above the beach. That no trace of leadership existed became arrested by the unchecked rush of half-dressed figures towards a low, bare and rocky ridge rising in the background.

Dogs, horses, cattle, poultry and pigs began to run crazily about among the shacks, effectively adding to the confusion. Once the stream of runners had dwindled to a few scattered figures Paddock ordered a cease-fire then in intense thoroughness, he and the mates studied the scene through glasses until satisfied no resistance was being organized.

"Don't spy anyone nigh them swivel guns on the stone building's roof," Mister Coffin's nasal accents observed.

Mister Winslow nodded, remarked in subdued voice, "'Tis a shining wonder our boys served the guns so smartly."

"They weren't being shot at," came Mister Hayward's dry observation. "Makes a heap of difference."

Only when fully satisfied that this settlement had been abandoned did the whaler's Captain order her anchored. Once a heavily armed landing party, brimming with excitement and voicing extravagant boasts, was mustered, were a pair of boats lowered and manned.

Meanwhile, Jedediah Paddock returned attention to *El Sangrador* long enough to note that her stern now was awash so much so her masts with loosely brailed sails raking backwards like those of a Chesapeake Bay skipjack. Her bowsprit was tilting skywards at an ever-increasing angle.

A few picaroons, evidently too badly wounded to escape, were screaming for rescue but the *Gladiator*'s Master paid them no attention; from what he'd seen, this harbor appeared too shallow to permit the schooner's sinking out of sight. Let the wounded picaroons clamber into the rigging if they could; if they couldn't, well, to hell with them.

From his boat Jed reconnoitered at close range before leading the men ashore. Musket held ready before him, he waded in with Te Ponapa splashing at his heels. The Maori was chanting a war song and making glittering steel windmills of cutlasses brandished by either hand.

After an interval of cautious skirmishing the invaders scattered to examine El Funesto's squalid little base. The only living things they came across were a few terrified curs and various sorts of livestock. No living human was discovered; only a few mangled bodies.

The sun was lifting above a range of lofty and very distant mountains when insistent blasts on a boatswain's pipe assembled the landing party looking let-down and grinning foolishly before the biggest building in the place; that same two-storey stone structure topped by a stunted watchtower already noted by Jed.

44
"—To the Victor"

Captain Paddock ordered a third boat to bring Lydia and a small party of reinforcements ashore to help in ransacking this rat's nest. Lyddie could list worthwhile plunder if such came to light.

On the Fourth's arrival the entire landing party was divided into three groups, each headed by a mate. There was to be no disorganized ransacking Jed announced. Every item of any value must, straightaway, be lugged down to the wharf.

Once the men dispersed, Jedediah dispatched Te Ponapa, Heetee, Fast Canoe and a few other dependables to make sure those swivels atop the stone building really were deserted.

He sent Big Pig Monahan and Beefy Pickleman along to arm and serve the swivels should the picaroons counterattack—which conceivably they might do. Nobody knew how many rogues had fled to the ridge.

Mister Hayward, happy as a dog with two tails, guessed the fugitives must outnumber the whalers four or five to one.

All manner of weapons, including a wide assortment of British and American harpoons and lances, were found in the hovels.

As foreseen, *El Sangrador* settled in water so shallow that not only her top hamper but also sections of her knightheads and bowsprit remained visible.

Even the most unimaginative among the whaler's crew went atavistic, waved weapons and shouted like vandal barbarians on being given license to pillage, generally run riot and set fire to all picaroon structures when they'd done looting. As Mister Winslow remarked after draining a bottle of powerful French wine, "Ah, me. I fear the passion for destruction lies scarce beneath the skin of most men."

With the exception of a very unhappy few gun crews ordered to remain aboard the *Gladiator* and stand ready, the whalers joyfully fell to work. Busy as ants, they ravaged huts and, whooping and yelling, staggered down the sandy beach bent under boxes, bags and ungainly, hastily tied bundles of plunder.

Everybody worked fast, there being no guarantee that other picaroons might not be using this lonely, well-protected little harbor. Another possible threat arose from the fact that owners of a few smacks and coasters on finding themselves ignored during the landing operations, slipped cables and, employing sweeps, had vanished through the harbor's entrance. Once free of the Cove of Oxen they'd hoisted patched brown-and-black lug sails to scatter at top speed. Should other pirate nests exist in the vicinity they might soon be alerted.

The landing party began by methodically ransacking huts along the settlement's edges; when they'd done they set them afire before turning attention to shacks next to the stone building.

From bare and rocky slopes above the anchorage, dogs, cattle and goats looked on, bewildered and sad-looking.

To Lydia, coolly excited, but taking in most of what was going on it was amazing to watch such slovenly hovels yield such a variety of valuable plunder.

Panting and sweating whalers staggered down to the beach carrying armfuls of silk and satin yardgoods, lace-trimmed garments and damask hangings, all to be tossed indiscriminately onto a growing, multi-colored pile. By twos and threes looters staggered out onto the wharf bent under casks, boxes, barrels and chests only to drop them, and go lumbering back for another load.

All morning the *Gladiator* lay, faithfully mirrored in the harbor's placid surface with a big red-and-black Paddock house flag dangling from her foretop and National Ensign limp on her mizzen gaff.

Until mid-afternoon whaleboats, gunwale-deep, continued to pull out to the bark. Beyond the littered beach the last picaroon shanties were giving off crackling clouds of smoke and flame to the delight of everyone—especially the Indians and the Maoris.

Tom Blue Fox, ludicrous in a woman's hat garnished with ostrich plumes started running towards Jedediah yelling, "Cappen! Cappen! Many hostiles on ridge!"

"In that case, Mister Hayward, take some hands and chase 'em off. Be sure there ain't others hangin' around once you've done."

Scarred features lighting the ex-Navy man cursed a hastily collected detail into a ragged line of skirmishers before starting up the slope whereupon a dense swarm of ragged figures on the skyline slunk back and disappeared into the bleak countryside of Chiloe Island.

Once the stone house's iron-banded door had been battered down, Jed beckoned the Fourth, surly through having been denied opportunity to prove her marksmanship. She followed her brother inside along with Te Ponapa, Purvis, Harrington and Hercules.

Jedediah and the rest halted, weapons ready to survey this stifling-hot and musty-smelling room which occupying the entire ground floor was piled shoulder-high in some places and clear to the ceiling in others with stacked boxes, bales, barrels and chests.

Jed noted the strength of many iron-bound coffers so detailed the blacksmith and Hercules to see what could be done about opening them. Noisily, they set to work. Whenever they came across a lock too complicated to be picked the Negro's maul would shatter it. On one occasion a massive iron padlock securing a beautifully designed wrought-iron coffer of medium size defied sledge and crowbar.

Jedediah, sucking on a captured pipe, turned to his sister, said solemnly, " 'Mister' Paddock, for time-out-of-mind you've been burnin' to exercise your pretty pistols. Let's see what you can do with 'em."

Shaggy, perspiring and weary whalers climbed up on the plunder about to watch the Fourth in apparent unconcern cock one of her silver-mounted weapons, retreat a yard, then sight steadily at the keyhole before firing. In this confined space the report sounded deafening as a carronade. When smoke cleared away, the blacksmith, grinning like a horse collar, unhooked the smashed padlock then threw back the coffer's lid.

A great, ringing yell exploded. Lydia gasped, burst into peals of hysterical laughter when a dazzling shaft of sunlight slanting through a small, high window struck into the coffer and drew breath-taking multi-colored flashes from a brimming hoard of jewel-and-gem-encrusted objects so jumbled together that quick identification at first glance proved impossible.

Half-deafened by the tumult about her, Lydia, nerves tingling, then succeeded in distinguishing rings, crucifixes, bangles, combs, bracelets, collars and necklaces; also pearl-and-jewel-encrusted gold monstrances adorning holy relics or paintings. What immediately caught and held Lydia's eye was a small and delicately wrought diadem set with a plethora of emeralds, diamonds, pearls and rubies.

Her dazzled eyes then sought her brother's and read in his expression incredulous delight mingled with overwhelming relief. The wonderful realization had just struck him that this treasure couldn't possibly have formed part of the *Amanda Alexander*'s rich cargo; this gleaming, scintillating hoard therefore constituted a pure bonanza which should go far towards erasing bitter memories of Vera Cruz and Yucatán.

Men outside quit what they were about to come crowding, shoving inside; all started yelling like lunatics when they glimpsed the hoard.

"God above! That there's a prince's ransom!"

"Move aside, damn you! Lemme see better."

"Hell! Don't fool yerselves, the most o' them jools can't be real!"

Roared the *Gladiator*'s Master, "Get back, you bastards! Back I say! Now start lugging this stuff to the beach. Move!"

Only continued pushing and shouldering on the part of Jed and his stalwarts started wild-eyed onlookers towards the door.

While superintending operations Jedediah felt the fine edge of his elation turned by a sudden realization that, with treasure aboard once more, there'd be danger of rekindling tensions, and plottings such as had bedeviled his voyage to Mexico. Now, the danger would be intensified; too many eyes actually had feasted on this dazzling, greed-inspiring treasure. Therefore, when another heavy, steel-strapped oaken chest came to light, Jed ordered everybody outside, excepting Hercules and the Fourth.

The cook's sledge having smashed its lock, the second chest was found brimming with gleaming gold and silver coins. Among the latter, to her surprise, Lydia recognized quite a few new-minted American dollars.

Pounding began on the door then Mister Hayward entered breathless and undoubtedly anxious for a view of the spoils. He jerked a salute "Sir, those picaroons on the ridge have scampered —wouldn't even tarry long enough even to exchange a few shots." The Third's eyes roved, commenced to shine. "Will you look at that? God above! We'll all be rich as bankers!"

"—Not unless we pull out of here fast," snapped Jed. "Go round up enough reliable men to lug these chests down to the wharf." He went to the door, stood outlined against blazing sunlight, shouted, "Hurry up that loading! We daren't miss the ebb."

By mid-afternoon the crew already were passing into the whale-boats plunder from a great pile dumped, helter-skelter, onto the wharf deck.

Once the ebb tide began to flow strongly boats were hoisted in, along with a pair of captured whaleboats. All hands, nearing exhaustion, moved slowly coughing amid acrid clouds of smoke drifting out from the beach.

Fire also had been set to picaroon smallboats. No point risking pursuit should this uncertain and feeble offshore breeze die out. But it didn't; it increased until the *Gladiator* bowled handily out of the Cove of Oxen and propelled by the ebb, entered that same narrow strait through which she had groped before dawn.

Clear of the strait and with Chiloe Island's barren silhouette rapidly receding Jedediah Paddock summoned smoke-and-sweat-streaked mates and boatsteerers to his cabin where, joyfully, he circulated a demijohn of prime Barbados rum. Meanwhile, the crew spliced the main brace with no less gusto.

"Well, Jedediah," observed Lydia Paddock Roach when at last she was alone with her brother, "your plan was brought off handsomely. I—I'm *that* proud of you—which I haven't been for a considerable spell."

"No more have I, Dark Sister." Chortling, he caught her off her feet and swung her around and around till her shoes grazed the desk and chart table. "B'God, girl, I still *can't believe* what's happened!"

"Well, *I* can!" she laughed. "But, remember, we're not home yet." She pressed a heated cheek hard against his bristly one. "Now put me down, you bully!"

While he was setting her down his sunburned features contracted. "And I'm mighty proud, too, Lyddie. Now that you're done with that would-be-female play-acting you've made as fine an officer as a skipper could hope for."

Flushing, she dropped her gaze, took a big swallow from her glass. "Glad I've pleased you, because I—I'm going to tell you something—" she looked at him steadily, "which you may or may not suspect. You see—"

—"Right now, Dark Sister, anything you do is fine with me." He executed a few jigs steps with all the grace of a dancing bear but only because he was so all-fired weary. "Oh God, Lyddie, ain't it grand to know I'm solvent again!"

"Yes, but—"

"But me no buts!"

He lit a pipe then, in high good humor, confided, "Things turning out as they have, reckon we'll make for the Line Grounds and start fishin' our way westward till we raise the Three Kings north of New Zealand.

"If Obed's lying in the Bay of Islands I'll transfer as much oil as he can take so's he can start home right away, beat the competition and get top prices."

High cheek bones suddenly prominent and with a desperate gleam in her oblique eyes, Lydia again attempted to break in. She failed, Jed being much too carried away by his theme.

—"Once the transfer's accomplished I'll head for Canton, full-tilt, and our banker friends' comprador—which is Portuguese for 'agent' or 'factor'. After that—"

He got no further because Abner dashed in to report a sail had been sighted.

Jedediah ran on deck leaving Lydia to quiver internally; it hadn't been easy to brace herself to the point of confessing a dreadful fact.

The stranger, Jed soon realized, was a big, full-rigged ship that suddenly had materialized from behind a headland; now she was crowding on sail so fast it was inescapable that her Captain must be hell-bent on overhauling the *Gladiator*.

Jed, abruptly sobered, ordered all hands on deck. The Mates and boatsteerers helped bone-weary men to crack on every stitch of canvas which might increase the whaler's speed.

45
Nuptials

On the second day after the *Gladiator* outdistanced that unidentified man-of-war which suddenly had appeared off the coast of Chile, Lydia Paddock grimly faced facts.

Since her abdomen seemed to become increasingly distended every hour she'd no choice but to brace for a hurricane and speak out to Jed. Craftily, she waited till he would be alone in the great cabin checking inventories of the plunder; at such a moment she reckoned she'd find him in a tolerably good mood.

When she entered he put down his pen and settled back casually to view the straight, slight figure in its customary male attire. "That's a rich coat of sunburn ye're wearin', Lyddie. Never seen you so red."

Said she tonelessly, "I hope you'll never again see me such a color." She drew a deep, deep breath, burst out, "Don't know how you're going to take this, Jedediah, but I'm pregnant."

To her stupefaction her brother nodded then burst into peals of laughter. "Been wonderin' how long 'twould take you to admit you've a bun in the oven."

"You *knew?*"

"For above a week I reckon. Off and on I've had—er, considerable experience with pregnant girls. Understand this, Lydia, I ain't going to take you to task for what's happened. Such happens to all kinds of women all the time."

She blinked, fought back rare tears and steadied herself against the *Gladiator*'s slow rolling. Also, she started to get angry. Why in hell hadn't this big brute let on and saved her this humiliation.

"How could you tell?"

"From the way you've been picking at your food lately; besides, I've heard you throwing up in your cabin some mornings." His amusement suddenly evaporated and his features assumed a stony, savage expression she knew—and feared. "Everbody will know about this come another few days if they haven't already caught on."

She stared with desperate intensity into piercing steely eyes illumined in sudden clarity by a flash of sunlight off the ocean. "Please, may I sit down?"

When he nodded she seated herself, gripping both arms of a swivel chair bolted to the deck.

"All right, speak up."

"For one thing I—I got assaulted—not once but twice."

"*Twice!* Holy jumping Jesus Christ! Who'd ever have guessed a cold, skinny fish like you would get snagged by more'n one man!"

"*I* didn't," said she defiantly, and color drained from her face. "But all the same that's what happened."

"When did this happen?"

"First time was on a moonlight night when we were passing Staten Island off the Horn."

"—And the next time?" He sounded eager, stimulated. "Go on."

"'Twas on the eve of the New Year."

Relaxing he settled back in his chair and began to chuckle. "Enjoy it better second time 'round?"

Dark eyes blazing, Lydia burst out, "Yes, damn you, I *did!* Guess I'm not your sister for nothing!"

"You're fairly sure 'twasn't the same fellow tumbled you both times?" Mouth slackening, he was relentless.

Gone scarlet again Lydia shook her head. "I—I can't explain, but somehow I'm positive it wasn't."

"Couldn't you tell by the size of the roger?"

"N-no. First time I was too scared, second time I guess I was too drunk to notice anything like that. Almost everyone was celebrating three sheets to the wind."

"I got drunk as a fiddler's bitch," he admitted. "Any idea who tumbled you?"

Lydia's olive-hued features relaxed into a bleak smile. "Know something? For a time I thought *you* might have been the first one."

Jed stared for a long instant then broke into a burst of delighted shouts, made the sunlit cabin resound. "Did you now! Well, I'll be damned!" He leaned forward, patted her hand. "Now I'll tell *you* something. After we left Mexico I was sore tempted to swarm aboard of you more than once. But I guess there's enough of Ma and old Micajah in me—" He broke off, spoke sharply. "Now then, who do you think your lovers were?"

Lowering her eyes Lydia murmured, "I'm by no means sure; but all during this cruise Te Ponapa's been attentive in a shy sort of way."

"You like him?"

"Yes," a trifle defiantly. "Ever since he came to our house in Nantucket I always have sort of favored him but I haven't dared show it, he being a savage."

Sun-cracked lips forming in a soundless whistle, Jed nodded several times. "Who else?"

"Well, maybe Mister Hayward. We had many a long talk together during night watches; for all that's happened to him he's educated and well-bred."

"True enough, therefore I'll post him as another prime candidate for your hand. Anybody else? Thought I've noticed that big Irishman Harrington giving you some pretty calculating glances."

She nodded in silence. "Yes. He—he appeals to me. He's so merry and so full of life."

"Anybody else?"

"Uh. No, no, no! What do you think I am?"

"—My pregnant sister who needs to get married in a big hurry."

A brief silence ensued during which the slow creak and groan of the ship's fabric and the dull thumping of feet on deck sounded distinct.

Briskly Jed said, "Now then, which one do you think most likely got you knocked up?"

"I—" She flushed furiously, "I—don't know much about such matters, you see. The two—two assaults came only about six weeks apart."

"Well, one thing's certain. We can't be sure if Ponapa's responsible till the baby's born, by which time we ought to have reached Canton. But that needn't concern us right now; main thing is to get you spliced straightaway. Now, Mister Paddock, you'd better send the cabin boy, go to your cabin and wait till I call for you."

By the time Abner appeared Jedediah had decided on playing a hunch and summoned Te Ponapa. He appeared from duty smiling, barefooted and wearing only a pair of work-stained canvas breeches.

The harpooner's tattooed bulk seemed to fill the whole of the white-painted cabin.

"You sent for me, sir?"

"That I did." He paused long enough to cause an anxious expression to appear on the Maori's broad, pale-brown features. "Now I'll not beat about the bush." In an ominous, harsh voice he demanded, "Did or did you not lie with my Sister?"

To Jed's infinite astonishment Te Ponapa nodded promptly, teeth gleaming amid the dark background of his face. "A very good time; the happiest night of my life."

"Nonsense! Lydia's always been a cold-blooded, skinny little bitch."

"You never noticed those fires that burn deep inside?"

"You still say you were happy?"

Te Ponapa beamed. "Yes, my Brother—I was overjoyed because, soon after we became blood-brothers, I began greatly to admire and then to grow fond, very fond of your sister, but I didn't dare reveal my sentiments. Instead, during nights on watch, I often composed and sang love songs to Lydia which only the night wind could hear."

"By 'admire'—what do you mean?"

"She is so capable, so self-possessed." Te Ponapa's voice rang louder. "Best of all, she has the gift of command such as a great chief needs in his consort." His enthusiasm faded and his manner became almost abject. "Oh my Brother I greatly regret what happened. I intended waiting until we reached Aotearoa when I could, as a great *rangatira* ask you for her hand."

Humbly he bowed his head. "Too bad I drank so much on New Year's Eve; you know what even a little rum does to people of my race. I—I grew lustful, went crazy. My Brother, I am ashamed of this and sorry beyond the use of words. Can you forgive? Can she?"

Jed hesitated then said with a half-smile, "Yes. Precious few saints sign aboard a whaler." A flood of relief warmed him. Now b'God there'd be no necessity to quiz and possibly threaten either Hayward or Harrington. Tomorrow Lydia would have a husband, and no ordinary one. The more he peered into the future, the better he felt. Considering certain ambitions 'twould certainly prove no disadvantage to have Maori royalty of a sort one of the family.

Early the next morning while the deck still was bright with dew all hands were summoned on deck; most looked frankly puzzled, others sniggering, offered lewd comments in cautious undertones.

In his capacity as Captain, Jedediah Paddock solemnly joined Lydia Paddock Roach and Te Ponapa, *Rangatira*, in holy matrimony.

II
Aotearoa

1

Three Kings Astern

Driven before a half-gale out of the northwest, the whaling bark *Gladiator* soon left astern a sinister trio of towering, surf-ringed islets known to those familiar with the waters about New Zealand's North as "The Three Kings".

Curtly, Captain Jedediah Paddock ordered Third Officer Hayward to steer the course he'd shaped for New Zealand, which should allow ample avoidance of a galaxy of largely uncharted reefs and sandbars lying off the North Island's coast.

At this stage of the cruise there seemed small point in running unnecessary risks to save a few hours' running time. Well, with any luck, before another sunset his lookouts should raise landmarks marking the Bay of Islands' eleven-mile-wide entrance.

'Twould prove interesting to find what might be there; Obediah more than once had stated that in and around Port Russell was concentrated the greatest number of rogues to be found in one spot anywhere in the universe.

The question plaguing him most at the moment was whether he'd find the *Morning Star* lying in one of several anchorages scattered about the spacious and fabulously beautiful Bay of Islands.

Lord! He was yearning to feel his twin's massive fists hammer his shoulder blades. Although Nantucketers seldom were given to open displays of emotion he and Obed had been so close over many years that, following long separation neither made much effort at restraint even in public.

He cast an eye aloft to make sure his smoke-smudged courses and topsails were well-trimmed and drawing steadily; in silent approval he noted Mister Coffin, whose watch it was, ordering another staysail set.

The *Gladiator*, her holds half recharged with sperm oil since they'd been emptied into the whaler *Nobadeer* long months ago, was driving steadily through long, evenly spaced and silver-crested rollers.

It had been pure good luck Jedediah mused while taking a turn across the oil-spotted deck that, on nearing the coast of China, he'd come across the whaler, *Nobadeer* of Nantucket. Her Captain, Levi Saltonstall, sourly admitted he'd suffered the goddamnedest run of bad luck; out three years, she was heading homewards with under three hundred barrels below hatches.

Saltonstall, long a close friend of the late Micajah Paddock, following a conventional backing and filling over terms, had proved ready and able to take aboard the *Gladiator*'s rich, rank-smelling cargo.

Jed had experienced no qualms over entrusting oil to Pa's old friend; if anyone could, and would, obtain fair prices for the *Gladiator*'s take it would be whiskery, sheep-faced old Levi Saltonstall.

Around midday the wind moderated somewhat; presently, the sun shone so warmly that Lydia soon appeared lugging her cheerfully gurgling owl-eyed baby.

Jedediah always anticipated Dark Sister's appearance for Lydia, in a maternal role, struck him as incongruous, if not downright funny. Not that his sister was unfeeling, yet, somehow, her movements when attending to her infant seemed hopelessly direct, quite unfeminine. To watch her nursing black-haired little Pehi through a seaman's checkered shirt inspired frequent fits of silent laughter.

Morning's first light revealed land as a series of dim, gray dots and streaks showing off the starboard bow.

The minute Te Ponapa, become Fourth Mate in place of his wife, sighted the North Cape his whole manner underwent decisive alteration; shouting at the top of his lungs, he hugged Heetee and so far forgot himself he actually did *kongi*—rubbed noses—with a servant! Both Maoris began a wild, stamping and jumping *haka* encouraged by the grinning crew who clapped hands in ever-quickening rhythm until the panting dancers were forced to quit.

"Hail, oh Aotearoa!" gasped Te Ponapa, tears streaming down his face. "Greetings, beloved Land of the Long White Cloud!"

Sure enough, in a short while a long, white cloud *did* form and cling about the pointed peaks of a blue-black mountain range.

Dark-red lips forming a thin smile, Lydia balanced her tawny-skinned infant upon the rail and pointed. "Take a good look, Pehi," and turned his head, "that's Papa's country. Reckon 'twill soon be home to us also."

She struggled to keep her voice level but it wasn't easy. Yonder lay a strange, barbaric land where, in all likelihood, she would spend the rest of her days; Lydia Roach Te Ponapa had no intention of fetching a half-caste child back to America. Well, she mused a trifle defiantly no one ever could claim with any justice she hadn't accomplished what she'd set out to do on quitting Nantucket.

Her thoughts reverted to the present. Did Te Ponapa's father, the *Ariki*, Te Pehi, still rule the Ngati Waikato and sub-tribes living around Waikato Bay? How would she react when a cannibal feast took place? That she was strong-stomached above the average Lydia was well aware, but even having to attend during the consumption of human beings—!

One fact recently imparted by her massive husband to whom she daily was growing more quietly devoted, offered a measure of reassurance; he assured her that, under normal circumstances, it was sternly *tapu* for a female even to taste human flesh.

From the quarterdeck Jed beckoned Mister Te Ponapa who, grinning, hurried aft. Whipped by a rising breeze the two big figures watched the North Island's mountainous outline rise, silver-gray, out of the sea.

"How does it look after all this time?"

The Maori drew a huge breath. "How can I say what I feel? Who knows what will become of me—and you—in this, my home country? Anything is possible."

"Hell, you're going to take over your pa's property. If he's dead I'll back you b'God with every gun I mount. Never doubt that." He fixed brilliant eyes on his companion while the wind tore at long yellow hair with invisible talons and his jaw went out.

"Tell you something, Brother, I don't mean ever to return to Nantucket or to New England for that matter—got myself into too much trouble; besides, I figure there's a rich fortune to be won out here provided one ain't over-choosy about how you go about it. Aye, and I can be just as tricky and tough as the next man, as you ought to know by now." His voice strengthened over the sea noises. "Yep. Once you're settled in yer rightful domain I count on you to give me all the men and supplies I need to get established, even if it means licking a hell's mint of savages and white bastards in the process."

Te Ponapa flung an impulsive arm about his companion, hugged him hard as they swayed and balanced to the motion. Eyes hard and bright as onyx he cried, "Together we *will* rise, though many battles may have to be fought. You shall have your empire of trade and some day I shall rule over the whole West Coast! I *know* that."

Newly appointed Gunner's Mate Abner Doane, deeply tanned and now standing five feet eight on his bare feet, was growing broad in proportion. He touched his cap to Lydia then, light-brown hair lifting easily under the breeze, continued on forward. There, Heetee and the ship's Indians, copper-brown and wearing blue-black hair knotted into tight braids, stood talking excitedly by the rail. All of them were peering over the heaving water at this fabled country rising slowly, grandly out of the ocean.

A long while back, Tom Blue Fox, John Fast Canoe, Billy Big Buck and big-nosed Dick Sun-in-the-Eyes had accepted Heetee as one of their group once the Maori exhibited a penetrating and intelligent curiosity concerning the American Indians' way of waging war.

Particularly he was curious concerning bows and arrows, the use of which, he confessed, was almost completely unheard-of on Aotearoa. The skillful employment of such silent and long-range weapons he felt offered military and hunting advantages too great to be neglected. He couldn't explain why an intelligent and war-like people like his own hadn't yet discovered the bow and arrow or, for that matter, the use of the wheel, block-and-tackles or even the forging of metal implements.

The Monomoy, Tom Blue Fox, in particular took pleasure in teaching Te Ponapa's squat, beetle-browed follower how to fashion a short, strong bow, string it and finally send an arrow flashing into a spot painted on a sack stuffed with straw and shaped into the rough outlines of a human body.

Young Doane, after studying the North Cape a while to memorize landmarks, strolled over to make funny faces at Lydia's baby who rewarded his efforts with a fixed, uncompromising stare.

The bark's after-guard had been surprised how quickly Sylvanus Doane's son mastered even difficult problems in seamanship and navigation; also, he'd grown skilfull in his handling of a harpoon or a lance.

Fine fuzz covering Abner's squarish chin gave off little bright flashes when he bent to pat the baby's head. "I declare, Mrs. Ponapa, I'm all of a twitter over the prospect of reaching the famous Bay of Islands. Think we'll see really wild Maoris thereabouts?"

"Shouldn't wonder. You'd better make certain-sure some cannibal don't take you for the main course of his dinner."

"I bet he'd a sight rather munch on Pehi—" he pointed to the black-haired baby, "—or you."

Lydia couldn't help laughing. "You've a point there, only I expect they'd find me pretty tough and stringy. Howsumever, I'm sure Mister Ponapa will see to it we don't get sampled."

Abner turned away to check log recordings on slate beside the wheel. The bark was really making time; if she kept on at this rate they'd enter the Bay of Islands by dawn and he'd get a real look at Te Ponapa's homeland.

Would it, could it be possible that in Russell he'd hear some word about Pa? He could hear himself asking for the thousandth time, "Anyone heard anything about a Sylvanus Doane of Boston, last seen in Port Jackson, Australia, about seven or eight years ago? He was Third Mate in the ship, *American Star* of Boston."

Of course someone would query, "What did this fellar look like?" and he'd have to answer miserably, "All I know is he was slim with a long, straight nose and wavy light-brown hair." This was all he'd ever been able to learn, Sylvanus was never discussed within the family.

Turning to the taffrail he wondered why he'd never been able to accept the plausible fact that Papa most likely must be dead. Still, if old Adam Masters of the *Amanda Alexander* correctly had identified Father as the Third Mate on the *American Star* who'd got himself in such deep trouble in Port Jackson, he *might* still remain alive, slaving out his sentence on Norfolk Island.

Maybe, if the Captain took the *Gladiator* to Australia later this year, as he'd hinted he might, he could learn something through the Courts in Port Jackson and determine what could be done to help his scapegrace sire.

As was his custom while entering an unfamiliar roadstead, Jedediah Paddock settled himself on the fore crosstrees, powerful legs swinging in space.

For the life of him he couldn't understand this peculiar sense of apprehension which had bothered him ever since the North Cape had been reported. Likely, he'd heard too many contradictory reports conerning this ruggedly beautiful country, and its intelligent, artistic and often fiendishly cruel inhabitants.

Then, at the back of his mind lurked his old ambition gradually to give up whaling with all its risks, personal and financial, and, getting in on the ground floor, establish a great trading business in this raw, naturally rich land.

Much depended, of course, whether Obediah's old *Morning Star* soon would be sighted in one of the Bay of Island's many well-protected anchorages.

Studying a distant island—or was it a headland Jedediah wondered how he'd go about trafficking the cargo of firearms, chinaware, cloth and iron goods taken aboard in Canton, now that he'd completed his duty towards Messrs. Doane, Welch & Peabody. One item he'd been advised always stood in high demand in New Zealand: Jews harps, of all things! Why a war-like people such as the Maoris would fancy such an instrument was beyond him; nevertheless he'd a good supply of them below decks along with many bolts of scarlet cloth, mirrors, paints and strings of bright brass, silver or copper beads.

For their part, the crew were aware that scrimshaw work was much-sought-after in Russell which intensified their use of awls, sailor's needles and scroll saws in shaping whale teeth into ship models, bracelets, rings, combs, brooches, hair skewers and other gewgaws.

Jed settled against the white-painted foremast. Would Port Russell, formerly Kororareka, the main port on the Bay of Islands, live up to its reputation? He hoped so. 'Twas high time for a free-for-all and a rousing time with local females. B'God these days his breeches were fairly bursting, morning and night.

Next morning Lydia who, although no longer an officer had continued to keep the *Gladiator*'s log, wrote in her clear, flowing script:

'October 30, 1832. Commenced with moderate wind at N.N.E. attended by dark, rainy Weather. Shortened sail at 7 a.m. Clear Weather, wind shifting. Jagged black Mountains and Hills rising to Starboard beyond a long and sandy Coast.'

She then glanced at a transcript made from the log of the whaler *Sam Robertson* during the long stay in Canton:

'The Bay of Islands open to N.E. to the W. Cape Pocock. The entrance is safe and very wide, a most commodious Bay.
Latitude obs. 36.00.00 south
Longitude obs. 168.38.30 east'

Aside from a few wandering rain clouds the day proved fair when the *Gladiator* reached the bay's entrance and left Point Pocock to starboard and Cape Brett, barely visible in the far distance, to port.

Under full sail the bark headed for a scattering of small, barren islands ringed by lazy surf.

As usual, Abnor was fascinated and later noted in the journal he'd recently begun to keep the presence of exotic sealife; huge black or striped marlins lazily paralleled the ship's course with dark, triangular dorsal fins neatly cleaving sparkling, dark-blue water. Several unfamiliar species of shark also were in evidence as well as great schools of playful, comical-looking porpoises.

What especially charmed the new gunner's mate were small squadrons of sedate little black-and-white Adalie penguins which, quite unfearful, cruised alongside and studied the *Gladiator* from bright black-and-yellow eyes.

Myriads of seabirds circled, screeched and dove all about the bark feeding on *kahawai* which, Heetee declared, was a tasty gamefish much resembling mullets in shape and color.

Here and there naked, bushy-haired natives were emptying nets into outrigger canoes dug from a single tree trunk. These small and muscular fishermen weren't nearly as dark-skinned as Abner had been anticipating—not by half. Laughing and calling greetings, they waved paddles and blew long, wailing notes on conch shell trumpets.

2

Port Russell

Recalling Obediah's advice, Jedediah Paddock took the *Gladiator* past a series of anchorages situated near the bay's entrance and occupied by a few anchored, slack-rigged whalers.

Lydia using a chart hand-drawn by Obediah and weighted flat before her, noted various havens—Tippuna, Keri-Keri, Rua and the rest.

The *Gladiator* sped past many small islands, mostly low-lying and covered with drooping palms, until Jedediah reduced canvas on leaving Tepekka Point to port.

Obed had advised: "To start with, it's a good notion to drop your hook at the river's mouth near Waitangi, the missionary settlement. The savages there are reasonable quiet and can supply you with food, wood and water at reasonable prices.

"When you need to visit Russell, go in a smallboat. Your crew will deserve a frolic in that hell hole, but mind you give 'em shore leave a few at a time. Don't let a second lot leave till every man-jack of the first party shows up."

Jedediah therefore cast anchor near the mouth of a small river flanked by a dense forest of enormous, pale-trunked trees.

A low, white-painted mission house dominated a group of clean-looking whitewashed huts and small storehouses scattered, hit-or-miss, among palm groves and green fields stretching away towards the forest, but for men craving lusty entertainment this anchorage didn't look inviting at all, at all.

Te Ponapa raged in disappointment. What news of importance, he demanded, could be garnered in so remote a settlement? He had to have information, accurate information and lots of it. Paddock's ambitions, he rasped, would suffer if he didn't find out promptly what might be going on.

A flotilla of canoes deep-laden with food and other trade goods soon put out from shore.

Abner studied them, hopeful they'd offer *paki-pakis*—preserved human heads—for sale. Once he displayed one the bays around Boston would *have* to credit even his wildest yarns.

Suppressing anticipation Captain Jedediah Paddock, next morning, ordered a boat. Among others he took along Mister Hayward, Tom Blue Fox, Te Ponapa and Heetee and set sail across the spacious blue-green waters of the Bay of Islands.

No less than fourteen stub-masted, smoke-grimed and bluff-bowed whalers and half that many merchantmen were lying off a narrow beach from which a number of jerry-built wharfs and docks jutted out into the translucent water like broken brown teeth. Behind these stood a row of unpainted, jerry-built warehouses which in Canton would have been termed "godowns". In disorderly fashion the palm-thatched roofs of many nondescript structures could be seen climbing a steep, half-moon-shaped bluff paralleling the beach.

Crudely lettered signs indicated that this hovel was a chandler's store and that yonder shack dealt in general merchandise. A few unpainted, two-storeyed frame structures brazenly proclaimed themselves "hotels". Many shanties advertised billiards and skittles but most bore signs reading "Tavern", "Bar" or "Ordinary".

Once his whaleboat's leg-of-mutton sail had been lowered and his men were getting out Jed recognized the *Pocohontas* and the *William Roach*—both of New Bedford—and then the *Julian* out of Duxbury, Massachusetts.

Farther inshore lay the *Cyrus*, a fellow Nantucketer he'd visited many times. Briefly, Jed wondered whether irascible old Ben Hussey might still be commanding her.

Other short-masted, carelessly-rigged and smoke-grimed ships showed faded and weather-shredded Union Jacks; among them the *Samuel Enderbury* of Liverpool, the *Duke of Norfolk* out of London and the *Corinthian* from Bristol, plus a scattering of equally graceless whalers showing Australian colors. The *Prince of Denmark* easily was the largest in port.

Between these whaleboats, dingies, canoes and clumsy, locally built shallops kept criss-crossing refuse-laden water. When such craft collided, their occupants bellowed insults, threats and drunken abuse.

To Jed's surprise he recognized a Church of England chapel, also a theater of sorts. Innumerable saloons and brothels even at midday, seemed to be doing a thriving business. Why not? A generous tot of villainous Jamaica rum or the favors of a dim-witted, worn-out native wench cost no more than ten cents.

Te Ponapa, after giving his solemn promise to report aboard the *Gladiator* before dark, promptly disappeared towards the back of town.

Again and again Jed heard his name called, then some bearded and generally blear-eyed New Englander would come swaying up to shake horny hands and beg for news from home.

"*Morning Star?* Ain't seen hide nor hair nor heard any report of her," drawled Dick Gifford of the *Pocohontas* who, back on Nantucket, had been switched by the same schoolmaster as Jed.

One chance encounter proved productive; a horse-faced Australian skipper claimed to have sighted the *Morning Star* cutting-in a whale not a fortnight earlier. He'd not spoken her but, judging by the fact she rode so deep in the water, he reckoned the American must be having a greasy cruise.

In quest of further tidings Jed, with Mister Hayward, roamed a succession of dusty and malodorous alleys, peered into many dark, fly-filled saloons and "hotels" to be hailed by hideously smiling, bloated, bare-breasted native females, raddled half-castes and a few bedraggled, pale-skinned harpies who might have been altogether white.

Over the years Jedediah and his Third had touched at some mighty tough ports but were in agreement that never before had they encountered so sordid a concentration of lawlessness, drunkenness and vice.

Brawls, mostly half-hearted, seemed endemic in these airless, sun-blasted streets and alleys. Serious fights, if they threatened to cause a dangerous and expensive riot, were broken up by a vigilante force of merchants organized by one S. J. Polack, a tough English Jew of considerable education and varied capabilities and a burly ex-convict named Ben Turner. Apparently these worthies were the only residents willing to make even a pretense at maintaining order.

Turner, Jed learned, had been in Kororareka some fifteen years and had started out as part-owner of a sawpit turning out ship planks. Through business ability and utter ruthlessness he now owned or controlled a good many bars and bawdy houses in addition to a shipyard, a careening dock and a wholesale chandler's business.

The effects of alcohol and venereal disease were written tragically upon the native population. In almost every alley once-handsome and stalwart Maoris lay dead drunk amid dust and refuse; flies crawled in and out of half-open mouths. Scarecrows crouched, dispirited, sick and befuddled wherever they could find a bit of shade.

Hercules, who'd pulled an oar in Jed's boat party, learned that somewhere along the town's outer limits lay several stockades in which a couple of enterprising "Government men"—as ex-convicts were euphemistically referred to locally—kept bevies of young female prisoners sold by their captors.

These rascals for years had been conducting a lively business by selling girls and young women outright to sealers, whalers and other seafarers. What later befell these chattels interested them not at all.

Hercules discovered Captain Paddock consulting price lists in Turner's chandler's warehouse and, eyes gleaming, described what he'd seen. "Cappen, dey got some likely wenches out back dere. Mebbe you lend de hands 'nough money to buy us a few 'gainst de next leg ob de voyage?"

A short laugh escaped Jed. "Maybe. I'll decide after all the hands have had a chance to plow furry furrows about town." He winked elaborately. "Now I'm going off-duty. See you at the landing."

Without further ado he made for the nearest and least noxious-appearing "hotel-bar". He strode through swinging doors roaring, "Turn out everybody! Drinks are on me 'till I've proved I can lick any bastard in the place! Come along, ladies, I've got something good for you, too!"

When early next morning Te Ponapa, *Rangatira*, appeared in a canoe paddled by muscular, half-naked natives he was being treated with obvious, almost obsequious respect, a fact not lost upon Jedediah Paddock who, sore and wearing a livid welt under an eye, was suffering from various forms of remorse—among them a splitting headache, badly skinned knuckles and a certain tenderness in the region of his groin.

He nodded only perfunctorily when Te Ponapa reported himself aboard but sat up on noting the Maori's manner and expression.

"What's the matter? Didn't you find yourself sufficient *vahines?*"

Te Ponapa fetched a deep sigh, said frowning, "After I heard what I did, I had no taste for pleasure—besides, am I not a married man and father of your nephew?"

Jed passed a damp cloth over his forehead, briefly tested his bruised eye. "You'll get over that in time. What's your news? Your father dead?"

"No. Te Pehi remains *Ariki* of my people—or was a few months ago."

Considerable of Jed's misery became forgotten. He sat up, blood-shot eyes intent on the broad, tattooed features before him.

"Then what's wrong? One of your brothers been named heir-apparent?"

"No. My informers said the Old Man refuses to believe me dead because the wisest of the *tohungas*—priests—have told him I still live."

"Then why the long face?"

Te Ponapa looked his brother-in-law straight in the face. "Because my father is full of years and a powerful new enemy threat-ens his borders from the north."

"'Powerful new enemy?' Who?"

"I could not learn much," Te Ponapa admitted, "only that this new war chief is a white man who, with a few other *pakehas*, prob-ably escaped convicts, seized rule over the Tari Mata tribe and have been conquering the West Coast. My father's land is next to be at-tacked."

"And who is this—this renegade?"

"My informers could not say his real name—only that he is known as 'Tahi Mata Kagatira', the One-Eyed High Chief. They say he never has been defeated because he owns an armed schooner and has plenty of muskets. He even conquered a great chief called 'The King of Bones'. My father is much afraid and he is so old. Without firearms of his own he knows he will be conquered. You understand why I am sad?" Then his face lit. "But the *Ariki* will not suffer defeat because you, my Brother, will fight on our side. But we must move swiftly. Can we sail tomorrow?"

Jed got to his feet fighting down a threat of nausea. "Take it easy, Brother, take it easy. Let's consider practicalities. Your news is weeks, maybe months old—your pa may have been done in by now. Anyhow, I intend to meet with my brother—have to, matter of business. That, with Paddock and Company, always comes first in case you've forgotten.

"Sure, I've promised to help you and I will to the limit, but only when the right time comes—which, pray God, won't be over-long in arriving."

Te Ponapa tried to break in.

"No. Don't try to galley me. I know what I'm about. Remember one thing—I'm just as keen as you to see you on your throne or whatever you call it and although I'm dead-set to start trading along the West Coast, I don't aim to go off half-cock even to help you."

He grinned suddenly, flung an arm about the other. "Te Ponapa, I'm only going to wait a reasonable time for the *Morning Star* so you'd better see it my way."

"I have no choice," Te Ponapa admitted bitterly. "I will wait. I must have your help."

Having wholeheartedly sampled the dubious pleasures and positive dangers of Port Russell, Jedediah kept the *Gladiator* at anchor off the missionary settlement.

However, he granted the crew shore leave in rotation and advanced sufficient cash to allow them, for a space of twenty-four hours, to run riot, drink and fornicate to the best of their means and ability. The next party was not allowed to shove off before the first lot had returned, generally in battered condition.

The only crew members he refused to allow to visit Russell were his American Indians. Too well he knew that even a few mouthfuls of well-watered rum could transform a steady, dependable harpooner into an insane, murderously-inclined savage. Shore leave for Tom Blue Fox and his fellow redskins therefore was limited to the flourishing settlement of Waitangi where Anglican missionaries headed by vigorous and practical-minded Reverend Mr. Fairbairns, applied effective restraints. Sensibly, blind eyes were turned towards certain erotic practices, so long as such were performed in the privacy of some convert's hut.

Concerning matters of the flesh—well, the *pakeha* priests were aware that not much could be done about combatting a hospitable custom through which chiefs lent nubile maidens and even attractive young wives as entertainment for a stranger within the gate.

3

Reunion in Aotearoa

In bluish shade cast by an awning rigged aft of the mizzen Jedediah Paddock lay sweltering and only half-awake, his vast muscular form sparsely concealed by a native loincloth. How much longer should he wait on Obediah? Um. Already a fortnight had passed without sight or report of the *Morning Star*.

Te Ponapa, his resentful impatience becoming more pronounced each day, got news that fresh tribal wars—some of them large scale —were being fought along the West Coast so grew withdrawn to the point of sullenness. Only when little Pehi was brought on deck did he relax and become his old self—a dusky Hector dandling Astynax.

Jed was sipping rum, water and lime juice when the anchor watch called out, "Mister Coffin's boat's headin' back."

Jed heaved his bulk from a hammock of flax netting, went to join Te Ponapa at the rail. Early that morning Lydia, bored and restless with this tedious delay, had wheedled the Second into taking her handline fishing off Motu Rua Island, along with Abner Doane and a pair of Indians.

Eyes squeezed tight against the glare Jed noted that the whale boat's sail was sheeted home so she was making good time before a moderate breeze.

Before the whale boat could arrive alongside Lydia hailed through cupped hands, "*Morning Star's* rounding Tapekka Point!"

"Sure of that?"

"Aye," boomed Mister Coffin, red-gray chin whiskers flaring. "Recognized her and yer private signal minute she ran out from behind the Point."

Te Ponapa roared relief; soon the *Gladiator* could resume her cruise.

Jed ordered the black sperm whale on its scarlet field to the foretop and a clean Stars and Stripes to the mizzen gaff.

Hands began betting on just how well the Old Man's twin had fared since quitting Nantucket Lord alone knew how long ago.

Jed donned a clean checked shirt and ran a comb through recently shortened yellow hair before ordering Number Two and Four carronades readied to fire six blank rounds—long the customary salute exchanged between Paddock ships in foreign waters.

Half an hour later the *Morning Star* veered into the river's mouth and under short canvas made straight for the Waitangi anchorage.

The large crowd collecting on shore watched a half-dozen puffs of gray-brown smoke burst thunderously from the bark's side and drift lazily off over the bay. Meanwhile, the National Ensigns of both vessels thrice were dipped.

As the blunt-bowed old whaler that had accomplished so very much towards founding Micajah Paddock's fortune drew near, men on both ships began cheering and waving any handy piece of cloth. Lydia felt resentful over the way her eyes kept filling. Damnation! Here was a small piece of a home she'd never see again.

Te Ponapa raised a chant of greeting before he and Heetee executed a wild, leaping *haka*. Tom Blue Fox and the other Indians danced too, treated the ever-growing crowd on shore to a series of screeching war whoops so blood-curdling as to impress the Maoris—themselves no mean raisers of ear-piercing battle cries.

The last of Obediah's canvas was being clewed up when a fiddle on the *Morning Star* struck up "Hail Columbia, Happy Land." In Russell some skipper must have identified the Paddock house flag for over in the distance began to sound the dull *boom!* of cannon saluting and the *crack! cracking* of muskets aboard whalers owning no wheeled ordnance. Many hoisted American National Ensigns.

British and Australian crews looking on expressed obscene amusement over such noisy demonstrations. The few foreigners in port paid no heed.

When the *Morning Star*'s stubby bowsprit entered the river Jedediah signaled for her to tie up alongside; in so sheltered an anchorage there could be little danger of entanglement and make it dead easy to transfer cargo, provided Obed had room for roughly a hundred additional barrels.

Jedediah, climbing into the main shrouds, shouted welcome; and when he made out Obed's huge figure waving a peaked cap it was hard not to let his voice thicken.

Gradually the expanse of clear green water separating the whalers diminished until Obediah halted his vessel's forward progress a short distance to windward by backing topsails; gently the smoke-blackened *Morning Star* then started to drift towards the *Gladiator*.

Behind him Jed heard Lydia's query, "Who's *that* standing beside Obediah?"

Intent until then only on the *Morning Star*, Jed had paid no notice to a short, trim figure lingering on the quarterdeck. Because of the stranger's slight build, white trousers and seaman's shirt he at first judged the figure to be a cabin boy; but then he took a second look and batted his eyes.

"B'God, Lyddie, damned if Obed ain't acquired himself a female creature!"

Lydia sniffed. "Knew that minutes ago. Wonder what a woman's doing aboard of Obed?"

The gap separating sides narrowed until, causing a gentle grinding sound, the *Morning Star* came to rest alongside. Once yards had been braced about to avoid fouling, watches on both vessels set about securing them together.

Disappointed, Abner Doane frowned at that small figure balanced on the other's rail. Hell's bells! Yonder was only a miserable female! What with those curly locks cropped so close to her head she sure had looked like a lad. Damnation. Now he wasn't about to find a youth of his age to gam with, man-to-man.

To his surprise Jed found himself staring hard into a girl's golden-tanned, delicately formed but rather squarish features, dominated by a full-lipped and rectangular pink mouth. Her small, round eyes were wide-set, very dark. Framed by ghost-pale curls they offered a most effective contrast.

As upon an apparition from some other world Jedediah stared at this diminutive creature balancing on the rail not twenty feet distant and became aware of unprecedented and confusing emotions. The man's shirt she was wearing had been unbuttoned low enough to disclose a deep cleavage between round, high-riding breasts large enough to have looked better on a bigger woman. She in the lad's clothing was looking about, gesticulating with quick, bird-like movements suggestive of intense vitality.

Then she noticed Jedediah's stare. When their gaze met and clung she became immobile. To both of them it seemed as if surrounding activities had ceased to exist and they were alone, absorbed in fascinated astonishment.

The hiatus was broken by Obediah's shout of, "Coming aboard! Rig me a gangplank."

Once Obed and his companion had started crossing Jedediah Paddock drew a deep, deep breath, looked hard at his sister. "Don't know what's come over me, Dark Sister, but—I—*I'm damned if I don't marry that girl!*"

"Get your head examined. To me she appears an extra flighty bird."

4

Aimée Dumont

While preparing supper Goober Pike, teeth gleaming like a piano's keyboard, outdid himself after sending Heetee ashore for native delicacies. After sundown a table was set up on the *Gladiator*'s after deck and loaded with a profusion of exotic fruits and local dishes in addition to sturdy American fare. The after-guard of both vessels, primed with plenty of Old Medford, applied themselves so heartily to the victuals they paid no attention to the melodious singing of converts in canoes alongside.

Crew members, openly or covertly, were curious about this pale-haired young woman who wore a dress of crisp yellow cotton when she came abroad in company with the *Morning Star*'s towering skipper. To Abner, the pair suggested a ship-of-the-line escorted by a dispatch sloop.

Who was she? What was she? They'd not seen her like before. She looked sporty and yet she didn't. From her escort's manner they couldn't tell a thing; Cap'n Obed appeared polite in an offhand way but he wasn't acting in the least formal or kiss-your-hand.

Lydia, her infant blessedly at peace below, attempted an unbiased estimate of Obediah's companion and found it difficult to arrive at. Owing to her limited experience among females she'd never encountered one so completely enigmatic as this annoyingly vivacious young woman.

Before long Aimée or "Amy", as she preferred to be called by English-speaking persons, cheerfully had identified herself in clearly enunciated accents as the only child of one *Capitaine de Vaisseau* Augustin Dumont, cadet son sprung from an ancient line of Norman seafarers.

The light of a cabin lamp picking out her lively, golden-brown features and silvery hair Aimée spoke incisively. "Like others of his position, Papa made the French Royal Navy 'is career. Through sheer ability 'e became Lieutenant Dumont. That was just before our Révolution changed everything. *Figurez vous!* Nevertheless, 'e survived the change not only from the Bourbons to the First Republic but also to the Navy of Napoléon.

"Papa 'ad become a *Capitaine* when 'e put in at the Island of Guernsey, in the English Channel. There 'e met and became enamored of a young English lady and, much against 'is family's objections soon made 'er 'is wife.

"Papa," Aimée continued, her expression sobering, "was killed off Toulon in a frigate duel with the English even before *Maman* 'ad been granted time to conceive a second child."

Full, coral-tinted lips compressed, Aimée averted her head as if to consider a cluster of fires glowing and leaping on the beach.

"After Papa's death," she continued, "*Maman* and I were penniless so she went to keep house for a crippled uncle of mine. It was near Fécamp that I grew up wild as a colt but better educated, I suppose, than most girls of my age. *Maman* being English I learned to speak English," she shrugged, "as you can 'ear, well, but not perfectly. I also can make myself understood in German and Spanish."

Listening in complete absorption to the young woman's discourse Jedediah judged her to be about twenty years—give or take a few months. The way she gesticulated, incessantly waved square, short-fingered hands; the way her round, black eyes kept darting about—damned if he'd ever seen her like. Why should he find himself goggling at her like a callow mooncalf?

Lydia meanwhile was deciding that although this lively young female *might* lend the impression of being soft and compliant like a friendly kitten, she nevertheless could, if need arose, make effective use of teeth and claws.

What most impressed her concerning Amy was the girl's sense of awareness, combined with an apparently inexhaustible vitality. To her surprise she commenced to appreciate, if not to approve of Amy who, like herself, seemed to be one of those rare females who knew what she wanted out of life and intended to get it.

Had Jed suddenly become one of her goals? Impossible. They'd scarcely met. And yet—and yet. Never had she seen her brother in such a silly maze; he barely sampled victuals passed by Abner and Goober. Perhaps he was too preoccupied in listening to his twin describe Aimée Dumont's arrival aboard the *Morning Star?*

Obediah's deep voice was relating, "We were fishing along the Line till a spell of hard gales drove us near five degrees south of my intended course; 'twas lucky for Amy I'd a sharp-eyed lookout in the hoops else he'd never have spied an empty-lookin' smallboat."

He nodded towards a gaunt, gap-toothed officer tearing at a chicken leg. "I ordered Mister Lincoln to lower. He discovered Amy and three others lyin' in a foot of water on the floor boards near perished through hunger and thirst."

Like an amiable sunburnt bear Obed beamed on the diminutive figure at his side and only then realized she was looking hard across the board where the triangular scar on Jed's chin was beginning to show red.

Mister Winslow paused, wiped gravy from his flowing gray whiskers. "Mind my askin', Miss Dumont, how-come you got found in such a sorry fix?"

She treated the gaunt First to a fleeting smile. "It was that I 'ad taken passage on a corvette from Le Havre with intention of becoming *gouvernante* to the children of an aunt who is the wife of *Monsieur le Governeur* of Noumea." Politely she added, "As m'sieu knows, Noumea is capitale of Nouvelle Calédonie."

This of course was only a half-truth. She'd been fleeing the intolerable boredom and the stifling life of a minor French port—as well as clumsy, provincial attempts at seduction. She'd succumbed just often enough to grow ambitious for more soul-satisfying experiences in a brighter *milieu* than that of Normandy.

She'd snatched eagerly at an opportunity to emigrate. *Vogue la galère!*

Again Aimée waved supple hands. "We 'ad arrived but a few weeks short of our destination when, during a terrible tempest, our ship took fire. *Hélas,* soon the flames reached that place where gunpowder is kept—what is it called?"

Without removing eyes from Aimée's face, Jed spoke for the first time. "It's called the 'magazine'. Expect your ship got blown to smithereens?"

Aimée's nod was brief. "If 'smithereens' means veree small pieces, that is the word correct. It was 'orrible. Only a few reached a smallboat drifting among the wreckage. We were fortunate. Everybody else perished."

While Aimée continued her account her small brown-black eyes seldom shifted from Jed. What had come over her? Here was not a man of rank, of fortune or of a great family—only a big American, as crude as the rest of his compatriots.

What confounded her was that although this fellow across the table was the mirrored image of her rescuer his attraction somehow was overwhelming, whereas toward his brother she'd felt only gratitude, intimately expressed on a few discreet occasions.

But this Jedediah!—*bigre!*—why did so many Americans have outlandish unpronounceable Hebraic names?—his appeal was an affront to a thoughtful girl's commonsense.

Why did she keep acting as if he were the only man at the table? She didn't wish to remain so aware.

But she did.

Chanting and the wild music of a *hakari* taking place on the beach floated out to the ships. Finally, Jed heaved himself to his feet.

"Come along, Bro, let's go aft and gam. Lyddie, suppose you show Miss Dumont 'e Ponapa's heir?"

Sucking pipes, Jedediah and his twin seated themselves on the poop, were briefly content to watch the leaping glare on the beach and listen to the pulse-quickening rhythm of a *poi* dance.

At length Obed scratched his nose, said without turning his head, "Well, Bro, am I mistook or hasn't that little Frenchie got you thrown into a clove hitch?"

Jed continued to regard the river's purple-black and starlit water, said steadily, "Never did believe in first-sight love. Don't know why but one way or another I've simply *got* to get Amy for my own." He shrugged. "Can't explain, but there it is. Now ain't that something?"

Obed sucked till his pipe's bowl glowed ruby-gold. "Guess the age of miracles ain't by yet. Howsumever, you won't get this one like Lucy Dismont and the rest, else I'm 'way out of soundings. Know something? You could do worse than to marry her. For all her soft looks and chatter I've found Amy as sensible as she's—she's warm and tempting. She sees things like they really are."

From under an elevated brow Jed considered his brother. "Just how 'warm and tempting' is she?"

A small chuckle escaped Obediah. "That's for me to know and you to find out."

Jed left matters at that.

Big fish jumped and plopped, huge bats skimmed silently about spars and rigging etched against the star-stippled heavens.

Finally Jed straightened, tapped dottle from his pipe against the taffrail. "You got room for some oil?"

"Depends. I'm pretty near full. How much you got?"

"—A hundred eleven barrels."

Following momentary reflection Obed's big, golden head inclined. "Reckon I can accommodate just about that much." He tapped teeth with his pipe's stem. "What're your plans, Bro?"

"Won't know certain-sure till I find out how things stand 'twixt Te Ponapa and his people." He broke off. "What's your opinion of his marrying Lyddie?"

"They get along? Love one another?"

"They're getting on better all the time. Lyddie's softened a bit and for her she's acting real tender towards him and their baby."

"Answer my question. What d'you *really* think of Sister marrying a brown fellow?"

"Can't say I'm overjoyed. People back home will never understand."

"She knows that, plans to stay out here for good. Lyddie's always needed someone to tame her so maybe matters won't turn out too bad, seeing as how he's royalty of a sort."

"Te Ponapa know yet what's going on in his home country?"

"Not for sure; he's all of a sweat to find out where he stands."

"His father still alive?"

"At last report he is, but he's very old and may have died. If he's dead I figure my pop-guns—as you call 'em—just might convince Te Ponapa's people—they're the Waikato tribe—that Lyddie's spouse is their lawful ruler."

Canoes kept circling the whalers so in a rare, mellow mood, Jedediah ordered natives be permitted to come on board—people under missionary influence should present no problems.

Thus far they'd appeared only eager to trade fruit, pets and beautifully worked greenstone ornaments in exchange for scrimshaw work and fancy-tied knots. Pretty soon a Portuguese guitar commenced to strum and dancing began on the starlit foredeck.

Obediah prompted, "Suppose our brother-in-law gets recognized as ruler—what follows?"

Jed's tattooed hand crept up thoughtfully to stroke his jaw.

"Why, I'll do what I've intended all along, explore the West Coast for trading possibilities. If I like what I find I'll set up a trading station in Te Ponapa's country though I don't mean to leave off whaling altogether. I—I, well, I don't intend to go back to Nantucket, either—too damn' pious and narrow for my taste."

He looked his brother in the face. "You're the one to keep the family going back home—respectable and prospering. Me—well, I just ain't cut out to be a Puritan ancestor.

"Whenever I stand in need of a refit and fresh trade goods I'll make for Port Jackson or Canton." He sat up and stretched hugely. "I'll have no competition on the West Coast so stand to make a fortune in due time."

Obed predicted, "'Twon't be all that easy. From what I hear, the West Coast is a confounded tricky and dangerous one and ain't been charted since Captain Cook did it back in 1769. All the tribes there are hard-fighting cannibals and hostile to strangers."

"Reckon that's true. Still, I intend to go see for myself. Never did mind a good dust-up now and then."

"'Pears like you've got your mind made up—till now." He laughed and reloaded his pipe.

"''Till now'?"

"Yep. Let's see how you and this Dumont wench fare."

Lydia's and Aimée's voices could be heard growing louder. When they reappeared on deck Obed stalked over.

"Come aboard of me, Lyddie. Got some scrimshaw might interest my nevoo. What's he called?"

"'Pehi'—after my husband's father," she informed teetering over an extra-wide plank connecting the whalers. "Seemed a smart move and it pleased Te Ponapa no end."

On the *Gladiator*'s stern the oddly assorted couple frankly scrutinized one another. Aimée, well-rounded, but scarcely half Jed's height, had to tilt back a small, pale head while he peered downwards.

Increasingly, he became enveloped by the indefinable physical appeal exuded by this petite young woman with the large, curvaceous and infinitely soft-looking bosoms. Her full-lipped mouth slowly was opening as if she were out of breath.

"Amy, I—I, well, I'm rated pretty handy with the gab when it comes to womenfolk, but right now, I—I'm taken full a-back."

By radiant starlight her teeth glinted. "*Je comprends.*" She frowned. "I understand, yet I do not. Why is it I seem to 'ave known you so long. Ah! Perhaps I 'ave it! It is because so much you resemble your *jumeau*—what you say, 'twin'?"

"Aye. That's the word."

"—And yet there is much difference between you. I—I never wanted your brother to 'old me close—neither he nor any other man."

" 'Other man?' "

She fell back a step. "Yes. There 'ave been others—a very few. So now you know; it is better to be truthful, no?"

"Sure, and I guess you can tell I'm no part of a plaster saint, either—no whaler is."

Jed cast a quick look about, saw that everyone had concentrated their attention on the foredeck and the erotic undulations of a trio of bare-breasted girls.

Suddenly his huge hands closed over her shoulders and held her steadily at arms' length. "Now that that's out, I—I hope you're agreeable to marrying me because, well, I won't have it any other way."

For a long instant she hesitated, then sharply inclined her small, bright head. "It may be a terrible, a fatal mistake for us to speed into marriage but I cannot believe that we are mistaken. *Je suis contente*. In you, *mon coeur*, I be'old the man I have sought so long in vain; one who is so very strongly determined, ambitious and, I think, capable of great love."

5

Rites

In his chapel's vestibule the Reverend Mister Fairbairns and his plump wife, both clad in Sunday best, stood awaiting the arrival of a curious little party making their way over a sun-seared lawn.

Captain Jedediah Paddock and Te Ponapa, who'd often been ashore, were the only people the minister recognized. When Obediah Paddock came close the Reverend Fairbairns blinked furiously believing himself abruptly afflicted by double vision.

Behind the towering American sea captains strode Te Ponapa ill-at-ease and turned out for the occasion in European clothes, tattooed features and all.

After them came a lithe, dark-haired white woman who, despite voluminous skirts, moved more like a youth than a female for all she was lugging a brown-faced infant in European swaddling clothes.

Beside her was a short, silver-haired young woman in a calicut gown of pale blue; she wore her home-made garment with an air—as if it had been created by a Parisian modiste.

A few paces behind the ladies trudged a small group of beaver-hatted, liberally whiskered officers looking mighty red-faced and uncomfortable in these unfamiliar go-to-meeting suits. Bringing up the rear was an excited throng of crewmen and grinning converts.

Sedate greetings having been offered, the Reverend Mister Fairbairns and his spouse led the visitors into the chapel—originally a spacious and handsomely carved *waka*—storage house. On the peak of its sharply pitched roof of straw-colored thatch gleamed a gilded Latin cross. Near an altar on which candles already had been ignited was waiting a quartet of round-eyed Maori boys wearing skimpy lace collars over surplices of coarse, red-dyed muslin. They kept squirming broad bare toes on the floor of hard-packed earth.

The Reverend Mister Fairbairns slipped on a stole and then,

flanked by a pair of native acolytes vigorously swinging censers that gave off the fragrant fumes of burning sandalwood, led the way deeper into the chapel's cool, dark interior in which clouds of flies droned in aimless circles.

Before a handsome altar of kauri wood the minister faced about, opened a well-used Bible which he made no pretense of reading and pronounced, "Dearly beloved, first we will christen a soul ready to be saved from damnation and accepted into the blessed community of our Lord, Jesus Christ."

He adjusted steel-rimmed spectacles and over them sternly regarded Lydia's wooden-faced husband. "Te Ponapa, *Rangatira*, approach and kneel before the font."

Christening rites soon were completed with the big Maori being given the Christian name of "John"—chosen at random because an ex-pagan had to have one.

Then Lydia brought forward little Pehi, whose round black eyes considered the proceedings with a lively curiosity. He squalled only briefly while the minister with Holy Water was tracing the sign of the Cross on his forehead.

Obediah, uneasy but cooperative, stood as godfather. It was he who suggested the infant's Christian name: " 'Peter' sounds godly and it's easy to say."

To Mrs. Fairbairns it came as a surprise that so many weather-beaten whalers, although sweating like draft horses, could recall correct responses and unhesitatingly repeat nearly forgotten prayers.

Once the christenings had been completed the Reverend Fairbairns blessed the congregation and was about to close his Bible when Jedediah Paddock, broad features aflame, took Aimée Dumont by the hand and led her forward.

"Reverend, sir, Miss Dumont and I—well, we'd be vastly pleased if you'd marry us."

"Of course. And when?"

"Right here and now."

For all she'd assisted at many a bizarre ceremony during long years of service in foreign lands Mrs. Fairbairns batted her eyes, then, summoning the best smile ill-fitting false teeth permitted, murmured, "You *will* accommodate these young people, Mister Fairbairns?"

The minister considered Aimée standing straight as a ramrod to her scant five feet of stature. "Miss Dumont, do you consent to enter into Holy Matrimony with this man?"

"*Mais oui*— But yes, of course, and with much joy."

Obviously more than a little puzzled, the Reverend Fairbairns noisily cleared his throat before beginning the marriage service.

6

Heir-apparent

Long hours of labor under a broiling sun were required to transship the *Gladiator*'s second cargo of sperm oil into the *Morning Star* and get barrels snugged down against the long voyage home.

Once Jedediah had bear-hugged Obed farewell he prepared to take the *Gladiator* over to Russell to replenish essential stores before heading for the North Island's West Coast.

While her crew were hoisting jibs and shaking out topsails the Reverend Mister Fairbairns, his wife, family and flock lined the shore. Maoris among them waved green branches and lifted the traditional chant of farewell: *"Fa'aroha mai to maru*—Grant us thy protection."

Aimée Dumont Paddock waved until those on the beach were no longer recognizable, then turned piquant features towards her bridegroom. "Ah, *mon coeur*, right now I paint in my mind this so lovely place where we 'ave met."

Jed slipped an arm about her. "Reckon I will, too."

To one side Lydia stared thoughtfully over the taffrail at the receding shore then her mouth tightened and her chin rose. Damned if this wasn't the start of another adventure. How would it end?

Since the last of the oil had been transshipped an amazing change had come over Te Ponapa. For one thing he'd stowed all *pakeha* clothes in his sea chest and had taken to wearing only a kilt. He went about his duties barefooted and with a pair of pointed black-and-white-tipped *huia* feathers stuck upright to either side of his forehead.

For the first time he openly wore his *tiki* of greenstone. Rapidly, the Maori sloughed off mannerisms acquired over years of exile.

The *Gladiator* remained half a day off Port Russell only long enough to take aboard European supplies and provisions then her anchor was heaved and her now badly weathered figurehead swung towards the bay's wide entrance.

Ensigns, house flags and private signals were run up and dipped and were duly acknowledged.

After weathering the North Cape the bark encountered a full gale which pounded her sides and flung heavy blankets of spray high enough to drench the foregallant's buntline hitches.

Deprived of the steadying weight of oil discharged into the *Morning Star* and not having taken on ballast, the *Gladiator* plunged and twisted like a harpooned porpoise.

Although in possession of charts brought reasonably up to date by his twin, Jed took care to steer well clear of the Three Kings, then continued to sail far offshore lest he pile up on some unmarked reef or shoal.

The *Gladiator* therefore sailed south so far from land that her lookouts saw nothing of Ahipara Island and that part of the coast which Te Ponapa explained was ruled by a ferocious chieftain called "the Bone King".

The weather continuing blustery and unpredictable, Jedediah remained cautious and wary along this wildly beautiful coast dominated by a range of towering, heavily wooded mountains running roughly parallel to the shore.

At long last Te Ponapa came aft saying, "I recognize that headland by the twin round hills near its tip." Excitedly he added, "I know this coast all the way to Waikato Bay. There are many dangerous reefs and sandbars." His big voice deepened. "The north boundary of my father's lands begin a short day's sail to the south."

Through his glass, Jed studied a double line of shoals foaming wildly off to port. "I reckon, Mister Ponapa, you'd best climb the hoops and conn us in."

During the night the weather modified until Te Ponapa declared it safe to stand inshore. For all his confident air the giant, on occasions, appeared a bit hesitant, which wasn't to be wondered over since he hadn't beheld this coast in years. Nevertheless he conned the bark through the entrance to a capacious bay rimmed by high, wooded hills. Just inside and in the lee of a rocky headland Jedediah ordered his bark anchored, but kept canvas loosely clewed so it might be cast loose in a hurry.

The ship's company watched Mister Hayward's boat lowered

with Te Ponapa standing in the same prow from which he'd so often seated a harpoon.

Lydia's heart lifted when she called, "Take care and come back soon."

Aimée murmured, "*Mon Dieu*, Lydia! Does 'e not make a figure of the most impressive—a noble sight?"

Te Ponapa, wearing a long-skirted kilt of flax, a plaited war belt and a colorful cape of yellow-dyed feathers, turned and saluted the Stars and Stripes floating from the signal gaff. On his chest gleamed a necklace of mako shark's teeth while into his hair had been stuck the usual pair of *huia* feathers.

Heetee to the best of his ability also had ornamented himself in Maori style.

Oars dipped and flashed when the whaleboat started her journey propelled by long, lazy rollers beating regularly in from the Tasman Sea.

Soon the whaleboat hoisted a triangular sail, became lost to sight beyond a group of small forested islands dotting Waikato Bay.

When the Third's boat had disappeared, Paddock ordered gun drill, the first in a very long time. Since Gunner Purvis had become stricken with rheumatics Abner Doane substituted for him. He had become so adept with carronnades that he now rated as a full gunner's mate.

By the time the sun had started to touch the horizon anxiety set in, mounted steadily until the sail of a seagoing canoe was sighted heading for the entrance's far side.

Jed decided against mentioning the possibility that were Te Pehi no longer reigning in Waiuka *pa* Mister Hayward's boat party well might meet a sanguinary finish.

Night fell and with it the wind; the boom and grumble of surf on distant shoals and reefs became distinctly audible.

Lydia, once she'd nursed Peter Pehi, climbed tight-lipped to the hoops and insisted on relieving the lookout. Sighing, she felt the familiar embrace of iron and peered desperately through purplish-gold twilight.

Strange, until now she'd never really appreciated how very dear her husband had become. To her surprise she found herself composing a silent prayer which appeared to be answered when, instants later, a pinpoint of clear white light—unmistakably cast by a sperm oil lantern—rounded an island masking the depths of Waikato Bay.

An icy skewer seemed to pierce her heart when, twenty minutes later, Mister Hayward's boat lay bobbing alongside. Although every white man in the boat's crew was present there was no sign of Te Ponapa or Heetee!

On reaching the deck Mister Hayward saluted the non-existent quarterdeck—time would never break him of that habit.

"Sir, I have to report that—."

"Mister, I'll hear your report below. Come along, Lyddie—if things have gone wrong I don't want you bawling in public."

"Damn thee, Jedediah!" she hissed. "I don't bawl—ever; thee knows that full well!" Full skirts asway, she followed him down the companionway.

The expression on Mister Hayward's battered features remained enigmatic while Lydia, outwardly impassive but struggling to keep her hands steady measured out three mugs of rum and tepid water.

In his deep, strangely cultured voice, the Third reported that once his boat was well into Waikato Bay—Te Pehi's *pa*—had come into view. Mister Te Ponapa who'd become very uneasy, had observed that some very unusual event must be taking place.

"When I asked him why, he pointed out that not a single fishing canoe was in sight; also that a landing below the town seemed deserted." Mister Hayward took a long pull from his mug, sighed and wiped his mouth on back of a saddle-colored hand.

"Nobody seemed to pay us heed till we were a half-mile offshore, then a big canoe filled with armed men put out. Mister Te Ponapa guessed pretty quick what was up; a funeral of great importance was going on. Mister Te Ponapa was sure the moment he saw the paddlers' faces freshly scratched and bleeding and that they were wearing heavy wreaths of green leaves jammed low over their brows."

Lydia suddenly grated, "Dammit, Mister Hayward, *will* thee stop beating the bushes!"

"Aye, ma'am. Your husband's safe; reckon I should have said so first off."

Jed peered through the cabin's gloom. "What bigwig's funeral was going on?"

"Te Pehi's, Mister Te Ponapa's father's. Seems three days ago he got killed in a battle. Well, the funeral was going on, full tilt, when we landed."

"Belay," Jedediah snapped. "How did the natives receive Te Ponapa? Friendly-like?"

"Yessir. With shouts of joy."

"They recognized him at once?"

"Straight away, sir." Mister Hayward nodded before draining his mug. "After a bit, Mister Te Ponapa learned how his father, the old *Ariki*—I think that was his title—died in an ambush rigged by a tribe allied to the top chief of Kaipara."

Lydia elevated narrow black brows. " 'The Chief of Kaipara'?"

"Aye, ma'am. He's that white renegade they call the 'One-eyed King'—the one we heard about in Russell."

"Go on," directed Jed, wide-set blue eyes intent. "What chanced when Te Ponapa reached the town?"

"Nothing at first," explained the Third. "Folks were too busy with mourning old Te Pehi; you should have seen how fast Te Ponapa joined in. Tore off his ornaments, he did, scratched his face, then howled and groaned louder than the best of 'em. Oh, I forgot to tell you; Mister Te Ponapa's next younger brother got killed at the same time."

"If Te Ponapa's Pa got whipped, how come his body was fetched home?"

Mister Hayward scratched at bristles standing silvery on his jaw. "Seems like the ambushers overplayed their hand and got chased off."

Jed signalled his sister to replenish drinks. "What happened then?" Damned if it didn't look now as if Micajah Paddock's daughter weren't about to become a queen!

"In the old *Ariki*'s honor the men of Waikato had sacrificed all the prisoners they'd taken and still were eating some when we came ashore. Well, sir, just afore I shoved off Mister Te Ponapa came down and told me he'd figured he'd best stay on shore on account of there'd soon be a grand council of some sort to decide whether or not he's the rightful heir."

"Any doubts on the matter?"

The former Navy man's scar-seared brown features contracted. "Who knows about savages? Oh, one thing more: as Mister Te Ponapa was bidding me farewell he whispered, 'Please ask the skipper to come in to the bay and anchor in easy range of the *pa*.' Mister Te

Ponapa claims while he don't *expect* trouble 'twould do no harm to kind of let the council understand he's got guns to back his claim. You'll oblige him?"

In the lamp light Jed's smile widened. "For a smart man, Mister Hayward, you sometimes ask ox-dumb questions."

7

Amelia Island

On a hilly, well-wooded island lying a short mile to the northeast of Waiuka *pa*, Te Ponapa, *Ariki*'s capital, Captain Jedediah Paddock and his men, aided by a horde of native laborers erected the first components for what he intended to become the finest careening place and trading center on the North Island—Russell included.

He'd selected Amelia Island because this island was blessed with a spring of never-failing fresh water and protected from attack on three sides by a crescent of shallows and reefs capable of discouraging the approach of heavy war canoes and European vessels of any size.

A pair of European-type houses were the first to go up; one was a dwelling for Paddock and his bride the other a sizable counting house built at the end of a sturdy wharf alongside a thatch-roofed warehouse.

Already increasing numbers of canoes from all along the coast had begun to appear to unload bundles of flax, kauri gum and baskets of greenstone ornaments.

Fine ship-building lumber felled along the bay's farther shore was towed to a crude shipyard in which a small schooner soon began to take shape.

Straight and flawless spar timbers were brought in to be weathered and cured for the benefit of those European vessels which in time were bound to appear once news of his venture got about.

Outside a large stockade of pointed logs a native village sprang into being and grew rapidly. At the stockade's center arose a two-storeyed blockhouse with the usual overhang to its upper floor.

After considerable deliberation Jedediah decided to mount a pair of carronades on platforms placed to protect his wharf and the stockade's main gate.

On the hot and sultry morning of New Year's Day, 1833, a scattering of buildings lining Amelia Island's deep little harbor had been decked with all manner of flags, banners, pennants and ensigns as well as streamers of gaily colored yardgoods and colorful floral decorations.

Visitors arrived in flotillas of canoes to join in a great *kanikani*—ceremonial dancing and singing. They stared, deeply impressed, on the fortifications, the like of which they'd never beheld. However the principal attraction proved to be the *Gladiator*—that great black-and-white *pakeha* sailing canoe so huge, so graceful and so dangerous because of its cannon. Many visitors also were moved to exclaim over the beauty of an unfamiliar starry flag fluttering above the block-house.

Since Jed's home had been built on a hillock behind the stock-ade Aimée Paddock enjoyed a fine view not only of the anchorage but also of that *marea* on which Mister Hayward and Abner Doane at the moment were putting on an exhibition drill presented by a company of musket men selected from a mass of volunteers.

From her verandah Aimée Paddock watched the drill in con-scious comfort. Her thickening waistline made it agreeable to occupy an armchair in the shade while a naked little slave girl fanned her.

Dieu de Dieu! How incredible. In a few short months her whole way of life, her philosophy and sense of values had undergone so many sharp and fascinating alterations. How kind fate had been since she'd taken the plunge, had abandoned the colorless, dreary security of the society into which she'd been born. How *could* she, for so long, have endured the bleak cold fogginess and winter gales of Fé-camp?

True, she'd almost died in that waterlogged boat, but she hadn't; now she could count herself among the happiest of women. Still she wondered where she'd found sufficient temerity to risk such a wild gamble as to marry a man she'd scarcely met. Bless that instinct! Day by day and night by night their devotion had become intensified to a deep-seated devotion and better yet to a respect and understand-ing of one another. And now, with a child in the offing, their inter-ests were becoming more securely interlocked.

"Oh, *bon Dieu*," she prayed silently, "please permit that we 'ave a son we can build and plan for. Let 'im in 'is time become a leader among men as is his dear father. Later, *bon Dieu* we will welcome all the girls you care to send us, but let *this* one be a boy."

From the parade ground rang Jed's voice as he gave someone a rousing tongue lashing. She only smiled; as a naval officer's daughter she understood the necessity for the unvarying and sometimes brutal application of discipline.

She found much comfort that Queen Lydia Te Ponapa, together with little Peter Pehi, so often appeared on Amelia Island. Gradually a bond based on outwardly different, but in fact, similar viewpoints had grown without comment.

That her enigmatic sister-in-law had become pregnant for a second time within weeks of arrival on Waikato Bay might have accounted for the swift deepening of their *rapprochement*.

For all Te Ponapa's forces were being instructed in new tactics built around Jedediah Paddock's élite handful of musket men, the *Ariki* never slighted the traditional mode of Maori warfare. Continually he hardened young warriors through exhausting forced marches and maneuvers in all weathers and over the most difficult terrain he could find.

Aimée was seven months pregnant when the day she'd been dreading finally dawned; the *Gladiator* was readied for a whaling cruise to Australia.

Ever since Te Ponapa's accession, except for short exploratory cruises along the coast, the *Gladiator* had remained at anchor off Amelia Island to permit certain of her crew to help construct Jedediah Paddock's trading station.

Somberly, Aimée watched mildewed canvas materialize on the *Gladiator's* recently scraped and white-painted upper yards; next her bow swung across the glimmering, green-blue water until it pointed towards the bay's entrance.

All at once an appalling premonition seized her. Could it be that she was viewing the *Gladiator* for the last time? Angrily she shrugged. What nonsense!

Eyes filling, she got to her feet and waved a kerchief when the *Gladiator* dipped her colors and fired a gun. The fort, now under Mister Hayward's command, returned the courtesy.

Fervently, Abner Doane cursed his luck over having been left to complete the training of Te Ponapa's company of musket bearers.

Now he'd find no opportunity, when the bark reached Sydney, formerly Port Jackson, of resuming the eternal question: "Have you seen or heard anything of an American merchant officer name of 'Sylvanus Doane'?"

8

Ruawai Pa

Eyes narrowed against the hot glare Sylvanus Doane watched the *tohunga moko*—priestly tattoo artist—use a frayed twig to apply a solution of charcoal and water and sketch a fern leaf pattern along the top of his stringy left thigh. When completed the design would match in perfect detail a graceful blue-black pattern already decorating his other limb.

The gaunt, gray-haired artist dipped his needle, a shark's tooth lashed at right angles to a wooden handle into a little, highly ornamented gourd filled with a thick pigment composed of water mixed with candle, nut ashes, charred caterpillars, gunpowder and *kauri* gum.

Naked save for a narrow red loincloth tucked between scrawny thighs, Sylvanus Doane settled a lean and wiry frame well back in one of the few chairs in Ruawai *pa*, one of the best fortified and strategically situated strongholds along the West Coast of New Zealand's lovely but rugged and mountainous North Island.

The one-eyed white man tightened his grip on the chair's arms then braced calloused brown feet against the first lancing pains which would begin once the tattooer commenced to use his little wooden mallet.

Impatiently the white man used a heron's wing to fan aside flies gathering at the first smell of blood and in so doing caused an ornament, incongruous on a Maori chief, to flash momentarily; this was a gold signet ring engraved with the Doane coat-of-arms—a greyhound gracefully leaping over a six-pointed star and a scroll bearing the motto, *"Toujours Fort"*. The ring, gleaming bright because tattooing had darkened the white man's skin, served as a single reminder of his past.

"Does the *Kagatira* desire to have this leaf completed at once?"

queried the tattoo artist blotting freely flowing blood with a swab of flax.

Doane, known to his people, the Ngati Tari Mata and a steadily increasing number of allies and sub-tribes, as "the Great One-eyed Chieftain" inclined a narrow, sandy-gray head. Its angular features by this time had become effectively disguised by intricate patterns of spirals, loops and whorls darkening a naturally fair complexion to an uniform and spurious swarthiness.

Privately, Doane thanked God that especially painful facial tattooing was over and done with; no longer would he be forced to subsist for a while on liquids fed through a wooden funnel because his features had become so swollen he couldn't part his lips even a little bit.

The victim drew a deep breath, traversed his remaining bright-blue eye along a green-blue river winding its way down to empty, a mile farther on, into the wide and shimmering expanses of Kaipara Bay. It flowed through an area of wide, level beaches below those low bluffs on which stood his modest capital, Ruawai *pa*. Well, if events kept on moving as intended, his wooden palisaded *pa* ought to double or maybe triple in size before long.

He was glad to be protected from the hammering rays of a torrid sun by an unusually wide porch fronting his *kaitangata*—small palace. Four intricately carved black-and-red-painted posts suggestive of short totem poles supported its thatched roof and created at least an illusion of coolness.

His gaze paused briefly on a boatyard across the river where, under the direction of a priestly canoe builder—gangs of stark-naked slaves, chunky brown-black bodies gleaming with sweat, were swinging adzes and using stone chisels and gouges laboriously to shape and hollow out a sixty foot log of *kauri* pine. Eventually this would form the middle section of yet another handsome and extremely seaworthy *waka taua*—war canoe.

The dull *thump* and *thud-thud* of crude tools rang clearly through the hot and windless atmosphere.

On wide, shelving beaches lining either side of the sluggishly flowing stream, rows of plain, unornamented canoes designed for fishing, for easy transportation on rivers and for other everyday uses lay drawn up like basking crocodiles.

Higher upstream on a strand just above a complicated fish weir, women and girls, smooth, light-brown bodies agleam and for the most part naked as Eve washed clothing or sat in the shade plaiting and knotting fishnets of green flax. Others were busy fashioning lobster pots and crab traps from bundles of well-soaked and peeled willow wythes.

Doane was recalled to matters nearer at hand by stinging pain when the *tohunga* went to work in a fresh area. The one-eye American gritted teeth but couldn't suppress grunts when, to the delight of swarming flies, blood began to trickle warmly down his haunch and patter onto a coarse floor mat of woven bulrushes.

He cursed himself for the hundredth time for having voluntarily submitted to so much pain—as if he hadn't already suffered more than his share in one lifetime. Still, if he hoped to become accepted as a genuine *Ariki*—Emperor or Chief of Chiefs among the Maoris —he'd best bow to local customs even if his surviving fellow ex-convicts, George Powys and Israel Bulloch conformed only half-heartedly and with bad grace about adopting Maori ways and beliefs.

As for Algernon Penny, Esq., as he styled himself, that otherwise astute young Englishman had announced his intention of remaining in all ways a *pakeha*—a white foreigner.

A small pink-and-gray scallop shell slung to a strand of plaited flax covered the brooding figure's right eye, effectively concealing an empty raw, red socket. His remaining eye of startlingly bright blue surveyed busy beaches of which he enjoyed a fine view from the porch of his palace standing on the uppermost of three broad terraces rising above the river and protected by a double row of palisades. Long ago ancestors of the Ngati Tari Mata tribe astutely had decided to fortify this hilly low headland jutting far out into Kaipara Bay.

On the *marea*, a wide and dusty parade ground lying between Sylvanus Doane's dwelling and the brown-thatched Tribal Meeting House—the largest and most lavishly ornamented structure in Ruawai *pa* a band of young warriors were practicing a complicated war dance supervised by a group of lesser nobles and veterans of common birth who had distinguished themselves in interminable inter-tribal wars.

Fearsome yells and blood-curdling shouts repeatedly ebbed and swelled in volume to the rhythmic beat of broad bare feet being stamped and to the drum-like booming of bare chests being vigorously slapped and thumped in unison.

Trying to forget his pain the one-eyed American watched the

sunlight flash on sharp-edged *tewhatwhas*—long-handled, feather-ringed tomahawks the blades of which were set cross-wise to the shaft like an adz, not parallel like the weapons of an American Indian, and on the points and blades of *taiahas*—fighting staffs—a weapon peculiar to the Maoris. These consisted of a heavy shaft about five feet long made of fire-hardened wood and tapering to a sharp point at one end; at the other it widened into a pair of broad, double-edged and razor-sharp blades. Decorated with scarlet-dyed flax streamers; a *taiaha*, could if handled dexterously, be used for slashing at a distance or reversed for stabbing during in-fighting.

In long lines the dancers grimaced, jumped nimbly into the air in unison and executed other maneuvers to the barked commands of naked officers whose hair was twisted into tall topknots secured by rings of bone or ivory. Into these had been inserted nodding clumps of brilliant yellow, red or green parrot feathers.

Clouds of yellow-white dust arose from under stamping feet to hang low over the sun-gilded *marea*. Whenever someone's foot missed coming down at precisely the right instant the drill master would bellow, "Heavy feet, wet skin" meaning that a slow or heavy-footed fighter was likely to find his skin wetted by his own blood.

Slaves bearing water from the base of a waterfall roaring among wooded heights behind the *pa* trotted past without looking up. They traveled, single file, bent under huge clusters of gurgling, dripping gourds and calabashes which to Doane suggested nothing so much as bunches of gigantic brown grapes.

Other slaves were bringing in baskets of fern roots and *kumaras* —native sweet potatoes, and bundles of firewood.

Hunters appeared carrying slender lances thirty feet or more in length with which they had speared birds roosting among boughs high above them; bedraggled strings of wood pigeons, parrots, kiwis and wood hens swayed over smooth brown backs. But the hunters carried no mammals of any species; when the canoes of the First Great Migration had reached Aotearoa, Land of the Long White Cloud, the wanderers had discovered not a single species of four-footed beast, only a bountiful variety of birds, many grown wingless through the complete absence of predators.

The only warm-blooded creatures encountered was a primitive, un-war-like people called "The Moa Hunters". These very soon had disappeared into Maori cooking ovens.

Completely enclosing the triple-terraced *pa* was a series of elaborate defenses consisting of alternating deep, spike-lined ditches and high wooden palisades bound together by sturdy vines and ropes of flax. At strategic points stood fighting towers, only rude platforms in reality.

For a long while it had puzzled Doane and his fellow fugitives that a people so martial-minded never had learned the use of bows and arrows or even sling-stones. True, Maoris on occasion did employ throwing sticks with which they could launch light darts a fairish distance; they greatly preferred, however, to join in bloody hand-to-hand combat.

And why hadn't the natives of Aotearoa ever discovered the principle of the block-and-tackle, the use of the wheel or the forging of any sort of metal?

Wincing under the needle's continued sting Sylvanus Doane returned his attention to the amber-yellow river and a row of red-and-black-painted war canoes hollowed from the trunk of a single tree to which sections had been added at the bow and stern. Some were two masted, double-hulled and secured together by a platform of transverse timber, on which was fixed a flimsy shelter of matting lashed over arched rods.

From such a distance Doane couldn't make out details of weird and intricate carvings decorating the ten-foot stern posts rising, vane-like, above the paddlers' benches. At the bows rose back-swept figureheads, smaller but equally lavishly ornamented. These varied in design only slightly from those sea-going canoes which, nearly a thousand years earlier, had transported the first wave of Maori immigrants across thousands of miles from *Hawaiki*—the Far Distant Land.

"Enough," snapped Doane fanning sweat-drenched privates with his loincloth.

The tattoo artist at once dipped water from a calabash bowl and, grinning satisfaction, employed a swab of soft linen to wipe away mingled blood and ink.

Over a shoulder Doane shouted to an adjacent sleeping hut, "Goddam it, George! You aim to sleep all day?"

George Powys suffering from overindulgence in a fermented palm wine decocted by himself emitted a volley of obscenities. "Ah-h lay off! Me bloody head's splitting for fair."

"An you don't turn out straight-away, you sodden swine, I'll make it hurt still worse!"

Sylvanus Doane cast a glance at the women's house, was pleased to see that Neti, his favorite concubine of the moment, was seated under a tree working a design done in bright red-and-yellow feathers into a ceremonial cloak. Neti's efforts were causing large but firm and well-formed breasts to quiver pleasingly.

Neti whose abundant and slightly wavy brown-black hair flowed freely over naked shoulders was pleasing in a chunky, golden-brown way; delicate blue tattooings covering her chin and upper lip didn't seem in the least objectionable. She was the perpetually good-natured daughter of a *rangatira* defeated by Doane in single combat soon after he'd usurped rule over the Ngati Tari Mata. What a pity Neti's much prettier younger sister had got knocked on the head and devoured in celebration of the victory.

Doane was bracing himself for the completion of another leaf when a conch shell trumpet started to wail an alarm from a watch-tower overlooking Kaipara Bay.

Brushing aside his tattooer Sylvanus Doane strode into the long, dim interior of his palace and from a battered sea chest pulled a telescope which he steadied against one of the carved posts supporting his porch. Quickly he focused on a tiny speck rounding a dim, blue-green headland separating Kaipara Bay from the Tasman Sea.

With insects buzzing about trickles of blood descending his leg the sandy-haired American steadied his brass-mounted glass and made out a large sea-going canoe speeding along under a pair of brown, triangular sails. The distant craft apparently was alone which was odd because, he couldn't discern any gleam of weapons aboard her.

Turning, he barked orders to a sub-chief on duty, then stalked over to the sleeping house to deal George Powys a kick in the ribs.

"Rouse, you lazy bastard! War canoe's entering the bay."

"Wha—wha's up?" Powys, jet hair awry, sat up, knuckled small blood-shot dark eyes and spouted a freshet of Australian Cockney oaths.

"Bugger me gently!" he snarled. "Wot for did yer kick so 'ard?"

"Strange war canoe's headed this way."

When Powys struggled to his feet, badly bowed legs and pre-ternaturally long arms lent him a distinctly simian appearance.

"How many canoes?" He yawned cavernously.

"Only one I said, but more may be hidden behind the headland."

Hairy as any chimpanzee, Powys pulled on a pair of canvas pants hacked off at the knees and then appeared, spitting and hawking.

"Where's Bulloch?"

"Aboard the *Scimitar* where *you* ought to be readying the Long Tom."

"If yonder craft's really alone can't be more'n sixty-eight cannibals yonder; no call to waste ammunition."

Powys shaded his eyes, peered at the *Scimitar*, that dingy little two-masted schooner overwhelmed off Norfolk Island.

Although the *Scimitar* continued to swing placidly to her anchor, men, white and brown, were swarming about the white-painted schooner's deck and stripping the canvas covering from her pivot gun.

9

Pourparlers

Joseph Algernon Penny, Esq., without appearing to hurry, arrived before Doane's *kaitangata*. As usual, the slightly built Englishman—he might have been in his early thirties—was wearing clean white canvas breeches, pewter-buckled shoes and a faded but freshly laundered blue linen shirt. A naked *tumau*—slave—was forced to trot in order to keep a lacquered paper-and-bamboo Chinese parasol shading his master's head.

Algernon Penny, Esq., halted, stroked a brief, neatly clipped goatee. Sylvanus Doane, he noted, was in conversation with several chieftains, among them Tuhea, a husky, handsome and splendidly muscled young chief who'd helped establish the one-eyed American as high chief not only of the Ngati Tari Mata but also of several subtribes owing allegiance to Ruawai.

Among the escapees from Norfolk Island Tuhea had become known as "Young Nick", or "the Young Devil" not because of his ferocity in battle but for his arrogant cruelty towards slaves and the humbly born.

Tuhea had a long and drooping silky brown moustache and large, wide-set jet eyes shining beneath bushy black brows. It had been he who'd persuaded his uncle, late ruler of the tribe, to launch a surprise attack on a powerful near-neighbor but only after said neighbor had been warned that he and his heir-apparent were taking the warpath. Why was it not reasonable for the Ngati Tari Mata to allow the one-eyed American and the other whites to rule until no formidable foes remained? Only then would come the hour for the foreigners to die.

Sylvanus Doane, who had known all about this bit of treachery, was among the loudest to howl grief, scratch his face and cut short his hair when the ambushed war party straggled back into Ruawai.

It hadn't taken Algernon Penny, Esq., long to perceive how well Young Nick appreciated the vast power and effect of gunfire.

At the moment Young Nick was squatting on his heels before a beady-eyed, yellow-and-green parrot anchored to its perch by a leg ring fashioned from an enemy's thigh bone.

Algernon Penny, Esq., ducked his narrow, dark head to enter welcome shade then looked about for a seat somewhere among an increasing throng of sweating and malodorous sub-chiefs. Not finding one he cursed Doane in crisp, faultless Oxford English for not providing even a stool. Decidedly, Yank was going too damned far with this determination to adopt native ways.

While he himself had proved adept in learning Maori, his skill was as nothing compared to the ease with which Sylvanus Doane had become fluent in most dialects in addition to learning and observing the countless forms and prohibitions of *tapu.*

He noticed at once that the tattooed American was wearing a new scallop shell to cover that raw, red socket created by a lead-tipped lash.

A pity. Once upon a time Sylvanus Doane must have been really handsome in a virile, classic way. Too bad the original fine planes and outlines of his well-modeled features had become ruined by scars and a crooked nose which when broken never had been set.

Grunting resentment, he in the white trousers at length seated himself cross-legged on a bulrush floor mat beside George Powys—dishevelled and unshaven as usual. With a curt gesture he signalled his slave to furl the parasol and start using a palm leaf fan. "What canoe is coming in?"

"Yer guess is as good as mine." The Australian's bloodshot eyes slewed sidewise. "All I say is this stranger's either bloody brave or a great fool to risk visitin' Ruawai in a single war canoe. Look yonder."

Young Nick was holding out a broad, blunt hand for Doane's telescope. Squinting, the broad-shouldered Maori surveyed the red-painted craft.

"That *waka tua* bears the device of the Ngai Wangape tribe. See? They wave green branches to say they come in peace."

"Very well. Let them land. We'll give them proper reception. Hoki! Bring me ornaments."

The slave presently hurried in bearing a magnificent mako shark tooth necklace; the American lifted it over his topknot then lowered it into position. Next, he secured to his shoulders a billowing cloak of emerald-green parrot feathers. Finally Doane ordered his most potent *tiki*, a greenstone pendant carved in the conventionalized form of a penis and testicles, to be slung about his neck.

Wooden-faced, he turned to Young Nick now decked out in a ceremonial mantle bright with scarlet feathers plucked from the underwings of parrots and a necklace of beautifully carved sperm whale teeth.

"Who is *rangatira* of the Ngati Wangape?"

"Te Hiko. His tribe lives three long days' paddle up the coast. They do not number many but his warriors are fierce, tireless and very crafty. Te Hiko is a giant."

"Do any of his men carry firearms?"

"No," Young Nick said. "But that means little. Doubtless he keeps well hidden any flintlocks he may own."

Doane fixed his eye to Algernon Penny, Esq., who, after working his way into the shade of the porch, lounged there looking faintly amused. "Why ain't Israel Bulloch here? Bastard's supposed to come ashore whenever an alarm's raised."

"Dear lad's lingering aboard the schooner I expect; he'd a batch of extra pretty *vahines* brought aboard last night."

"Nevertheless," grunted Powys, "bugger's on the job, carouse or no carouse."

From the porch Sylvanus Doane and the rest watched the stubby-masted schooner's jibs and main jerkily hoisted, saw her swing away from her mooring on a course calculated to thwart any attempt by the stranger to run back out to sea.

To the population of Ruawai *pa* this inexplicable appearance of a foreign war canoe proved a most welcome escape from monotony. All through the *pa* shouting warriors raced among houses to assemble on the *marea*; they were waving spears, long-handled tomahawks and short, blunt-headed, sharp-edged swords chipped out of greenstone, a species of jade.

Doane turned and strode to a rack from which he selected a light musket; next, he jammed a pair of French pistols into a belt of plaited dogskin.

"Penny!" he barked. "You and Young Nick go down and make welcome the Wangape chief. Act friendly but aloof; see that no conceivable offense is offered, then escort him and *not more than six* of his followers up here."

Once the sparely built, black-haired Englishman and his massive Maori companion started for the landing Doane checked the priming of his firearms then seated himself, cross-legged, before the entrance. Silently, his principal adherents squatted, to either side.

Silent and expressionless on his *kaitangata*'s threshold, the American attempted to recall what he'd heard concerning the Ngati Wangape. Um. According to Young Nick they by no means were the largest tribe along this coast but, under the ambitious leadership of a new war chief, it recently had subjugated several neighboring peoples.

Consulting a mental map Doane recalled that the territory of the Ngati Wangape lay to the north. Um. And what tribe lived along the northern limits of Te Hiko's domains? Ah, yes! The Ngati Waro who, reportedly, were ruled by Te Wainga, a fierce and resourceful adventurer from the South Island.

According to Young Nick, this potentate was better known as "the King of Bones" because of a high pyramid of human skulls and bones reared before his *kaitangata*.

Doane scratched a particularly irritating flea bite while searching for the reason why a chief so wily as Te Hiko had dared to approach a rival's *pa*. *Why?*

As often in the past when faced with so important a problem, Doane attempted to place himself in Te Hiko's position. Before long he arrived at a tenable explanation. Still and all, he couldn't be positive that such was Te Hiko's real purpose.

Continually, Young Nick's men jumped high into the air screeching and scowling ferociously just to prove they were fit and eager for combat. All the same they kept glancing at the landing where the visitors now were occupied in pulling up their long red canoe.

Biting down a grunt of pain, Doane placed his carbine, fully cocked, on the ground handy to his right, but took care to lay a cermonial fighting staff in the place of honor across his lap. Frozen into impressive immobility, the American then watched a little group of visitors lugging a pair of heavy baskets start climbing towards the *pa*'s uppermost terrace.

The strangers toiled upwards amid a silence so profound that the buzzing of flies could be heard; that, and a distant screaming of pigs about to be butchered.

Doane beckoned Rewa, better known as "Young Nick's Brother"—a handsome, intelligent, young fellow from among a rank of sub-chiefs. "Stand beside me, warn of any lies or trickery they may attempt. Explain what I may not understand; if I ask for advice, advise me."

A few yards behind the basket bearers strode a figure towering a full head above his superbly muscled companions. It struck Sylvanus Doane that beyond doubt Te Hiko must be one of the hugest human beings he'd ever come across. When the giant drew nearer it was seen he was wearing a magnificent *mere* of greenstone in his war belt and a thick war cloak adorned with strips of black-and-white dogskin.

Into this strutting figure's topknot was secured upright the usual pair of black-tipped white *huia* bird feathers. As Doane had foreseen, Te Hiko's broad, strongly delineated features were covered by incredibly intricate coils and whorls of blue and black tattooing.

The foremost visitors deposited their baskets outside the porch and stood panting; in Algernon Penny's unvoiced opinion they appeared apprehensive. Setting his feet down heavily Te Hiko strode up to Doane who appeared to accord him not the least recognition, then called out in a loud voice the ceremonial greeting accorded only to a great chief, "*E tohu mata ra koe!*"

For several long instants Doane pretended to have heard nothing. Finally he fixed his visitor with his single vivid eye and made reply, "*E koro! Tena ko Te Hiko.*"

Again a silence descended encouraging the tame parrot to rock back and forth a few times before stretching a gleaming blue-green wing along its perch.

Te Hiko tattooed features impassive announced, "I, Te Whiro Kanohi, ever-victorious high chief of the Ngati Tari Mata have brought you fine gifts."

Obedient to a quick gesture his companions uncovered both baskets and tilted onto the floor mats perhaps twenty *paki-paki*—cured human heads—each distinguished by tattooing of the most elaborate sort.

"*Euh!*" grunted Young Nick's Brother then in an undertone added, "The head lying nearest you is that of Te Arowa, a very famous warrior—truly, a most splendid gift."

Doane treated Te Hiko to a curt nod before beckoning his

visitor into shade created by the overhanging roof. He signaled Algernon Penny, Esq., and Young Nick's Brother to sit inside the Meeting House together with a surly mannered and enormously broad-shouldered individual who apparently was Te Hiko's second-in-command; on each of his muscular buttocks was tattooed a huge bullseye target pattern of concentric circles.

Young Nick's Brother felt offended by the visitor's omission of certain courteous preambles for Te Hiko came directly to the point. As Doane had foreseen it proved to be a circuitous invitation to form an alliance for attack on Te Wainga, "the Bone King" of the Ngati Waro.

Penny bent over Doane's shoulder, muttering, "Like you, I'm attempting to figure out why this bloody cannibal should seek help. Why doesn't he fight the Ngati Waro on his own? If he wins he wouldn't need to share the spoils."

"I reckon he daren't tackle the Ngati Waro alone because, lest I miss my guess, he's got few firearms of any account, let alone a schooner mounting a Long Tom."

Penny turned to Young Nick's Brother squatting comfortably beside him. "What about this Bone King and his people?"

"They are seafarers much feared for surprise attacks by water. Te Wainga, their chief, is famous for craftiness and cruelty."

Once the conference ended, refreshments—unusual during the middle of the day—were fetched from a nearby cooking house.

Te Hiko was offered a golden-brown and succulent-smelling suckling pig bedded in a new basket lined with fresh leaves. Although the steamed meat appeared uncommonly well-cooked and handsomely garnished Young Nick noted a fleeting grimace of disappointment cross the visitor's heavily tattooed features.

Nevertheless the huge chief of the Ngati Wangape helped himself generously to baked native sweet potatoes, gulped raw fish and swallowed whole many song birds preserved in fat. These he washed down with hugh draughts of *ava*, a mildly intoxicating drink brewed from pepper root.

While Te Hiko ate in silence his protuberant jet eyes flickered ceaselessly about the *pa*—beyond a doubt estimating the nature, extent and strength of its defenses.

After wholly nude brown handmaidens wearing crowns of bright flowers on waist-long and wavy brown hair had cleared away the broken viands Te Hiko got to his feet and, belching loudly, addressed Doane in almost truculent tones. "As my valiant host, Te Whiro Kanohi, has learned, the Bone King's warriors are famed for skill in combat. His *pa* is strongly placed and so skillfully fortified in an open mass attack a large army would find much trouble in capturing."

Doane's piercing blue eye probed the other's glaring black ones.

"Long have I thought on how best the Ngati Waro can be defeated and eaten up."

"Explain your intentions. If I find merit in your plan—then we shall see."

"My plan is of so secret a nature few should hear of it." Te Hiko sent his lieutenant out into the blazing sunlight to join a semi-circle of sub-chiefs squatting impassively before the palace.

Doane thereupon dismissed his own staff with the exception of Algernon Penny, Esq., and the wily Tuea.

At once the principal negotiators came to the point. As foreseen by Doane, Te Hiko needed reinforcements in the form of a contingent of veteran warriors and especially of a band of musketeers.

When the visiting *kagatira* had concluded, everyone sat in silence ignoring myriad flies droning about their topknot feathers. Irritably, Penny fanned the pests away by using his broad-brimmed hat.

At length Te Hiko rubbed his chin and slitted his eyes. "What are your thoughts, O valiant *Ariki?*"

The use of this title, of course, was rank flattery. Not yet did Sylvanus Doane dare to style himself as "*Ariki*", an exalted rank tantamount to that of Emperor or King of Kings. At present, it suited Doane to be saluted merely as "*kagatiri*", a paramount chief.

"I have been listening well, O Te Hiko: it is possible that I—and you—together can win a great victory."

The other's big, ivory-hued front teeth gleamed. "How many warriors can the *Ariki* send against the Ngati Waro?"

Algernon Penny, Esq., barely suppressed a grin.

"In person I will lead fifty of my finest warriors."

"Only *fifty!*" Te Hiko's eyes bulged, his bull neck swelled and enormous fists tightened convulsively on a ceremonial war club. "You insult me!"

Doane's tattooed chin deliberately elevated itself. Said he in grating tones, "I offer Te Hiko no insult. I need no more warriors; twenty of my followers will carry good muskets which they know how to fire."

"*Heu! Heu!*" the Wangape blinked, apparently reassured. "Still, my friend, that is not enough men for the task. I command only ten time ten stout veterans ready for war."

Both Young Nick and Doane judged this a gross understatement but made no comment.

"As I have said, the Bone King's *pa* is very strong. He can summon ten times a hundred warriors whenever he wishes."

Doane's single eye closed deliberately and he spoke to the floor before him, "If you agree to the plan I have devised, no more than one hundred men can capture the Bone King's *pa*."

"And you, O mighty *Kagatira*, how many muskets do *you* possess?" Algernon Penny, Esq., interjected smoothly, "I mean muskets which can be fired, not just used for dancing."

Scowling, Te Hiko bent forward, jerked a splinter from the side of a thickly calloused and pink-soled foot. He spat angrily onto the floor mats. "Only two."

The one-eyed American permitted himself a contemptuous smile. "Only *two*! You amaze me. But, no matter. My twenty muskets, well-handled, should ensure victory *provided* your followers justify their fame as mighty warriors.

"Now listen well, Te Hiko. We will sail up to Waro not in war canoes but in my mighty ship of war." Without turning a hair he thus dignified the dingy little *Scimitar*. "Your warriors and mine will lie hidden below decks so that strangers here will think I am departing on no more than a peaceful trading expedition."

He stared steadily at his massive guest. "Never forget one thing. I, Te Whiro Kanohi am all-powerful because I can bring into battle more firearms than any other chief in all Aotearoa—more even, than many whalers who visit the Bay of Islands."

Te Hiko said, "Why boast of your power? You cannot impress me."

Under his splendid cape of green-and-red feathers Doane shrugged. "That's as may be." Tactfully he added, "To throw fear into so valiant a warrior as Te Hiko would be impossible. I speak as I have because, within a year's time, I plan a war so great I may even invite the ever-valiant *Kagatira* of the Ngati Wangape to fight by my side."

Instantly Te Hiko flashed, "Who will be your enemy?"

Algernon Penny, Esq.'s always elevated opinion of the American soared to new heights when Sylvanus Doane replied evenly, "After the Bone King has been eaten up I may tell you."

Te Hiko bent forward as if to rub noses. "So you and I will fight the Bone King together?"

"Such is my intention," Doane announced coldly.

The giant leaped to his feet and, yelling his pleasure, stamped so hard on the mats that puffs of dust spurted up through them. Te Hiko knelt and extended both hands; the two cloaked and feather-decorated leaders then rubbed noses in ceremonious *hongi*.

Young Nick appeared pleased by the way things were going yet retained reservations; not for nothing was Te Hiko reputed to be not only valiant in battle but also wily and treacherous.

While the new allies were striding through mellow, late afternoon sunlight Young Nick muttered in Doane's ear, "Te Hiko was not pleased with the midday meal. I think he wishes to feed upon the 'Fish of Wharo'. It would be wise to honor him."

The one-eyed American stared an instant, then, grasping his lieutenant's implication, jerked a half-nod. The importance of Te Hiko's good will was well worth the life of a slave or two.

10

Te Hiko

Outwardly Sylvanus Doane relaxed, commenced to apologize; thus far his guest's reception had been unworthy for one of his exalted rank. A pity Te Hiko hadn't sent messengers to warn of his imminent arrival; the ruler of the Ngati Wangape would then have been treated to a great feast with much dancing and singing and plenty of tender young slaves on which to sate his hunger. As it was, the one-eyed *kagatira* genially remarked, he trusted his guest would overlook this unintended slight. He would attempt to make amends.

Could Te Hiko make an inspection of this *pa* of which he had heard so much?

Almost eagerly Sylvanus Doane declared himself willing but before setting out he delayed long enough to emphasize that not so much as a whisper concerning the impending foray must escape. The *Scimitar* would sail the following night and pause to pick up Te Hiko's followers, at present encamped outside the bay.

Alas, that the raiders would be forced to risk the wrath of Tu and the other gods of war through omitting the customary dances and other propitiatory rituals. For a moment Te Hiko looked uncomfortable about running so grave a risk but ended by agreeing.

In full panoply the new allies then quitted the Meeting House together with Te Hiko's second-in-command, Young Nick's Brother and Algernon Penny, Esq., looking mighty aloof and casual under the shade of his parasol.

The sun had begun to nudge the horizon and the evening sea breeze to rustle towering pines and fern trees shading haphazardly sited groups of low, thatch-roofed family dwellings.

Long since, the survivors of Norfolk Island had learned that no Maori house, even the most pretentious, ever was partitioned off; therefore privacy, even on intimate occasions was not missed; no one paid attention to copulating couples.

Food never was consumed indoors no matter how foul the weather but under the roof of a wall-less cooking shed. At the moment women were bringing in mounds of fresh green leaves and mats under which they would cook the second and last meal of the day.

Chattering, gossiping and laughing females of all ages crouched beside beehive-shaped earthern ovens, heating stones which soon would line the bottom and sides of the stoves to generate steam. Also brought in were fresh-woven platters stacked high with raw food of varying sorts—shellfish, fish, crabs, fowl, vegetables and fruit.

Soon a public crier would cup hands and bellow, "*Ka Tahu!* Light up your ovens." Not until then would the women really settle down to cooking.

Now that heat was waning children were returning from the fields. Some drove pigs on leads, others carried woven fiber bags of kumara, fern root, and other vegetables. They whooped and frolicked along past impassive slaves bearing baskets of crushed and calcined human bones destined to fertilize fields beyond the palisades.

The afternoon having been excessively humid and hot men, women and children unconcernedly went about stark naked except an occasional female who for some reason—never for modesty— might have secured a loose-woven kilt about her loins, or some grizzled old man sheltering his scarred and withering body under a ragged cloak.

Laughing women kept running up to proffer wreaths of freshly plucked flowers. Young Nick made sure to select the handsomest floral crowns for Te Hiko and Kingi, that giant's gray-bearded but brawny lieutenant.

Quite without appearing to the slender, dark-browed Englishman perceived the interest with which Te Hiko and his lieutenant were surveying the defenses of Ruawai *pa*; almost visibly, they were noting the position of "murderers" or swivel guns easily seen against the bronze-blue sky. These had been mounted on stouter than usual fighting platforms and placed at strategic intervals along the ten-foot-high triple line of palisades encircling the town.

The one-eyed American found satisfaction in noting how impressed his guests were with the extent of his defenses and the engineering skill evident in the *pa*'s fortifications.

Once the party leisurely had circled the topmost terrace and had inspected an impressive number of well-carved food storage houses standing clear of the ground on four-foot piles, Doane noted how Te Hiko's gaze kept shifting from one group of good-looking young slaves to the next.

At length the *Kagatira* of Wangape stroked drooping mustaches and announced, "I hunger for my favorite food."

"It is a pleasure to satisfy your craving," Sylvanus Doane remarked through acrid-smelling smoke rising from dozens of freshly kindled ovens.

"Make your selection, my friend. The best I have to offer is none too good for so mighty a war chief—who now is also my dear brother. Is there no *vahine* in this *pa* who whets your appetite?"

"When I see one that pleases me I will say so." The giant slowed sufficiently to permit peering into weaving and cooking sheds and to study slave families with care. At length he paused between two hideously carved votive effigies which, like small totem poles, rose at random about the *pa*. He stared at a thatched shelter in which a trio of slender, quite naked young slave girls were busily weaving crowns and garlands from bright pandanus and *kahawai* blossoms heaped before them.

One, Algernon Penny, Esq., perceived, had delicate features and she looked to be about fifteen. She was considerably paler skinned than her companions and also was remarkable for pronounced red tints glowing in fine, abundant hair which floated rather than fell over smooth, brown shoulders.

When Young Nick's Brother spoke to the group the reddish-haired girl looked up with a gay smile revealing small and very white; teeth. Luminous, doe-like eyes gradually rounded themselves.

Sylvanus Doane knew what to expect but experienced no trace of compunction—on Norfolk Island "pity" had become a forgotten word.

Wearing an amused half-smile, he halted and watched Te Hiko's huge bulk swagger over to the thatch-roofed shelter. Stooping, he jerked the red-haired slave to her feet. She tried to keep on smiling when, like a marketing housewife who knows what to look for, the chief pinched her buttocks and thighs, upper arms and small, conical, beige-tipped breasts.

Te Hiko turned away. "This one."

Doane nodded whereupon a pair of guards ran forward. Expressionless, the three girls watched their approach. Born slaves they, since childhood, had been taught and had accepted, humble and without question, the belief that they lived from day-to-day only to serve their owner in any fashion he chose.

As the guards closed in, the red-haired girl rose to her feet and in a graceful gesture which elevated immature breasts donned a flowery crown. Next she bent her head and stared fixedly at the ground until a guard's hand gripped her shoulder. She then sank to her knees in a graceful, fluid movement, even smiled timorously at the knot of dignitaries.

A guard wound fingers in her hair and forced her head forward. His companion then raised a war club and brought it down sharply on the back of the small, dark-red head. The victim collapsed, lithe limbs quivering like those of a stunned bullock.

Sylvanus Doane remarked casually, "It is too late in the day to prepare this *vahine whare*—eating slave—in a fashion worthy of so distinguished a guest."

Licking thick lips, Te Hiko watched the slender corpse dragged out of the shed while the remaining girls resumed weaving flowers. "True, her flesh will taste better tomorrow."

11
Nightmare I

Towards the rear of his *kaitangata* Sylvanus Doane's long and rangy body lay supine upon a magnificently woven sleeping mat spread upon deep layers of soft and fragrant dried fern leaves packed within a carved wooden frame. On his right reposed the solid bulk of Riua, his First Wife whom he'd married after defeating, and eating, her late husband—a powerful neighboring chieftain.

While Riua wasn't exactly handsome she nevertheless was good-natured, expertly amorous and, most important, connected by close blood ties with the ruling families of several tribes along the North Island's West Coast.

On his other side breathed Neti, his smooth-skinned, eighteen-year-old Number One Concubine. In every way she was more exciting and desirable but this night was so sultry he pushed both women out of contact.

Damn! Why would sleep persist in deserting him like allies in a losing battle? Why wouldn't this welter of semi-conscious worries disperse? Um. Likely he'd partaken too freely of the main course of the great feast in honor of his unbidden guest. To have consumed less of the red-haired slave than Te Hiko would have been to offer an affront not to be risked at so critical a stage in certain long-range plans.

Mosquitoes whined and pricked without let and his stomach rumbled and griped so insistently that, in futile irritation, he slapped Riua's perspiring rump and made her turn over in order to discourage resounding snores.

Restless and uncomfortable though he was, there remained one alleviating fact; he'd successfully abandoned his origins and now was thinking and acting exactly like a genuine Maori.

It was typical that neither Israel Bulloch nor George Powys had taken trouble to acquire more than a few absolutely essential Maori nouns, verbs and adjectives.

Joseph Algernon Penny, Esq.'s attitude, however, had proved to be different. While he was, as the New England saying went, "hair-hung and breeze-shaken" by various uncertainties, he'd proved ready to bend with the wind and, with few reservations, to adapt himself to this barbaric society. Nevertheless he insisted on three meals a day instead of two and, whenever possible, took tea in the afternoon. Only on the greatest of ceremonial occasions did he make even a pretense of devouring human flesh.

Further, he'd refused to endure tattooing and even in the hottest weather he'd invariably turned out clean-shaven, in shoes, fresh shirt, trousers and a broad-brimmed, low-crowned hat.

The sharp-featured and slow-moving Englishman had limited his handmaidens to three sloe-eyed nymphs he was patiently instructing in the rudiments of English and Latin!

The favorite bastard of a minor nobleman owning immense holdings in Surrey and Ireland, Joseph Algernon Penny, Esq., had only been lent his mother's family name.

Only because he'd noticed Te Hiko's wide-set and bulbous eyes fixed challengingly upon him had Penny quit gnawing a wood pigeon's carcass and, used a bone skewer to impale a piece of the main course. The moment the visitor's attention became diverted he'd promptly spat it out unchewed.

Long ago Sylvanus Doane had come to favor the taste of well-cooked human flesh. Its flavor, he'd decided suggested a pleasing combination of pork, veal and chicken while its texture resembled that of venison. The best cuts came from buttocks and thighs of a young person of either sex.

Also favored was the tongue and filets carved from along the backbone. But for a cannibal gourmet the finest of *bonnes bouches* were the palms of a victim's hands. Surprisingly, the firm breasts of even a young female invariably proved too fatty and glutinous to bother with.

A resounding belch somewhat relieved painful pressures lancing Doane's abdomen. He felt sweat trickling in rivulets. Damn! There wasn't even a breath of air flowing through his shadowy *kaitangata*.

When Riua commenced to snore again he employed a calloused foot—he'd gone without shoes for many months—to push Number One Wife onto her side then, sighing, slapped futilely at persistent mosquitoes.

How odd to reflect that, in all likelihood, another and very different Mrs. Doane probably must be living in the vicinity of Boston. Unbidden, but in surprising clarity, Sally's image sprang to mind.

Delicately pink-and-white of complexion and with flashing green eyes, vivacious Sally Anderson had attracted plenty of attention some seventeen years earlier but he'd won her.

What had become of the only fruit of their brief union? What name had been given the child? It had begun with an "A"—was it Adam, Alfred, Azael, Albert or Abner? *Abner!* Christened after a rich old uncle who, at last report, unobligingly had refused to depart this world.

Sighs and sleepy noises arose from near the front of the building where body servants lay on their bed mats.

That he'd not the least recollection of his son's appearance was understandable since he'd been forced to flee Boston so soon after Abner's birth. A pity that, in self-defense of course he'd grievously wounded the outraged husband of his current innamorata when that gentleman had unexpectedly returned from a business trip.

Undoubtedly it was just as well that Sally, their family and friends must believe him lost at sea. Pretty, charming and well-connected, his presumed widow proably had married again—probably to someone better fitted to rear Abner as a Boston gentleman.

Damn those night birds! In a raucous, demonic chorus they continued chortling and laughing crazily in the forest beyond Ruawai *pa.*

Doane's hand sought and touched his empty eye socket, uglily concealed beneath its sagging lid.

Unbidden, his mind's eye formed a mental picture vivid in every detail. He was standing in chains before a purple-faced, white-wigged judge in Port Jackson—now known as Sydney. He was listening to His Worship intone: "Sylvanus Doane, you stand tried and convicted of manslaughter in the second degree.

"Possibly I would be more merciful were I to sentence you to be hanged forthwith, but, since I despise all Yankees and always will, I sentence you to fifteen years of servitude at hard labor in His Majesty's penal colony on Norfolk Island—and may God have mercy upon your soul."

12

Nightmare II

Air in the convict hold remained stiflingly hot and lifeless, pungent with the reek of urine, stale sweat and slimy layers of faeces coating the deck.

Dully, Sylvanus Doane rubbed pus and mucous from swollen and yellow-granulated eyelids to peer about. Only dim light penetrated the heavily barred hatch securing the convict ship's forehold subdivided by bulkheads into four intolerably cramped compartments.

He and nine other prisoners sat half-collapsed on the filthy deck of the H.S.M. brig *Trident*, 8-guns. For two prisoners to lie anywhere near flat was impossible shackled as he was by one hand to a stout chain running through the ship, fore and aft.

How long he'd existed amid this indescribable squalor he couldn't determine; must have been at least a fortnight.

The prisoner chained next to him on the right was Welsh-Australian, a twice-convicted thief and highwayman. He called himself "George Powys" and admitted that he once had served a hitch in the Royal Navy a fact attested by a lumpy, criss-cross pattern of scars running across his hairy back and shoulders.

Recently Powys had suffered flogging so severe that in all probability his back would never completely heal. Grotesquely bow legged, he had such long arms that his fingertips hung on a level with his knees, lent him an ape-like appearance. The stumps of a few yellow-black teeth remained and leathery shreds of a mangled ear clung to his head.

Bracing against his shackle, Sylvanus Doane struggled to sit more erect since it was time for an ex-convict deckhand to appear lugging a wooden bucket of warm and incredibly foul-tasting water —the twice-a-day ration for ten men. God! Wouldn't the fellow ever appear?

A large gray-brown rat thrust its head from a hole in the compartment's corner, peered about with bright, bulbous eyes then darted out and drove yellow teeth into the nearest foot.

Spouting blasphemies a blond young fellow lashed out with amazing quickness and smashed the rodent flat. Limited by his shackle, he had to strain to reach the broken carcass from which he eagerly sucked at a trickle of blood.

"Cor!" Powys begged. "Be a good lag; lemme jerk off 'is 'ide and take just one little bite."

The prisoner, crouched on the chain's opposite side, growled, "Nah! Ye're too mean to give a duck a drink if ye owned a lake."

"Ah-h. Up yer arse wi' a branding iron!" Body yielding to the brig's slow roll, Powys turned aside to peer up at the barred hatch. "'Ow much longer afore we reach bloody Norfolk Island?"

The double row of chained scarecrows made no reply, only remained with heads bowed, elbows on knees.

Dull commotion sounded on deck, then a voice far above hailed, "Land ho!"

"Where away?"

"Eight points to looward."

"'Ope to God that's Norfolk," panted Israel Bulloch. "Can't stand it in 'ere much longer."

Sentenced to twenty years for murder, ferret-faced Bulloch wore a halo of thinning, ginger-colored hair and a stringy beard of the same hue.

The convicts of course couldn't sight a group of sharp, purple-blue volcanic peaks lifting above the heat-shimmering horizon. Soon the island's steep hills showed dark-green under a growth of evergreens, unique survivors of paleolithic ages which during the next century would become known the world-over as "the Norfolk pine."

Grunted Bullock, "Pray God we'll soon be off this 'ell ship, anything's better."

"Don't count on it," rasped an old lag—a twice-convicted jailbird. "Heard tell the worst we've suffered ain't nothink like wot lies in store."

Doane roused enough to query, "Who told you so?"

"Time-expired 'government man' in Hobart; 'e'd survived 'is sentence on Norfolk but 'e were white-haired and half-dotty."

H.M.S. Trident's anchor chain rattled out of its hawsehole amid brief clouds of rust-colored dust. Feet thumped overhead and muted the curses of officers berating seamen slow or awkward in furling sail.

Blinking in the hot glare on deck Sylvanus Doane, to a jangle of leg-irons, stood gulping deep of faintly fragrant air. Kingston Harbor proved to be small, round and hemmed in by steep wooded hills behind which jagged black mountains raked a blazing, bronze-blue sky. Scatterings of small, whitewashed stone cottages dotted a shoreline which for the most part looked flat and rocky.

Dominating this stark settlement stood a large and bleak white-painted structure of two storeys. Since a faded Union Jack hung limp from a flagstaff before it Doane deduced, correctly enough, yonder was the Governor's Residence.

Presently a large unpainted barge pulled by a gang of gaunt and heavily manacled wretches put out from the dock. The convict oarsmen wore only shapeless straw hats and filthy sailcloth breeches; many shoulders were raw-red with sunburn.

A guard in a dirty red uniform jacket ranged the length of the barge pausing now and then to lash some wretch without apparent purpose. "Faster, you lazy buggers! Put yer backs into it."

Once the ungainly craft arrived alongside began the business of driving half-dazed prisoners through the gangway and down into the barge.

Rowers, watching new arrivals scramble aboard, awkwardly because of their fetters, called out, "God's butt! Now 'ere's a pretty pack of narks, plump pimps and whoremasters. Whilst ye've the chance, Alf, ye'd best pick yerself out a noo bugger boy."

The guards, to Doane's surprise, were garbed in shakoes, ill-fitting scarlet tunics, white crossbelts and baggy blue-and-white seersucker pantaloons. They suggested slovenly soldiers rather than prison warders. Whatever they were, they made liberal use of brass-shod musket butts in disposing convicts about the barge.

Blinking like so many owls suddenly exposed to daylight the newly arrived prisoners were herded ashore and lined up between a double line of soldiers. Later, it turned out that most of these hard-faced infantrymen themselves had done time.

"Nah then, *form* fours!" barked a sergeant cutting the air with a heavy leather strap attached to a wooden handle. "*Move*! Ye goddam mother fuckers!"

That something unusual must be taking place in the prison's central block was attested by the fact that gangs of shaggy and heavily fettered prisoners were being driven in from outbuildings to converge on an iron-bound main gate.

Once Sylvanus Doane and his companions had shambled through the entrance they were greeted by a sight they'd never forget.

In dingy double ranks drawn up along three sides of a small, sun-lashed square known as the "punishment court", slouched some three hundred hopeless-looking and indescribably filthy convicts.

Behind these sagged half a dozen offenders, spread-eagled by means of cords secured to a double tier of iron ringbolts let into the courtyard's masonry. Each victim had had his ankles spread as far apart as possible and secured to a lower course of ring bolts while his arms were stretched to their limits above his head.

The spread-eagled wretches kept begging for water, made piteous lowing sounds, like thirsty cattle. No one paid the least attention.

In a space left clear in the center of the punishment court loomed a gallows of freshly sawed timbers; from its crossbeam three nooses dangled starkly.

A chorus of groans, howls and curses greeted the arrival of a dark-complexioned individual wearing white riding breeches, glossy tasseled boots and a spotlessly clean red tunic adorned with yellow cuffs, collar and facings. On the back of this official's bullet head was canted a huge gold-bound cocked hat above which nodded a single scarlet plume.

"'E bloody goddam Guv'nor," a voice growled. "Satan roast his balls forever!"

Followed by a neatly-turned-out lieutenant and a drummer boy, Lieutenant-Colonel J. T. Morisett halted a few feet short of the gallows. After staring deliberately about him he signalled the drummer to beat a long roll; it continued 'till comparative silence prevailed in the sun-baked punishment court.

"Mister Becker," he instructed his lieutenant, "I want these new jailbirds brought close by the scaffold. They'll profit from an object lesson; may discourage any of 'em from fancying they're about to enjoy a holiday among us."

The assembled convicts parted to permit the "fresh fish" from *H.M.S. Trident* to shuffle up to the scaffold's base. Sylvanus Doane, still unable to adjust his vision to this blinding glare found himself squinting up at a scaffold of rough boards upon which were waiting a trio of wild-haired convict-executioners in urine-stained white duck trousers.

"Proceed!" Lieutenant-Colonel Morisett directed the subaltern at his elbow.

To a dull clanking of fetters the onlookers were lashed back to create a passage to the prison's principal entrance.

Sighing groans went up when into the sunlight tottered three condemned felons with hands bound behind them. Swaying, they were being haled along by a squad of red-coated guards who dragged or shoved them up a short flight of steps onto the scaffold.

Tortured by hunger and thirst, Sylvanus Doane from a distance of twenty feet couldn't avoid witnessing all that was taking place.

One of the condemned, he realized, was red-haired and looked to be about twenty years of age. He began to sway like a tree ready to be felled, then tilted a twitching freckled face towards the brazen sky and raised peal on peal of shrill and mirthless laughter.

The second prisoner was a brown-bearded hunchback. Once he'd been shoved onto a trap door he began, in a rich, true voice, to sing a Wesleyan hymn.

The third man about to die was a moon-faced young man who apparently was half-witted for he grimaced, bobbed his head and, cackling, attempted a few jig steps when pushed onto his trap.

Doane overheard a sear-faced executioner suddenly exclaim to the red-headed youth, "Why, Jacky-Jacky, is it really you?"

The doomed man broke off his laughter, nodded, "Aye, Bill. Nice of you to send me off."

"Sorry, chum. I've no choice but to do yer in or get me fuckin' back flayed again."

"Don't fret yerself, Bill. I'm real happy to be shut o' this god dam hole."

The hangman reached out briefly to grip one of the felon's hands pinioned behind his back. He muttered, "Sorry, me lad, this can't be helped."

Then he lowered a yellow-brown manila noose over Jacky-Jacky Westwood's head and adjusted the hangman's knot under the red-haired man's left ear before slipping a black cloth hood into place.

By this time Sylvanus Doane had learned that if a condemned man had any luck his neck would be snapped and he'd die instantly once he'd plunged through the released trap door; otherwise he'd swing for minutes, slowly strangling to death. Now a steel lancet seemed to be penetrating Doane's brain severing nerves controlling the emotions of pity, mercy and decency.

The half-wit broke into peals of laughter and quickened his jigging. "Which o' you lads 'as brought the hamper o' food? May as well enjoy this 'ere picnic."

Even after the black hood had been put in place the hunchback continued to intone his hymn. Why was so grotesque a creature about to die like this?

The courtyard began to tilt and whirl about him. Doane gasped, struggled to retain sanity.

The three executioners then squatted each gripping the handle of a bolt securing the trap door before him.

Legs straddled, Lieutenant-Colonel Morisett stood with head cocked to one side. A huge, delighted grin was spreading between silky, mutton chop whiskers and over smallpox-pitted features. Although, as former Chief of Police of Port Jackson, Morisett must have witnessed dozens of executions he obviously had lost none of his taste for them.

Later on, Doane learned that the Governor professed to be deeply religious, so much so that on Sundays he often read the lesson in the prison chapel.

The shock-haired and sunburned executioners remained kneeling, the condemned men swaying, awaiting the signal Morisett deliberately was witholding.

At length the Governor wetted already moist lips and called out, "Sling those bastards! This will teach you blackguards what happens if you dare to strike or defy a warder."

Once trap bolts were drawn, the hooded prisoners plummeted a short distance to the end of their rope.

Only the hunchback proved fortunate enough to suffer a broken neck. A sound started as a low moan and swelled into an eerie, blood-chilling howl while the red-haired convict's body spun, jerked and struggled for all of five minutes before it hung still and a thin stream of urine began to drip from its rigid toes.

13

Nightmare III

The plaint of a lovesick food dog complaining to a gibbous moon roused the one-eyed *Kagatira*, sweating and shaking, from his tortured half-sleep.

Cursing, Sylvanus Doane sat up, used the side of a hand to scrape an accummulation of cold sweat from his forehead then shadow-boxed a swarm of invisible, whining mosquitoes.

The long-drawn cry of a sentry posted on the palisades to assure the *pa* that all was secure failed to reassure his tormented mind. The floodgates of memory seemed to have become unbarred and jammed open.

In vain the one-eyed American attempted to command thoughts sufficiently to concentrate on present considerations. What should be his attitude towards Te Hiko? Could he risk treating that arrogant and ambitious giant as an equal in this projected campaign or, with reservations, as an honored partner?

How many men should he take with him? How numerous might the dreaded Bone King's forces really prove? How strong were the defenses of Te Wainga's *pa*? So much remained to be determined.

At length Doane settled back sweating heavily between wife and handmaiden; both audibly were enjoying their slumber.

He thumbed away stinging drops of perspiration slipping under the sagging lid into his empty eye socket. A grateful sigh escaped when, at long last, a cool wind commenced to blow in from the moonlit sea and penetrate his shadow-ruled *kaitangata*.

But soon his thinking relapsed into a blur of incidents on Norfolk Island—scenes ineradicably branded into his memory like the time he'd first experienced, for some minor offense, the tortures of a "whistling gag"—a block of wood drilled through by a very small augur.

Jammed in and strapped into position such a gag completely

filled the victim's mouth; if his teeth got in the way they got broken off. No description could fit the acute agony of attempting to draw breath through an aperture less than half-an-inch in diameter. In short what one suffered was tantamount to slow suffocation—especially when spread-eagled against a hot stone wall. That many a convict had died from the whistling gag was a matter of no consequence to the authorities.

There were innumerable brutal floggings administered for no reason beyond the whim of a sadistic warder. Never less than twenty and usually fifty strokes were layed on with a lead-tipped cat-o'-nine-tails, an innovation introduced by the pious Lieutenant-Colonel Morisett.

Often when a severe flogging ended and the senseless wretch was cut down a dull, yellow-white gleam of bone showed through lacerated flesh.

Doane, again drifting helplessly amid semi-consciousness, was one of fifteen convicts crammed into a cell designed to accommodate four inmates; there being no room to lie down prisoners spent endless night hours jammed against the sweating and foul-smelling bodies of his fellows.

Should anyone be forced to answer a call of Nature he'd no choice but to relieve himself where he sat. It was during those hours Doane's reason only was preserved by the possession of one small article—a gold seal ring bearing the family's coat-of-arms—a greyhound leaping over a six-pointed star—and a motto which, on a flowing scroll read *"Toujours Fort"*.

Aye, "Always Strong" was a fine, a noble sentiment but a mighty difficult one to live up to on Norfolk Island. He managed to keep his signet concealed in a prisoner's only secure place—his anus.

A new Governor, one Captain Fyans, deemed it good discipline to halve the convicts' already starvation rations and to pocket the difference against that happy day when he'd quit Norfolk Island forever.

The convicts, literally starving, attempted a series of mutinies, but Doane if approached shook his head. "Lest you plan better, the troops will rally, hunt us down and hang every last rebel. No. Bad as things are, we'd best bide our time."

Doane's prediction proved correct; a rising, successful to begin with, failed once it got out of hand and mutineers wasted priceless time in an orgy of pointless killing, looting and burning.

The hard-pressed garrison, reinforced by troops from outlying labor camps, used musket butts and bayonets to drive rioters and non-participants alike into the punishment yard. Employing lead-tipped whips, guards beat a path for Captain Fyans through the mass of cringing, despairing, howling convicts.

As neatly as the blade of a surgeon's scalpel the leaden tip of a hard-swung lash flicked out Sylvanus Doane's right eye and dropped him, dazed and agonized, onto the dusty earth. In this he was fortunate; prisoners were dying by the dozen under the indiscriminate thrust of bayonets.

Garbed in clean white clothes by order of Captain Fyans in order that dying contortions on the gallows might be more readily visible presumed ringleaders were executed the next day.

During the next year and a half the one-eyed convict called Sylvanus Doane, inevitably nicknamed "Yank", was lashed and spread-eagled more times than he accurately could recall. Only the existence of his signet ring, that fragile link with the past, preserved his sanity.

One cold winter day while their gang was felling pines Doane beckoned Algernon Penny, Esq., aside, whispered that present conditions seemed to favor a scheme tested in theory time after time.

Doane, Penny, Bulloch, Powys and a few other selected jailbirds were to feign sickness and so gain admittance to the prison's squalid infirmary.

Poignantly, the tortured sleeper relived those crucial moments during which the infirmary's drowsy night guards one-by-one had been overwhelmed.

Leaving the redcoats trussed and gagged, the plotters muffled fetters with bandages then armed themselves with the guards' muskets and, drifting like stinking shadows, hurriedly launched one of several small canoes pulled up on the beach. By hugging the shoreline they managed to escape the harbor in silence and unobserved.

Once their craft had begun to pitch and roll in the Tasman Sea they paddled westward, parallel to a cliff-ramparted coast against which surf endlessly boomed and roared.

On the second day following their escape the fugitives, sunburned, thirsty and starving, put into what appeared to be the mouth of a small creek. Concealed from the sea by a bend in the creek the fugitives, laboriously freed of fetters, watched a small and bluff-bowed two-masted topsail schooner sail by, head inshore and disappear behind a low, wooded point.

Doane and the rest agreed that this was no pursuer, only a small merchantman which, probably short of wood or water, had put in to resupply herself.

Cautious reconnaissance along the shore revealed the schooner at anchor off a short rocky point forming a pretty little cove into which a falls spilled tons of clear fresh water.

From a clump of shrubbery Sylvanus Doane waited until two of the schooner's three boats shoved off, deep under men and an assortment of water casks to vanish behind the wooded peninsula.

It seemed only reasonable to assume that so small a vessel which at the most might have displaced a hundred tons, would not carry a numerous crew: therefore only a handful of unwary men were likely to have remained on board. Crawling back to his companions, Doane set them to breaking off plenty of heavily leafed branches.

When the size of the pile satisfied him the one-eyed American donned a hurriedly contrived head wreath, announced, "Algy, you and I will paddle. The rest will hide under the boughs; don't make the least move till I tell you. Take care your priming's dry."

The paddlers then shoved off and, in a fine pretense of deliberation, sent the canoe sliding over the emerald green water. From time to time Algernon Penny, Esq., flourished a green branch to create the illusion that here came only a couple of settlers intent on trading.

Since the schooner lay anchored less than two hundred yards off the point, not much time was required to close in on what Doane felt sure must be an island trader distinguished from the ordinary, however, through having a Long Tom cannon mounted on her fore-deck.

In dingy yellow lettering across her stern was painted the name "*Scimitar de Lorient*".

From under the boughs the convicts swarmed over the schooner's low rail so quickly that three half-naked and heavily bearded men on deck died before they'd any idea of what was taking place.

In the old days Sylvanus Doane never would have participated in the merciless shooting down of three wholly surprised seamen; as it was, he hesitated not at all, instead, experienced savage joy over seeing the Frenchmen sprawled on the deck and draining small rivulets of bright scarlet blood into the scuppers.

It all had been so quick and easy the convicts paused in stunned immobility till Doane dropped a still-smoking musket and lumbered to the helm shouting, "Get cracking you fools!" The scarecrows snatched axes from a rack and through a series of feeble blows barely managed to hack through the anchor line.

The *Scimitar*'s shore party, having heard shots, appeared, pulling hard.

Gasping, Powys and Algernon Penny, Esq., managed to hoist and set a pair of jibs; then, through an united effort the fugitives sent the mainsail jerking upwards, but it stirred only slightly under a feeble offshore breeze. Finally the main boom creaked slowly out to port and the mainsail filled barely in time to give the prize sufficient steerageway to outdistance her pursuers.

By sunset the jagged volcanic peaks of Norfolk Island had been lost to sight. Only then did the fugitives find time to appreciate the magnitude of their luck. Not only did this trader mount a powerful, long-range gun but in her hold lay many cases of French-made muskets, cutlasses, pikes, dirks and swords; all priceless items of trade.

14

Nightmare IV

During a short space Sylvanus Doane's mind mercifully ceased spinning and went blank. Again he sat up, rubbed itching red cicatrices left by too many floggings, then realized he'd perspired so heavily his rush mattress and bed mats were soaking.

A few roosters scattered about the *pa* began to proclaim the approach of dawn and somewhere a bell bird raised melodious notes. Mechanically, he wiped out the empty eye socket, stretched out again after resolving this time surely to remain awake, but soon he'd relapsed into half-consciousness to re-experience a stormy week spent aimlessly cruising the treacherous Tasman Sea. The *Scimitar* had yawed, bucked and plunged like a spurred bronco along a generally southeasterly course decided upon by her one-eyed Captain.

During this interval Sylvanus Doane while achieving a new philosophy, spoke seldom, often revolved the seal ring now permanently decorating his left hand.

Followed a succession of fine days. Soulful-eyed seals and grotesque sea elephants surfaced to stare at this grimy, white-painted schooner lumbering along under badly trimmed sails. In their fashion porpoises, flying fish and seabirds convoyed her.

The moody one-eyed Captain kept the *Scimitar* well to the south of a rhumb line running between Norfolk Island and New Zealand; pursuers were almost certain to search along this short and obvious course.

The speed with which Sylvanus Doane regained his skill in celestial navigation amazed him. Although forced to rely upon the *Scimitar*'s antique charts, obsolete instruments and a chronometer of dubious accuracy, he felt able to reckon the schooner's position with reasonable confidence.

One blustery afternoon Algernon Penny, Esq., sable hair now

neatly clubbed over the nape of his neck, appeared in the Captain's cabin and languidly seated himself. "Well, Yank, d'you mind confiding where we're going?"

"From what I've been able to glean I believe the northwest coast of New Zealand's North Island, still largely unexplored, seems to offer the best haven for the likes of us, although the local tribes are reputed to be fierce and treacherous cannibals."

Penny drew a deep draught on a long-stemmed pipe, coughed on rank French tobacco. "You'll not make for the Bay of Islands?"

"I'll decide that all in good time."

"Do we start to peddle arms, take to buccaneering or go black-birding?"

Doane treated his companion to a stare. "Are you out of your fucking mind? We number only eleven and the half of us ain't fit. Even using the Long Tom we'd be hard put to stave off a pack of cannibals."

Her fresh water supply all but exhausted, the *Scimitar* raised pale-blue peaks on the North Island two days later.

"It is my intention," he informed his shaggy companions, "to cruise southwards along this coast, well offshore, till we discover a river's mouth on some stretch of what looks to be an uninhabited country. Our water's almost gone so we've no choice but to stand in and risk attack."

Powys shuffled forward. "Cap'n, I were 'ere in *H.M.S. Lion* years ago; think maybe I might reco'nize parts o' this coast."

"Better be right. The French charts I've been studying must ha' been drawn either by Noah or Ananias. You'll say the instant you recognize a landmark for sure?"

"Aye, aye—sir," the title escaped before the Australian realized and, surprisingly, he knuckled his brow.

Next day the schooner negotiated a perilous barrier of reefs and shoals and, under reduced canvas, stood in towards a lovely looking stretch of green-blue coast.

Doane was scanning a low, heavily wooded headland on the south side of the bay's entrance when he noticed a cloud of blue-gray smoke commencing to spiral into a sky of brilliant blue; soon more smoke columns appeared close to the first.

"Looks like a forest fire," Bulloch hailed from the bow.

Algernon Penny, Esq., on joining Doane disagreed. "Not likely. Separate clouds like those are climbing too near together. What's your thinking?"

"I judge that maybe some village is under attack. We'll keep on till I get a better notion of what's taking place."

The Englishman raised a quizzical brow then picked at the small goatee he'd started. "If a fight really is going on, which side do we support?"

"The one which seems to be losing—an underdog's more likely to prove grateful."

When well into a large bay Doane ordered Powys to ready the Long Tom. Soon he was able to make out a long rank of big, red-painted canoes drawn up on a beach below a palisaded village built on the summit of a conical hill.

Along the shore palm-thatched huts were giving off furious clouds of smoke and flame. Knots of attackers still were splashing ashore to join in a *mélée* raging before the *pa*'s main gate defended by warriors on crude fighting platforms.

Under a faltering breeze the *Scimitar* closed in until war cries, howls and shouts became distinguishable.

Sylvanus Doane through his glass saw the disputed gate's valves start to sag inwards.

Immediately he called, "Powys! Open fire on those men and canoes on the beach."

Spouting obscenities, the Australian pursed leathery lips and blew on a slow match before lowering its ruby tip against priming smoothed in the cannon's touch-hole. To a deafening roar the sixteen-pounder recoiled savagely against its breechings as dazzling, orange-red flame flashed from its muzzle and a doughnut-shaped cloud of grayish smoke started drifting out over the water.

Echoes of the report caromed about among blue-green hills hemming in the bay.

Fortune nodded. The Long Tom's round shot smacked squarely into a concentration of canoes, sent clouds of splinters and sand flying high into the still, hot air.

"Cannister!" roared Doane, nostrils flaring like those of a winded horse.

Since few of the combatants before ever had heard a cannon fired the effect, on both sides, was terrific.

Cannister smashing into men and canoes caused the attackers to howl and begin shoving off in frantic disorder.

Apparently dazed, the besieged hesitated then, raising war cries, sallied out of their *pa*.

The fight ended with only four canoes paddling frantically. They gave the *Scimitar* a very wide berth and at top speed made for the entrance to the bay.

By the time the little schooner had anchored a cable's length off the landing place half-naked brown men already were busy beheading and quartering fallen enemies. Up in the *pa* a hideous wailing sound somewhat similar to the keening of Irish peasants arose. Again and again the doleful cry swelled.

That this lament was being raised for the *kagatira*—high king— of Ruawai *pa* who, with his heir had just been killed, wasn't yet comprehended by the escapees.

Before long Sylvanus Doane was able to learn, from a native who'd acquired a smattering of English through having shipped aboard a whaler, that the Ngati Tari Mata, the defending tribe, were profoundly grateful for the *pakeha*'s well-timed intervention. Especially, they had been impressed by the awesome havoc wrought by the schooner's Long Tom.

Like all Maori tribes, the Ngati Tari Matas held the white man's *pu*-musket in awe thanks to the noise it made and the amount of destruction it could cause. This huge, super-*pu* was so overwhelming it must be a weapon consecrated to Tu, all-powerful god of war.

The slain *kagatira*'s second oldest son with a mourning wreath of green leaves riding low on grief-torn hair and a group of local nobles paddled out to the schooner to be warily greeted by Sylvanus Doane. With impressive gravity the deputation invited this all-powerful one-eyed warrior to come shore and attend a great tribal council.

In the *pa*'s large and grotesquely carved Council House waited chiefs, sub-chiefs and allied dignitaries who begged Sylvanus Doane to become their *kagatira* and employ his terrible magical powers against their enemies.

The insistent crowing of a nearby rooster ended Sylvanus Doane's succession of nightmares and returned him, gladly enough, to the consideration of more immediate and pressing problems.

15

Ahipara Pa

Forty-eight hours after the *Scimitar* sailed out of Kaipara Bay in the dead of night, Sylvanus Doane—who had been keeping the schooner far offshore—ordered her over-long bowsprit pointed towards a barely visible gray line marking the North Island's shore.

Doane, swaying to the little schooner's motion, picked a path aft among the crowd of grinning, tattooed brown warriors squatting on the deck. Said he in perfect Maori, "Everyone will go below and *stay out of sight* except Te Hiko and Young Nick's Brother, Mr. Penny and Mr. Powys, who will pretend to be Captain and Mate of this trader."

Half an hour later an albatross soaring above the *Scimitar*'s top-masts would have spied only a few kilted Maori seafarers loafing about an untidy deck and a pair of bearded white men in jerseys and canvas pantaloons slouching near the wheel.

Presently the schooner closed in on a pair of fishing canoes; Maoris on the foredeck commenced to wave faded green branches.

A flying fish, gleaming blue-and-white, went skittering off over the waves towards the nearest canoe as Te Hiko, smiling, flourished a *kauri* branch and called, "Fame in producing food will always remain."

The fishermen grinned and offered the choicest of their catch as gifts and, in open curiosity steered outrigger canoes close to the *pakeha*'s vessel.

Intently, Doane listened to Te Hiko explain that the great canoe's sole purpose in visiting these shores was to trade arms and ammunition for flax, pigs and *kauri* gum and perhaps some choice preserved human heads.

Te Hiko gestured to Penny, who pipe in mouth, stood listening. "The Captain yonder will pay fair prices but will carry on trade *only* in his own fashion."

Firearms! Broad brown faces lit when Te Hiko held up a Tower musket with its brass mountings brightly burnished. The *pakeha* Captain, explained the giant, was planning early next morning to anchor his great canoe off the entrance to Ahipara Bay and the Bone King's stronghold; however, he would do business only if canoes came out one by one. Once the first canoe arrived alongside the next must wait till a green branch was waved; each canoe must wait its turn.

Should more than one *waka* attempt to approach, the ship's great gun would blast the Ngati Waro out of the water.

The fishermen then were told to head homeward and inform the Bone King of the conditions.

Next morning Sylvanus Doane navigated the *Scimitar* through an angry pattern of reefs and sandbars and dropped anchor off the entrance to Ahipara Bay.

When the first canoes could be seen shoving off from a beach below Ahipara *pa* sparkling morning sunlight clearly revealed tall palisades encircling a high round hill dominated by an impressive Council House. What immediately commanded the one-eyed American's attention was a dirty-white triangle at least fifteen feet high standing before the Council House. Focusing with care, Doane soon realized that this pyramid indeed had been entirely constructed from human bones and skulls.

An ordinary fishing canoe carrying a mound of produce and six dark-faced men waited for a branch to be waved and only then paddled alongside, smiling and calling greetings.

Algernon Penny, Esq., Israel Bulloch and Te Hiko excited cupidity by displaying carbines, a variety of muskets and pistols, also cartridge boxes, powder horns, bullet moulds and bars of lead. The cannibals needed no further invitation to climb over the schooner's rail, agile as apes, leaving their canoe to bump alongside.

In the *Scimitar's* dark and stiflingly hot forehold warriors from Ruawai and Wangape gripped war clubs while listening to a party of six flax-kilted visitors clamber up the side and drop onto the deck.

Tattooed human heads—always in great demand aboard *pakeha* ships of war, whaler, traders—first were offered.

"Those heads really first-class?" Algernon Penny, Esq., demanded, shoving a broad-brimmed straw hat more comfortably onto the back of his head.

"Not poor—not fine," Young Nick's Brother said.

Thanks to heavy tattooing and the fact he was wearing only a *pareau*—a long-skirted kilt—Sylvanus Doane continued to crouch unnoticed in the lee of the wheelhouse.

Presently Te Hiko suggested the visitors go below and inspect at first hand an assortment of firearms. One by one Maoris were guided down a ladder to the main hold; at once they were tripped and their hands lashed behind them. If any man tried to cry out he immediately was clubbed into insensibility.

The first lot having been hauled behind a pile of chests, the next group were lured below.

In less than an hour a cluster of empty canoes lay alongside and close to eighty captives lay bleeding and writhing in the main hold.

Once the last cannibal had disappeared Doane ordered the main hatch battened down.

"Te Hiko! Summon the warriors on deck, but tell them to keep their weapons hidden. Pray God there's no telescope in the *pa*."

In short order the crew, armed with muskets, spears, clubs and fighting staffs, dropped into the canoes from Ahipara, and commenced leisurely to paddle over shimmering, dark-green waves towards the Bone King's citadel.

Indistinguishable from a Maori, Sylvanus Doane occupied a big, sea-going canoe speeding in towards the stronghold; apparently it remained unalarmed since a considerable crowd had gathered at the landing place and were calling greetings.

Doane glanced over his shoulder at the *Scimitar* and was relieve to note a dark cluster of figures busy about her Long Tom. Fervently he prayed the Australian would hold fire till he flashed a small mirror as a heliograph.

Algernon Penny, Esq., had been left aboard to make certain that Powys obeyed orders.

Drawing a deep breath, Doane faced about and slowly tilted his mirror back and forth; a cloud of smoke smothered the schooner's foredeck a split second before the deep-throated *boom!* of her Long Tom came rolling over Ahipara Bay.

A round shot arched into the sky, screamed over canoes in which paddlers put on a burst of speed and hitherto concealed warriors rose brandishing weapons and screaming threats.

Whatever George Powys' faults, and they were legion, poor gunnery was not among them; the first shot landed at the entrance to the Council House precisely in line with the pyramid of bones.

Carved door posts and beams snapped, the thatch roof collapsed and out into the open rushed a stream of men so terrified many were weaponless. Others, stricken by jagged splinters, lurched and reeled about squalling like scalded wildcats.

The Bone King himself appeared with a heavy splinter sticking into his shoulder like a broken lance. He ran out into the glaring sunlight roaring futile orders.

Te Hiko ran out his tongue to full length then, eyes bulging in a terrifying grimace, led a rush through the main gate.

The Long Tom boomed for a second time while Sylvanus Doane was wading ashore and using a long-barrelled pistol to wave forward his musketeers. The tumult became frenzied once the raiders penetrated the palisade and a massacre commenced; smoke poured from dozens of dwellings.

The gigantic Te Hiko, howling like a hungry wolf, sighted the Bone King desperately defending himself.

Combatants in the immediate vicinity fell back, leaving Te Wainga, critically hampered by the splinter sticking out of his shoulder, to face an enemy who leaped in and, striking hard with his long-handled tomahawk, landed a blow at the base of the Bone King's muscle-corded neck.

Eyes rolling, Te Wainga staggered backwards clasping his neck, vainly trying to staunch the jets of bright arterial blood which kept spurting from between his fingers. His knees buckled then he sprawled, quivering convulsively, at Te Hiko's feet. A great wail arose. "*Ki patu Kagatira!*—The great Chief is dead!"

Nevertheless, defenders reinforced by warriors running in from fields and forests attempted a rally which soon was broken up when Doane sent his musketeers among the huts with instructions to shoot only leaders and handsomely tattooed fugitives. Here and there knots of defenders started fighting back-to-back, whereupon the musket men simply mowed them down.

Te Hiko, sweating and blood-smeared, flourished the Bone King's dripping head then raised a bragging chant which ended abruptly when from somewhere among the blazing dwellings a pistol cracked.

Te Hiko collapsed with a small, bluish-red hole between his bulbous eyes. Such was the dust and confusion no one ever knew whence the shot had come or even less who might have fired it.

Sylvanus Doane emerged from behind a cluster of huts casually reloading a fine French duelling pistol noted for accuracy at long ranges.

16
News from the North

When, after the passage of twelve weeks, the *Gladiator* still had failed to put in an appearance, *Kuini* Lydia Ponapa persuaded her sister-in-law to await the bark's return in the sociable security of Waiuka *pa* where a large and airy dwelling had been readied near the royal palace, complete with a swarm of servants and essential pieces of European furniture.

By now Aimée Paddock's belly had grown so rotund and her breasts so big that she suggested, with a quick grimace, that she resembled nothing so much as a series of superimposed circles.

The two women spent most of their time on the porch of Te Ponapa's lavishly carved and red-painted *kaitangata* about which Peter Pehi, innocent of garments, staggered about in the wake of his round little belly.

It had begun to warm up after a cold and blustery morning with a half-gale roaring in from the Tasman Sea.

To settle herself more comfortably Aimée squirmed in an armchair and pulled a native shawl higher over her shoulders. "What is taking place in the great Council 'Ouse? I 'ave seen so many 'igh chiefs and warriors hurrying in."

Informed to the minute as usual, Lydia compressed dark-red ruler-straight lips and stared out over the bay. "This morning one of the *Ariki*'s—" nowadays she invariably referred to Te Ponapa that way, "—spies reported on a trip made up the coast." Intense black eyes delved into Aimée's clear blue ones.

"—And so?"

"Apparently he's brought bad news."

Aimée anticipated. "The One-Eyed King—Te Whiro Kanohi—is preparing for war?"

Lydia's sleek head inclined. "From the little the *Ariki* told me I judge that's about it."

Without conviction the Frenchwoman suggested, "Is it not possible that this renegade may be arming against others than ourselves?"

"Hardly possible. No. It could only be our Waikato tribes the One-Eyed King means to attack; already he has conquered or made allies of all his neighbors." Peter Pehi, owl-eyed, clambered onto his mother's narrow lap but she paid him no heed. "For example, only a year ago this renegade crushed the Ngati Toa and the Ngati Mutunga and so added hundreds of fine warriors to his forces. Frankly, I'm badly worried."

Reaching into a linen bag Aimée produced a tangle of knitting then merged winged, pale-brown brows while her needles began to flash. "*Chérie*, it is best to remember one important fact. Although your 'usband commenced his campaigns at a later time 'e, too, always 'as triumphed. Take for example that last clan 'e defeated. What was its name?"

"The Raukawa—but they were a subject tribe which tried to break away when old Te Pehi got killed."

"Oh, my dear, if only my 'usband would return! What *can* 'ave 'appened to him?"

"God knows. Still, I fully expect Jed to turn up any time now."

Aimée stared at the floor mats. "*Chérie*, I 'ave not told you before of a presentiment I suffered while watching the *Gladiator* depart."

"A premonition? What was it?"

"That I will never again behold the bark."

Kuini Lydia Te Ponapa's jaws clicked shut. "Bosh! And double bosh! Jed's in no trouble, you silly creature. Likely, the greedy rascal's lingered to take a few extra whales on the way home. Mark my words. He'll come sailing into the bay in ample time for this campaign."

Aimée's fetus gave a kick strong enough to spill her knitting bag onto the floor mats.

Lydia laughed. "Like his pa. Impatient and lusty already."

"''Is'? You believe it will be a boy?"

"Certain-sure since you're carrying him so high. 'Twas the same with Peter Pehi. But this one," grimacing, she tapped the gentle roundness of her lower abdomen, "I hazard will prove a snivelling little female."

Among cool shadows in the Tribal Meeting House Te Ponapa

Ariki heaved himself onto broad bare feet and stood so tall a pair of albatross feathers at the back of his head scraped a chiselled beam.

Tattooed features impassive, the giant in great deliberation surveyed the semi-circle of intent chiefs squatting on the floor of hard-packed earth.

The only whites present were Mister Hayward and Abner Doane.

Clenching hands, Te Ponapa thumped himself on the chest several times, then jerked a handsome *mere* from his belt and waved it above his head declaiming: "It is war! May wrath and I join together. All warriors of the Waikato will assemble here in seven days' time.

"Tomorrow, to each *rangatira* will be given a sacred war cloak with the hole of Tu burned through it. Show these in all your towns and villages. Bid your warriors tirelessly to practice war dances. Order your *tohungas* to cleanse your followers of all *tapus*. Bring with you many slaves strong but young enough to eat should we grow hungry." Contorting his features into a hideous scowl the ex-harpooner flourished the *mere*, screaming, "*A, a, te riri*—it is war!"

Abner Doane would be a long while forgetting the orgy of dancing, posturing and bragging which then spread through the *pa* with the speed of a grass fire fanned by a high wind.

Mister Hayward, outwardly impassive, was impressed by such exhibitions of raw violence until Heetee remarked, "Mister Third, you think this little noise something? Wait till all the *Ariki*'s warriors prepare for the fighting."

During the paddle out to the fort on Abigail Island Abner frowned. "Mister Hayward, you got any idea why the Skipper's not showed before now?"

Brow furrowed, the Third spat over the side. "No, I haven't and that's a fact. Te Ponapa's going to have need of the *Gladiator*'s arms and ammunition to bring off this war and, from all I hear, this promises to be a tough campaign; everyone claims old One-Eye's mighty shrewd, capable and merciless."

"If he's white I wonder who he really is—or was?"

"All I've heard is that he led the party of escaped convicts who now rule tribes around Kaipara Bay."

"How many convicts are there?" Abner demanded as a flock of comical little penguins surfaced nearby to stare fearlessly at the canoe.

"No one knows for sure; still, I hear they don't number over five or six."

"Heard tell the cannibals call you 'Kapene' nowadays. Must feel pretty good at your age to be called 'Captain'."

"I can't help that, sir, they're only stupid savages."

Mister Hayward exposed the yellow-brown stumps of teeth. "Well, *Kapene*, how many men you got in your musket company?"

"Around thirty, sir. Most of 'em have become better than average shots."

The Third checked himself as he started to turn away. "How are Fast Canoe and Heetee makin' out teachin' these bloody cannibals to use bows and arrows?"

"Pretty well. Seems like the tribesmen take to such easier than to firearms. Fast Canoe allows some can even shoot a parrot out of a tall tree and others are good on running targets."

"'Running targets'?"

"Aye, sir, slaves running as fast as they can. Though I don't believe him, Heetee claims some of his recruits can nail a runner at seventy-five yards. He's got a party at practice right now. Want to go take a look-see?"

The older man peered curiously at his companion. Lord! This smooth-faced youth with yellow fuzz sprouting all over his jaws couldn't have been more casual had he been inviting him to attend a boxing match!

"No," grunted the older man. "Got to get back to the island. I'll send a canoe for you in an hour's time."

In a shallow gully Abner came across Heetee and a young warrior crouching over a headless corpse from the side of which protruded the shafts of two arrows. Heetee jumped up and saluted, European fashion. The movement sent scarlet drops to spattering the underbrush.

"How are things going?"

"Good, *Kapene*." Heetee's pleasant, broad, brown features lit. "My fellows brought down four *tamaus* running fast as they could. This one we think is pretty enough for trading." By its long, brownblack and wavy hair he held out a severed head.

Using the back of his hand Heetee's grinning companion casually wiped blood from his lips; obviously he'd been drinking it.

To his surprise Abner didn't feel in the least sickened while watching Heetee secure the neck's skin about a roughly contrived hoop of *kareao* wood. Next, the skin at the base of the skull was parted to permit the blade of a European dirk to be driven upwards and employed in a circular, churning motion which, before long, excavated the brain and splinters of bone. Then the victim's tongue and eyes were removed.

While working, Heetee explained that later on the trophy would be immersed in boiling water just long enough to permit the skin to separate from the flesh. Next, to preserve its shape the head would be tightly stuffed with flax and, after the lips had been sewn together it would be impaled on a stick to be smoked over a slow fire until properly cured.

Before being offered for sale such a *paki-paki*, fixed on a stake, would be degraded through being planted before the village latrine.

The victim's hands also would be smoked once its fingers had been bent inwards to serve as pegs or hooks from which garments and weapons could be suspended in much the same fashion as deer and moose trotters were used by the Indians of North America.

The sisters-in-law, once more enjoying the quiet and European comforts of Amelia Island, took turns scanning the bay's entrance through a light spyglass but caught never a flash of distant topsails.

Early one morning Aimée was awakened by the *boom!* of a swivel gun on the watchtower. Throwing a cloak over her nightshift she ran onto the porch in time to sight a pair of battered-looking whaleboats gunwale-deep with people standing in under sail.

Her heart gave a mighty surge on recognizing the huge figure handling the lead boat's steering oar. *"Bon Dieu, je vous remerci!"*

17
Survivors

Kuini Lydia Paddock Roach Te Ponapa never once had found reason to question the strength of the bond between Te Ponapa and his blood-brother so she wasn't in the least surprised at the abandon with which her husband hugged Jedediah's gaunt and dreadfully sun-burned frame. Once they'd rubbed noses in prolonged *hongi* Jedediah broke free, ran to his wife who, hugely swollen and ungainly of gait had started towards the landing.

Weeping and laughing at the same time, she passionately kissed her husband.

Once the scarecrow smallboat crews began straggling up from the trading post's dock Lydia missed the presence of Aaron Winslow, Charley Coffin, Goober Pike, John Folger and all-too-many familiar faces. It came as a sharp relief, however, to recognize Adam Masters and Purvis, the British Master Gunner. Best of all was the sight of Hercules' shiny, sable countenance. Then she spied the copper-hued features of Tom Blue Fox, Dick-Sun-in-the-Eyes, Billy Big Buck and John Fast Canoe.

Jed stood, massive hands clutching Aimée's sloping shoulders and for long instants peered into her bee-brown features. Lord! Lord! She'd never appeared so unutterly precious. Subconsciously, he noted that the whites of her eyes had a vitreous, milky-blue tinge peculiar to pregnant women.

After dinner Lydia tautly asked how the *Gladiator* had been lost.

"Tell you later," Jed grunted.

"No, now, now. As part owner I've the right to a speedy re-port."

"Plague take you for a goddam sea lawyer." Nevertheless, he stood, legs braced apart, as if facing a Board of Inquiry. "Made a fast passage to Port Jackson for all I tarried to take half-a-dozen medium sperms; tried out one hundred and six barrels. Sold 'em when we reached Sydney."

He picked up a glass of brandy and slowly revolved its stem between thumb and forefinger. "Laid in a stock of likely trade goods and plenty of flintlocks. Next, I restocked the magazine and shot-lockers.

"I was runnin' ahead of time so decided to try my luck along the Line but didn't meet with much success. In a month's cruising about I came across only a few lone sperms so I shaped a homeward course and figgered on reaching Waikato in a hurry.

"Left Phillip Island astern and was expectin' to raise The Three Kings come three-four days when the goddamnedest typhoon you *ever heard tell of* struck us 'thout warning. That infernal blast came roarin' in from all directions."

He began to talk faster. "At noon the sun shone bright and hot with a light to moderate breeze blowing; by one the sky had turned blacker'n Zip's ass and all the devils in hell were screamin' through the rigging."

Jed commenced to stride back and forth. "That goddam tempest hit us so fast I'd no time to secure and batten down proper-like; never have seen seas build faster.

"Maintop was first to go and its weight damn' near capsized us. Don't know how many men got swept overboard whilst they were choppin' to free us of the drag. Then we fell into the trough of the seas and began to roll fit to sicken a Turk."

In a still, flat voice Lydia prompted, "What then?"

"Next, the foremast went, then the mizzen's shrouds ripped right out of the chain-plates and everywhere stays snapped like grocery twine. Some carronades fetched loose and smashed great holes in the sides. By this time most of the deck was under two-three feet of water; God alone knows how much there was in the hold."

In smothered voice Aimée queried, "Then, *mon pauvre coeur*, you—you 'ad no mast left?"

"Only the stump of the main up to the trucks," Jed told her. "Well, about then the typhoon commenced to slack off and I was beginnin' to figure we might save the bark after all when we struck some bloody big reef shown on no chart I'd ever seen.

"We struck so hard I knew the ship had broken her back and that that was the end of her."

Miserably Lydia commented, "A poor finish for a damned expensive ship. What followed?"

"When the storm finally eased off we rigged and supplied two unhurt boats. I say 'supplied' though we'd barely time to take along whatever came handy. As it was, the bark began breaking up even as we were shoving off."

Jed swung over to stand in the doorway and stare at canoes tied up to his dock. "I calc'lated our best bet was to make for the North Cape which we reached in under two weeks time. 'Twas a good thing, too; we were tasting the last of our food and water."

Aimée got up, lumbered over to kiss the compass rose tattooed on her husband's big bronzed hand.

Lydia demanded, "I presume you refreshed yourselves on Cape Marie van Dieman?"

"Aye. Managed to keep enough firearms to make the cannibals give us what we needed."

Jed faced his listeners, a bleak expression on deeply lined features. "That's about all except we've had the devil's own time working south. Never realized what a mean coast this is; reefs and shoals everywhere, strong tides, crazy currents and rocky shores. I can understand why Russell's favored for refitting."

A knock sounded. Abner entered, cap held before him. "Sir, did —did you—?"

"I was pretty well occupied in Sydney but I did ask whenever I thought of it."

Eagerness faded from the former cabin boy's long, freckled face. "You didn't hear word of Pa?"

"Never a one; even the magistrates hadn't heard of a Sylvanus Doane—which ain't surprisin' after a lapse of so many years. Sorry. Better face up that your pa's disappeared for good—or bad.

"Even if you'd come along with me I doubt you'd have learned —" He broke off when a lookout in the blockhouse sounded a series of moaning blasts on his conch shell.

Lydia shaded eyes to peer in the direction of Waiuka *pa* and made out a sleek scout canoe being paddled towards Abigail Island so fast spurts of lacy white foam kept leaping from under its figurehead.

A man balanced in the prow cupped hands shouting, "*Kagatira* Paddock! *Kagatira* Paddock! Spies say the One-Eyed King has learned your great gun canoe is no more! Three days ago he sent out the burnt fighting cloaks and gathers men for a great war!"

18

Preparations

Never before in the vicinity of Waikato Bay had martial preparations been conducted on such a scale.

Abner Doane happened to be in the *pa* when a large contingent of warriors from the Ruakawa tribe appeared and stolidly stood awaiting a ritual welcome.

Already Te Ponapa, his sub-chiefs and *tutuas* were marshalling a detachment of home troops at one end of a wide parade ground lying outside the palisades.

Howling war cries and brandishing spears, tomahawks and stone short swords, the *tutuas* and *ponogas*—free men of humble birth—four-abreast formed into three columns.

Once the visiting force, shouting and chanting, had deployed along the parade ground's opposite end three stalwart "challengers" selected by Te Ponapa raced to the *marae*'s middle. There they halted and began to leap like demented jumping-jacks with tongues run out and white-ringed eyes popped and glaring defiance.

A brief pause ensued during which both contingents glared and made faces before raising a terrific concerted yowl. Only then did they charge headlong at one another. At the last expertly timed second the Raukawans suddenly veered to the right while Te Ponapa's followers with a shout of "*hurihia!*" also took an oblique right turn barely in time to avert a collision.

All at once laughing and friendly both parties trotted off the field.

The newcomers then were made welcome with wailing, speeches and much pressing of noses among leaders.

The two forces then combined in welcoming in similar fashion bands of warriors coming in from allied and subject tribes.

At a solemn council-of-war presided over by Te Ponapa *Ariki* and Jedediah Paddock it was decided that, in view of the One-Eyed King's hasty preparations for war, it was no longer advisable to delay

for the arrival of war parties coming from distant parts of Te Ponapa's dominions. On the morrow the great war dance of departure
would be performed by the entire Waikatan force. This done, warriors could consider themselves freed of *tapus* and ready to take the
field.

From armchairs set on the porch of Te Ponapa *Ariki's kaitangata* Lydia and Aimée watched the proceedings. Between them stood
thick-bodied Tuki Kutene, consort of Te Aukawa, commander of
the powerful Raukawan contingent. Tuki was middle-aged, sedate,
and well-fleshed but with very handsome pale-brown features; only
her chin and upper lip were adorned with not-unattractive tattooing.

Since Lydia and her sister-in-law had grown fluent in the local
dialect they had small trouble following Tuki's description of the
ceremony about to begin.

Feather headdresses nodding and dogskin war capes asway,
companies numbering around one hundred and forty men began to
trot out and take up positions on the sun-baked *marae*.

Quite casually, Lydia noted that most warriors went stark naked
except on occasion some fighter wore a loincloth tucked between
thick and powerful legs. Some carried long capes to be used either as
a protection against the weather or as a shield when wrapped around
the left forearm.

Amid clouds of whirling yellow-red dust detachments ranged
themselves before a low dais on which stood the *Ariki* in company
with Captain Paddock, recently given the exalted title of *Kagatira*.

While Te Ponapa, *Ariki*, resplendent in a nodding crown of
blue-dyed heron plumes and a magnificent cloak of kiwi feathers,
ranked as sole Supreme Commander, or *Te Heu-Heu*, the fact remained that he never made an important decision without consulting
his blood-brother.

Tuki Kutene's chattering discourse pointed out certain unprecedented aspects of this ceremony; for example, there was the arrival before the royal dais of a band of red-kilted musket carriers.
Commanded by Mister Hayward and Abner Doane they wore white
crossbelts and black leather cartridge boxes, which lent the only note
of uniformity among them. Also appeared a handful of bearded and
canvas-trousered survivors of the *Gladiator's* crew armed with cutlasses and flintlocks.

To Jedediah's amusement Mister Hayward barked a command which caused the musket company awkwardly to present arms, European fashion. Maoris among them improved the salute by running out pink tongues and making all manner of war-like grimaces.

In the background log drums commenced to thud and thump; conch shell trumpets wailed and moaned like so many lovesick tomcats.

Jedediah Paddock, *Kagatira,* then suffered further astonishment when out onto the parade ground bounded what very much resembled a war party of American Indians. Red-tipped white war feathers had been lashed into Tom Blue Fox's greasy blue-black hair while across his aquiline features ran horizontal bands of red-and-black war paint. The Monomoy brandished a short war bow in one hand and an iron-headed tomahawk in the other as he whirled across the *marae* amid startled outcries from Maoris who'd never seen such a sight. A quiver of brown-and-white dogskin rattled its contents between the red man's sinewy, copper-hued shoulders. Blue Fox suddenly halted, threw back his head and raised a whooping, ear-piercing war cry such as, for generations, had accompanied death and destruction along the coasts of North America.

Quickly he was joined by the leaping and whirling figures of Billy Big Buck, John Fast Canoe and Dick Sun-in-the-Eyes. Caparisoned and painted like braves on the warpath they stamped in a tight circle waving weapons on high and all the while making screeching, gobbling noises.

Heetee and a party of Maori bowmen then ran out and attempted to imitate the Indians' gyrations but quickly reverted to movements learned in boyhood.

The exhibition reached its climax when, to conclude their dance, the archers whipped arrows from quivers and at amazing speed loosed a series of shafts into the blazing hot sky.

Thunderous roars of excitement went up when most of the red-feathered arrows buried themselves in the *marae's* hard surface so close that the bowmen could retrieve them without moving more than a pace or two!

Heu! Heu! Was this not a form of sorcery capable of wreaking great havoc among the enemy? Truly, omens for the impending campaign seemed to be favorable beyond an expectation.

Wooden war drums thundered and long wooden trumpets

wailed and groaned like a chorus of doomed souls. In ever-increasing density dust clouds began to swirl about the *marae* once the combined forces of Waikato commenced the furious leaping dance of warriors departing for war.

Still panting, Tom Blue Fox and the other red men watched, deemed it a fairly impressive performance for a pack of ignorant cannibals.

Once companies of breathless, sweating and semi-hysterical warriors commenced to quit the parade ground, Lydia turned to Tuki Katene. "What comes next?"

The aristocratic woman smiled. "They parade to the latrines."

Lydia's oblique jet eyes widened. "The backhouses! For the land's sakes what for? *All* those men can't be took of a need at the same time!"

"No, *Kuini* Ponapa," laughed the guest. "Our fighters only go to perform a next-to-final rite."

"In a latrine?" Aimée looked amused being aware that, as in all Maori settlements, the communal latrine consisted only of a number of stout posts connected by crossbars to which a user clung while suspending his posterior over a gully or deep ditch.

Jed's wife, always curious about earthy subjects, added, *"Ma foi!* And what could warriors expect to accomplish in such a place?"

"They bite the crossbars to prove themselves willing to suffer any humiliation in order to win a victory."

"—And after that?"

"The fighters will go down to the river where *tohungas* will sprinkle enchanted water on them to free them from the observation of all *tapus*. Also, they will rededicate themselves and their weapons to the service of Tu, our god of war."

Observed Lydia in a swift aside. " 'Pears like a lot of time-wasting mumbo-jumbo but I reckon it's no greater nonsense than our benedictions, band concerts and parades." She considered Aimée closely then arose. "You're going drawn and white, best come and lie down. I'll have my women sponge and fan you."

Through strenuous efforts backed by threats and promises, Te Ponapa *Ariki* and his fellow chieftains succeeded in assembling an impressive fleet of canoes of many sorts; from sea-going double-hulled war canoes hewn out of a single tree trunk and equipped with lofty, elaborately carved prows and sterns; to fast but tricky *waka tiwai* designed for use in rivers and bays; most numerous of all were sturdy outrigger fishing canoes.

While the first opalescent streaks of dawn were tinting the sky the armada put to sea lest spies, undoubtedly present, might speed warnings to the One-Eyed King who, according to last minute intelligence, already had completed his mobilization. If favored by a fair breeze his seaborne forces, probably escorted by the *Scimitar*, might already be at sea.

To Jedediah Paddock it proved exasperating that Te Ponapa's informants should all be simple fishermen lacking ability to estimate numbers; the enemy's actual strength therefore remained a critical question.

Eventually Jed, Te Ponapa *Ariki* and his chief subordinates reckoned that old One-Eye and his fellow renegades must be leading an army of between 2,000 and 2,500 men, of these possibly fifty might be armed with muskets.

Should this estimate prove accurate the forces of Waikato must proceed with great caution; canoes, sliding and dipping over long, dark-blue swells, were transporting only about 1,800 warriors, including some 200 brawny slaves taken in war. If necessary these could be armed and sent into battle inspired by hopes of freedom if they acquitted themselves with distinction.

Um, mused Jed, if God always fought on the side of the heaviest battalions the Waikatans were in for a bitter struggle—especially if the schooner and her Long Tom were in evidence. A bitter taste entered his mouth at the thought of his beautiful *Gladiator* wrecked and her carronades at the bottom of the sea.

Around midday a brisk southerly wind sprang up and soon made it impossible to keep the flotilla in a compact formation.

Inevitably, canoes straggled into a perilously disordered mile-long column.

19
Gathering Storm

Beneath an awning of raw linen rigged above a platform joining the red-painted double hulls of a huge war canoe Sylvanus Doane sat with Algernon Penny, Esq., Israel Bulloch, Young Nick and Young Nick's Brother.

Thanks to a fair wind blowing strongly out of the northwest sweating paddlers were glad to ship blades and allow a pair of triangular sails to drive their craft swiftly down the coastline.

For the One-Eyed King it had been a real temptation to use the *Scimitar* as a flagship but the little schooner had become so dangerously worm-eaten and otherwise decrepit she no longer could be considered even remotely seaworthy.

Nevertheless, he very likely would have risked taking the schooner had it not been reliably reported that the Captain of an armed whaler, known to base in Waikato Bay, had returned to Waiuka *pa* minus his ship and accompanied by only a few of her crew.

Sylvanus Doane was forced to sit in a half-crouch because the awning had sagged so low that the *huia* feathers bound upright to his head kept scraping the material above him. His hair now more silvery than sandy had been twisted to a topknot pulled through a heavy ring of fancifully engraved whale ivory.

He slipped from under the canopy to stand with yellow-and-red-feather cape streaming bright to ascertain the position of his scout canoes. He grunted satisfaction; the screen, skillfully conned, was skimming along midway between a series of surf-lashed beaches and an irregular line of barrier-reefs. Close behind the scouts and not far in advance of his own craft sailed a brace of a double canoes carrying musket men commanded by George Powys. Astern bobbed a thick, half-mile-long column of canoes surging along over hissing, ultramarine-blue seas.

He crooked a bony finger at Young Nick's Brother. "Signal the leaders to slow down. We're getting too strung out." He glanced at Algernon Penny, Esq., "Where are we?"

The sunburnt young Englishman distinctive in the usual clean white ducks and fresh blue shirt unrolled a map drawn by him during a furtive surveying expedition made months earlier.

He spoke in clear, drawling tones, "From the shape of yonder rock I judge, if this breeze holds, around two hours' sail will find us off Manukau Bar which marks the entrance to Carry-Over Bay."

Doane gathered his cloak tighter about him and blinked his single cold blue eye.

"That's good. I don't want to arrive off Manukau much before dark." He turned to Young Nick. "You spoke to a fisherman a while back; what did he say?"

"*Ariki*, he said that all remains quiet around Waikato. Te Ponapa remains unsuspecting."

A school of silver-blue flying fish burst out of a wave and flashed across the flagship's prow. One landed, flapping wildly, amongst the paddlers who raised shrill cries over so propitious an omen.

Doane smiled thinly. "Let's hope this means something."

His tattooing long since completed, Sylvanus Doane, decided Penny, except for his blue eye and gold ring was indistinguishable from a Maori noble.

"Penny! What was our last strength return?"

"Around 2,000 men give or take a few dozens."

"Your opinion, Israel?"

"Add a couple of hundred head," Bulloch called over the rhythmic *hiss-hiss* of waves alongside. "Since we've no longer got that damned armed whaler to reckon with, we'll handle the Waikatos right handsomely."

Signals on conch shells gradually collected the fleet into a compact, egg-shaped formation behind a screen of scout canoes.

Doane returned to his red-painted stool and absently revolved his signet ring. Well, with luck, the *Ariki* of Waikato soon would be totally crushed.

He determined his next move; come sundown he'd land his warriors just inside the entrance to Manukau Bay and spend the night there. Before daybreak tomorrow, he'd despatch an important-appearing flotilla manned by slaves and inferior troops down the coast as a feint calculated to delude the *Ariki* of Waikato into expecting an assault from the sea. Meanwhile, the bulk of Doane's army by forced marches would descend the coast fast enough to deliver, another of those classic dawn surprise attacks which had kept the slave pens of Ruawai *pa* well filled and the tribal coffers glutted with tribute.

The one-eyed white man's lean, tattooed hands tightened gradually on his lap until the ring bit in. With Waikato crushed, what forces would remain to prevent later conquest of the Taranakis and thus bring the entire West Coast under his sway?

The lowering sun was creating purplish shadows in the troughs of long, lazy rollers when Algernon Penny, Esq., spoke up. "Look alive, Yank; should sight breakers off Manukau any minute; the pilots will need good light to navigate tricky currents around the entrance."

"True enough. Anything else in your mind?"

"Where do you intend to land for the night?"

"Near the entrance on the bay's south side. Know of a more suitable spot?"

"What's your intent?"

Doane planted a finger on his map. "There's a wide sand beach here, with wood and fresh water close by which should serve our purpose."

"Seems a likely enough landing place."

Doane looked hard at Young Nick's Brother. "You *sure* Te Ponapa's got no idea I've moved out?"

"Spies report that because the *pakeha* ship has been lost Te Ponapa's people are not getting ready for war."

There was, of course, no way Young Nick's Brother could be aware that, around noon of that same day, the Waikatan expedition had landed on the banks of a small river flowing into the Tasman Sea just below the entrance to Manukau Bay.

Te Ponapa *Ariki's* canoes had disappeared behind a cluster of islands and a camp made on the river's bank. No fires were allowed so after sundown the Waikatans were tortured by clouds of whining mosquitoes, sand flies and nearly invisible midges which could bite like tigers.

The Monomy felt years drop from his wiry body when, an hour before daybreak, he started to wriggle, flat on his stomach, through chill, dew-soaked sandgrass covering the summit of a high dune.

On reaching its top Tom Blue Fox gently parted a clump of low bushes to peer intently through gray half-light. *Wagh!* This was a miracle! He was feeling so much like a young brave on his first scout. Soaked through, he felt glad he'd made his bowmen wrap their bows in oily linen lest moisture slacken strings of expertly cured dog gut.

Turning his head, the old harpooner glimpsed Fast Canoe's dark outline crawling only half a length behind him. Also he was pleased by Sun-in-the-Eyes' absolutely silent progress; nor was Billy Big Buck making much more noise.

This couldn't be said about the advance of Heetee and other Maori archers scrabbling along a few yards behind and doing their best to imitate the red men; still, they weren't doing too badly for warriors untrained in the fine art of stalking an enemy over comparatively bare ground.

Once Blue Fox gained a clump of wind-twisted shrubbery he inched onto his knees the better to scrutinize his surrounding vicinity by the light of a waning moon. It was encouraging to perceive how ignorant these cannibals were.

What appeared to be the enemy's principal outpost of all things had been stationed *in plain sight* on a low hillock only slightly higher than long, low dunes all about. The warriors on duty up there were so plainly silhouetted against the stars that even the stirrings of capes under the wind was visible.

Better yet, the Maoris appeared to be incredibly unalert—real sitting ducks. Scarce-remembered surges of fierce anticipation warmed the old harpooner; he breathed joyous thanks to the Great Spirit for having made it possible for him to lift a few more scalps before departing for the Happy Hunting Grounds. Ever since reaching New Zealand the Monomoy secretly had planned some day to lift Maori hair—so tempting thick and luxuriant.

His breath levelling out, Blue Fox resumed his patient advance through dew-soaked beach grass around a foot high. Yes, it was most encouraging to see how utterly unwary the pickets remained; best of all, he and the other stalkers noticed nothing to indicate the existence of other outposts. They did however catch certain noises other than the roar of surf in the distance which convinced Blue Fox that the One-Eyed King's main camp must lie close behind a rampart of pale yellow dunes.

"Everything," Jedediah Paddock had warned, "depends on the noiseless killing of all pickets or sentries you find. They must *not* be allowed to raise an alarm. Minute the job's done to your satisfaction send runners back so's we can begin deploying troops in a hurry."

Obedient to hand signals from their leader, the archers in the depths of a little gulley unsheathed bows and slewed quivers into the ready position between their shoulder blades.

When Blue Fox, heart thumping but outwardly impassive, judged the cannibals were looming against the sky some fifty yards distant he checked the advance and considered the situation.

The five hostiles standing on the knoll seemed more concerned keeping their backs to a cold wind blowing from the sea than in keeping an even half-way sharp lookout. Of course there *might* be enemies sheltering behind the hillock but the old Monomoy decided to risk that.

Easily as serpents, Sun-in-the-Eyes and Fast Canoe slithered up to Blue Fox's either side, arrows on string, followed by Heetee and a pair of tribesmen, incongruous in American Indian war paint.

Blue Fox whispered, "Five hostiles up there. When I say 'loose!' shoot only warrior most opposite you. Fast Canoe and I will slay the tall brave standing in their midst."

The wrinkled harpooner, war feathers twisting slowly in the wind then made a lifting motion with his right hand. "Now!"

As one the archers sprang to their feet, bows bended into tight arcs; followed a series of humming twangs and the hiss of arrows flashing upwards.

Three of the five pickets instantly went limp and collapsed with the suddenness of marionettes whose strings have been cut; their bodies rolled to the foot of the knoll. The other Maoris, topknots swaying, staggered about, apparently too shocked to cry out. The tall warrior on wavering legs was tugging at an arrow sunk into his solar plexus; then Blue Fox's second transfixed his chest and silenced him forever. The other Kaiparan struck in the throat, tumbled off the skyline without outcry.

20

Battle I

It proved most unfortunate for the plans of Captain Jedediah Paddock and his blood-brother that Blue Fox's extermination of the Kaiparan outpost had not gone entirely unobserved; a detachment ordered to relieve pickets on duty were within a hundred yards of the hillock when, before their unbelieving eyes, the warriors they were to relieve all at once collapsed or staggered briefly about before falling. The complete silence with which the outpost had perished was both awe-inspiring and terrifying. *Why* had there been no visible assailants? Why no clash of weapons or roar of *pakeha* flintlocks?

Black sorcery of some sort must be the answer. The relief officer, gibbering in terror, took to calloused brown heels and raced, white-eyed, back to the bivouac sprawled along shelving beaches behind a barrier of tall dunes. Possibly some wizard might be found able to explain and nullify effects of this astounding *tapu?*

Blue Fox and the other Indians, their blood racing, became so pleasurably occupied in the time-honored rite of lifting hair that for a while, they quite forgot the importance of sending back runners to report on the situation.

When wild tales of sorcery having destroyed his principal outpost reached Sylvanus Doane the renegade, accompanied by trembling bodyguards, ran to the knoll and viewed the dead. Unbelievably they had *retained* their heads; moreover, those were arrows protruding from their bodies! Instantly, he grasped what had happened nor it didn't surprise him when by the increasing light of dawn, he saw that the top of each dead man's skull gleamed shiny-pink—like a baby's bottom.

What really shook Sylvanus Doane were belated reports that the *Ariki* of Waikato not only had learned of his departure from Kaipara but had stolen a march. At once the One-Eyed King commenced to revise his strategy in view of the fact that Te Ponapa must have landed the day before and lay encamped not far away among the scrub-covered and sandy hills so characteristic of this stretch of the coast.

It now would be sheer folly to feint a sea attack on Waikato so, being utterly ignorant of the enemy's strength, he decided to hold his present position until he could ascertain the Waikatan's numbers. He knew better than to retreat even a short distance. His *mana*— prestige—would suffer irreparable damage in the eyes of his chiefs and warriors.

Appearing quite unshaken, Doane assembled his principal chieftains and while the pink-gray light of dawn intensified made plans for immediate attack. He reminded them that the Kaiparan forces on the beaches mostly were veterans, proven warriors accustomed to victory. Further, they were to be supported by a band of musketeers supposedly capable of coping with enemies bearing firearms.

A west wind grew stronger, colder just before the sun peered in a glorious burst of radiance above the steep, volcanic mountain range inland.

Suffering belated misgivings, Tom Blue Fox trotted up to a huge tree under which Te Ponapa, his blood-brother and a cluster of chieftains had collected for a last-minute council. Warned by his Captain's expression, the Monomoy braced himself for a blast.

"Why didn't you report earlier, you mangy red bastard?"

"Please, Cappen, me not remember," said he surreptitiously wiping fingers on his kilt.

"I'll bet: too damned busy lifting hair."

Painted features set in a scowl, Blue Fox offered a scalp with brownish-black hair so long it brushed the ground.

"Me take *coup* for Cappen. Fine."

Jed batted aside the proffered gift. "You *did* wipe out their outpost?"

"We kill all, Cappen—no noise," broke in Fast Canoe shouldering forward. A pair of scalps hung dripping redly from his belt.

"Please not get mad, Cappen. Delay only short time to count our *coups*," Sun-in-the-Eyes pleaded.

"You pulled all arrows out of the men you killed?"

"No, Cappen."

"You bloody stupid idiots!" Jed started to cock a fist, barely controlled himself. "If there's an American among those jailbirds you've given the show away."

Te Ponapa motioned Jed aside. "Since our dog-sired enemies must have learned we are here we must strike before they can arrange in order of battle."

The tarnished patent leather bill of Jedediah's cap dipped in a sharp nod. "Sure, we'd better hit the sons-of-bitches right away."

Te Ponapa's big front teeth glinted. "It would make great my *mana* to surprise the enemy, but even greater will be my fame to crush him in open battle."

The assembled *Rangatiris* grunted agreement.

The new-risen sun revealed both armies running into position along the crests of a series of low ridges roughly parallel and separated by about half-a-mile of bush and wind-dwarfed trees. The soil of this narrow plain was rather more sandy than earthy.

The onshore wind increased, grew colder and brought with it patches of fog and a series of rain squalls which prevented any attempt on the part of Sylvanus Doane to send a squadron of canoes through the entrance of Carry-Over Bay to take his enemies in the rear.

Standing on a tall rise with Te Ponapa, sub-chiefs and runners Jedediah Paddock never had felt more clearheaded and calm now that he'd a clearer grasp of the situation—even if the odds appeared far from equal. Tom Blue Fox, his Indians and native scouts had counted canoes on the far side of dunes masking Manukau Bay. They estimated the invaders must number not less than 2,500 warriors. Against these which the Waikatans couldn't field more than around 1,800 men.

With the sky turning a brighter yellow-red the situation became clarified; along the crests of almost parallel ridges separated by gently undulating, sandy and bush-grown terrain, the opposing forces noisily were gathered for simultaneous assaults.

Many warriors had become so frenzied they were becoming difficult to control. Howling, they brandished fighting staffs or whirled long-handled tomahawks about their heads. Since few warriors had eaten in hours hunger lent an edge to their hysterical fury.

Jed, armed with a brass blunderbuss equipped with a bayonet which could be folded back above the barrel and released by pressure on a spring button, scarcely noticed the drag at his belt of a regulation Navy cutlass and a brace of boarding pistols.

A hurrying rain squall briefly but viciously pelted dunes, caused Tom Blue Fox's bowmen hurriedly to case weapons and tie down quiver lids.

Once the downpour had subsided to wind-driven, silvery mist, Te Ponapa cast a quick glance at his brother-in-law. Jed, satisfied that the bulk of the Waikatan array had arrived on the dune's crest, jerked a nod. The *Ariki* beat his enormous chest and roared, *"Tuia! Tuia mai totou! —*Bind! Bind us together! *E tawa!* Fight a war!"

His whole array roared, *"E tawa! E tawa!"*, hurled volleys of taunts, insults and challenges. The enemy replied by raising an even louder chorus of yells, ululations and howls of "Give them the axe!"

By hundreds Kaiparans jumped high enough to lift feet off the ground and hammered themselves so hard on the chest that a bass, drum-like booming came rumbling across the little valley.

Jed ignored the tumult and used his spyglass to make sure the musket company under Mister Hayward and Abner Doane had reached station on the Waikatan extreme left flank then reassured himself that Tom Blue Fox's Indians and native archers had arrived at the opposite end of Te Ponapa's line.

Both units had been instructed to devote their principal efforts towards killing enemy leaders, for when a chief who, as a rule led, rather than commanded his followers, went down, his followers were very apt to turn and flee in panic-stricken confusion.

Te Ponapa, *Ariki*, impressive in a blue-and-white cape and tall headdress of nodding white heron feathers suddenly postponed an order for a general charge and instead ran down into the valley and halted there. Shaking a fighting staff collared with scarlet parrot feathers he insulted the Kaiparans, defied them to send forth a champion worthy of duelling with him.

"Ko taku ure! Be my penis!" he bawled all the while jumping up and down. "Sons of eaten men, come kiss my arse before I send you to the cooking fires!"

Shouts of outrage rose from the enemy line but ended when a towering *Rangatira* broke from the center of the enemy line and came plunging down the sandy slope flourishing a fighting staff even sturdier than Te Ponapa's.

Both forces fell silent once the two champions neared one another and began nimbly to circle, feinting tentatively.

Algernon Penny, Esq., was reminded of the Iliad, of the classic duels between Ajax and Myrmidon, Hector and Achilles and similar paladins.

One of Te Ponapa's principal lieutenants, standing restlessly at Jed's elbow, commented on the impending combat once the *Ariki* bounded forward to precipitate the duel.

To begin with both men held their *taiahas* in the horizontal or on-guard position with the pointed, spear-like end to their left and the razor-edged double blade to their right.

Weapons held at arms' length both champions grimaced and ran out their tongues. Both emitted cries like those of fighting stallions then leaped in at the same instant switching their fighting staffs' blade end up and point down; the shafts thus protected the front of a warrior's body at the same time threatening a lightning slash at his opponent.

"See! Now they take the guard position," cried Jed's companion. "*Heu! Watch!*"

Jed saw Te Ponapa's weapon rise vertically even as he kept dancing and swaying from side to side.

"Ho! The enemy thrusts!" The Kaiparan crouched then with incredible speed drove the pointed end of his *taiaha* at Te Ponapa's belly. The *Ariki* parried strongly and instantly countered by using his blade in a short, lightning slash at his opponent's neck who parried and leaped back a pace. Both men resumed the on-guard position.

Jed then noticed that both combatants were looking downwards as if watching the ground instead of each other's eyes. He mentioned this.

The other explained quickly, "They watch each other's big toes. A feint is made from bent elbows with no need for a firm stance but a real blow comes from the shoulders for which a fighter must take a firm grip on the ground with his toes.

"Ah-h!" The Maori's hand clamped hard on Jedediah's elbow. "Watch well. See? Our *Ariki* lowers his guard; watch his hands cross in turning his staff which seems to leave his head and chest unprotected and open for another blow."

The tempting low guard proved an effective lure; the Kaiparan whirled up his blade for a lightning-quick, right-handed blow at the head. Te Ponapa's weapon flashed up, deflected the other's blade.

A split-second later he reversed his *taiaha* and making an underhand lunge drove its pointed end into the other's solar plexus so hard that the tattooed champion doubled up and staggered backwards, hopelessly off balance and exposed to the sweep of Te Ponapa's blade which landed at the base of his enemy's neck. Blood from the severed jugular artery suddenly sprayed far and wide over the trampled gray sand.

A deafening clamor rose from both ridges when Te Ponapa jerked a *mere*-stone club-sword from his belt, planted a foot on the fallen chief's chest and emitted a hair-lifting screech of triumph. Two hard blows sufficed to lop off his opponent's head. He then kicked it contemptuously aside before trotting back to his array.

Since halting at the musket men's station, Abner Doane had been trying to identify the One-Eyed King but failed, unaware that the enemy leader had had himself tattooed out of all resemblance to a white man. He did, however, glimpse an occasional white man among the enemy now running to form wedge-shaped units. These, together with famous warriors and renowned chiefs stood at the apex of each triangle, roaring defiance, brandishing weapons and otherwise preparing to charge.

The only formation remaining in line-abreast was a small group of Kaiparans carrying firearms.

In grating tones Mister Hayward ordered his men formed into a compact double rank. "Their musketeers are near opposite and moving out. *Let 'em come to us!* Hold your fire till I give the word."

He glared at his wild-haired, nearly naked and liberally tattooed followers now beginning to raise horrific war cries. "Remember! I'll surely blow out the brains of anyone firing without orders."

Steadied by the presence of five *pakeha* whalers, the Waikatan musket company wearing only crossbelts and cartridge boxes lined up European-fashion, shoulder-to-shoulder on the rain-spattered sand; one rank knelt awkwardly before the second.

While the din raised by both armies swelled to an ear-numbing crescendo Abner clung to his composure by reminding himself he'd heard shots fired in anger at the Cove of Oxen.

Suddenly a young Maori pointed to a tall, angular figure wearing a short scarlet-and-yellow cloak ranging along the dune crest opposite. "There goes Te Whiro Kanohi—One-Eyed Conqueror of the north!"

Before Abner could get a really good look the distant dominant figure became lost behind a dark avalanche of screaming warriors racing down onto the scrub-dotted plain. He returned his attention to the Kaiparan musket company now trotting in an irregular line—abreast towards the Waikatan position.

Every now and then one of their musketeers would halt, shoulder his piece and let fly without taking aim. Sometimes the whine of a musket ball sounded chillingly close. His voice suddenly gone high-pitched he joined Mister Hayward in yelling, "Steady! Steady. Let 'em come real close, then for Christ's sake aim low—*low!*"

" 'Low's' the word—waste no balls in the breeze!" yelled one of the *Gladiator*'s crew.

Grimacing enemy musketeers were less than ten yards away before Ed Hayward whipped up his flintlock and yelled, "Ready! Present! Fire!"

A succession of booming reports drowned out a confusion of strident noises swelling, spreading wider over the little plain.

Abner sighted a bandy-legged almost hairless white man in dirty canvas breeches and a ragged brown shirt plunging towards him with bayonet levelled. Choking with excitement, he squeezed off his trigger. Whether or not he killed the fellow he never knew so dense became billows of rotten-smelling powder smoke from his companion's guns.

For a long instant fumes obliterated all sight of the enemy but from behind them arose a chorus of agonized screams. Mister Hayward's could be heard roaring, "Reload! Reload quick! Stand fast and reload!"

To keep Maori musket men in ranks proved all-but impossible; both armies had become locked in furious combat, stabbing, swinging fighting staffs, *meres* and tomahawks. Such was *pakeha* discipline that the Waikatan musketeers stood fast just long enough to fire a ragged volley before snatching sword-clubs from their belts and plunging gleefully into the *mêlée*.

With other white men Abner fell back a few paces in order to bite off the end of a paper cartridge and tilt powder down the smoking barrel of his piece. After tamping home the charge, he spat out a bullet stowed in his cheek and dropped it down the bore.

Once his ball had been seated Abner dashed tears from his eyes and squinted through the shifting battle fog in search of a worthwhile target. The dull *smack!* of axes, swords and *taiahas* being driven home occasionally was punctuated by the dull reports of firearms.

The uproar of war cries, screams and yells of mortal agony became deafening. Abner lost his hard-kept self-control and became confused but not sufficiently as to forget to snatch out a pistol and fire from the hip at a nightmarish figure rushing towards him with gory sword-club raised.

The apparition's glaring eyes and working features disappeared behind a dazzling flash and a blast of whirling gray smoke. A wave of screaming demons then closed in so fast the youth couldn't reload, was forced to club his musket and lay about with such desperation that attackers ringing him in fell back over ground littered with fallen and writhing bodies. During a momentary respite he watched Mister Hayward's knees buckle because the back of the Third's head had been stove in by the crunching sweep of a whalebone club.

From behind sounded a new chorus of battle cries—reinforcements were arriving. At once Te Ponapa's warriors commenced to gain ground for all the One-Eyed King's men continued to fight with ferocious energy, slashing, hacking and stabbing.

Jedediah Paddock, sweating and short of breath, was enjoying the fight of his life. Effectively, he swung a brass-guarded Navy cutlass to parry the slash and hack of razor-edged *meres* and *patuas*, then followed up with powerful sweeps of his broad blade. B'God this was what a man was born for! Exultation filled him; didn't the urge to kill or be killed lend the finest edge to existence?

His sword arm began to grow numb while, breathlessly, he braced to counter the charge of a wide-shouldered warrior wearing a shark tooth necklace and a tall headdress of hawk feathers.

The Maori lunged with a feather-decked spear, Jed uttered a hoarse yell, put his whole weight behind his cutlass and sheared off the other's shaft just back of its point. His attacker's momentum carrying him onwards, Jed sprang backwards shortened his cutlass and drove its blade deep into his assailant's belly an instant before a swirl of Waikatans came charging in from the left and carried him, half-berserk, into the *mêlée*.

Gradually the One-Eyed King's followers started to fall back over the corpse-littered plain.

Dashing trickles of bitter sweat from his eyes, Jedediah Paddock took care, while catching his breath, to reload both pistols. This done he realized that, although the enemy forces were being forced back, here and there knots were standing fast, howling and fighting like demons; warriors on the verge of retreat regained courage.

Jedediah led a handful of followers against the densest of these rally points and had started to swing his cutlass again when something happened to his left leg; it suddenly gave way and sent him sagging helplessly onto the trampled gray sand. It was exactly as if his limb had been carried away by a cannon ball, but of course there were no cannon anywhere.

Helpless, Jedediah watched Hercules swing a clubbed musket to brain the wounded Maori who'd been lying on the ground shamming death. Somehow, the fellow had recovered sufficient strength to make one last slash with his razor-edged *mere* which, as neatly as a surgeon's knife, severed the Achilles tendon of Jedediah Paddock's leg.

On witnessing the giant *pakeha*'s fall, a swarm of Kaiparans came bounding back into the fray. Jed attempted to rise but, finding this proved impossible, propped himself on one arm and, jerking a pistol from his belt, fired at the vast red mouth of a warrior.

He felt the jar of his weapon's recoil then lightning seared his eyeballs and darkness descended like a smothering curtain.

21

Battle II

From the summit of the dune nearest Carry-Over Bay Algernon Penny, Esq., was deciding that on the whole this battle appeared not to be going well. In command of Sylvanus Doane's small reserve force, his responsibility was to protect the expedition's canoes unless summoned into combat.

Thus far he'd been able to remain comfortably aloof from the ferocious struggle taking place on the plain below so his heart sank on watching a runner come speeding up the sandy slope to the crest.

As anticipated, the fellow brought orders for the reserve to charge the enemy center where a critical see-saw struggle was taking place among tangled windrows of wounded, dying and dead.

Gulping down a rising tide of fear, Penny delayed long enough to tighten his belt against the drag of boarding pistols and forced himself to shout in a voice he scarcely recognized, "*Hei! Tuki! E tawa!* Strike! Strike! Join the battle!"

Raising a carbine at arm's length Penny waved forward his men before starting down the slope at a slow trot. This he maintained until the reserve, screeching and yowling like banshees bounded past him and joined in the deadly struggle below.

Gradually the Englishman slowed his pace, halted and then, forcing a measure of calm on himself, took stock of the situation; he decided it was time to consider the best interests of Algernon Penny, Esq.

From his position half-way down the dune it wasn't difficult from time to time to catch flashes of Sylvanus Doane's red-and-yellow war cape amid a shifting pattern of fighting figures. Um. Intervention of the reserve wasn't affecting the issue; slowly the Kaiparan forces had commenced a retrograde movement. As he well knew, Doane's followers at any minute were apt to lose heart and, raising wails of despair, race from the battlefield.

Accustomed to Sylvanus Doane's unbroken succession of victories he cursed himself for not having foreseen that some day the One-Eyed King might suffer defeat. But perhaps he wasn't going to lose? No telling; Penny fingered a yet undischarged carbine and studied fighters eddying inconclusively about the valley's corpse-littered bottom.

Hopes rising, he thought to sense uncertainty in the Waikatan ranks; they were wavering and had pulled back a little.

Sylvanus Doane's gaudy war cloak reappeared and moved towards a clear space. He was swinging a clubbed flintlock. At that same moment a squad of Waikatan musket men led by a slight figure in European clothing appeared from the left. Both sides left off fighting to watch another single combat when a stocky *rangatira* from Waikato sprang into the open with tomahawk poised and offered to duel with the One-Eyed King. The renegade flung aside his empty musket and freed a cutlass.

Nearby combatants glad of an excuse to stop fighting, watched the duellists leap, spin and slash at one another.

Penny saw Doane's opponent in a headdress of green feathers begin to give ground, pressed back by his enemy's glittering steel, but then a tall young European ran out, levelled and fired a pistol at his old cell-mate.

Penny saw Sylvanus Doane drop his cutlass then lurch backwards clutching a shattered shoulder. The Waikatan, screaming, leaped in to clinch his victory but a swarm of combatants surged forward and hid what followed.

Shrill, concerted wails and shouts of "*Tahuti! Te Whiro Kanohi!* All is lost! The One-Eyed King has fallen!" began to arise. Kaiparans by hundreds started fleeing in the direction of their canoes behind the ridge.

For a while fighting continued here and there on the edges of the battlefield, but the main body of Kaiparans were slain immediately or surrendered to a grisly fate.

Algernon Penny, Esq., was clever enough to not join in a general retreat towards the canoes he'd been guarding; instead he started running at an oblique angle from one patch of scrub to the next. He'd hide when neccessary then sprint on towards a dense clump of woods.

During one of these halts he unavoidably witnessed the end of George Powys. Ringed about, the bandy-legged little Cockney-Australian effectively was wielding a boarding pike but his enemies were too many. A warrior slipped in from behind and impaled him between the shoulders on a spear fashioned from a whale's rib. The ex-convict disappeared under a heap of screaming, stabbing brown figures.

The flight of Algernon Penny, Esq., ended when a band of big nosed, bronze-skinned savages, painted and be-feathered like no Maoris he'd ever beheld, ran him down and clubbed him to the ground.

As from the depths of a blinding fog he heard a guttural voice saying, "Not kill! Him white. Tie up, bring back."

To Abner Doane it appeared incredible that this battle, like most Maori conflicts, had been so brief: lost and won in less than half an hour. For the first time since the struggle began he again was able to think with some degree of clarity. So, anxious to learn the effect of his shot, he started searching for the body of a chief wearing a red-and-yellow cloak.

To recognize so bright a cape among the tangles of corpses should have proved easy but it wasn't; scores of bleeding, mangled and usually headless bodies lay scattered over a considerable area.

Eventually Abner came across what he sought. A long, wiry and extravagantly tattooed body lay supine among remnants of a red-and-yellow cape. It still slowly was draining blood into a puddle near the end of a severed neck; the head was missing. The dead man's tattooed left hand fingers, spasmodically, had dug deep into lumpy, red-streaked sand—the right ones hadn't articulated, undoubtedly paralyzed through a heavy wound in the shoulder.

On stirring the corpse with a booted toe Abner noticed a flash of gold on the dead man's left hand. Stooping, he worked free what appeared to be, of all things, a European signet ring.

For a moment he stared on the ornament, too confused fully to appreciate how strange it was for a Maori chieftain to be wearing such a seal. Narrowing eyes against increasing glare, Abner scanned his find and noted that, as if in red-brown enamel drying blood had picked out the design of a greyhound leaping over a six-pointed star and a motto on a scroll reading *"Toujours Fort"*.

Shaken, he recalled reports that Te Whiro Kanohi was both white and an escaped convict. Then his mind flashed back to that day the burning *Amanda Alexander* had been discovered and Adam

Masters had told of Father's having been tried for murder in Port Jackson.

Recalling his shot at the Kaiparan in the red-and-yellow cloak he felt like throwing up, but he didn't on recalling he'd only wounded, not *killed*, the man who in probability had been his father.

He was foiled in his search of a head with one eye for the victors already were dismembering bodies for easy packing into food baskets.

Finally he gave up, dropped the signet into his pants pocket then got so busy rounding up musketeers it wasn't 'till around noon he found time carefully to re-examine the ring. When he did his pale-blue eyes rounded.

Here was the family crest. —He recognized it because Mother always had kept a cross-stitched replica of the hound-and-star device hung in a dark corner of the library.

When he'd departed for New Bedford half a lifetime ago, along with Mister Welch and Mister Peabody, Mother had promised him a ring of his own if Father couldn't be found. Lord God above! Hadn't he just become head of the House of Doane?

He hurried back to the place he'd left Father's headless body. But it had disappeared, probably to become the object of ceremonial degradation. Before long the fallen *kagatira*'s thigh bones would be fashioned into rings and flutes and his hands smoked for use as clothes' pegs.

When Abner finally discovered his father's head it was impaled upon a stake, set before a hurriedly contrived shelter in which Jedediah Paddock lay unconscious and bleeding from a cracked head, a broken arm and deep gash above his left heel.

Although Te Ponapa, *Ariki*, his principal chiefs and a few survivors from the *Gladiator* stood about in anxious consultation Abner paid them no heed, went over to stare through a cloud of blowflies into his father's weirdly tattooed features. There could be no mistake; the head had a sunken depression where the right eye should have been; the other, glazed and half-open, showed bright blue. He caught up an abandoned cape and quite unemotionally wrapped it about the grisly object; perhaps Father's head was entitled Christian burial of some sort?

This decided, the new head of the House of Doane tucked the head under one arm at the same time working the seal onto the third finger of his left hand.

22
Twilight

The afternoon was well advanced before a hammock conveying Captain Jedediah Paddock's bulk arrived on Amelia Island escorted by solemn-faced dignitaries. For all great care was being exercised so many agonizing barbs of pain were shooting through the wounded man that groans escaped teeth locked to suppress outcry.

If his bodily sufferings were poignant the Master Mariner's mental anguish was more severe. By now he'd become aware that, beyond question, his seafaring days were numbered. No point in deluding himself there was any hope of repairing a severed Achilles tendon.

To all intents and purposes he now had a permanently useless leg and an arm shattered in so many places he'd be lucky not to lose it.

Not Aimée but Lydia, thin, dark features rigid in anguished lines came running out to guide the hammock bearers indoors.

Abner, Tom Blue Fox, Heetee and Hercules lugged the giant figure into the darkened bedroom. Then with Te Ponapa *Ariki*'s help eased him onto a huge four-poster he'd had constructed to permit complicated amusements between his bride and himself. At a signal from *Kuini* Lydia Te Ponapa the bearers silently withdrew.

Drowsy with laudanum Jedediah Paddock peered confusedly from beneath a thick crown of bandages. Something, someone wasn't on hand who should have been there.

Lydia, bending, touched his cheek, murmured in husky accents, "Well, Big Bro, seems like thee has got considerable knocked about, but I reckon thee is sufficient tough to come 'round, like thee did back home."

"Where's Amy? Ought—be manning—side—welcome conquering hero."

"Don't go fretting thy self, Jedediah. Save for one thing Satan himself couldn't have kept Amy back."

"'One thing?' Wha' that?"

"Late last night she bore thee a fine son; account of her size and build she had a long, hard time. She'll be along first moment she's able; early tomorrow, likely."

The heavy eyes widened. "So 'tis boy?"

"Aye, and a real buster."

Jed lapsed into semi-consciousness and didn't wake till after dark to recognize the massive figure of Te Ponapa towering beside his sister. The *Ariki* bent, rubbed noses in a gentle *hongi*, saying, "The *tohungas* promise you will be well and strong again."

"'Well an' strong'? To what purpose? What's health to a useless, stove-in wreck like me?"

Lydia squeezed his good hand harder than she intended. "Jedediah Paddock! Has thee forgot thee has a wife and now a son to provide for? Whatever our faults, Paddocks aren't quitters."

"Provide for 'em? A cripple like me? How?"

"By building that trading business thee always has hankered for. Suppose thee can't follow the sea? With Te Ponapa thee still can command all trade along this coast. Mark my words, thy business will *flourish!*"

Eyes full and shining she hurried on. "With the sale of thy oil Obediah has brought back, thee will have ample credit 'round Boston and New Bedford to buy ships and whatever trade goods thee needs!"

From the background boomed Te Ponapa, "So long as I and my heirs rule this land no other *pakeha* ever shall trade along this coast. This I swear to on my father's grave."

A noise sounded at the bedroom door then Aimée Paddock entered supported by a beaming young *vahine*; following her came another woman bearing a small white bundle.

'Ah! *Mon coeur! Oh mon coeur!* What 'ave they done to you?" Aimée shook off her servant. Huge-eyed and sobbing she tottered over to rain kisses and tears on those broad, brown features showing up so sharply against a bank of bolsters and pillows. Jed used his undamaged hand to pat her head.

"Well, Mate, what kind of games you been up to whilst my back's been turned?"

"For you, *mon âme*," she half-laughed, half-sobbed, "I 'ave been laying one small foundation to the great Family Paddock of New Zealand which is to be."

Aimée lowered the little bundle beside him then parted coverings to permit the battered giant to see his son's tiny, puckered and plum-colored features.

"*Mon coeur*, I take great pleasure in presenting our son. 'Ow shall he be called?"

Gradually a grin widened on Jed's lips. "Why, as to that, seems to me 'Micajah Paddock' might do very well."

K33